THUNDER RIFT

THUNDER RIFT

MATTHEW FARRELL

An Imprint of HarperCollins*Publishers*

This one's for Denise
Only. Again.
You helped me through this, as you have with everything.

EOS
An Imprint of HarperCollins*Publishers*
10 East 53rd Street
New York, New York 10022-5299

Copyright © 2001 by Matthew Farrell
ISBN: 0-380-79915-4
www.eosbooks.com

First Eos paperback printing: May 2001

Eos Trademark Reg. U.S. Pat. Off. and in Other Countries, Marca Registrada, Hecho en U.S.A.
HarperCollins® is a trademark of HarperCollins Publishers Inc.

Printed in the U.S.A.

10 9 8 7 6 5 4 3 2 1

ACKNOWLEDGMENTS

The quotations from the *Tao Teh Ching* are from the Shambala Dragon Edition (St. John's University Press, New York, 1989), translated by John C. H. Wu. For the sake of consistency with Mr. Wu's translation (and because I lack the requisite knowledge to perform my own translation), I've retained the exclusively male references found in the Shambala edition, despite the fact that I personally find them limiting. Please feel free to substitute pronouns—I do assume that Taoist philosophy applies to both genders.

Thanks to Kamera Raharaha, sysop for Maori Organisations of New Zealand, who came forward with help when I inquired about Maori songs. All the Maori songs quoted in the text of this novel are in the public domain. Check out the Maori website at *http://www.maori.org.nz/*—they've put together a wealth of information, resources, and links for the Maori. I did much of my research on the Maori with this link as the starting point. *Kia ora,* Kamera! Please be aware that any mistakes of fact or mistranslations in this book regarding the Maori or their language are of my own making, and are not the fault of either Kamera, Maori Organisations of New Zealand, or their website.

Thanks to Maureen F. McHugh, who helped me to understand some of the nuances of Mandarin as a language. As with the Maori, any mistakes made in the book regarding Mandarin are my own and not Maureen's. You should really go out and buy one of her books, though—Maureen's a fabulous writer.

Thanks to Ron Collins, a writer whose work (both fictional and non-) I admire, who gave me an insightful critique of the first section of the novel and helped smooth over a rocky place or two. If you see Ron's work in one of the magazines, pick it up—you'll be rewarded.

The *Grimm's Fairy Tales* referred to in the novel are taken from a version that recounts the tales in their older, unsanitized, politically-incorrect incarnations. If you're familiar with the Grimm tales only in the Disneyfied versions, you should find a copy of the original translations and read them. These are dark stories with images of sudden violence and strange psychological undercurrents.

The Elegant Universe by Brian Greene (W.W. Norton and Co., 1999) is an interesting book on the latest theories regarding the underlying structure of the universe, and it also provided a few sparks for the events in this book. An excellent book on the new physics for those with an interest in the latest findings, but whose math (like mine) isn't quite up to the intricacies of string theory. (Actually, my math skills are sometimes not up to balancing the checkbook. . . .)

Thanks also to Jennifer Brehl, my editor. Her enthusiasm, energy, and support are much appreciated!

If you're connected to the Internet, my web page is at http://www.farrellworlds.com—you're always welcome to browse through.

SUMMER 2061

The softest of all things
Overrides the hardest of all things.
Only Nothing can enter into no-space
Hence I know the advantages of non-Ado.

Few things under heaven are as instructive as the
   lessons of Silence,
Or as beneficial as the fruits of Non-Ado.

—Chapter 43, *Tao Teh Ching*

Thunder arrived as a stunning burst of light.

On the fourteen-thousand-foot summit of Hawaii's Mauna Kea, it was 1:36 in the morning, well into in the scientific staff's usual working "day." The flash just south of zenith was brighter than the full moon, dominating the night sky and utterly ruining the Gemini Northern telescope's exposures of the spiral galaxy NGC 4565, but the astronomers in the complex hardly cared. The immediate supposition was that they were witnessing a nearby supernova, and the news flashed around the astronomical community via neural links as the Mauna Kea staff quickly reprogrammed all available instruments to record the event.

The sensavid networks picked up the Mauna Kea bulletin and decided that full sensory reaction to a supernova might be worth a ten second slot or so on the early morning news feeds for North America, so cameras and recorders were trained on the sky, and emoticasters did their best to give their viewers a heartfelt response to the images (though in at least one case, the 'caster could not avoid sending a peeved "it's a goddamn bright spot in the sky—big fucking deal" over the links).

That was before the astronomers realized there were no candidate stars in the area where the quickly fading burst had appeared, and that the spectrum of the light indicated the source was far, far closer than any star—in near-Jupiter space.

This was no supernova. It was something very, very different.

Then the first, furious electromagnetic tsunami hit the Earth. The invisible storm wrecked global communications, destroying the eyes and ears of every satellite in the sky, taking out radio, television, and networked communications, destroying most computerized safeguards on equipment and systems, causing any device with an embedded computer chip (which was, as the anachronists grumpily declared, damned near everything) to immediately fail. In the first few hours perhaps ten thousand people died: in half a dozen airline collisions over crowded metropolitan skies; from failed medical systems; in train and subway crashes; in suddenly dark and silent cities . . .

The odd light in the night sky would change the way society worked. Nothing afterward would be quite the same.

It was almost eleven-thirty P.M. in New Zealand, and Gloria Spears had little interest in the stars or the night-wrapped landscape of steep pastureland outside Mangaweka. She was far more interested in the landscape of Trevor, who reclined on the blanket alongside her. Well down the hill the windows of her parents' farmhouse cast long rectangles of yellow light over the broken ground, and Gloria could smell the wood smoke coming from the chimney. "It's beautiful out here," Trevor said. She loved the sound of his voice, the strange deepness of it. *He sounds like some bloody foghorn*, her dad had said the first time he'd come to visit, but that foghorn had wakened a resonance deep inside her. They'd dated for five years, until she graduated from college in Wellington, then were married. They'd celebrated their first anniversary only three months ago, and just the sound of him still made her shiver sometimes. "We should be getting back. Ruth and Carl are going to wonder what happened."

"My folks are asleep by now," Gloria answered. "And

they don't worry about me. Not out here. Not with you."
She kissed him, lightly once, then more urgently, her hand
trailing down his chest, then lower.

"Gloria . . ."

"Be still. God, I hate the zipper on these pants of yours."

"Here . . ." The rasp was loud in the darkness, and Gloria laughed.

"Now all of a sudden we're anxious, are we?"

"You're the one starting things, love. So no complaining
about rocks in your back or the chill."

Gloria lay back and pulled him on top of her. "Does it
seem that I'm complaining?" she whispered into his ear.
They fumbled with clothing, giggling in the dark like adolescents, and she gasped once as he entered her. Their lovemaking was quick, which was fine for her—the rocks *did*
stick up a bit through the soft grass, and she was after the
comfort of being with him and not the release.

Afterward she pulled the blanket up around them in the
darkness and kissed him again, suddenly pulling away
with startled breath. "What's the mat—" Trevor started to
ask her, then he saw the shadows and the light on her face,
and turned to look at the apparition on the eastern horizon.

"My God," he said, "ain't that something . . ."

They watched the strange light in the eastern sky blossom and fade again to darkness as it rose over the next
hour. The two of them had no hint of the carnage that was
occurring elsewhere around the globe. There was only the
blue-white flash and themselves, and the quiet of the night.

Much later they would tell their daughter Taria that she
had been conceived on the very night Thunder appeared,
and they would smile, remembering.

Even after what happened during the next few years,
they would still smile.

The world was a hundred or more light-years away. There,
a being lifted her head toward the sky. Her vision was so
myopic that she could not distinguish details a hundred

meters distant nor see the swirling curls of brilliant colors that dominated the sky. But her hearing was acute, sensitive to wavelengths well above and below those a human being could notice.

It was the day of her Acceptance. Others of her kind stood with her in the courtyard: her Mother-of-Name, her elderly Guardians-of-the-Right-Spirit. Even the Neritorika was there. They had gathered to watch, and the moment of Acceptance was here. The Keeper-of-the-Acolytes had stroked the crystalline rod she had given her until it rang with a note of pure tone, and the massed voices of the order were calling her name to the winds, but the sound of their chorus was lost in the drone of the watersingers in the distance. The sound of the watersingers was enormous, far louder than any song she or any of her kind had heard before, laced with the profound volume of several of the Greater Singers. It was an omen that such a chorus would come now, as she was about to become Baraaki. The roar of the watersingers nearly drowned out all the other sounds.

It was her moment.

But she heard the sudden bright, insistent hiss from the emptiness above her, as did the others, and the voice of the chorus faltered, and the rod fell from the Keeper's hands to shatter on the ground.

She knew her fate had just changed with the cacophony of the sky-voice, and she wondered what had just been decreed for her . . .

TIME OF MOST LIGHT

Without going out of your door,
You can know the ways of the world.
Without peeping through your window,
You can see the Way of Heaven.
The farther you go,
The less you know.

—Chapter 47, *Tao Teh Ching*

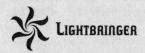 **LIGHTBRINGER**

It was the night before *Lightbringer* would go through Thunder into the unknown.

Still sweaty from lovemaking, Taria Spears glanced at Kyung's face and found herself wondering. "What?" Kyung asked, brushing strands of damp, sand-colored hair back from Taria's forehead. Lines creased between his eyebrows, and smaller ones furrowed the corners of his cinderblack eyes. He smiled uncertainly. "You're staring at me."

Taria tried to return the smile. "It's nothing," she said.

"You're supposed to be basking in the afterglow. Are you telling me it's missing?"

"If you can't tell, you shouldn't ask," Taria answered. She'd wanted the words to sound flippant; somehow they only sounded sad. She cradled against Kyung, enjoying the feel of his body on her own but suddenly not wanting him to see her face, afraid that she couldn't hide what she was feeling. She hugged Kyung, kissing his neck, his ear. "Kyung," she whispered, "does it scare you, to be going through Thunder?"

"No," he said, so quickly that Taria knew he'd either long ago come to that conclusion or that he'd given the question no thought. "Not at all."

"You're going to be doing something that no one's ever done."

"I'll be the *second* one to do it—Mahaffey has the point,

9

and her Firebird goes first. I'd say it's because Commander Merritt's got a thing for her, but that'd be unfair; she's good. Then me, then Davies in the third 'bird. Then *Lightbringer* herself—with you and everyone else. Right behind us."

"And if the Thunder Makers are on the other side waiting, you're going to be the first to deal with them, whatever that means. That doesn't make you a little scared, or apprehensive, or . . . ? I don't know. Something."

Kyung tried to roll out from Taria's embrace. She wouldn't let him, holding him tightly so he couldn't see her eyes. After a moment he relaxed, stroking her back as she lay her head against his shoulder. "Taria, we've sent dozens of probes through Thunder without any Thunder Makers showing themselves—hell, you've put a half-dozen probes through yourself. We've sent ten or more chimps through in the last two decades, and they all came back fine. The system's a sun, a gas giant, and a few big dead rocks—that's all. Chances are *nothing's* going to happen. I've been through every simulation SciCom could throw at us, looked at every possibility. I can't imagine running into anything we haven't already prepared for."

And that's the problem, Taria thought, still holding Kyung and staring at the walls of her room without seeing any of it. She wanted fire; Kyung was ice. She wanted fear and passion and apprehension; Kyung was nonchalance. She wanted wonder and ferment and doubt; Kyung had only certainty. She wanted imagination and excitement; Kyung couldn't imagine anything beyond the sims.

Taria could imagine more. She could imagine much more.

Thunder is a bridge. We know that now. You don't build a bridge if you don't want someone to cross over. The Thunder Makers are there, whoever they are. They're there on the other side, waiting for us.

For three decades they've been waiting for us . . . It wasn't until the first probes from Earth reached Thunder in the early seventies that anyone realized that the monster shadowing Jupiter in its orbit, whose wild emanations had unraveled the last two hundred years of technological progress on Earth and nearly destroyed the social and economic structure of the planet, was the throat of a wormhole. More compellingly, it was an artifact. A construction. A pathway to another solar system light-years away.

Taria pulled away from Kyung, gazing at him. He looked back at her, still smiling, and she knew from his face that he couldn't tell anything was wrong, and that was worst of all. "What?" Kyung asked again.

"Nothing," she answered. She hugged him again, hiding her face in Kyung's shoulder once more. "Nothing." She pulled his head down to her, kissing him with a desperation born of the mingled fear and yearning in her heart.

"Hey," Kyung said. "I know it's been hard for you. I really do. But you'll be fine. I promise."

Taria wished she could believe him.

The next morning, in her own room, Taria watched in her wall-holo as the three Firebirds pulsed away from the rotating bulk of *Lightbringer*, their flickering plasma jets an aching blue-white against Jupiter's painted face.

Her stomach churned. She could hear blood pounding in her ears, and her hands were cold. She wondered if Kyung, despite his protestations, might feel the same, out alone in his little craft.

She watched the Firebirds turn toward the blacker-than-blackness that was Thunder, and she felt *Lightbringer* shift underfoot to follow the small fighter scouts. Alarms wailed through the ship, alerting everyone that the living quarters were about to stop rotating, leaving them in zero g for the transit through Thunder. Taria reached for the brooch hanging around her neck, clutching the picture of her mother until she could feel the case digging into her palm. "I wish you really were here, Mama," she whispered. "I wish I could find you on the other side, the way I used to pretend."

In the holo, Thunder yawned like a satin mouth, a veil over the stars behind. As Taria watched, one of the Fire-birds banked away from the others, then slid back to loop around its companions: a hotdog maneuver. She knew it was Kyung, and Taria knew he did it for her, to make her smile. But she didn't. She couldn't. Taria only watched—as the first Firebird went through, the hull sparking orange as it passed the wormhole's entrance; as Kyung's Firebird did a final plasma burn and arrowed toward Thunder.

Taria watched, thinking she should be feeling more as Kyung approached the unknown. *He's your lover. You should be agonizing, you should be thinking more of him than of yourself*... But her thoughts were more of her mother and her own impending transition through the wormhole.

"Is something wrong with me, Dog?" she asked her Personal Interface Avatar, sitting alongside her. Dog, a holographic projection of a tan and white mutt that appeared to be mostly Australian shepherd, stared at Taria, her head cocked sideways with one ear lifting, her eyebrows curled in canine puzzlement. She whined in Taria's head. "Is it me?" Taria asked again.

There was no answer from her PIA as *Lightbringer* made the final course adjustments and fell into Thunder.

Thunder was a coldness that seeped into the marrow of your bones, a cold so intense that it burned.

Thunder was a maelstrom of aching, brilliant colors.

Thunder was a roar and a wail that may have been Taria's own voice, and then . . .

. . . quiet.

Taria was floating, held into her chair by the restraints. The wall-holo flickered, but she could see nothing but static. She felt a moment of panic, not knowing where they were or what had happened to Kyung. Dog barked a warning in her head, and *Lightbringer* groaned as the living quarters began to spin once more. Taria felt her body being slowly pressed back into her seat as a sense of gravity returned. Dog whined, and Taria reached for the sensory net draped over her chair's arm and placed it over her head.

She had always imagined that the moment of First Contact would be momentous and glorious. A spaceship of strange and wonderful design would appear alongside *Lightbringer*, emerging from a shimmering of veiled stars. The holotanks and monofoils all through the ship would shift from static to a sudden clarity, and a face both wise and alien would peer out at the humans. "Welcome," it would say in Shiplish with a voice deep and dark. "We have been waiting for you . . ."

That was the fantasy.

In her nightmares, the ship would materialize, but there would be no words. Instead, lines of burning light would flare from the spires of the alien ship, painting glowing stripes of molten steel in *Lightbringer*'s hull. Inside, it would all be chaos as everyone scrambled to respond to the unexpected attack. Firebirds would streak away from *Lightbringer*, raining their own destructive hail on the intruder. The halls of *Lightbringer* would be awash in blood and fire and screams . . .

Reality didn't match either fantasy or nightmare. Reality, in truth, was slow. Reality was virtual.

The sensory net contacts wriggled and snugged themselves tight to her head. White static bombarded her optical nerves while the spinal override dampened her tactile senses. For a moment she was a disembodied entity, blind and paralyzed, and Taria felt her heart pounding. It seemed to last far longer than normal, and she started to scream, knowing she couldn't control her hands and arms to lift and pluck the net away from her head. Then the system flooded the inputs with sound and light and vision, and she gasped.

She seemed to be floating in space just outside *Light-*

bringer's hull. She could see the mouth of Thunder in brilliant false colors, only a few hundred kilometers away. X rays streamed away from the opening in searing white arcs; blue and violet clouds of electromagnetic emissions billowed outward as if ejected from a volcano's steaming caldera. Even as Taria watched, Thunder was closing, as if exhausted from the effort of ejecting *Lightbringer*, the throat of the wormhole constricting beneath the seething boil until it was a black pinprick from which a glowing, radioactive hell surged. The sound of it in her altered hearing was tremendous, and Taria thought the volume down until it was a dull, constant hiss. She didn't want to move, staring at Thunder high above her, but finally she did.

Stretching out ahead and behind her was *Lightbringer*: the long tube holding the basic systems, surrounded by the rotating torus of the living quarters. Connected to the rest of the ship by a quartet of tubular corridors which seemed too frail to hold it all together were the radiating spires, fins, and manifolds of the drive unit. Taria saw with relief that the three tiny Firebirds were stationed like hawks nearby, ready to protect *Lightbringer* at need. The weapons systems of *Lightbringer* were also powered up and ready, glowing at armored points on the hull. The ship was on full alert, all its sensors out and probing, ready in case the Thunder Makers turned out to be less than friendly. Until they knew more about the Makers, they would stay on alert.

Taria reached out and opened the Firebird comlink channel, listening. Kyung's voice was among the babble that emerged. Taria's virtual point-of-view was the midship telescopic array, and she had the array take her in closer, so she could see Kyung's helmeted head through the cockpit windows of the fighter scout. She seemed to be hovering outside his craft, and she wanted him to turn, to see her there and smile.

But she wasn't there, not really, and though Kyung's head swiveled around, he looked through her. His voice was flat and uninflected, and she could hear disappointment just under the surface.

". . . nothing here. Sensors zeroed, Tower. Loading Nav Yin and standing by . . ."

Taria pulled back away from Kyung's Firebird, the starfield receding dizzily, and as she swiveled the array to the port side of *Lightbringer*, the visual display immediately overloaded. They had emerged from Thunder close to the gas giant they had dubbed Yang, which was half again as massive as Jupiter, its atmosphere a turbulent swirl of yellows and oranges, with a faint ring encircling the planet. Peering over Yang's shoulder was Yin, the sun around which Yang orbited; unlike Jupiter, Yang did not keep its parent sun aloof but huddled close to its fire, not much farther out than Earth.

There were a dozen or so balls of various colors coalescing around Taria—the other members of ExoAnthro, riding the sensory inputs of the probes and instruments studding *Lightbringer*'s hull: Colin, Alisa, Suni, Zachary, Matthew, Akiko, a half-dozen others . . . They gathered to one side of Taria, leaving her conspicuously outside the rough globe they formed. She scowled: this was the usual pattern of the physical meetings within ExoAnthro. With the exception of Alisa, all of the other team members were uniformed naval personnel, and Alisa had been a reserve officer at one time. This wasn't particularly unusual, as the vast majority of *Lightbringer*'s crew were unis. If Taria had become used to the unsubtle discrimination against the civies on board, the snobbery still annoyed her. She pushed herself into the larger group; it danced away, leaving her outside once more.

Early on she'd talked to Colin, who seemed the most approachable of the team members, about the attitude. "You unis discount everything I say because I'm not wearing a fucking uniform. It's like you don't even hear me half the time."

Colin shook his head. "It isn't us," he answered. "It's

you, Taria. Maybe if you made half an effort to fit in, if you weren't so goddamned arrogant when you say something—"

"Stating my opinion is arrogance? And when Suni or Zach do the same thing, it's not."

"Taria . . ." Colin sighed, and gave her the answer she'd heard most of her life: "You need to fit in, Taria. You need to change, Taria. Open yourself up, Taria."

You don't understand, Taria wanted to rage back. *You don't know how much it hurts . . .*

Another ball of light appeared, slightly larger and holding a core of brilliant, rich scarlet: Commander Allison, the head of the ExoAnthro team. His voice spoke in her ears. "We're all here? Good." His light danced around the group. "ScienceOps reports no sightings, and the Firebirds saw nothing coming in. We're seeing no obvious artificial structures within visual range."

Allison's clipped voice held the same disappointment as Kyung's. Even though none of the probes had encountered the Thunder Makers, whoever they were, most of *Lightbringer's* crew had expected—some with hope, some perhaps with fear—that a reception party would be waiting on the other side. *If we built Thunder, we'd sure as hell have an alarm system to let us know when someone used it . . .* But if they'd triggered an alarm, no one had shown up yet to investigate, and by any of the hypotheses regarding the Thunder Makers' expected behavior, that was strange and disturbing. The basic assumptions of ExoAnthro had been codified before *Lightbringer* had reached Jupiter orbit:

Within reasonable parameters, they will be like us. They might be reptiles, they might be intelligent spiders, they might be something entirely new, but if evolutionary pressures are to drive a species to intelligence, there are certain minimal physical requirements that we must share.

Within reasonable parameters, they will have language. They might talk in hand signs, they might be psionic, they might wave nasal appendages, but there will be ways to communicate with them that will be recognizably words and language.

Within reasonable parameters, they will think like us. Beings who could create Thunder would know science and mathematics. They would understand logic. They might (and almost certainly will) have different cultural and societal beliefs, they might worship divine cockroaches, but there will be overlaps in our thinking patterns and theirs.

Within reasonable parameters, they will have recognizable technology. Their technology might seem like magic to us, as our technology would seem magical to a Cro-Magnon. But it wasn't magic that built Thunder, it was technology. Massive technology, yes. In fact, damned near unimaginable technology. But Thunder was *built*, as we build bridges ourselves.

Since the Thunder Makers had declined to meet *Lightbringer*, that last tenet would drive the efforts to locate them. Technology and civilization—in all human experience—gave off heat as a by-product, and it was in the infrared as well as visible light spectrums that *Lightbringer*'s crew searched. After all, human cities burned like great fires in orbital infrared cameras. Power plants were searing points in the normal landscape, and heated waste water tinged the rivers and bays. Yang had among its attendant moons a world significantly larger than Mars, which they'd dubbed Little Sister: the initial photographs brought back by the robot probes had been startling, for Little Sister showed clouds and liquid water.

Little Sister was a prime target in the initial search pattern because it was a world that spoke of Earth.

Others speculated that the Thunder Makers lived in the outer atmosphere of the gas giant—after all, Thunder had appeared near Jupiter, not Earth. If Thunder was indeed a bridge, wouldn't you put the exit right where you want to go? Both ends of the wormhole contained within Thunder emerged close to a gas giant—therefore, there was a better-than-even chance that the Thunder Makers lived there. Several of *Lightbringer*'s instruments had turned immediately to Yang, attempting to penetrate its sunset-dyed clouds.

There were other possibilities. Thunder may have been only one "span" of a much larger bridge, a portal among many portals linking many systems—in which case there would be another Thunder somewhere close by, spewing its cosmic screech into the void, and some aboard *Lightbringer* searched for evidence of another wormhole.

Perhaps the Makers had been a spacefaring race for aeons, perhaps having evolved on a planet but then leaving it for the unlimited expanse of the stars. A ship or free-floating colony, if that's where the Makers lived, would also leak heat, and the drive unit would flare like a galaxy against the unimaginable chill of space. Some searched outward for signs of another ship.

And there was the slim chance that the Makers were simply hiding somewhere else in the system and could be discovered through some anomaly in the normal background data. Maybe they'd hide so they could observe whoever came through Thunder; maybe they'd hide to see if we were advanced enough to find them; maybe they'd hide for reasons we couldn't fathom. Most of ExoAnthro thought this unlikely. Worse, the search for hidden Thunder Makers would be arduous, boring, and unglamorous. It was not the option any of them wanted to pursue.

Commander Allison's ball pulsed red, a beating heart against the backdrop of *Lightbringer*. "I've loaded your in-

structions into the net. Access them now, please . . ." Dog
barked once in Taria's head and ghostly numbers scrolled
across her vision while coordinate lines painted themselves over the landscape, moving with her as she turned.
A sector of sky pulsed yellow—her target area: out of the
ecliptic plane where Yang orbited, outward from the sun
Yin, nowhere near Thunder. Dead space.

"Commander Allison, this has to be a mistake," she said.

The ball that was Allison rotated, gleaming. "No,
Spears," he said. "It's not."

*SHUT THE FUCK UP, SPEARS, AND LET US GET TO
WORK* . . . The words skidded across her vision as Allison
spoke, and Taria clamped her jaws together, furious. *Dog*,
she thought, *who sent that?*

A woof. *Don't know*.

Taria took a breath. The ExoAnthro cluster quivered
near her. "Commander, there's nothing there. It's a waste
of time. Let the AI program take it and alert us if it sees
something. It'd be better if I were with the Yang group, or
Little Sister—" Taria heard her voice go hollow as she was
cut out of the main link into privacy mode, and simultaneously Allison's voice dinned in her ears.

"Spears, I've put up with your insubordination because
you're a civilian and a damned smart team member, but no
more. Not on this side of Thunder. You have your orders.
Are you going to get on with it, or should I cut you out of
the search program and ExoAnthro entirely? It's your
choice, and you have about two seconds to make it."

"Commander—"

"One."

"Fine," Taria spat out. "I have my coordinates. Sir."

"Good." There was a momentary spatter of static as Allison took them out of privacy mode. ". . . she's an ass-
hole—" Taria heard someone say as the ExoAnthro link
opened, and then the voice went silent. "You each have
your coordinates and you know what we're looking for,"
Allison said. "You have four ship-hours for the initial

sweep, and then we'll meet in the EA conference room at 1800 to debrief. Let's go, people. This is what we came here for."

With that, the cluster of lights went out as one. Taria was suddenly alone again. "Upload the program to my array, Dog," she said, and heard the acknowledging bark from her PIA. The sector Allison had given her zoomed toward her in her sight, as if she were flying toward it at impossible speeds. There would be nothing there, but it would take hours to prove it. "Dog, give me the Yang and Little Sister feeds in separate windows, please."

Dog whined once. *They'll know.*

"Half of *Lightbringer*'s going to vampiring those feeds. Use the hack module, keep yourself low, and pull out if you notice someone paying attention. I'll take the chance."

Dog yipped, and her vision split into a several different windows. She kept her own sector centered but watched it very little, letting the AI search program do the bulk of the work. Around her, she watched as the other members of her team sent their own arrays to searching the huge face of Yang or to touch the marble of Little Sister. False colors switched often as they looked for signs of the Makers in various spectrums: infrared, ultraviolet, radio, hydrogen emission, visible light. Voices chattered in Taria's head as she watched, occasionally making her own verbal notes. It was Zachary and Alisa, probing Little Sister, whom she observed the most. Little Sister was so tantalizing, so familiar despite the backdrop of its giant parent. The infrared there showed no large heat sources, and the visual scan displayed no artificial satellites around the planet, as they would have seen on Earth. Yet . . . something nagged at Taria, even as the hours went by and the Thunder Makers remained hidden.

Nothing. The answer was always the same. Nothing.

"No anomalies in Yang's lower cloud strata."

"Our first pass shows no obvious wormhole leading out of the system."

"No evidence of anything in Yang's ring debris."

"Nothing to report in Yang's northern quadrant."

"Little Sister has biomass, but nothing worth a priority look. The atmosphere's clean and cool and the skies are empty."

One by one the windows winked out. Taria scowled. "Dog, move the array. I want to take a look at Little Sister."

The universe whirled around her, *Lightbringer*'s drive unit sweeping past her eyes and Yang's shoulder appearing. Little Sister, blue and white, loomed larger in her sight. "Shift to infrared," she told Dog. "I want you to increase the color differential by temperature and narrow the range. I'm looking for differences of only a few degrees. Keep going in, as close in as you can take it. Yes, I know the image is breaking up. Don't worry about it, just keep taking me in. Concentrate on the western coast of the main continent and keep the enhancement as high as you can."

"Spears, what the hell are you doing?"

The sudden voice in her ear would have sent her jumping out of her seat had Taria been in her body and not in the network. At the same time, she felt someone else sharing her feed from the array. "No one really checked out the biomass on Little Sister, Commander. There has to be a reason the concentration was slightly heavier on the coast."

Allison's voice held honed and sharpened scorn. "No satellites, Spears. No radio emissions, no electrical transmissions of any sort. No large scale structures. No industrial pollution in the atmosphere. The planet's metal and oil poor. It has plant life and maybe animals, yes, and that's very interesting but I don't see the Makers. You're wasting time we could be spending finding them."

During Allison's lecture she'd continued to increase the scale of the infrared image of Little Sister. Allison did nothing to stop her, though he could have easily cut her off from the array's input. Taria was staring at a fuzzy world, as if she were severely myopic. She blinked, and the world got even fuzzier. But there was something there, in the blurred, pixelated outline of the coast, where the cool water slid into a bay. There were islands, and on the islands . . .

"Commander?"

"I see them, Spears." His voice held a tone she'd never heard before.

She hovered high up in Little Sister's sky, staring down at the brown, indistinct smudge of an island. There, along the edge, were blocks of tan and yellow, showing that they were slightly warmer than the rock around them. The edges of the blocks bled into the colors around them, but distinctly geometric.

Buildings.

Two ship-days later . . .

Commander Allison stood before the ExoAnthro team for the evening report. Taria always thought that Allison moved as if he had a steel pole rammed up him from ass to neck. He never slouched, never leaned, and he always looked as if he'd just been decanted from a steam press. Everything about him was precise, and you could cut yourself on the creases of his trousers. Even his voice was clipped and shorn of anything resembling friendliness. His PIA was a simple, unadorned gray cube—the Cube, which was the team's nickname for Allison as well as his PIA.

"Daniels, what do you have?"

Colin was seated next to Taria. He cleared his throat nervously. "We completed the initial sweep of the entire ecliptic last night, sir," he said. "I've gone over the data again this morning. Nothing's changed from the prelim report I sent you, and my group's in agreement: there are no artificial constructs anywhere in the system—no ships, no satellites, no visible signs of the Makers at all."

Which makes no sense, Taria thought, knowing she wasn't alone. *Who would go to all the trouble of building Thunder and then not use it, or not be here waiting when someone came through?*

Allison only frowned. "It's important for all of us to bear in mind that we still have the vast bulk of the system to scan, though, from above and below the plane of the ecliptic," Colin hurried to say. "We've already begun crunching some of that data, but it's going to take time. The ecliptic was where we thought they'd most likely be, but there's no particular reason that they *have* to be there."

Allison was already turning away, his eyes finding Taria. "Spears. What've you got?"

Taria felt the attention of the ExoAnthro group turn to her, and some of the gazes were less than friendly. Zachary, a few people away from her, sniffed loudly. *Okay, Dog,* she thought to her PIA. Dog wasn't visible here; Allison didn't like having an entourage of holograms in team meetings. Dog woofed in Taria's head, and a projection window opened in the air at the front of the room. There, Little Sister spun slowly in front of the orange-swirled arc of Yang, with Yin glinting over the shoulder of the planet. The image of Little Sister dissolved and was replaced by a figure: bipedal, with finely textured skin the color of the Mediterranean on a sunny day; a crest of vibrant, mottled orange that echoed Yang's colors running from forehead down the back, a ring of flesh studded with eyelets circling the entire head; a long, lipless mouth; hands with long fingers, four on the left and six on the right. The creature's torso was wrapped in a winding of dirty white cloth. The shape rotated like a model on a turntable, moving its arms and legs, the head-crest lifting and falling again.

The basic body structure was familiar enough. Beyond that, little was "human" about the creature. The ExoAnthro team had dubbed them the "Blues," after the predominant skin color.

After Taria's discovery of buildings on the west coast of Little Sister's one large continent, *Lightbringer*'s ScienceOps crew had sent down orbital and atmospheric probes, and they'd found small cities scattered here and there, always on the coast, and in those cities were the

Blues. For a brief, hopeful moment Taria and the others had thought that meant they'd also found the Thunder Makers. But . . .

"Everything indicates that our general impression is correct and the Blues aren't the Makers," Taria said. "The Blues are definitely sentient. There's no question about that—we've found our first truly alien race. However . . ." Taria shrugged. "The buildings in their cities are no more sophisticated than those in medieval Paris or ancient Greece. Maybe less so. They don't have motorized vehicles, don't have air travel. We already knew there were no radio, television, or any other electromagnetic emissions from the planet, and no artificial satellites. There doesn't appear to be any power grid—in fact, no signs of power plants of any sort: coal, steam, nuclear—nothing. No large-scale smelting operations; therefore little or no metal use, and in any case there isn't a lot of metal ore on Little Sister. All the settlements are restricted to the coast; our best guess is that the population's less than half a billion on a continent the size of Eurasia." Taria shrugged, and caught Allison's chilly eyes. "From all appearances, the Blues aren't the Thunder Makers. They don't even know we're up here."

"We're all agreed on that?" Allison asked, turning stiffly as he looked at the others. Heads nodded around the room, and finally Allison nodded himself. "Then for the time being we link with ScienceOps and focus our priorities on continued searching through the arrays. We'll continue to monitor Little Sister, however—"

"No," Taria said sharply, interrupting Allison. She'd thought the word, certainly, but had been as surprised as anyone when it tumbled out of her mouth. She felt everyone turn to look at her: "I mean, yes, but . . ." Allison swiveled and gave her his best uni glare.

"Exactly what *do* you mean, Spears?"

"I think . . ." Taria glanced around the room.

Everyone was staring now, and she could feel a flush warming her neck. *"Careful . . ."* Colin whispered from his seat next to her.

"I think," Taria continued, "that the Blues deserve a certain priority." She waited, but Allison only blinked, continuing to pin her with his stare. "I know I just said that they're not the Makers. But they're *here*. If the Makers *are* somewhat like us, then I'll bet they also knew that the Blues were here. Maybe they contacted them. Maybe the Blues know who they are and where they live."

"I'm hearing a lot of maybes in that," Allison said.

"And they're going to continue to *be* maybes until we make the effort to find out," Taria answered, then added belatedly: "Commander." She heard Alisa chuckle at that. The flush touched her cheeks as Allison regarded her with his expressionless gaze.

"So you're suggesting we initiate First Contact procedures with the Blues, who 'maybe' know something about what we're here to discover. You believe we should expend the people, hours, equipment, and limited resources necessary to initiate First Contact procedures on a race that isn't the one we came here to meet. Is that an accurate representation, Spears?"

Taria grimaced and forced herself to hold his gaze. "I'll add another maybe, Commander," she answered. "Maybe it'd be good practice, so we know what we're doing outside simulations and theory when we actually find the Makers—or they find us."

Allison grunted; several people around the room chuckled. Taria knew that everyone expected him to proceed to verbally rip her head off. She expected it herself—Allison's reputation as being abrasive and curt was well founded, and she had been on the receiving end of his displeasure long before they'd come through Thunder. To Allison, the civilian members of the expedition were an annoyance who didn't understand that orders were given to be obeyed, not questioned. Taria pressed her lips together. Dog whined in her head as she steeled herself for the onslaught, closing her eyes and taking a breath. The image of the Blue at the front of the room blurred and faded.

"I'd agree with that assessment," Allison said.

"Sir?" She didn't have breath to say anything else.

"I said I'd agree with you, Spears. Are you suddenly having trouble with your hearing?" His pale, icy eyes moved away from her to sweep over the rest of the room. "I'll speak with Admiral McElwan and ScienceOps, and we'll start putting together the specific protocols. In the meantime, Spears, I want a full report on the Blues up on the system so we can all look at it. We'll meet back here at 0830 tomorrow. That's all."

Allison swept out of the room. As the door irised closed behind him, the ExoAnthro group turned in their seats to look at her. "Well, our workload just got increased," Zachary, across the room, muttered.

Taria spread her hands. "Sorry," she said. "I just thought it was the right thing to do."

"And you're always right, aren't you, Spears?" Zachary answered.

After the satellites were put in place around Little Sister and the main cities were identified, bugs were released: tiny winged probes modeled on native insects, with cameras for eyes and microphones for ears. For several ship-weeks they silently watched, while at the same time the ExoAnthro staff continued to search for the Makers, who could not be the planet-bound and technologically inferior Blues. Still, a few in ExoAnthro, with Allison's tacit support, slowly came around to Taria's point of view. The Blues were native to this system—there was no "exit" from this solar system, no other Thunder leading to yet another system, so it seemed logical that the Makers *must* have come from here, that the Blues might know them and could perhaps help *Lightbringer* find them.

So they watched. They listened. And Taria supposed that it was actually good "practice."

Without a Rosetta stone, without any cultural linkage at all, understanding what they were seeing and hearing was a long, slow, and tedious process. There were vociferous arguments among the ExoAnthro staff at times as each argued their interpretation of what they'd seen. Language was the hardest to decipher—the Blue voices overloaded the sensors of the first generation of bugs, distorting everything they heard, and with the second generation, someone noticed that the voices were still using the entire frequency range the bugs were capable of reproducing. The third generation had microphones sensitive to acoustic wavelengths above and below that of the human ear, and only then did they realize they'd missed half the "words" the Blues were speaking: grunts and bellows below human threshold, and piercing shrieks that could have functioned as dog whistles.

And even when they finally decided they were "hearing" everything that was spoken, there was still the problem of assembling a vocabulary and grammar. Nouns were easiest—when enough Blues used the same word when obviously referring to an object, another name was added. The ship's computer system was indispensable, interfacing with a linguistic avatar they called, appropriately enough, Rosie—their own Rosetta stone.

For Taria, it was the hardest task she'd ever undertaken. It was also some of the most boring work she'd ever had to do, poring through hours and hours of recordings from the bugs and trying to compile the stolen fragments of alien life into some understandable and reproducible pattern.

"Play back that 'hello' sequence, Rosie."

Rosie looked like somebody's maiden aunt, dark hair pulled back in a severe bun, a reserved stance and a total lack of humor. Taria thought she should have been more idiosyncratic, more strange. But Commander Allison had had the final say on Rosie's appearance. Taria always suspected that Rosie was actually a simulacrum of some Allison relative.

Rosie answered Taria's request with a barrage of sound. Kyung, reclining on Taria's bed, chuckled. "Okay, Taria. Now you try."

"Not a chance." Taria sighed. "God, we're never going to be able to talk with them. Not really."

"Don't *need* to talk to them," Kyung answered. "They're not the Makers. They're not who we came here to find, so fuck 'em."

"If all you're going to do is spout uni nonsense, you're welcome to leave," Taria told him. She managed to keep the tone light enough that Kyung missed the edge concealed within.

They were in Taria's room, the monofoil showing three separate recordings of Blue interchanges and scattered note files on a second screen unrolled on her bed, and Rosie standing sourly near the door. Dog had been told to disappear for the time being. Kyung looked at the chaos and shook his head. "So what'd that mean? 'My, you're looking especially azure today'?"

Despite herself, Taria laughed. Rosie answered with stiff reproof. "No. That was 'I hear and acknowledge your presence.' "

"It sounded more like an opera singer competing with a foghorn to me," Kyung commented.

"Rosie, you can leave now," Taria said. "I'm done working for the moment."

Taria could have sworn she heard an audible sniff just before Rosie vanished. She touched the monofoil on her desk and a chorus of Blue voices suddenly went silent. Taria caught a glimpse of herself in the wall mirror: she looked tired and bedraggled. She ran fingers through her hair. "Rosie's gone. You staying?"

"Depends. What you got in mind?"

"Sleep."

Kyung didn't quite manage to keep the disappointment from his face. It had been at least a ship-week since they'd made love. "You're still set on going down there?"

"Allison told me that I have a good shot at making First-Team. I plan to be on it, yeah. Meeting an alien race is what I came here for."

"So you'll go down to the Land of Bad Opera?"

"There's nothing wrong with singing. My mother—" Taria stopped, surprised at the sudden welling of emotion the word evoked. *After all these years . . .* "My mother always sang to me."

Kyung didn't notice the film of moisture that she quickly blinked away, or the slight catch in her voice. He wasn't even looking at Taria; he was toying with the monofoil on the bed—he'd closed Taria's note pages and brought up one of the network games. "You'll never be able to sing like that," Kyung said through the crackling of electronic gunfire. "You'll never be able to understand them on your own."

"Does that mean we shouldn't try?"

Kyung looked up from the monofoil. "If I can't sing, I probably shouldn't try to join the band." From the monofoil there was loud gunshot, followed by a dramatic moan and a crash. "Shit," Kyung said. "I just got killed."

Taria's hand had gone to her throat. For a moment Kyung and her cabin shivered in her gaze. "Hey," Kyung said. He was looking at her quizzically over the top of the monofoil screen. "What's the matter?"

"Nothing," Taria said quickly, and took a breath. "Nothing. I just . . . I just was remembering . . ."

 TARIA WAS FOUR . . .

Mama sat on one side of her, Gramma on the other, the cake in front of her. There were three candles already set in the dark swirls of frosting. The kitchen was still fragrant with the fish stew Gramma had fixed for supper, and Grampa and Papa, after washing the dishes, had gone outside on the porch so Grampa could smoke his pipe and Papa could drink his beer. A television sat on the kitchen counter—a useless anachronism, since Thunder had blown out all the satellites, and standard transmissions were hopelessly static-ridden with Thunder's continuing racket. At least once a day Grampa turned on the set, disregarding Gramma's inevitable protest, "just to check." Every day, there was nothing but white noise and cracklings. "That damned Thunder's still there. Well, at least one good thing came out of it," he'd say, then wink at Gloria, who shook her head in mute reply. At least she no longer blushed.

Mama was singing as she pushed a fourth candle into the frosting, and Taria was already imagining the sugary sweetness in her mouth. "Do you feel four?" Gramma asked Taria. Gramma was half Maori, and told Taria that her Maori part was uneasy with the *Pakeha*, European, parts of her—if Gramma didn't follow some of the *Maoritanga*, the Maori customs, the war inside her would kill her. Mama aways tried to hush Gramma when she talked that way, but Taria loved listening to her. Gramma even had a *moko*—a chin tattoo—and the blue-black swirling lines in her tanned, wrinkled flesh fascinated Taria. The *moko* bobbed up and down whenever Gramma spoke.

"I guess so," Taria answered. "But I won't have skin like yours until I'm seven, Gramma." Taria touched her grandmother's wrinkled cheeks, and Gramma leaned her head back and laughed, a hearty roar of amusement that made Gloria shake her head and stop singing.

"Mother, really," she said.

"What? Aren't I allowed to laugh when my granddaughter says something amusing? Or are we supposed to be all solemn and pouty-faced because you're leaving Monday?"

"Mother." More sharply this time. "We weren't going to discuss that. Not tonight. It's the girl's birthday."

"Well, fine, then," Gramma said, and Taria thought she heard irritation in the older woman's voice. She'd heard that tone creep into Gramma's words more and more since Mama and Papa said that they were going to China for a few years.

Thunder's appearance on that summer night nearly five years ago had ended any hope that the Pacific Rim would emerge from the economic recession in which it had wallowed for the past two decades. Instead, recession swelled and bottomed into full depression. China's economy, the linchpin of the East after the economic collapse of Japan in the early twenty-first century, was already unstable. The civil war in Pakistan boiled over to envelop India as well, furthering weakening the region. The loss of consistent and dependable supply lines to and from the West was a blow from which Asia could not recover. A ferocious drought hit China, Indochina, and Australia a few years later, which lasted two full seasons. Parched crops failed; a pall of smoke from brush fires covered the region.

Taria knew none of that. She knew only that Papa lost his job and Mama lost hers at the university. The bank, Mama told her, had to take back their house in the city.

Now it was Mama's job that was taking the family to

Nanjing: her master's degree was in archeology and her preferred field of study was China. There were pitifully few jobs in academia available during the Great Asian Depression, but the University of Beijing had undertaken an excavation of the Ming Temple, whose foundations dated back to the time of Chu Yüan-Chang in the fourteenth century—even in the face of disaster, some mundane tasks were funded. One of Gloria's professors was associated with the project, and he managed to secure a place on the team for her, a menial job that paid something slightly more than nothing, but it was a job. Trevor found employment with the Chinese government as a low-level tech working to restore the communications systems throughout the country.

"There's always room here," Gramma said the first night Mama had told her parents of their decision—Taria had heard, listening from her bed in the night darkness. "You can just stay with us."

"Mom, you have to understand. We appreciate the fact that you let Trev and me come here after we lost the house, but this is a chance for us to get back on our feet, to do the work we're both best at."

"But China . . ."

"It's only for a few years. Maybe then things will be better here, and we can come back . . ."

Taria thought China would be exciting, even if she was worried that she wouldn't to be able to speak Chinese. But Mama and Papa were taking lessons, and she was learning, too. In fact, Mama kept saying that she was doing the best of all of them, but she still worried, and she'd had a few nightmares in the last week. She didn't tell Mama, though. Mama hardly smiled at all anymore. Maybe she would smile when they were in China . . .

"I guess we should light the candles," Mama said, then raised her voice to call: "Trevor! Dad! Time for the cake!" Taria heard chair legs scrape against the wooden porch, then the sound of Grampa knocking out his pipe against the railing and the screech of the screen door. Gramma lit

the candles and slid the cake closer to Taria, and they all
sang "Happy Birthday" to her. Gramma Ruth sang in
Maori, the others in English. "Make a wish and blow out
the candles," Mama said.

The wish was easy. Taria puckered her mouth and blew
out all the candles with one sweeping breath. "What'd you
wish for?" Papa asked, and Mama shushed him with a smile.

"Trevor! You know that if you say the wish out loud it
won't come true. Don't you tell him, Taria."

"I won't, Mama. I know all about wishes."

I want to be back here for my next birthday. That was
what she'd been thinking as she blew out the candles. It was
a simple wish, the wish of a little girl sad to be leaving the
only home she'd known and the grandparents she loved.

It was a wish that, unfortunately, would come true.

> *"Po atarau, e moea iho nei*
> *E haere ana koe ki pamamao*
> *Haere ra, ke hoki mai ano*
> *Ki te tau, e tangi atu nei."*
>
> *Oh moonlight, as I sleep here*
> *You (my loved one) are going to a distant land*
> *Farewell, but return again*
> *To your loved one, weeping here.*

Mama liked to sing. It was a rare morning when Taria
didn't awake to her mother's soft, gentle voice. She
thought Mama's voice was wonderful and perfect. She especially liked it when Mama sang the Maori songs that
Taria remembered Gramma Ruth singing. They were
pieces of home in the midst of the strange, frightening
landscape of Nanjing.

"Why are you singing 'Po Atarau,' Mama?" she asked.
"That's such a sad song."

Her mother's mouth twisted a little, almost a smile. "I'm
sorry, Taria. I didn't want to wake you. I was singing that

because I was thinking about Gramma Ruth, and I heard her singing that to herself the night before we left, at your birthday party. It made me feel close to her again, I guess."

"Why do you always sing, Mama?"

"Don't you like it?" Mama sat on the bed alongside her. Outside, vendors called in high voices, and children squealed and laughed on their way to school—Taria knew she would be going with them in a few days, but the noise and clamor mostly scared her now.

"Oh no, I love it, Mama. I do. But why do you sing? Are you happy?" Mama seemed to shrug. "I'm happy to be with you, and with your papa. But I'm . . . I'm not really happy here. It's not home. As long as I'm singing, I know that Gramma and Grampa are still there, and I feel like I'm part of them. Sometimes I imagine that they can hear me." Mama laughed. "Like they can *feel* the sound of my voice. Here . . ." Momma took her hand and put it close to her lips. She sang a phrase, and Taria could feel the air moving, softly striking her hand.

"A song is carried in the air, and I sometimes think that Gramma and Grampa are outside and a breeze touches their cheek, and that's my song, carried all the way across the ocean to them."

"Mama, that's silly," Taria said.

Mama smiled at her and stroked her cheek. "I guess you're right, darling. Do you want me to stop singing?"

Taria shook her head. "No."

"Why not?"

"Because when you're singing, I know you're there."

Mama laughed at that. "Then I'll sing some more," she said. "And you can sing with me and we'll both know each other is there."

"You could tell me a story instead, Mama." Taria fumbled under her pillow and brought out a bedraggled book with brightly colored pasteboard.

"What's that?" Mama asked.

"Aunti Li gave it to me," Taria answered. Li Xouyin—

Auntie Li—lived one flight down with her husband, mother-in-law, a sister-in-law, two daughters, and three sons. Auntie Li watched her while Mama and Papa were working. She told lots of old Chinese tales in her accented Mandarin, bringing Taria memories of cuddling with Gramma in the big soft chair in front of the fireplace in New Zealand and listening to her read from a book spread open on her lap.

But Mama didn't like fairy stories; she especially didn't seem to like the ones Gramma told. Auntie Li had somehow come across a musty copy of *Cinderella* in English and had given it to Taria. Now she gave the book to Mama. The resulting sigh and frown had made Taria ask: "What's wrong, Mama? Is it a bad book?"

"I don't think I can explain it to you so you can understand it now, Taria. Fairy tales . . . well, the real ones can be awfully violent, and the way they present the world isn't the way I see it or the way I want you to see it."

"Gramma read them to me."

"I know. And I didn't like it, particularly."

"Why not?"

"They . . . they seem to say that all mothers are jealous of their children, that stepmothers are evil, that old women who choose to live alone must be evil witches, that being beautiful and marrying someone rich is the single most important thing in the world, that being of royal blood somehow makes you a superior class of people." Her finger tapped the brightly colored jacket of the book on her lap. "I guess I always wondered what would happen if Cinderella didn't manage to escape the ball at midnight. Would they all hate her when she turned into a filthy, ugly cinder girl dressed in rags? Would the prince still be enchanted by her, or would he be disgusted by the fact that he'd been deceived, that he'd been dancing with and touching this . . . this *thing*? How would Cinderella feel, hearing the curses and whispers from all the rich people gathered around her?"

"Mama," Taria persisted, blinking at the torrent of

words, not really comprehending what her mother was saying but understanding perfectly the tone in which she spoke. "It's just a *story*." Pouting, she started to turn away.

"Taria . . ." She glanced back over her shoulder. Her mother lifted the book so that the dancing couple on the cover vanished in the shimmering of the single overhead light of the apartment. "Would you like me to read this to you? Without the commentary, I promise."

"Yes, Mama." Taria smiled, and jumped up into her mother's lap as she sat down on the chair nearest the window.

"All right, then," Mama said. The book, opening, sent Taria a wonderful, singular aroma of old paper and must, and the brown-edged leaves made a lovely rustling as they turned. " 'The wife of a rich man fell sick . . . ' "

"We're trapped here. You know that, don't you?"

Taria's father's voice carried in the darkness. They thought Taria was asleep, but the storm outside had awakened her. Half dozing, she lay silently on her side with her knees drawn up on the small futon that served as her bed, and which in the morning went under her parents' bed. Through the screen of her lashes Taria could glimpse the curtains of the bedroom window in their two-room apartment. Outside, the streets of Nanjing were awash in monsoon rains, and blue-white lightning painted quick shadows on the wall.

Her parents' voices were comforting in their familiarity, and Taria hardly listened to the words at all.

"Trevor . . ." Taria heard her mother sigh, and the bedsprings protested as she turned. "We didn't know what to ask when we came here, and that was a mistake. I know this isn't what we expected, but in another year both of our contracts are up. We'll get our exit visas then, and we'll leave."

"If they don't exercise the extension clauses." A long sigh. A gust of wind tossed rain at the window in a quick, cold pattering. Taria's eyes closed, then half opened again when her father spoke. "We never should have signed those contracts, Gloria."

"I wanted to do something in my field, Trev. It was the only chance I could see to do anything like fieldwork. There wasn't anything for us back home, not since Thunder wrecked things. This was work, real paying work, and with Taria and the job they promised you . . ." Taria thought her mother might be crying; there was a catch in her voice now, a tremor. "I'm sorry it hasn't turned out the way we expected. We'll leave. In a year. Professor Yuan won't renew my contract if I tell him I want to go. He understands."

"We could leave now," Trevor insisted. "Just quit. Both of us."

"Then what, Trev? Even if we could afford to fly back home, what then? Where do we work? My parents are just barely making it with the money we're sending them now. If that stops, they'll lose their land, and then we have nowhere to go. What happens to us then? What happens to Taria?"

Thunder rattled the window, growling in the darkness. Taria always imagined that the deep rumbling was like the unheard sound of the other Thunder, the thing out by Jupiter that everyone always talked about. The noise of Thunder that had nearly destroyed them . . . But this thunder was receding already, the storm front passing. Taria closed her eyes.

"Half the time, I never even get to see you or Taria. Next week I'll be in Beijing for God knows how long."

"I know, I know," Mama said softly, the way she talked to Taria when Taria skinned her elbow or came home crying from school. "But it won't be long. Not really. A year will go by before we know it."

"Then what?"

"We'll leave, if that's what you want to do. We'll go somewhere else. Maybe home, maybe to the States. They say there's work there, if you can get a green card—"

"Fucking Thunder," her papa said, his voice growling, but Taria knew it wasn't the thunder outside he was talking about.

"Shh . . . You'll wake Taria," Mama told him. "As long as you're here, I don't care if we're trapped or not. And there are some things about Thunder that I'll always remember fondly . . ." Taria heard her mother kissing Papa, then he laughed, quietly. Then neither of them talked for a long time, and the quiet shush of rain on the roof tiles carried the drowsy Taria quickly into sleep.

Taria knew that Thunder was important, as any child did. Mama and Papa talked about it occasionally, and the news reports were always full of something or other that had to do with Thunder. "Why do they call it Thunder?" Taria asked once. The sounds of a Nanjing evening were quiet outside her window. She was playing with a bell that she'd brought from New Zealand. Once, it gave forth what Taria thought was the most beautiful, resonant sound she'd ever heard, but she had dropped it on the floor and the metal cracked. Now it went "just clunk," as she had told Mama, crying. She still played with it, but she'd taken off the clapper because she hated the sound. "I don't hear anything in the sky, Mama."

Mama laughed, hugging her. "Well, Thunder is out by Jupiter, and Jupiter was a god whose weapon was lightning bolts. And Thunder *does* make noise, Taria. We can't hear it, not with our ears, but it's there. Someday you'll understand that."

She wanted to understand it *now*, but she was tired, and it was easier to put the cracked bell on the arm of the chair and lean against her mother's warmth. A silver brooch hung around her mother's neck on a fine chain. Taria wound the chain around her fingers. "Could you really *see* Thunder, when it first came?"

"Yes, darling," Mama answered. "Your father and I were outside, and we saw it, almost as bright as the moon, and we knew it was kind of a special sign for us, because not too long after, you came."

Taria snuggled closer, enjoying the feel of the worn

lamb's wool sweater her mother wore every night at home, and the fragrance of soap and perspiration, but her nose was wrinkled in confusion. She wasn't sure she wanted Thunder to be special for her. "But everyone hates Thunder, Mama. Everyone."

"Well, the noise Thunder makes has caused problems here, darling. Lots and lots of people died because of Thunder, and lots of things that we used to have don't work anymore." Taria felt her mother's chest lift and heard her sigh. A hand stroked her hair, and Taria closed her eyes. "That's what your father does here. He's helping put things back together."

"Auntie Li says that there are awful monsters on Thunder. She says there are dragons and ogres, and that they'll come here and eat us."

"Auntie Li has an overactive imagination, Taria, and she loves to tell fairy tales."

"Gramma said there were monsters back home."

Mama smiled. "That's your Gramma's Maori part talking, Taria. She likes to tell the old tales sometimes. They're just stories, like Auntie Li's. There aren't any monsters on Thunder. It . . . it isn't even a *place*, like New Zealand or China. No one's sure what it is."

"If no one knows what it is, then there *might* be monsters there," Taria persisted. Turning her head, she could just see the window, and the night sky outside. There were no stars, all washed away in city glow.

"If there are monsters on Thunder, they wouldn't hurt you, Taria. Not you, they wouldn't. I promise."

"But if Thunder's a bad thing, and the monsters are bad, too—"

"Shh . . ." Taria felt her mother's lips brush her hair. "I don't know if you'll understand this yet, but the truth is, Taria, that things are only rarely black and white. Good people sometimes do bad things, and people you think are mostly bad can do things to help you. You never know."

Taria nodded, not entirely convinced. Auntie Li had

wonderfully awful stories, and told them so well, and in *her* world, at least, evil was always totally evil . . . "Mama, do you know what I want for my birthday?"

Another stroke, pressing Taria's head against her mother's soft chest. "No, darling. What do you want?"

"I want us to go back home to where Gramma and Grampa are. That's what I wished for on my last birthday—that we'd go back there when I was five."

A sound almost like a sob escaped her mother's throat. The hand stopped moving through Taria's hair, and began again. "That would be nice, wouldn't it? Someday, soon, we will. Soon."

"Why not now?"

"It's not that simple, darling."

"For my birthday?"

"We'll see," Mama said. "We'll see."

For the moment, Taria was four. She would be five in a month and a half.

Taria's memories of China always contained crowds. The streets of Nanjing were constantly stuffed with people, loud with an eternal din of voices and conversations, redolent with the smells of spices hung in market stalls and shops and the open charcoal fires of food vendors. She was too young to understand most of what was going on outside their apartment building. Taria's days were spent with Auntie Li, who spoke very little English, and none at all when she was watching Taria. After nearly a year in China, Taria spoke Mandarin nearly as well as her native tongue.

Taria also knew that hunger was constant for her, though even she noticed that her rice bowl was usually more full than that of her either of her parents', and that there was often a treat of a piece of grilled chicken or fish on top of her bowl. She knew that her parents talked of leaving Nanjing soon, that the government might shut down Mama's work but that Mama couldn't find a job back where her grandparents lived in New Zealand, and the Chinese government might not give her father the visa he needed to leave.

The summer of 2067 had been a landscape of cloudless, unrelentingly hot days in the Yangtze delta. With the heat and accompanying drought, rice paddies became broken, cracked mudflats, while the numerous lakes around Nanjing evaporated to puddles. Market days were more chaotic than usual, with screaming, pushing throngs fighting for what little food arrived in the city—there had been food riots in nearby cities, Taria would learn later.

She only rarely accompanied her mother on her trips to the market. Usually she stayed behind with Auntie Li or her father, but Auntie Li was visiting relatives across the Yangtze, and Papa was working in Beijing for the weekend. So Taria went along with Mama, who admonished her to stay close. As foreigners, the two of them were painfully conspicuous in the throngs. For the most part they were well-treated, though from time to time they could hear a muttered curse or feel the pressure of stares. Still, the people who knew Taria and her mother greeted them with a loud *"Chi fan le ma!"* to which Taria would reply just as loudly: *"Chi le!"* Her mother just smiled back and nodded. Taria enjoyed talking with neighbors and acquaintances as they pushed through the lanes near the old Chang Gate. There were pats on the head and pinches on the cheek, and smiles. Taria was laughing and smiling back.

A fruit shipment had just arrived by boat from Shanghai. Taria could see a heap of muskmelons through the shifting bodies, surrounded by milling people with hands stretched toward an unseen vendor, clutching handfuls of brightly colored money, and shrieking in high voices. "Hold onto my coat, Taria," Mama whispered. "Tightly now . . ." and they plunged into the fray.

In her memory there were quick images of the next few minutes, snapshots of chaos:

. . . faces contorted with shouts all around her, a waving, moving forest of arms and legs and white cloth.

. . . Mama snatching a muskmelon from the ground where it had momentarily rolled free of the pile. She smiled, even though Taria saw the mottled bruise on the pale skin of the fruit. "Look, Taria! This will taste good at supper tonight . . ."

. . . a hand, a man's hand, snatching at Mama. Taria clearly remembered the hand, fisted around Mama's small wrist. The fingers were grimy, and the nails were shattered, thick and yellow. *"Neige shì wo hamigua!"* he shouted at Mama in Mandarin. "That's my melon! Give it to me!" Mama pulled away, and for a moment the man was lost in the crowd.

"Come on!" Mama said to Taria. "Quickly now!"

The man was still shouting in Mandarin behind them as Mama's hand caught hers, her adult fingers interlaced with her small ones as she tugged her away. "Mama," Taria said, "that man . . ."

But Mama only looked concerned and a little frightened, and she didn't listen. Her head was tossing from side to side, and she let go of Taria to pull a fistful of change from her pocket. "Where's the vendor?" she said, almost angrily. "I want to pay and get out of here."

"That's what I'm trying to tell you," Taria said. Mama didn't understand Mandarin anywhere near as well as she did. Mama still stumbled over the simplest phrases, and she never got the tones right. Taria pulled at her mother's coat, trying to pull her back. "That man's the—"

"Ta tou le hamigua!"

Taria looked back to see the man—the vendor—emerge from the crowd. "She has stolen my melon!" he cried again, but Mama didn't understand the stream of fast, high words. She only heard the tone and saw the tight anger in the man's face. Change jingled onto the concrete as Mama grasped at Taria's hand and her mother started to run. *"Tíng!"* he shouted: Stop! Only Mama didn't stop and she was pulling so hard at Taria that she nearly fell, looking behind at the melon vendor.

There was a glint of metal in the man's hand, and someone shrilled in alarm as everyone moved away. There was a *bang* that sounded like a cough, then another one, and Mama staggered. Her hand pulled away from Taria . . .

. . . there was blood on Taria's hands and spattered over her clothes and people were shouting and screaming and Taria couldn't understand anything except that Mama was sprawled in the street, her eyes open, and she wouldn't move, wouldn't move at all, and just out of reach of Mama's outflung hand the melon lay smashed and broken, the pale juice running out to mingle with the dark, dark blood . . .

"Ni hao ma?"

The old man from the apartment down the hall stuck his head in the door of their rooms and asked how she was. Taria screamed, seeing a male Chinese face through the screen of hovering women, afraid that he would shoot her the way Mama had been shot by the melon vendor . . .

Taria always wondered why she remembered so little of the events following her mother's death—how could she forget something so horrible? The world had changed around her in that instant, and her memory of it was fogged like an old picture. She sometimes thought that she should go to a hypnotist and let herself be taken back to that moment, but she was afraid.

For a long time she was afraid.

A few things she could recall: the loud scuffle as several bystanders wrestled the melon vendor to the ground; a wall of concerned faces all speaking in fast Chinese; an unknown woman picking her up and taking her away from her mother's body, whispering "Poor baby, poor baby" in heavily accented English; the wail of sirens; shouting . . .

For a long time she could not stand crowds, nor the sound of firecrackers, and sudden loud shouts could startle her for years afterward.

Her father returned to Nanjing that night. Taria remembered that moment: the way the crowd in the front room of their apartment suddenly went silent, then dissolved away as if they were smoke, leaving her alone with him.

"Papa, the melon vendor shot Mama. He thought she was stealing, but she wasn't. She just didn't understand him and . . ."

Silently, he nodded, and went to where she sat on a nest of pillows.

He hugged her for a long time, and she realized he was crying. She could have stayed there in his arms forever, but finally his arms loosened around her and he sat back. A forearm swiped at his eyes, and he ran his fingers through his hair. "Your mother's gone away, darling," he said, his voice soft and trembling, as dark as the room. Light from an oil lamp limned his face with yellow.

"Yes, Papa. She's gone to Thunder. She went there to wait for us."

He looked startled, his face ruddy in the lamplight of the room. "Why would you think that, Taria?"

"Because," Taria replied, with the earnest seriousness that only a four-year-old can muster, "Mama always said that Thunder was the best thing that ever happened to her, no matter how bad it made things for everyone. So that's where she'd go to wait for us."

Her father never told her that she was wrong. Instead he turned away for a moment, staring into the darkness of the room with his back to her, and he sighed, as if—somehow—the answer satisfied him.

 **LIGHTBRINGER**

The shape came closer, and familiar arms went around her and she was suddenly small again, a four-almost-five-year-old again, and Mama was clutching her. "You knew I would be here, didn't you?" Mama said, and they were both crying as they hugged each other. "You knew and you came for me . . ."

Taria woke, and found herself crying.

"Hey . . ." Kyung's voice came quietly from the darkness on the other side of the bed, and a hand stroked Taria's back. Kyung snuggled closer so that she felt the warmth of his body along her back. Taria sniffed, burying her face in her pillow. "What's the matter, love?"

Taria sighed. "I don't know," she said, which was a half-truth. *The dream . . .* But she didn't want to talk to Kyung about the dream. In the talks they'd shared, Taria had told Kyung about her mother, about her senseless murder in Nanjing. She'd even told him about how the little girl she'd once been had believed that Mama had gone to wait for her at Thunder.

But she hadn't mentioned that the dreams still came. She hadn't mentioned the illogical sense of disappointment she felt ever since they'd gone through the wormhole. She'd kept all that to herself, armored deep inside where the sharp spines and points of memory couldn't hurt her.

"I don't know," she said again, more softly this time.

She could hear Kyung's breathing in the blackness, could feel the faint thrum of the ship, the grumble as the living quarters spun in their endless rotation. Soft lips brushed the back of her neck, lightly kissing; a hand brushed hair from her temples. Taria caught the hand, pressing it against her lips so she could kiss the palm: a callused hand, a working hand, not soft like hers, the skin sallow against her own. *Like the hand of the melon vendor . . .* Taria let the hand go. "I'm all right now," she told the darkness and Kyung. "Go back to sleep."

"We're all a little scared here." Kyung's voice was honey, slow and thick. "I'm scared, too. So far from home . . ."

It's not that, Taria wanted to say. *Not really.* "You don't ever seem scared," she said instead, speaking to the darkness in front of her.

Another kiss, this time on the shoulder. His voice was a dark whisper in the night. "I get scared. I was terrified—just before I got into the Firebird and fell into Thunder. I went into the prep room and sat down, my hands shaking and sweating, just thinking of the immensity of it all. I wondered whether the others did the same thing. I wished you were there so you could tell me it was all right, that I didn't have to worry, that you'd be there for me when I came back."

"I wish I'd been able to do that," Taria said. "I do. And I'm glad you're here now. I'm sorry I woke you up."

Kyung almost laughed; Taria could feel his breath on her back. "Hey, don't apologize. It's almost time to get up for our shifts, anyway." A finger stroked the curve of Taria's breast, circled her nipple, then slid down the curve of her hip. Another kiss on the back of the neck, then at the ear, more demanding this time. Taria turned, found Kyung's lips, and pressed desperately against him as if she could obliterate the last shreds of the dreams with his touch, with the heat, with the passion.

For a little while, lost in Kyung's embrace, she forgot everything.

In time patterns began to emerge. The ExoAnthro team would watch a tape of two Blues interacting and—with Rosie's assistance—try to respond as if they were the Blue being addressed. Sometimes Rosie's translation program would work; more often the conversation went on some other tangent. But they had a greeting sequence; they had the beginnings of a Blue dictionary.

It was the moment for First Contact . . .

The disagreement over how to make that initial contact was raucous. There were volunteers enough to go down to Little Sister, but the regulations under which *Lightbringer* operated called for strict medical isolation for anyone returning from contact with an alien species or planet. Biohazard suits were the required uniform for those "performing extravehicular excursions to alien spacecraft or worlds." Taria, along with several others, argued that the Blues might be frightened if someone appeared in a biosuit. At best it would give them a false indication of what humans looked like. The air on Little Sister was eminently breathable—a touch more oxygen than Earth, slightly less CO_2, a variant mix of noble gases, but definitely able to support and sustain terrestrial life. Biosuits were simply paranoia, Taria argued. Lab animals aboard *Lightbringer* had been exposed to Little Sister's air, and soil samples brought back by the bugs, and none of them had exhibited any ill effect at all.

That argument was overruled. The regs were the regs.

Taria remembered all the books she'd read, the movies she'd seen: the space traveler stepping down from a sleek craft to greet the waiting aliens, like a futuristic Columbus stepping triumphantly from his boat with the Indians waiting curiously on the shore. That's the way it was in all the books, in the movies. But it wasn't the way it would be here.

First Contact was made by Commander Allison, as a hologram.

Allison stood against a green screen in *Lightbringer* with an array of holocameras set around him. Down on Little Sister, a holoprojector had been dropped outside the main door of what they called the "Cathedral." They'd identified one of the Blues there, one to whom the other Blues deferred, and referred to with the title of "Baraaki." As near as ExoAnthro could figure, the Baraaki was something close to a priest or archbishop, since her duties seemed to be largely ceremonial and religious in nature. When the Baraaki came from the entrance of the Cathedral, as she did every morning, Commander Allison struck a pose with hands open in a gesture of friendship; on the planet, his image did the same a few seconds later. Taria, as well as the rest of the ExoAnthro team, watched the monitors, as did most of *Lightbringer*'s crew. This was, after all, a momentous occasion, even if the Blues weren't the Makers. This was the moment where humankind would finally interact with another race.

The speakers of the holoprojector bellowed the greeting phrase.

And the Baraaki went over to the holoprojector, touching its metallic surface as she answered, and ignoring the image of Commander Allison entirely.

Taria wasn't sure where the laughter started, but it rippled through the room, through the ship, growing louder with each moment. Taria chuckled herself, watching the Baraaki inquire gravely of the holoprojector who it might be. Before the green screen, Allison's cheeks flushed.

As a First Contact, it was hardly grand or majestic.

"Here you go."

Colin tossed the bundle of ship-scrip toward Taria; as usual, she misjudged the parabola thrown objects always took in the centripetal force that served for gravity in

Lightbringer's living quarters. The bundle landed on the floor next to her terminal, at Dog's feet, and she picked it up as Dog cocked its head inquiringly. "What's this?"

"You haven't heard? You won the pool."

"No kidding?"

Colin pulled a flimsy from his pocket and squinted at it over his glasses. Taria always wondered how, with his eyesight, Colin managed to get chosen for the mission, even if he was a uni. Colin's PIA, a small blue dragon, was curled around his neck like a scaled scarf. It lifted its head as if it were also reading the flimsy. "Yep. You were right about the eyestrips—the new computer models indicate that the Blues can't see for shit. No focusing ability at all. That's why the Baraaki ignored the holo of Allison. Which also means no books, no written history: the current bet is that everything's orally transmitted. McDermott's still claiming that's impossible even for their minimal technological level, but Allison's already adjusting the contact protocols accordingly. You win."

Taria fanned the scrip before putting it in her pocket. "So when do we go down?"

Colin glanced down and away, and that told Taria more than words.

"Goddamn it," she said. "I'm not part of FirstTeam, after I found them, after all the analysis I did from the surveillance? After I was the one who told Allison we should contact the Blues? After my call on Blue eyesight?"

Colin at least had the grace to look uncomfortable. The dragon wriggled around his throat, hiding its head under its tail. "Allison wants FirstTeam to be unis."

"Fuck."

"Taria, I'm sorry—"

"So when the hell was Allison going to tell me? After FirstTeam left? Never?"

Colin's face was flushed—this was obviously a conversation he hadn't intended to become involved in. His PIA lifted its head and hissed. "Look, don't shoot the messenger here, Taria. In fact, I'm not even the messenger. All I wanted to do was hand you the goddamn pool money. The commander was planning to tell you the rest at the end of the shift."

"Yeah. I'll just bet he was." Taria shoved her chair away from the terminal; the monofoil slid back into the desk in response.

"Where are you going?"

"Where do you think?—to talk with Allison."

"I wouldn't."

"Of course you wouldn't. That's why you're a uni." It came out more sharply than Taria intended, but she didn't care.

By the time she reached Allison's office at the end of the ExoAnthro deck, the door was already dilating open. *"Come on in, Spears,"* Allison's voice spoke in her head, relayed from Dog, who was no longer trotting alongside her but had suddenly disappeared. The Cube, Allison's PIA, sat on his desk. The door closed and opaqued behind her.

Allison sat behind the desk, one small light casting illumination on the dark surface. One finger nudged his nameplate, which was already in perfect alignment with the desk's edge, and motioned to the side of the desk, where a chair was already rising from the floor. Taria ignored it, standing in front of Allison's desk. She put her hands down on the faux-wood surface, taking pleasure in knocking the nameplate askew.

"I've been given to understand that I'm not on First-Team."

Allison looked in dismay at the nameplate and ignored it with a visible effort before looking up at Taria. His pale blue eyes always seemed vaguely sinister to Taria, with their lightness in an otherwise swarthy face. "That's right," Allison said, two syllables spit out with precision.

"Commander, I think I have every right to be considered . . ." Taria's voice trailed off; Allison was holding up a hand, waiting.

"Do you suddenly think these Blues are likely to be the Makers?"

"No sir, but—" The hand came up again, and Taria exhaled loudly, but went silent.

"Then this is hardly the most important contact we'll make, is it?"

"Maybe not, but it's still the *first* actual contact we'll make with an alien race. This is going to be a historic moment. Why is the picture going to show nothing but a bunch of people in uniforms?"

No answer. Only the flat, pale, unblinking stare.

"Look, I know you don't like me," Taria continued, "but my work—"

"Your work has been exemplary," Allison finished. "I have no problem with your work."

"What *do* you have a problem with?" Taria straightened, lifting her hands from Allison's desk, and Allison reached forward to straighten the nameplate again.

"Let's go off the record, Spears," he said.

"If that's what you want, Commander—fine."

Allison glanced at the Cube, which pulsed once brightly and then vanished. At the same time Taria heard Dog bark, and her connection with the network went dead as her neural web disconnected. Allison put his hands flat on the desktop and leaned forward toward her. "I don't know what you want. I don't think you do, either."

Taria almost laughed. "You don't know what I *want*? What kind of asinine logic is that?" A breath. "Commander."

Allison hardly moved at all. He steepled his hands under his chin and stared up at her. "It's not logic at all. Right angles don't necessarily imply logic, Spears, only obsession. I watch you and how you interact, and I look at your dossier, and I think you have a lot of emotional baggage invested in this mission, enough—since we seem to be talking frankly here—that I'm mildly surprised you weren't washed out in the first psych profiles before your file even got to my desk. But it did, and *I* chose you—that should say something to you about how I feel."

"I'd rather hear you say I'm part of FirstTeam."

"No."

"That's it? No?"

"You'll get your turn downworld, but not on FirstTeam. You want it too much—or you wouldn't be here now, would you?"

"C'mon, Commander. That's not fair: if I come to you and plead my case, then I want it too much; if I say nothing, you just go ahead and leave me off FirstTeam. Seems to me I lose either way."

"I'm sorry you feel that way."

"I don't think you're sorry at all, Commander. I don't think you like me or trust me."

An eyebrow raised slightly.

It was the only answer she would get.

Taria could feel Kyung's gaze on her as she paced. She glanced over at the uni, and the half-amused look on Kyung's face only stoked her anger. "I don't find it funny in the slightest," she said.

"I don't know what you expected, Taria," Kyung answered. "*Lightbringer*'s a military ship."

She wanted support. She wanted to be held, to fold herself into Kyung and tell him all she was feeling, to cry if she felt like it, and to have Kyung tell her that she was right and Allison wrong, that he understood—even if he didn't.

Taria wanted the lie even if they both knew it was a lie. But Kyung wouldn't give her the lie, and that made Taria angry, also.

"*Lightbringer*'s supposed to be an exploratory ship," Taria answered. They were speaking Mandarin, as they usually did when alone. Back and forth: Taria strode between her bed and the door, gesticulating extravagantly. Dog watched her, too, his holographic head swiveling as he sat patiently near her dresser. "The unis are here in case there's trouble, but we're supposed to be conducting a scientific mission. That's what the public was told. That's why I came." Taria stopped, slamming her open hand against the wall, then grimacing at the sting. "I'm the only one who said anything in the last meeting. Everyone else just fucking sat there and listened . . ." The obscenities were pure Shiplish in the midst of the Mandarin. Taria snorted in derision.

"We don't know anything about the culture of the aliens down there on Little Sister, Taria. There's nothing wrong with being careful."

"They haven't *done* anything to us," Taria retorted. "From the recordings I've seen from the survey satellites, they *can't* do anything to us. Hell, they still don't even seem to know we're here at all, even after the incident with the holo. They're on a medieval level, technologically. You unis want to set up a goddamn satellite weapons system before we go down, and Allison's talking about sending an all-military contingent to make the real first contact, ready to blast them out of existence if they look at us strangely."

"You're exaggerating, Taria, and you know it."

"I'm not far off, and you know that."

Kyung was shaking his head. "So you'd go down there unarmed and open? And if in their culture people with light brown hair are all demon-spawn and are required to be boiled in oil and dismembered, you'd be fine with that, too?"

Taria gave him a look of disgust and resumed pacing. "I really love the support you're giving me here, Kyung. In any case, it's a lot more likely that in their culture people who show aggression and display weapons are considered hostile and dangerous."

"I'm comfortable with their having that perception. It's the same impression I'd want to give the Thunder Makers when we meet them. Taria, I understand what you're saying. I really do. And I *do* support you, when I think you're right. This time, though, I think you're letting idealism get in the way of common sense. I've been in combat, and I've seen that a little healthy paranoia can save lives. We've had this disagreement before, I know, but I love you too much not to want us to be careful." Kyung rose from the bed and shrugged on his uniform jacket. He started to take a step toward Taria, and she saw uncertainty cross his face as he studied hers. He stopped, his hands still lifted in the beginning of an embrace.

They stared at each other; at first it seemed they were each waiting for the other to speak. Taria knew that if she'd smiled then, the mood might have changed. They might have hugged and kissed and, if not ended the discussion, at least shown some sympathy toward the other's viewpoint. But she didn't smile, and then it seemed they'd been staring too long, that it had shifted from intimacy to contest, neither one of them willing to break the eye contact.

It was Kyung who finally blinked. "I have to go. I'm on duty in fifteen minutes. Meet you back here at 2200?"

Taria looked at him. It was like seeing a stranger in front of her. All she saw were the bars and crossed muzzles on his lapels. "I don't think I'll be here then," she answered.

Kyung didn't move. "I'm not the uniform I wear, Taria. If you think that, then you're making the same mistake you're accusing Allison of making. Or am I just the next casualty in your long list of failed relationships?" He put his hand on the door plate, looking back at Taria as if waiting for her to say something.

Taria shook her head and shrugged simultaneously. A dozen different answers were all crammed together in her throat and she couldn't say any of them.

"Maybe tomorrow night," she managed at last. "Maybe."

Kyung hit the door plate. The door shushed open.

"Taria, if you can't even communicate with me, how the hell are you going to accomplish it down there?"

His dark, silent eyes were the last thing Taria saw as he left.

Taria watched the initial meetings with the Blues over the network along with everyone else. It wasn't the same as being there, and she remained angry that Allison hadn't named her to FirstTeam, but at least she could observe the events. All the meetings took place within a structure erected by the unis—an airtight inflatable building, with a transparent membrane and positive air pressure separating the humans and the Blues. Though they appeared to sit at a table in a room together, the truth was that they were segregated, each breathing their own filtered air, neither environment permitted to intrude on the other. In addition, returnees to *Lightbringer* from Little Sister went through Decon first: stripped naked, their clothes incinerated, their bodies scrubbed with antiseptic sprays and low-level radiation. No one wanted an alien virus or bacteria loose aboard the ship.

The monofoil on Taria's desk gave her an array of views from the video feed; she bounced from one to another, watching more than listening—this particular meeting was mostly to clear up linguistic problems.

Though it was already obvious that no human would be able to reproduce the Blues' speech without massive artificial aids, the Blues had demonstrated a remarkable facility for language, becoming semifluent in Shiplish within a month, though all of them mimicked Commander Allison's unmistakable Alabama accent. The Blues learned a little *too* quickly for some of ExoAnthro—their facility with a language bereft of any common roots or experience spoke of an intelligence that their society and scope of knowledge seemed to contradict.

There were still difficulties; at the moment it was pronouns. The Blue language itself had no sexed pronouns and the use of *he* and *she,* and *it* confused them. There was only one generic pronoun, and it was used rarely—the name of the person being referred to was generally used, unless the single pronoun's reference was unmistakably clear.

Taria watched as Allison pointed to one of the warrior caste—they were always present, always lurking in the background, even though it was the Blue Baraaki, whose name was Makes-the-Sound-of-East-Wind, who seemed to be their lead negotiator. Warriors wore no clothing at all except for a wide leather belt with hammered strips of silvery metal as decoration, and they were decidedly male: the Blue male genitalia was complicated and almost comically elaborate, with six pairs of bulblike structures arranged in a V from hips to mid-thigh, a rasplike horn surrounded by fleshy nubs at the junction of the legs, and another long, brilliant red whiplike structure emerging from somewhere below the horn, the length of which, in the case of the males in front of Taria now, was coiled two or three times around each of their right legs down to the knee. How the various bits lined up with the corresponding female parts, no one yet knew.

Allison pointed to one of the warriors. "For instance, that one is a male, so we would use 'he' as the subject, 'him' for the object, or for the possessive, 'his,' " he said.

"You are a male, also, Allison-Who-Is-Commander?" Makes-the-Sound-of-East-Wind asked.

"Yes."

"And you have the same genitals?"

There was a distinct pause. "Mine are . . . smaller," Allison said finally, and Taria heard Colin, in the next cubicle, snort with laughter.

She hit the cubicle wall with her fist. "Grow up," she said.

"C'mon, Taria," Colin's voice answered. "Tell me you didn't at least smile at that."

She had. She was grinning so hard her cheek muscles ached.

"The human penis looks very different," Allison was explaining with an expression of deadpan seriousness on his face. "But essentially it performs the same function, yes."

The Blue Baraaki made a strange, hooting sound which they'd already decided was an acknowledgment of understanding. Even over the limited sound reproduction abilities of the network, the range of tone in the sound was impressive. "So if a person is not-male, they are female and you would not use 'he'?"

For a moment Taria had felt a prickling crawl along her spine, a nagging unease at something Makes had just said. But then Allison's voice answered Makes. "Correct. Then you would use 'she,' 'her,' or 'hers.' And for a nonsexed thing, like this table, we use 'it,' 'it,' or 'its.' "

"But you just referred to your male genitals as 'it,' and they are definitely sexed. Why didn't you say 'essentially *he* performs the same function'?"

Taria grinned at that, and there was more laughter from the cubicles. Alongside her, Dog barked once. "I think Makes got him, there," Colin called over the cubicle wall. "I'll bet Allison's even got a cute little pet name for it, too."

"Colin . . ."

"Sorry," he said, but there was still laughter in his voice.

"You should be. Besides, no one ever said language was logical," Taria replied. "No nice, neat right angles for the Cube, just lots of curvy, squiggly bits." A chuckle answered her. "Though I guess that does answer one question," Taria continued. "Makes is female. I wonder how it all fits together—all that fancy stuff wrapped around the warrior's leg?"

"Now who has a dirty mind?"

On the monofoil Allison waved his hands as he explained that body parts were not considered to have a sex. "My mind's not dirty. Just scientifically curious," Taria answered Colin.

"Right."

"Hey, sex is important to *every* species."

"That's what I keep telling my partner. But does he listen?"

"I was talking about reproduction, Colin. Besides . . ."

"Who said sex had anything to do with reproduction?" Colin snickered. "And besides what?"

The uneasiness Taria felt had vanished. The thought that had precipitated it was gone. Allison was still talking to Makes on the monofoil, explaining the use of pronouns in excruciating detail. Taria wondered how Makes managed to listen without yawning.

Maybe when she reviewed the scene at the staff debriefing, she'd remember . . .

"Nothing," she answered Colin. "Nothing."

The butterflies were worse than Taria had thought.

After all, she'd watched the previous meetings with the Blues as they happened, she'd been an active part of the debriefing meetings, studied the Blues as hard or harder than anyone on *Lightbringer*.

But the knowledge that she was about to meet them herself for the first time made her stomach churn and her throat dry.

She wondered how Commander Allison felt. If anything, after four previous meetings already, he looked bored—which might actually be the truth. In their meetings, it had become apparent that the Blues had no idea who had made Thunder. They knew something was out there—they spoke of hearing a "Voice-From-the-Emptiness-Above-Us," which could only be Thunder. But they attributed this Voice to their deity, not to another race.

Contact with the Blues was to be *only* practice. Period.

The solution to the mystery of Thunder lay somewhere else. The Blues were a way to test their methodologies and perceptions regarding alien contact. But the Blues weren't important, not anymore—the *Lightbringer* unis had mostly lost interest in them since the Blues were also hardly a military threat to anyone, while ScienceOps and ExoAnthro had turned back to searching for signs of the Makers and trying to unravel the mysteries of Thunder from this side of the wormhole. The Blues were unusual, but the novelty had worn away like the finish on a cheap piece of costume jewelry. *Lightbringer* was not a colony ship. Little Sister might be an Earthlike world, but no one on this ship intended to live there. Ever. An ExoAnthro uni, Ensign Alex Coen, had been dispatched to explore the interior of the continent, and his first reports indicated there was nothing particularly unique to recommend Little Sister. The interior of Little Sister's continent seemed to be uninhabited by anything other than native animals—there was no sign of the Thunder Makers there, either.

While the Thunder Makers were still Out There Somewhere, the Blues and Little Sister could only be peripheral to *Lightbringer*'s main mission.

While the attention of *Lightbringer* and the ExoAnthro unit began to drift away from the Blues, Taria continued to find them fascinating, though she wasn't certain why. Maybe it was the orchestral quality of their voices, which reminded her of a chorus, or their quaint faith in a nature God they called She-Who-Spoke-the-World. Maybe it was simply the chance to untangle the warp and woof of their society and see how it worked.

Taria looked at Allison as they prepared to greet the Blues, his face set in a stony neutrality, and knew that he, at least, felt none of that allure.

The meeting took place, like all the others, in the environmental tent. A tubeway ran from the shuttle to the structure. The Blues were already there on the other side of the massive table dividing the tent's main room; beyond, Taria could glimpse the landscape of Little Sister. The Cube sang the multivoiced greeting sequence, though the rest of the meeting would be conducted in Shiplish. The humans nodded to the Blues, who stretched out hands toward them in their own greeting pattern, but those hands could never meet human skin. This was a negotiation that would never end in a handshake—not unless those hands were gloved and sealed.

Normally, the sessions were choreographed: the greetings, the exchange of information asked for in the last session, the agenda and timetable for the next meeting. For the most part the interchanges had been prosaic and unremarkable—some basic history, sociology, customs, beliefs. On the human side, Taria knew, ExoAnthro had controlled the information carefully. While no one had precisely lied, no one had precisely told the truth, either. They'd concealed the military aspects and capabilities of *Lightbringer,* they'd wrapped the location of Earth in studied misinformation—though it hardly seemed necessary for such a poorly sighted and technologically backward society as that of the Blues—they'd emphasized the successes of human civilization while downplaying its excesses and violence.

Every one of them fully expected that the Blues had done the same.

There were five Blues present: three of the "priests" seated on the far side of the table and two naked "warriors"—flamboyantly male—standing well back near the Blue entrance. The priest on the left side, which in Blue society was the place of prominence, was the Baraaki, Makes-the-Sound-of-East-Wind. The Baraaki was second in social stature only to the Neritorika, the ultimate head of Blue society in this city. No one had yet met this Neritorika.

Taria took it all in as she seated herself well to the right of Allison. Seeing the Blues closely was far, far different from seeing them through the eyes of the cameras. She could see the leathery texture of their aquamarine skin, could catch the glinting of the eyestrip and the way the earlets on their head-crests flexed and curled. She even thought she could smell them, a faint, spicelike and pleasant odor, though with the precautions ExoAnthro was taking against infection, that was more likely an artifact of the environmental barrier than actual Blue-scent.

The end of the Cube's greeting sequence trailed off, and Makes responded in simple Shiplish. "Hello." Her voice was soft after Allison's barrage of language.

In each of the past sessions, Makes had allowed Allison to lead after the initial greeting. This time, unexpectedly, the Baraaki continued. "I would like to ask a question of each of you," she said. Her head-crest swelled and earlets fluttered, as if she were listening to each of them. Taria saw that most of the earlets were cupped in her direction, and the Blue's hand lifted and a finger pointed to her chest. "I would like to know from you why you have come here," the Baraaki said.

"Me?" Taria asked in surprise, looking more at Allison than the Blue.

"Yes. Tell us why you-singular have come here."

Allison nodded, faintly. Taria let out a breath, started to speak, and stopped. She waved her hands. "I . . . I just want to understand," she said. "That's all, Baraaki." She stopped, wondering whether she should elaborate, but the Baraaki gave her no chance. She grumbled deep in her chest, and the earlets swiveled to face Colin, seated next to Taria at the table.

"And you?" Makes asked.

Taria didn't remember the exact words Colin used, or any of the other replies. She could feel embarrassment hot on her cheeks as Colin smoothly went through a long, flowery string of evocative phrases that each of the others, on down the line, echoed in their own words. Taria hated her own spare words, hated the fact that she'd been caught totally off guard and unprepared, and each person's grandiloquent summaries of their goal only seemed to make her bald sentence seem more barren and sparse.

But after Commander Allison's short speech on the glories of interstellar friendship and the expansion of a shared pool of knowledge, the Baraaki turned back to Taria.

"Will you stay here with us?" Makes-the-Sound-of-East-Wind said. "We will help you understand. Will you come here to stay with us?"

"Yes," Taria answered. The word required no thought. There was no hesitation in her, no caution. She felt the rightness of the answer and didn't even glance over at Allison, who she knew would be glaring at her. "Yes. I'd like that."

In the end Taria was reluctantly granted permission to go down to Little Sister. She had to sign a dozen forms relieving everyone from all responsibility and liability should one of those alien viruses decide to leave her dead. She put her name on a half-dozen releases asserting that she was going downworld of her own free choice, that she understood and accepted the risks involved. She signed an addendum to her *Lightbringer* contract outlining the year-long isolation that would result as a consequence of her exposure to Little Sister's environment, should she survive. She'd endured interview after interview with everyone from Admiral McElwan to a lowly medical staffer who'd wanted to review her psych profile—again. She'd agreed that the unis would monitor her PIA link to *Lightbringer*'s network.

Alex Coen's neural web went dead in the network the same day, and the shuttle sent down to look for him in the vast wilderness of the interior was unable to locate Coen, his body, or the land buggy he used as a base. The Blues in all probability had nothing to do with Coen's disappearance, but Taria agreed to delicately probe for any answer to Ensign Coen's whereabouts. "Yes," she'd said to everything they'd asked. "I'll do it."

If the unis found the Thunder Makers, she might kick herself for missing the real show, the true work of the expedition. She might be in isolation then, or trapped on Little Sister, or (yes) dead. But this was what she'd come for.

"I'll do anything you want, sign anything you put in front of me. Yes."

Kyung's reaction was more visceral.

When Kyung heard she was going to Little Sister, he said, "Taria, you've got to be kidding."

"Do I *look* like I'm kidding?" she replied, gesturing to the backpack sitting by the door, stuffed almost to bursting. Dog sat next to the pack, listening with her head cocked to one side, a pink tongue lolling in her open mouth. Dog almost looked as if she were smiling. Kyung seemed more irritated than anything else. They were speaking Mandarin. "Listen, it's not a big deal. I'll be back aboard *Lightbringer* in a month. Two at the most."

"I think you're crazy to be going in the first place, Taria, and *especially* crazy to do it alone when we've already lost contact with Coen. You're looking at a ship-year in medical isolation when you get back, for Christ's sake. I'm going to talk to Commander Allison—"

"No, you won't. I'm not going to be alone. I'll have Dog if I want her, and I'll be with Makes. You can talk to me whenever you want to over the comlink."

"Right." Kyung sighed. "You think this Makes person or any of the Blues are going to help you if you get into trouble? Maybe the Blues will *start* the trouble—we really don't know them at all. What if something happens to you, some simple accident? A virus crossing species, a sting from an insect, a poisonous bite, a reaction to chemicals in the air, or just tripping over a tree root and hitting your head on a stone. Taria, I can think of a thousand ways for you to die down there."

"That's comforting. Why don't you share a few more of them and really make me feel good?"

Kyung ignored that. "I could have asked Commander Merritt for a leave, maybe . . ."

"The Blues asked for *me*, Kyung. They met our delegation, they spoke with Commander Allison and Admiral McElwan and all the precious little unis running *Light-bringer*, and they asked for *me* to come back to Little Sister and learn about them. How can I *not* go?"

"You could have asked me before you said yes."

So that was it, Taria thought. Kyung wasn't so much worried as he was annoyed that she hadn't consulted with him before making the decision. *I didn't have* time *to ask you*, she started to say. *We had to tell Makes yes or no right then.* But even thinking of telling Kyung all of that made the statement seem like an apology, and she had no intention of apologizing for her choice. Taria clenched her jaw and jammed a packet of water purification tabs into the top of the pack. She could feel Kyung's gaze on her back. *You weren't* asked *to go*, she wanted to say, her chin lifting with the words. *They only want* me, *no one else.* "Since when are you interested in anything to do with the Blues? The Blues aren't the Makers, nor do they seem to be able to help us find them, so the Blues aren't important. You know what, Kyung," she said, looking away from him, "I can even figure out that that's the reason I get to go—because the Blues aren't a high enough priority for your superiors to deal with anymore."

At least Kyung had the grace to admit she might be right. "Maybe. But I'm interested in *you*, Taria. Not them."

Taria turned, still crouched down by the pack. "You're not interested in what I'm interested in. You don't have the slightest curiosity about the Blues now that it's been decided they're too backward to even get off their own world, much less construct something like Thunder. All anyone cares about is finding the Makers."

"I thought that was what you cared about, too. What the hell are you looking for down there, Taria? What is it you think you can find? You always said you wanted to find the Makers—that bit about you being conceived when Thunder appeared, about your mother—"

Taria stood up a little too quickly. *Mama lying on the*

ground, sprawled out like a broken doll . . . *"Shì de,"* she said. "Yes. But the Makers aren't making themselves visible right now, and I'm not so quick to dismiss the Blues. Maybe they know more than they're telling us. Maybe we just haven't asked the right questions. I don't know. *None* of us do, not really."

Kyung made an exasperated face and spread his hands. There was a touch of anger in his dark eyes, even though Taria knew he was trying to keep it hidden. "Taria, you have to admit that right now, the work I'm involved in is a bit more—" He stopped, finally noticing the irritation that was spreading like slow red tide across Taria's face, a heat she could feel both on her cheeks and inside.

" 'Important.' Is that what you were going to say, Kyung? Sending probes back and forth through Thunder is more important? Scanning every last rock in the system for some sign of the Makers is more important? Making sure all your lovely weapons are oiled and gleaming in case you need to use them is more important?"

He didn't even try to deny it. Kyung sighed instead, letting his hands drop to his sides. "I don't want you to go," he said simply. "If you're hurt—"

"Then I'll have Dog call for the shuttle and an autosurgeon. Unless, of course, I'm dead. Now that *would* be inconvenient for you. You'd have to ask Dog to download my preferred funeral arrangements, though of course you could have great fun blasting the nasty aliens into green goo in retaliation like the good uni you are. I'd take so much comfort in knowing you'd avenge my death. Maybe you could wipe out the whole Blue civilization in revenge, sterilize the whole fucking planet so there won't even be any microbes to bother you. Hey, they're not the Makers, so it wouldn't matter, right? It would be such the uni thing to do."

Kyung had been charged with supervising the placement of satellite weaponry in orbit around Little Sister—a move ordered by Admiral McElwan not long after the initial contact with the Blues. Taria had been among the civies who loudly voiced their objection to the Admiral, that such a provocative and threatening move would only increase the possibility of violence if the race below turned out to know the Makers. The Admiral hadn't even bothered to respond to her protest. But Kyung's cheeks colored nicely now. Taria patted Dog's head, whose large ears were standing upright as she listened to the two of them. Taria's fingers tingled as they passed through the holographic field.

The corners of Kyung's nose crinkled in anger.

"You know what, Kyung?" Taria continued, and shifted from Mandarin to Shiplish without realizing it. "I think you just don't want to lose the convenience of having me around, of being able to see me when you're done with your important goddamn work, all those lovely phallic weapons you keep nicely polished. I'm just stress relief for you, something to play with after a hard day kissing your superiors' goddamn asses."

His face flushed. "Christ, Taria, you don't need to talk that way . . ."

"Now you're worried about my fucking *language*, too?"

It was her fault. She knew it. The calmer part of her inside reminded her that this was how it was every time with her lovers. This was what happened whenever she felt someone getting too close. *How many have there been now? Do you want the litany? Eric, Nikki . . .* Lately, with Kyung there'd been that critical moment, a flashpoint in all their discussions when the conversation wildly careened into argument. They were both too much and not enough alike, sharing similar passions and stubbornness but not the same obsessions. One or the other of them would take a fatal verbal step, would load just enough annoyed fire into their voice that it kindled anger in the other. Taria sparked flame this time. She knew it even as she said the words, but the realization didn't stop the words from being said.

Maybe, she thought, she didn't really *want* to stop them. Maybe it was time to admit that—like all the rest—this relationship was never going to work, that she was too egocentric to make the sacrifice of self that was required.

By her backpack Dog whined once and faded away.

The rest of the quarrel followed the usual hopeless and standard script, the two of them seeking increasingly polarized positions until any possibility of compromise or graceful apology was lost. In the end Kyung stormed out of Taria's room with a curse and a shout that caused a few doors in her quadrant to open. Taria allowed herself to cry afterward for a time, and told the rematerializing Dog to set the comlink to "Refuse Calls, No Messages." She heard the 'link buzz twice during the night, and told herself that she didn't care.

She'd never been a particularly good liar.

She saw Kyung once the next day, as she was boarding the shuttle. Kyung took her backpack and put it in the cargo bay. "I put something in your pack," he said when he'd come back. "Ask Dog about it." Kyung kissed her once on the forehead, almost like a brother.

"What?" The word sounded short and too sharp. She hated the tone, hated the way it made Kyung's face scrunch up momentarily. She wanted to take it all back, but she didn't. Couldn't.

"Ask Dog," Kyung repeated. He touched her cheek with a hand and stepped back from the shuttle door.

She wanted to tell Kyung that she loved him, then, before she left. But the words, like all the rest, wouldn't come.

Taria waited for *Galileo*'s engines to slide from a banshee roar to aching silence. Servos whined inside the facing wall, and the cargo bay door pinged metallically. *"Good luck, Taria."* Benander, *Hawking*'s pilot, spoke in Taria's head as Dog barked and a line of light streamed from the bottom of the opening door. Exit doors to the cargo bay hissed shut, and Taria was alone. The bay door yawned wider.

She was breathing unfiltered Little Sister air. Unless the still-missing Coen had opened his helmet against orders, she was the first human to do so.

Little Sister air was cooler than ship air. It smelled of brine and tasted sweet.

She wondered, if Little Sister was going to kill her, whether it would be slow or fast. Taria took in a deep, deliberate breath. Nothing happened, and suddenly she was certain that nothing would. She smiled. "I'm out of here, Ruth. Thanks for the ride."

"No problem. Good luck. Give us a holler when you're ready for pickup."

Taria fit the vidcam recorder over her left eye. The vidcam sent sparks through her visual cortex as she snugged it against her skin contacts, and she tapped it once, then harder when nothing happened. Her vision settled again. She checked to make sure the vidcam was recording, and stepped down the stairs. Makes-the-Sound-of-East-Wind was waiting for her, maybe fifty meters away near the coastal cliffs. Out in the foggy bay, Taria could see the islands that made up the city, some connected by narrow bridges, all of them sprouting the irregular, gray buildings of the Blues. Someone—or several someones—seemed to be singing far out in the distance, like a chorus heard down a maze of city streets. The Baraaki was alone; there were no other Blues with her.

"Taria-Who-Wants-to-Understand," Makes said. "Welcome."

"Thanks for allowing me to come here, Baraaki," Taria said.

She was within a hand's reach of Makes. The Blue's hands lifted, and as they reached out for her, Taria took her hands in her own.

The true First Contact: the Blue's skin was warm and

soft, covered with a fine down that made it almost silken. Taria could feel fine muscles working under the skin, and Makes's fingers—one too many on the right hand, one too few on the left—clutched at her forearms, the grip tight enough to cause Taria to grimace. For a moment she was frightened at the touch, wanting to pull away, but she waited and Makes's hands released her. The Blue hissed and sputtered like a teakettle at full boil, though she didn't seem agitated, and there was a smell of licorice and spice to her that the bioshield had not let through during the initial meetings.

"You're apprehensive, Taria-Who-Wants-to-Understand."

"A bit," Taria admitted.

"Aah," Makes said, though the exhalation sounded more like venting steam than understanding. "You should be."

Taria felt the hairs suddenly prickling the back of her neck. "Excuse me? Why should I be apprehensive?"

"I am the Baraaki," Makes answered. "It's part of my burden to know things others don't. And I know that you will not be the same when you leave here."

Taria didn't immediately answer, and Commander Allison's voice sounded in her head. *"Spears, if you're not comfortable . . ."*

"I'm fine, Commander," Taria subvocalized back to him before he finished, and his voice continued over her reply. *"That's not a threat. It's only the truth."*

". . . with this, especially considering Ensign Coen's situation, then all you need . . ." Allison paused. *"It's your call. We'll continue to monitor, but once the shuttle's gone we're at least two hours away. Remember that."*

Benander's voice broke in then. *"Taria. You coming or staying?"*

"Staying."

Makes had not moved, standing almost motionless—though not silent—near the cliff. She didn't appear threatening, and the curve of Yang was a gorgeous, luminous backdrop to the bay, the islands, the mountains, while the distant chorus reverberated in the background. It was the beauty of the scenery that decided Taria. She glanced back at the shuttle; she waved. Benander waved back from the cockpit, and the engines shivered into life again, the downward-pointing jets kicking up an enormous gout of dust. Taria covered her mouth and nose with a sleeve. Makes seemed unperturbed. Taria watched her last physical link with *Lightbringer* rise, then turn to meet the clouds as the drive jets flared.

For the next ship-month she would be the only human on this world. She would be profoundly alone. Taria glanced back at Makes, still rumbling and grumbling deep in her stomach. "I'm guess I'm ready for that change," she said.

The strange song wafted in on the wind, momentarily louder, then fading again.

TIME OF LESSER LIGHT

Look at it but you cannot see it!
Its name is Formless

Listen to it but you cannot hear it!
Its name is Soundless

Grasp it but you cannot get it!
Its name is Incorporeal

—Chapter 14, *Tao Teh Ching*

✺ LITTLE SISTER

The small things were the most startling.

Taria wondered if it was one of those small things that had been the cause of Alex Coen's disappearance.

A ball of what looked like miniature salad sprouts sat in the corner of the ragged open space that served as a window to the small cabin. As Taria bent over to look closer, her breath moving the mass slightly, the sprout-ball suddenly wriggled and fell apart into a hundred tiny, hair-thin worms, with iridescent red beads at the end of their bodies. As one, the bead-heads turned in her direction. Surprised, Taria drew back; a serendipitous movement—at the same time, the window worms hissed as one and exhaled a fine mist in her direction. The spray rapidly solidified into a tiny silken net that fell to the stone sill. For a moment the worms waited, as if waiting to see if their soft trap had caught anything. Then, as if drawn by some magnetic force, the worms collapsed back into a ball once more, their net dissolving into a fine dew.

Taria reached out to touch one of the droplets. It stung her fingertip, like acid.

She thought of Alex, whom she'd known fairly well as a member of the ExoAnthro team. There were thousands of unknown life forms here on Little Sister, and any one of them could have killed him. She wondered if anyone would ever know what happened to him.

So far the Blues requested only one thing of the humans, in the same meeting Taria had attended: other than those who were part of the human delegation, they were not to send anyone down to Little Sister without the Blues' express permission. Commander Allison agreed—they didn't mention that Allison and Admiral McElwan had already sent Ensign Alex Coen down. But Alex Coen had vanished, and now they couldn't even mention it to the Blues, not without admitting they'd violated the Baraaki's request.

"They're about to sing," Makes-the-Sound-of-East-Wind said behind her, and Taria turned away from the window.

The Baraaki's head-crest, studded with twin lines of ear-let holes, rose to display its splotched orange and red markings, as if an alien Jackson Pollock had splattered her ridged flesh with paint from a dripping brush. The rest of her skin, before it plunged into the stained off-white windings of cloth around most of her body, was the blue of the deep ocean seen at the horizon. The flame colors of the head-crest shimmered against the background of cool azure, and the translucent eyestrip circling her head under the wide, lipless mouth glittered. Muscles in the wide neck pulsed around the prominent larynx. "I'm going down to where-water-slaps-smooth-pebbles now, Taria-Who-Wants-to-Understand."

Her hands stroked Taria's arm—the Blues all seemed to crave touch, the tactile contact obviously important to them. Taria knew that the intimacy would bother most of the humans. She found the constant stroking and patting irritating, but forced herself to ignore it. *It's their culture; you have to accept it.* It wasn't easy, and she didn't think that she'd ever enjoy the touching the way Makes seemed to. Makes's voice, deliberately pitched to the midpoint of the human range of hearing, sounded processed, like music with both the high and low ends of the spectrum rolled off.

"That's called a 'beach,' Makes."

That netted Taria a quick, low rumble of laughter from

Makes. The Children-of-She-Who-Spoke-the-World who had learned the human language found either amusing or insulting the human tendency to dramatically shorten their properly translated birth names, and Makes was of the former inclination. It was a tendency the humans shared, since the crew of *Lightbringer* continued to refer to the aliens as "Blues" even though they'd learned the literal translation of their own name for themselves: Children-of-She-Who-Spoke-the-World.

For their part, the Children-of-She-Who-Spoke-the-World usually added their own appellations to the human names, or strung together long phrase sequences to approximate their own words for things. The Blues called humans "Those-Who-Speak-Without-Saying-Anything."

"Would still be a 'beach' if it was Where-Quiet-Water-Washes-Over-Soft-Sand, or if it was Where-High-Surf-Crashes-on-Large-Rocks?"

"Yes," Taria told Makes, and the Blue chuckled again.

"This language of yours is a poor one," Makes commented. "You force your words to mean too many things. Are all your languages the same?" Her hands swept down Taria's waist, drifted behind to caress her buttocks. Taria forced herself not to move, not to slap away the offending hand. She tried to imagine that it was Kyung's hand instead. Makes grunted, a slightly louder rumbling from low in her throat.

Taria hadn't yet learned what happened to Alex Coen in her hundred hours or so on Little Sister, but she had discovered that Makes and a few others of the Blues spoke Shiplish—primarily English, with a few foreign phrases and words stirred in from the cosmopolitan mix of crewmembers—better than anyone aboard *Lightbringer* spoke Blue, with perhaps the exception of the network-linked PIAs. Taria herself knew only a few hundred of the long, complex words of Blue—a smaller vocabulary than a two-year-old might have. It was much easier to converse with Makes in Shiplish.

"I don't know *all* of our languages," Taria answered. "But they all have their quirks."

"How can you not know all your languages?" Makes asked, then gave a snort. "I will walk down to the 'beach,' then." She brushed Taria's hair like a mother might stroke her daughter's, then turned and snatched a tall wooden pole from the wall of the hut. At the end of the pole, a long, curved blade glittered, made of either a greenish metal or some local stone.

It was the first obvious weapon Taria had seen in Blue culture. She knew that the Blues had their own conflicts, that murder was not unknown to them, and there was the separate warrior caste. Still, seeing the weapon made her feel uneasy. For just a moment she froze, wondering if she were about to suffer Alex's fate, and very aware that her own little flechette gun was nestled somewhere in the bottom of her backpack. The gun had been Kyung's idea, the item he'd secreted in her pack—totally against regulations and ExoAnthro guidelines. Taria's stomach lurched at the thought of using it, and she took an involuntary step back from Makes.

"I'll be right with you," she told Makes, still eyeing Makes's spear. Taria snatched the vidcam recorder from her belt pouch and fitted it over her left eye. Her skin tingled as the contacts pricked her skin; static glistened in her visual cortex, then settled into blurred double vision. "*Shit! I thought Allison said Systems had fixed this damn thing,*" she muttered, tapping the vidcam with a finger and cursing her inability to see. *Where the hell's Makes? All she has to do is swing that damn spear and I'm dead* . . . "Dog, can you please compensate for this garbage?"

There was an anxious delay of two or three seconds before Dog's faint *woof!* sounded in her head. Without the ubiquitous sensors and projectors in the *Lightbringer*'s hull, Taria's PIA link to the ship's computer network was only an auditory signal in her skull, with a noticeable gap in response due to the distance of *Lightbringer* from Little

Sister. *Lightbringer* remained in orbit around the throat of Thunder. With a crackle and a burst of white overload, the woven cane-grass walls of the hut finally melted into acceptable focus. "Good Dog," she said. "That'll do. Let's go, Makes."

But Makes wasn't there.

Taria whirled around, suddenly afraid that the alien was behind her, ready to strike with that ugly pole arm. *You're getting paranoid now, girl* . . . She startled an insect on the back wall of the hut, which buzzed her head once before whining away—a fisher-fly, with a wriggling, iridescent "lure" hanging from the end of its long tongue. "Makes?" she called. The hut was empty except for the swaying curtain of dried seed pods over the door. The constant low drone from deep in Makes's chest, more felt than heard, was missing.

Feeling foolish at her sudden fright, Taria half ran out of the hut into the persistent offshore breeze, which tasted of brine and impending rain. It was Time-of-Full-Light, with both the sun and the arc of the gas giant around which Little Sister orbited cascading light down through the thin clouds: Yin and Yang. The waves were breaking hard on the pebbled beach, with a fine spray plucked off the whitecaps by the wind. Just out of the reach of the breakers, above the seaweed and foam markings of the high tide line, Makes was standing with the butt end of her spear jammed into the wet ground. In front of her, like ebony hillocks, were the dark, sinuous bodies of the watersingers. Taria hurried forward, already zooming the lens of the recorder.

The bodies of the watersingers were black. Not simply jet sable, but a color that was darker and more intense than any black Taria had ever seen before, a black that seemed to take the light of the sun and the great gas giant and swallow them both. Taria decided that a fur made from watersinger pelt would be beyond price. There were four of them, all about the same size, a meter and a half long, with muscular bodies that Taria could barely have encircled with her arms. The rear of the creatures tapered into a tail with a wide horizontal fluke, segmented by what might have been elongated toe-bones. Two pairs of flippers protruded from the body, also marked with prominent and long fingerbones between the webbing, perhaps a legacy of an evolutionary past on land.

Taria and Makes had been there when they flopped out of the phosphorescent surf last night (no, not "night"—Makes had called it "Time-of-Lesser-Light") at low tide, with the margin of the sea nearly two kilometers away from where it now pounded the land. Yin was full on the horizon then, throwing mottled orange light down through the clouds, making midnight nearly as bright as full day. Makes had broken sourgrass stalks and drawn several large geometric figures in the sand—"Because that is what you have to do when you ask 'singers to come to you," Makes had answered when Taria had questioned her, and Taria muttered a quick note to Dog about Blue religious rituals.

An hour or so later Taria had watched the 'singers—darker than any night—flail their way up the slope of the beach to where the snarled roots of the plant she had secretly named Fat Man's Hands (thick, pink tubes that wriggled when touched) snaked into packed sand. On land the 'singers were clumsy and slow; in the water, Makes told her, they flew like great birds, swooping and darting in small flocks of a half dozen or so.

Makes had "watched" the 'singers, too—though of course no Blue ever "watched" anything. Makes's eyestrip, like that of all her race, could not focus visual images well—the eyestrip was sensitive to variations in lightness and darkness, but Makes would have been incapable of recognizing Taria from her facial features except at extremely close range. Instead, the intricate array of earholes pocking the ear-ridge served as the primary sense for interacting with the world around her. The ridge ran from just above the mouth—centered on the front of the head—and up and over to end at the rear base of the skull. In the few local days Taria had been with Makes, she had never once seen the Baraaki act as if she were particularly "blind"— the Children-of-She-Who-Spoke-the-World constructed a detailed three-dimensional aural landscape around them from the ambient sounds and the delicate changes as it reflected from the objects near them, aided by the nearly constant low frequency sounds they emitted.

"When are they going to do this singing you wanted me to hear?" Taria asked when the watersingers had finally come to rest.

"When both the Greater and Lesser Light are in the sky," Makes had answered.

"Why is that?"

"Because that is when they will sing."

It was the best answer she would get. "Great," she muttered under her breath. "I'll remember that the next time I need a Zen koan."

She'd forgotten how keen the Blue hearing was.

Makes turned slightly sideways to the group of watersingers as she listened to them—Makes never looked directly at Taria when she spoke to her; she was always talking to one side or the other of her, a trait Taria found even more disconcerting than the constant touching. "That is a tautology, not a koan," Makes said. It was difficult not to hear amusement in her filtered voice. Taria winced. She ignored Makes and zoomed in on the largest of the 'singers with the recorder.

The watersingers had no eyes that Taria could see, though they had a row of earholes ringing the body just back from where the eyes might have been on a terrestrial animal. From what Makes and the other Blues had told her, in their long-winded way, the 'singers could "see" the world aurally, as they did. This was unusual for Little Sister's wildlife, most of which had at least rudimentary vision. Yet every other large animal on the planet used vision as their primary means of interacting with the world around them, as did most animals on Earth—the Blues and the watersingers were anomalies on their own world.

The watersingers had arrayed themselves in a wide circle, their heads facing inward. Their raven fur glistened, highlights sparking like stars. Makes was standing outside the circle formed by their bodies; when Taria started to move to stand in the center, the hand that had been rubbing her shoulder suddenly gripped her tightly. "No, Taria-Who-Wants-to-Understand. You must stay here. No closer."

Taria shrugged. She willed the recorder to zoom in on the face of the watersinger across the circle from her. He was a large bull, with a touch of gray flecking the dark fur of his muzzle. As the image of the bull's face grew larger in her vision, he lifted his snout to the sky and nasal vents flared as he took in a slow, long breath. His mouth opened in a comically wide O.

He sang.

No music Taria had ever listened to before prepared her for this. The first note slammed into her chest like a fist, an impossibly deep sound, most of the overtones of which, she knew, were below the range of her hearing. But she *felt* them. The first concussive blast sent her staggering backward with an involuntary step, the sound twisting in her gut and lungs and pressing against her eardrums: a physical, palpable assault. The bull's entire body shook as it roared its subterranean cacophony. In the midst of the song, Dog barked in alarm in her head. "It's all right, Dog," she whispered into the torrent of sound. "I'm okay."

The bull continued to bellow the long note, his body trembling on the stones; as his nostril vents flared again, the volume dropped slightly and Taria recovered her balance. The bull droned on, the pitch of the note rising and falling slowly, sending a rippling sensation down the front of Taria's body, as if a giant hand were brushing up and down, down and up, against her.

Now the other three raised their heads and added their voices. Unlike a human voice, each of the watersingers produced several notes at once, their voices slightly higher than the bull's, though still in the bass and baritone ranges. The melodies their multiple voices sang were more intricate: slow legato notes drifting and intertwining like vines around the massive, unmoving trunk of the bull's undertones.

Taria thought it sounded most like a medieval chant, though scored with discordant and too-close harmonies and not in any musical scale she had ever heard. The four watersingers sounded like a chorus of a dozen or more. The voices rose and fell in cascading, flowing patterns, and so loud that she wondered whether her hearing would be the same afterward. But she had no inclination to cover her ears. The song held her in a trance—she forgot the recorder, forgot Makes standing alongside her, forgot the startling vision of Yin dominating the sky.

The dissonances vibrated, shivering the air, sending wavering cadences flowing over the beach. "There!" Makes shouted, her voice startling Taria, one hand sliding down her back. "It's happening! In the center of the circle."

Taria squinted. The air did seem to quiver above them like the heat waver above a summertime road, as if all the complicated harmonies of the watersingers had concentrated there. But she noticed nothing else. Makes gasped alongside her, taking a step forward. Her head-crest was fully extended and her mouth open. She reached upward with her hands, as if trying to touch something. "Isn't it exquisite?" she said. "The shapes, the way they move in the Emptiness-We-Breathe . . . And look, that one *there* . . . that's what I wanted you to see . . ."

"What shapes?" Taria asked. "I don't see anything. Dog, are you getting anything from the recorder I'm not, maybe in infrared?" A faint whine—*no*—answered her after a moment. The song of the watersingers was drifting higher now and Makes gasped, obviously in awe of what she was witnessing. Taria still saw nothing. The music of the alien creatures was hauntingly interesting, almost hypnotic, but Taria perceived nothing beyond the sound itself. Makes stretched out both her hands as if caressing something in the air above her. After a moment Taria did the same. She could feel waves of focused sound buffeting her hands, as if she'd placed her fingers in front of a bass port on an immense speaker system, but there was no solidity.

Yet . . . yet . . . As Taria reached forward, invisible fingers intertwined with her own. She could feel them, warm and achingly familiar, and a voice called in her head, a voice that wasn't Dog or Kyung. *Taria*, it whispered, as familiar as the touch on her hand. *Taria* . . .

Sudden, hot tears sprang in Taria's eyes. Her hand, unbidden, went to the brooch hidden under her uniform shirt.

And the song ended.

As one, the watersingers went silent: as Makes sighed, as Taria cried out in a half sob. Her body tingled as if from a deep massage, and she realized she'd been holding her breath. She looked at her hand, turning it in front of her in wonder and disbelief, and cradling it to her chest again, feeling the outline of the brooch under the cloth.

The 'singers had rolled to their sides, panting great gulps of the salt air, seemingly exhausted by their efforts. The long flanks of the bull quivered, small muscles twitching just under the thick mat of ebony. Slowly, the sounds around them came back to Taria: the flying beach lizards with their wailing mewls as they swooped over the breakers, the hush of the wind through the fronds of the Fat Man's Hands, the soft aspirant clicking of the trishelled mollusks as they breathed through their snorkle tubes, poking up from between the rocks . . .

"You saw *nothing*?" Makes asked, and even through the artificial sound of her voice, Taria could hear a very humanlike disappointment. Makes's face was still lifted to the center of the watersingers' circle, her head-crest fully raised, the orange ridges around the earlets turned toward the same area, as if she were watching the last fading images of whatever had been there for her. "We thought . . ."

Taria was empty of words. *Did you really hear that voice, feel that touch? Was it really there?* "What did *you* experience, Makes?" she asked. She heard the trembling in her voice, and wondered if Makes heard it also and knew what it meant. "You said something about shapes? What shapes? How did they appear to you?"

"It's . . ." Makes hesitated. The protective roll of flesh over her eyestrip convulsed all at once: a massive blink. A hand touched Taria's left breast, then moved up to her face. "It is very difficult to describe, Taria-Who-Wants-to-Understand. I am not certain how to translate into your language. Just as we do not understand what you mean by your word 'color,' I am not sure that I can tell you what I heard-saw. Many different shapes, some with lines-that-do-not-curve, some that seemed more Things-That-Are-Found than Things-That-Are-Made, all changing from one to another. Sometimes they were all things at once, and at others . . . All so beautiful . . . And one that is much like you . . ." Makes stopped. Her hand fell away. "Have I helped you to understand?"

"No." Taria clenched her hand into a fist. "I don't understand at all."

"Your Eyes-That-See-Forms showed you nothing?" Makes asked again.

Taria shook her head, though she knew that Makes couldn't visualize the gesture. "No," she said, and Makes's head-crest lowered with the word, the blazing colors fading into the aquamarine skin.

She said nothing about the rest.

"Then perhaps we were wrong," Makes said, sounding so disappointed that Taria wanted to touch her, to reassure her. *There was something, Makes. Something. And it scared me.*

"What do these shapes mean?" Taria asked Makes. She

stared at the watersingers. "Why do the 'singers create them? Is this how they talk to each other?"

"The 'singers don't talk," Makes answered. "I thought you might be able to tell me. I thought that because you have Eyes-That-See-Forms you could sense what I cannot, that you could help me to 'see' what I can't." A loud breath wheezed from Makes's nasal vents, placed on either side of her neck. "Nothing. You saw nothing."

I heard her, felt her . . . Mama . . . "I'm sorry, Makes. I heard the song—hell, I *felt* the song—but visually . . ." Taria shrugged: another useless gesture.

Makes crouched down so that her hand trailed along the flank of one of the watersingers. The creature seemed to enjoy her touch, rolling slightly toward the Blue with an unmelodious grunt. Taria found herself wanting to touch the watersinger herself, to feel the startling softness of its coat. She did not. She still held her hand to herself, remembering the touch of fingers.

Makes stood again. "Have you ever witnessed a miracle, Taria-Who-Wants-to-Understand? Has your god ever reached out and touched you?" Makes's hands fluttered at Taria's shoulders.

I didn't come down here to get into comparative theology, Dog, she thought to her PIA, and was answered with a faint whimper. *Be ready to patch me through to* Lightbringer, *maybe to the ship's chaplain . . .* "Makes, there are some humans who are extremely religious, and as a species we worship more gods than you have rocks on this beach, some of them about as old. But I personally don't believe in a god. Any of them. Sorry. I know that as the Baraaki you're some kind of priest—"

Makes didn't seem to be listening to her. Her voice boomed over Taria's. "She-Who-Spoke-the-World is shaped like a vast Singer-From-the-Water, only She swims in the Emptiness-Above-Us, always, and Her song is eternal, keeping the land solid and whole and rippling the waters. You must have heard Her. You must have *seen* Her."

"No, Makes," Taria answered softly. "As far as I know, we didn't see Her, and we didn't hear Her. I'm sorry. I don't know, maybe to human eyes She's just invisible, like the shapes you said the watersingers made."

Makes's face turned pale, then darkened; Taria wondered what emotion that signified. "No." Makes's skin darkened further, so that the blue was nearly black. "You simply don't know how to look. You're just shadows to Her."

With that, Makes pulled her long-bladed spear from the ground, holding the long shaft in both hands and raising it high, the blade shining in Yin-light above the head of the bull watersinger. In the instant before Taria realized what Makes intended, long muscles flexed in the Blue's arms as she brought the blade down hard onto the bull's neck. Blood spurted from a long, deep cut, and the bull groaned in its multitone voice, though neither the bull nor the other watersingers made any motion to flee.

A purple and gold phosphorescence—*sparks?*—flared and crackled along Makes's spear and down the flank of the watersinger, and Makes grunted as if in pain. The spear shivered, the metallic blade groaning like a saw blade caught in wet wood. A nimbus of fluorescent yellow started to climb the shaft to Makes's hands.

What the hell . . . ?

In Taria's head, belatedly, Dog whined.

Makes raised the weapon again, the blade drooling blood and what looked like glowing embers as it came up. The horrified stasis that held Taria broke, and instinct overrode training. *"No!"* Taria shouted, rushing forward. "Jesus God, *stop*, Makes!" She caught the Blue's muscular arms, and Makes lowered the weapon slowly.

"What is the matter, Taria-Who-Wants-to-Understand?" There was bewilderment in Makes's voice.

The voice, the touch . . . Adrenaline and emotion shook Taria's voice. "Makes, you can't . . . Just slaughtering the defenseless things . . . After what they did . . ."

"The meat of Singers-From-the-Water tastes good," Makes answered. "I thought humans killed animals for meat, too."

"Yes, I know, but . . ." Taria let go of Makes's arm. She took a long, slow breath. "It's not the same, Makes. Not the same at all." She was shaking. *You just blew it*, a part of her was screaming. *It doesn't matter what you just heard or saw, or how strange Makes acts. This is not your world. You have no right to judge what's right or wrong for them, or to interfere in their way of life.* But she knew she hadn't been thinking, only reacting, and that after what had happened during the watersingers' display, she couldn't let them be hurt. "Makes, I'm sorry. I guess . . ."

The watersingers had started to waddle away toward the distant line of breakers, a trail of blood dappling the pebbles behind the bull. Taria would have sworn that a copper mist gleamed around the wound as she watched them leave. Makes made no effort to follow their slow retreat. She said nothing to Taria, just let her weapon drop to the ground and started walking back to the hut.

Dog yipped and whined in her head. "I know, Dog," she answered aloud. "That was really, really stupid of me, but . . ."

Taria looked at her hand once more. She thought she could still feel that other hand. *Taria . . .*

The voice had called to her, and she knew it. She knew it.

Taria took in a breath that sobbed in her throat.

Taria caught up with Makes near the hut. "Makes, I'm really sorry. I shouldn't have done that. I'm here only as an observer and I don't have any right to interfere with your customs like that."

Makes gave a rolling, slow blink of her eyestrip and gave voice to a low, tiger's purr. Her skin darkened slightly, but she said nothing. Taria had no idea what all of that meant. *"Dog,"* Taria subvocalized, *"help me out here. Give me an apology phrase I can use."*

A delay, then a yip echoed in her head, and the phrase rolled in front of her, a transparent overlay over her vision. She spoke the syllables haltingly. The word was long—hardly unusual for the Blue language—and she stumbled over the syllables. "*Wermasthaibrezhzorilak*. Makes, I'm very sorry."

Makes halted. Her hand brushed the beaded curtain to the doorway of the hut, and the beads clashed together musically. "Do you know the literal translation of what you just said, Taria-Who-Wants-to-Understand?"

"No," she admitted. "You know the Voices-Only-Taria-Can-Hear? The PIA link to the ship that's in my head? I got it from there. Why? Was that the wrong phrase, or did I say it badly?"

"You said it very badly," Makes answered. "But you also said it as well as a human could. *Wermasthaibrezhzorilak* means . . . let me think how it would be best said in the language you've taught us . . . 'I-have-wrongly-placed-my-will-on-you-and-offer-the-repentance-desired.' Did I ask you for an apology?"

"No. But I know that what I did was wrong. I had no right to interfere."

Makes's torso swiveled. She seemed to be looking somewhere beyond Taria's left shoulder. "You're right. You shouldn't have interfered. You didn't trust me when trust is what we've asked of you. I knew that you realized your mistake and that it was a human thing only, so I didn't ask you to give me an expression of regret. Now you impose your will on me again by forcing me to listen to your apology. Three times you said 'I'm sorry' on the beach, and I had never asked you; this is now the fourth time."

"Shit." Taria cursed softly, forgetting the Blue's keen hearing.

"I cannot tell if that is noun or verb. Do you need to relieve yourself? Or are you asking me to do so?"

"Neither. That was a profanity, Makes, something we say when we're not sure what else to say. I'm sor—" She stopped herself. Makes stared into the distance impassively, unreadable. Her earlets wriggled on her flame-colored head-crest. *So you don't apologize unless specifically asked to do so, or you just amplify the insult. You need to change your reflexes—fine, you can do that; you've had a lot of practice over the years. Deal with it, because you're stuck down here all alone on Little Sister for at least another month and you don't want to disappear like Coen. It was your own choice, remember?* "Makes, I'm all alone here. Things are strange, and I guess . . . I guess all of a sudden I'm a little more scared than I thought I'd be, and trusting is a little harder."

Makes *hmmm'd* softly. "Then we are more alike than you think, Taria-Who-Wants-to-Understand."

With that, Makes started walking away from the beach hut toward the main road that led to the nearest city, three or four kilometers away around a knob of rocky coastal bluffs. Taria knew the landscape from the aerial maps the survey satellites had made of Little Sister, but that was all. No human had ever actually walked here.

The road toward the city was more path than highway— irregularly flagged with glassy orange field stones, over-grown with Fat Man's Hands and what Taria thought of as sticky-weed: a grassy growth whose lacy seed pods were liberally coated with a gluey sap. The road, with muddy water pooled in the bottom of the deepest ruts, was heavily furrowed by the sledges and crude wheeled carts used by the Blues and drawn by the legless, muscular creatures the humans had dubbed horseslugs. Once they'd rounded the sea-bluff, the tidal flats on either side became fields of hip-high, hollow-bladed sourgrass, tended by Blue workers toiling under the watchful glare of Yin. Taria could hear the humming drone of the Blues as they moved through the tall fronds bending to the breeze. To the right a cloud of fleasnappers hopped across the field, thankfully moving away from them—Taria had been bitten by a swarm of them yesterday, and they'd left itching, hivelike bumps

over her arms that two vials of antihistamine cream barely
managed to quell.

Makes didn't speak as they walked. Taria lagged a little
behind the Blue, whose long-legged walking pace was almost too ambitious for her. She'd taken the vidcam off after the incident with the watersingers, mostly to give her
optic nerves a rest; she put it back on again now to record
the agricultural work around her. The recorder sputtered
and gave static, and her vision blurred again, slightly out of
focus, but Taria persisted, wanting a record of the scene:
Little Sister Pastoral.

Ahead, the road curved into a stand of trees as they approached the coastal hills. The trees were spindly, with a
tangled snarl of trunks rising for six or seven meters, after
which they exploded into a canopy of bright yellow, aquamarine, and pale orange leaves. Entering into the shadow
of the trees, the doubled light of the gas giant and the sun
dimmed, and Taria's vision became even more myopic for
a moment as the vidcam adjusted. When her eyesight fluttered into equilibrium, she noticed that Makes had
stopped, and that a quartet of Blues was standing in the
road several paces on.

Taria caught up with Makes in a few quick steps. The
Blues ahead of them were a half meter taller than Makes,
with ripplings of lean muscle in their arms. They wore
leather belts studded with silver. All four were male, one of
them noticeably taller than the others. Taria focused the
vidcam on that one, zooming in. A steely glitter attracted
her attention to the hands: each of the fingers was tipped
with a curved blade, like long nails. The teeth in the Blue's
face were filed to points, the enamel scraped away so it appeared his mouth was crowded with gray spikes. His chest
and face were crisscrossed with fine, pale blue lines of
scars, and the ridge of his head-crest was marbled with
swirling tattooed symbols. Taria felt the quick buffeting of
a subsonic bellow, almost like a challenge.

Warrior caste.

The translucent letters swam before Taria's vision, and she nearly laughed. *I'd already figured that out, Dog.*

During all the meetings, the warriors had never spoken. Conversation had taken place only with those like Makes, members of what seemed to be a semireligious organization: the baraalideish, which translated as Those-Who-Speak-With-Her. All negotiations had gone through the Baraaki and the baraalideish, but the warriors had been in attendance also: always in the background, always deferentially off to one side, always silent. Aboard *Lightbringer* there had been some speculation, especially among the unis, that the warriors were the ones really in charge, that the baraalideish were merely a front for the initial negotiations.

Taria had scoffed at that. She wondered now if the power structure was really as clear-cut as it had seemed.

The Blues were standing in a group and conversing; when they noticed Makes and Taria, the rumble of their conversation stopped, and one of them started toward them. "Makes," Taria began to ask, but the Blue gave her a steamy hiss.

"This is not a time for talking, Taria-Who-Wants-to-Understand," Makes said. Her voice was quiet, rushed. "It is a time to do nothing at all unless I ask, then to do it quickly. Do you understand this?"

"Yes," Taria answered, feeling the same sense of unease she'd felt when Makes had picked up the spear in the hut. "Absolutely." *Dog*, she thought. *Pay attention. I may need translation here.* After the usual lag, Dog barked once in her head.

With the Blues, it was difficult to determine what they were "looking" at, but it was obvious that the tallest warrior's attention was on Taria. He started to move past Makes toward her, but Makes interposed herself. The male nearly ran into Makes before he stopped, then he spoke: a rushing torrent of words that Taria could not follow at all. Listening to Blues talk was like listening to a collision of orchestras. The full tonal range of their voices was staggering, and Taria knew that the pitch of the voice conveyed much of the emotional context, something no human would ever be able to accomplish unaided.

Dog, where's my translation? she asked.

The PIA whined. *Can't translate. Unknown dialect.* Taria cursed silently, remembering linguistics and the speculations they'd all had aboard *Lightbringer* about potential communication pitfalls with the Thunder Makers, once they found them:

Damn it, then we have a diglossia. I'll bet there's a separate language for formal occasions and another tongue for casual speech. That's been a common enough attribute in human societies. And it's a real fucking pain in the ass for me right now . . . Tell Allison that we need to get someone in ExoAnthro working on this right away.

Sympathetically, Dog whined again.

The male hooted another discordant crescendo at Makes and placed his daggered fingertips on her chest with enough force that Makes took an involuntary step backward. The gesture seemed universally threatening enough for Taria: Makes was about to be attacked. The other three Blues were coming toward them now. Taria shrugged her backpack from her shoulders, wondering how long it would take to excavate the weapon Kyung had given her from her pack. She could feel her hands starting to tremble with the first onrush of adrenaline. *You can do this if you have to. Sure, they move awful damn fast, but you can probably take out all four of them before they realize what's happening. It'll take the* Lightbringer *shuttle maybe twenty-four hours to get the unis here, but you can stay hidden that long, and you can deal with the shit that will happen afterward as a result. You'll make it . . .*

When she ripped opened the pack's seals, the argument between Makes and the male stopped with the sound.

"You should do nothing, Taria-Who-Wants-to-Understand," Makes said, turning slightly toward her. Taria stopped; her fingertips could feel the cool plastic of the grip between her folded clothes. "No matter what happens, do nothing," Makes said again.

"Makes—"

"Do nothing," Makes repeated.

With a loud burst of noise, the male warrior bellowed something at Makes, his bladed left hand gesturing in Taria's direction. Taria heard Makes give the low grunt of negation as her head-crest rose. Her hands moved over the warrior's scarred body as she spoke—not a sexual touch, not the invitation it would be if the two of them were human, but more as if she were reassuring herself of where the warrior was.

The warrior bellowed again. This time his hands moved more harshly than before, and Taria saw the razored nails slash four separate lines along Makes's arm. Taria gasped in sympathetic pain, but Makes didn't react in any way Taria could see. The cuts drooled dark red blood; as the warrior continued to clutch at her arm, his fingers smeared the rivulets.

Which is when he finally seemed to notice that he had wounded Makes. The male uttered a long ululation that rose in pitch, and he backed away. He tried to move around Makes toward Taria once again, and again Makes placed herself between the warrior and Taria. Another exchange followed, this time with the others joining in, so loudly that a flock of beetle-birds dropped from their leafy nest just off the road, their wings opening noisily as they flew away. Taria could *feel* the argument, the lowest bass notes shivering the flagstones under her feet, the high squeals making her wince.

Abruptly, it ended. The male who had first confronted them stepped to one side of the road; one of the others followed him. The other two took up station on the other side of the narrow road. "You should follow me now, Taria-Who-Wants-to-Understand." Makes's voice, pitched to

Taria's ears again, sounded thin and weak after the full
sonic range of her own language.

"What about them?"

"They will not harm you. That is not their intention.
That was never their intention."

Taria wasn't convinced. She stared at them, letting the
vidcam, still riddled with static, record the scene for *Lightbringer*'s files as she panned from one group to the other.
*Is this what happened to Coen? Could he have run into
these bastards? Is this what they'd do to me?*

"We must go now, Taria-Who-Wants-to-Understand."
Makes had moved past them already, turning back to call
to Taria.

Taria reached up and pulled the vidcam away from the
contacts on her eye socket. The static went away; her vision cleared, and she realized that she had a pounding
headache. She picked up her backpack and put it back on,
watching the warriors. They seemed to be listening to her,
the earlets twitching on their head-crests. They made the
usual grumbling and mutters of the never-quiet Blues, but
their dangerous hands remained motionless at their sides.

"All right, Makes. Let's go, then."

As Taria walked between the warriors, their muscular
torsos swiveled, as if they were tracking her. Taria could
feel sound waves being focused on her, and she stayed to
the center of the road, though she was easily within an
arm's reach of them and she could feel her skin tingling
along her spine. She glanced from side to side, watching
for any sudden movement, any flicker of those edged fingertips. She was ready to leap, to run.

Then she was past, and she hurried to catch up with
Makes. Blood was dripping down Makes's arm, droplets
falling from her fingertips to hit the flagstones and dapple
the leaves of the Fat Man's Hands. "Makes, you need to
bind up that wound. I have sterile bandages in my kit. Let
me—"

A deep *haroom* interrupted her. "We must walk farther first," Makes answered. "Until the others can no longer hear our presence."

There didn't seem to be any arguing with Makes on the subject, and in any case the Blue was striding too fast for Taria to do more than try to keep up with her. She glanced over her shoulder at the quartet. "Just who were those people?" They had moved out to the middle of the road again, standing in a huddle watching Makes and Taria walk on toward the city. Taria could hear the booming rumble of their conversation.

Makes staggered, with a huffing exhalation. "Makes!" Taria clutched the alien's good arm, holding her upright as her knees buckled. Her skin was cool and leathery, and a smell like anise hung around her. "Sit down here and let me stop the bleeding. Dog, I need you to patch me through to Medical."

"No!" Makes hooted again, urgently. "You understand very little, Taria-Who-Wants-to-Understand. Let yourself learn from me now. We must keep moving away. We can't stop now, not while they can still hear us."

"Makes—"

"Help me, Taria-Who-Wants-to-Understand. You do not show weakness to the kagliaristi. Not much farther . . ."

Leaning on Taria, Makes continued to walk for another few minutes. Finally she stopped and her head-crest lowered. "They're gone," she said, and nearly fell to the ground. "I will rest here."

"Good." Taria let her pack fall from her shoulders and rummaged through it to find the medkit. She cracked it open and *tsked* at the quartet of long cuts down Makes's arm. The edges were clean, but for a hand's length the two middle cuts gaped wide, with blood streaming down along Makes's arm—the warrior's fingertips were scalpel-sharp, if nothing else. Taria's vision blurred for a second—*so much blood*—and she took a slow, calming breath. *You can deal with this,* she told herself. *You have to deal with this.*

"I'll need to glue some of these cuts, Makes, or you're going to have some nasty scars . . ."

"Scars . . ." There was amusement in Makes's voice again. "Is appearance so important to you that scars would frighten you?"

"Makes, you're really bleeding a lot."

"All right, Taria-Who-Wants-to-Understand." Again there was more amusement than concern in her voice. "If it will make you feel better, save me from blood and scars."

Taria opened the medkit and sprayed her hands; a few seconds later the spray had air-hardened into a sterile, flexible film. Gloved, Taria was about to inject Makes with an antibiotic, then stopped—there was no way to know how her metabolism would react to the drug, or if it would have any effects at all on the local germs. She doubted that either her superiors or the Blues would enjoy the irony of accidentally killing Makes while trying to help her. She considered asking Dog to link her with the *Lightbringer*'s medical staff, then decided against it—*do the first aid, and let one of the Blue doctors deal with the rest*.

Taria broke open sterile wipes and began to gently clean the wound. Makes sat quietly; if Taria's ministrations pained her, she made no protest. Taria wondered if she might not be in mild shock. "Tell me, Makes," she said. "Who were they? Kagli-something?"

"Kagliaristi: Those-Who-Will-Protect," Makes answered. "You have them, too. I have met them."

"The unis?" Taria thought of *Lightbringer*, up above. "The military, I mean. Oh, yes. I know them *very* well. Why were they bothering you, though? Why did they do this to you?" Taria gently touched Makes's arm above the wounds.

"The kagliaristi do not hear things in the same way we baaralideish do. The shape of the world is different for them, and they react to it in their own ways."

"I understand that, yes. But I had the sense that they actually wanted to confront *me*." Taria opened the surgical glue and started to knit together the edges of the wound. Makes didn't answer, letting her work. The glue set, and Taria quickly bandaged the arm. "There. That will hold it for now. You have doctors, yes? I'd check with one when we get back. I'm afraid to give you painkillers or any of my medicine; all I did was clean it and close the worst parts."

"Thank you, Taria-Who-Wants-to-Understand. I'm sure you have saved me from scars." Makes stopped. Reaching over with her good hand, she touched Taria's face with almost a caress. Taria smiled, and touched Makes's own face. For the space of a breath the gesture held, alien hands to alien faces.

Then Makes stirred. "We should get back now," she said.

"You're not going to answer my questions?"

"Right now we must get back," Makes repeated. "Sometimes true understanding only comes much later than the event."

Land of the Long White Cloud. . . .

Papa had Mama's body shipped back to New Zealand for burial. When Taria left for the funeral, she was excited about flying on an airplane to see her Gramma Ruth and Grampa Carl, and so didn't realize that she was leaving behind Nanjing, Auntie Li, and China forever. She would not go back there again, though her father would return to finish up the last months of his contract. She would stay behind in New Zealand, then go to the States with her father.

The funeral took place on an ironically lovely day, with a warm, soft breeze fluttering the leaves of the beech trees on the hilltop. Gramma and Grampa had wanted Gloria buried there on the farm, her grave overlooking the fields and the small stone house where she'd grown up.

This was the same hilltop where Gloria and Trevor had watched the appearance of Thunder, where Taria had been conceived, though Taria didn't know that at the time. Gramma kept calling the hillside their *marae*, which Grampa said was a Maori word for the place where the ancestral spirits gathered.

It was Gramma who came into her room that first night back, when the nightmare had wakened her screaming from sleep again. In fact, Taria had been experiencing nightmares nearly every night since her mother died. "Ahh, poor child," Gramma said, holding Taria and rocking her.

"To see your poor mama slaughtered right in front of you. How terrible, how awful . . ."

"I miss her, Gramma," Taria sniffed, wiping the back of her hand across her nose. Her nightgown, one of her mother's old ones that Gramma had kept, was frayed around the elastic cuffs, and Taria picked at the worn spot, imagining her mother doing the same thing years and years ago. "I want her back."

Tears started in Gramma's eyes then, too. "We both do, darling. We both do. Maybe I can help a little, eh? Let me sing you a song I used to sing to your mama, back when she was your age."

Gramma began to sing then, in Maori.

"Po karekare ana
Nga wai o Waiapu
Whiti atu koe hine
Marino ana e."

The sound comforted her, and she eventually drifted back to sleep, her dreams filled with images of *Aotearoa*—the Land of the Long White Cloud—before the *Pakeha* came.

Not many people came to the funeral: a few neighbors, Taria's great-aunt and -uncle from Wellington, a smattering of cousins Taria didn't remember at all. She stayed next to Papa, or with her Gramma and Grampa, as much as she could, almost angry at the way the other kids who were there ran about, laughing and playing. The adults talked mostly about other times, their voices quiet and low as they drank coffee and ate pastries, and occasionally someone would cry.

When the priest arrived, they all went up to the hill. Papa helped carry the simple wooden coffin, and Taria walked in front between Gramma and Grampa. The priest spoke a few words, and Gramma said something over the coffin in Maori, and they lowered the casket into the earth. Papa, Gramma, and Grampa sprinkled earth into the grave, and they started back down the hill, the gravediggers remaining behind to finish the burial. Taria walked between Gramma and her papa, holding each of their hands.

"Are you all right, Taria?" Gramma asked.

Since her nightmare the night before, Taria had been devoid of tears. It all seemed surreal to her, a dream. It was only a box stuck in the earth; it was not her mother. "She's not really dead, you know," Taria answered, looking up at the old woman. She saw Gramma glance at Papa.

"I know," Gramma answered. "We'll always remember her."

Taria shook her head vigorously. They didn't understand. "No," she insisted. "I mean it. She's waiting for us at Thunder." She looked at her father, at his stricken face. "Isn't she, Papa? Tell her. Tell Gramma."

"Ruth . . ." Papa started, then shook his head. "No, Taria. I can't tell Gramma Ruth that, because it's not true. Your mother's gone, honey. She's dead, and we can't bring her back." He swallowed hard, and his hand pressed hers so much that Taria pulled away. "Nothing we do can bring her back."

"That's not *true*!" Taria shouted. She stomped her foot on the ground. "It's not! I won't let it be!" She tugged her hand away from Gramma Ruth and started to run back up the hill. She heard her father start after her, and Gramma's voice.

"Trevor, let the girl go. Let her go. You walk on down with Carl and the others. I'll go talk with her. Go on, now. It's all right. She's upset. We're all upset by this."

Taria felt Gramma settle down beside her with a groan on the grassy hillside. Gramma didn't touch her, didn't speak. For long minutes they did nothing but watch the workers shoveling dirt into the grave. When it seemed enough time had gone by, Taria shifted on the ground. She sniffed. "She's not in there. She's not, Gramma."

"That's what the priest would have said, too," Gramma Ruth answered. "It's just her body."

"Is that what you think, Gramma?"

"Part of me, yes. The *Pakeha* part." Gramma took a long breath; another shovelful of dirt landed softly in the grave.

"What about the rest of you?"

Gramma plucked a tuft of grass from the ground and let it fall back, the breeze carrying it away from them. "The rest of me feels Gloria here. Right here. Not in some priest's heaven. Not away in the sky at Thunder, either. But here. Wherever we are."

Taria shook her head. She blinked away sudden tears. "I don't feel *anything*, Gramma. Why don't I feel anything?"

Gramma pulled her close, hugging Taria fiercely. "You will, darling," she whispered. "One day you'll listen in just the right way, and you will."

"You need to find some friends."

They hadn't stayed long in New Zealand. Not long after Taria's fifth birthday her father had taken a job offer from the United States. After a few months, when her father had settled into an apartment and made arrangements, Taria joined him there, first in California, then in Santa Fe, St. Louis, Cincinnati, and Nashville, as he was transferred. It seemed they rarely lived in one place more than a year or two, and each time, Taria faced the task of leaving the few friends she knew and making new ones. It was not something she did easily, not anymore.

At the age of ten, Taria and her father were living in the Florida panhandle outside Pensacola.

As always when her father suggested that she should be more outgoing, Taria lifted her shoulders as if she were about to shrug, hiding her face behind thin bones. She was playing in the backyard of their house. Wiry clumps of grass clung to sandy dirt, with two sadly leaning pine trees in either corner of the lot throwing a few scraps of shade in the heat. A speckled gecko cocked its head from a palmetto bush nearby and peered sidewise at her. Taria watched the lizard rather than her father. "I have friends," she protested. "I know lots of kids at school."

"You never invite them over. I never hear you talk about them, either. I don't even know their names."

"*I* know their names," Taria answered, but the truth was that none of them were friends, not in the way Papa was suggesting. She knew their faces, knew their seats in the classroom, but at lunch they all sat with other friends, and on the playground they didn't invite her to play unless one of the teachers made them. *"I don't like her,"* she heard one of them—Lisa—say one day when Ms. Kirsten suggested they ask Taria to be in the four square line. *"She's weird, and she talks Chinese all the time."* That wasn't fair—she only spoke Mandarin when she wanted them to go away, because she knew it bothered them. "I don't need to invite them over. I see them at school every day."

"I never see you playing with anyone," he persisted. "Kelsey next door—"

"I don't like Kelsey," Taria broke in. "She's stupid."

"Taria—"

"She is, and I hate her, and I don't *need* any friends. I'm fine alone." The gecko ducked its head and skittered away from under the palmetto, kicking sand as it fled. Taria folded arms over chest and lowered her head, staring down at the ground and rocking from side to side. After a moment the lizard returned, looking tentatively out from the bush a few inches from her foot.

Taria could hear her father breathing above and behind her, as if he weren't certain what to say. He seemed less and less sure how to respond to her with each passing year. They grew apart like two trees leaning in different directions. "Everyone needs friends," her father persisted finally. "Taria, if I hadn't had friends after Glo—after your mama died, I don't know how I would have gotten through it."

"None of those friends of yours changed anything, did

they?" Taria's head came up then, eyes hard and dry. "Did they, Papa? Mama was still *dead*." With the last word, she stomped her foot angrily on the ground where the gecko was crouched, and felt instant regret. She'd wanted to kill it, to take the fury she felt and use it to hurt something else, and now she was afraid, afraid to lift her foot and see the smashed body, wanting the lizard to be somehow alive and unhurt. Tears made the grass shimmer in her vision, and one drop fell glistening from her eye to land on the top of her sneaker, the canvas top darkening in an irregular circle.

Taria lifted her shoe, biting her lower lip and steeling herself for the sight of the mangled corpse. She told herself it wouldn't hurt, seeing the smashed body of the lizard.

She wouldn't let it hurt.

There was nothing below but the print of her sole.

The nightmare of her mother's murder, which still sometimes brought her screaming and sobbing from her sleep, receded somewhat over the years, but on nights when she was worried or upset, it could still come to her.

Taria was worried and upset more often in recent months, mostly because of Judy.

Her father had dated a few women in recent years, but Judy had been a constant part of their lives for the past seven months. She was a short woman with long red hair, active and lively, with a percussive laugh that sometimes hurt Taria's ears. Judy was nice enough to her, but Taria sometimes thought she glimpsed a pained look on Judy's face when she would interrupt Judy's conversation with her father, to request help with homework or to ask if someone wanted to play a game. Judy and her father went out a lot—which meant that Taria was left with a babysitter, and usually by the time they came home, she was already asleep.

She could feel the split in her father's attention. If she didn't actively resent it, the knowledge still tugged at her soul, making her eyes fill with tears when he and Judy were lost in each other and to her. "But Dad, what about Mama?" she asked once when she learned that—for the third time that week—Judy was coming over for dinner. "Have you forgotten her?"

Her father's eyes had gone soft and wet at the plaintiveness in her voice. He pulled her into his lap on the couch, something he hadn't done for a while. "I can never forget your mother," he told her. "Never. She was a wonderful person, and I loved her very much. I still miss her every day, I always will. But she wouldn't have wanted me to stop living my own life because she was gone. She would have wanted both of us to be happy, because she *did* love us. Can you understand that, honey?"

"I guess so," she'd said, and wondered even as she said the words if they were a lie.

Sometimes the small things were the worst. In their living room was a carved wooden chair with a rattan seat that her dad had shipped from China after they'd left, a chair Taria remembered her mother sitting in at night, reading with her legs curled underneath her and a pool of light in her lap from a lamp. Once, Taria had found Judy sitting in the chair. She said nothing, but it seemed heresy to her. Afterward, Taria always made sure that several of her stuffed animals occupied the chair whenever Judy arrived.

If her father noticed, he never said anything.

It was summer, not long after school was out, when the dream returned again. Taria woke with a start, her heart pounding and the sound of a cry—*"Mama!"*—fading in her ears. She sat up in her bed, momentarily confused by the dark quiet of the room, still seeing the man's hand on Mama's wrist, and the bloody sprawl of her mother's body on the street. She was breathing loud and fast, afraid to go back to sleep, afraid of what she'd find on the other side of consciousness.

From down the hall she could hear the soft, familiar sound of her father snoring. She swung her feet over the side of the bed and padded into her dad's room. The door was closed, and she pushed it open. "Daddy—" she began, then stopped, still holding onto the doorknob.

A glow from the streetlight outside knifed in through the window and slashed across the bed. There were two humped shapes under the blue afghan, and red hair spilled over the coverlet on the right, gleaming in the pale yellow light. Another softer breath punctuated her father's snores.

Taria stood there for what seemed an eternity, rocking back and forth on the rug, her hand clasping the cold bronze of the knob, caught between wanting the comfort of her father's presence and hating the betrayal of another woman's presence in his bed. Judy's clothes were folded over the footboard; the room smelled of her.

Taria went to her father's bureau and slid open the middle drawer, wincing as the wood squealed softly. In the tangle of cuff links, tie clasps, and chains was a small velvet case. Taria lifted it out of the drawer and let a silver brooch slide out onto her palm, the fine chain curling around it. She slid it quickly over her head. The silver was chilly for a moment on her chest, then quickly warmed.

Taria closed the door quietly and went back to her room. She dressed in the dark. She slid open the window to her bedroom, dropping down onto the dewed, cold grass of the side yard. Predawn gleamed on the horizon, washing out the stars in aquamarine, but she could still see Jupiter, where Thunder lurked, bright on the western horizon. Taria always knew where Jupiter was. Always, because that's where Mama was. Tires squealed somewhere off in the distance; birds were loud in the trees, and a low mist rising from the nearby lake drifted like lost dreams between the houses.

She started walking down the street, heading toward the intersection with East 12. She wasn't sure where she was going or why. It was just that the known was suddenly more frightening than the unknown. She had vague thoughts of getting to the harbor, where she might find a boat that would take her back to China, or maybe to New Zealand where Gramma and Grampa lived.

She walked. No one stopped her. None of the cars that passed her paused to check on a ten-year-old girl strolling determinedly and alone in the dawn. She walked for what seemed to be hours but was probably no more than two, and stopped to rest on the benches outside a Dairy Queen. She must have fallen asleep—the next thing she remembered was being awakened by a police officer, who shook her gently, crouching down alongside her. The woman asked her name, asked where she lived, and took her home.

Afterward, in the wake of the mingled anger and relief, her father asked her why.

"I don't know," Taria answered, aware of Judy leaning against the doorway of her father's bedroom, one of her father's robes around her. "I just . . . miss Mama. I thought . . . maybe I'd go back to China . . . I don't know . . ." She sniffled and blew her nose. Then she lifted the brooch from around her neck. "Here, Daddy. I should give this back to you."

She set the brooch in his upturned palm. He stared at the jewelry for a moment, then opened the clasp. Two tiny figures seemed to stand above the bowl of polished silver: their wedding picture. Taria heard her father's long, shuddering intake of breath. He gazed at the brooch with a strained look, as if Taria's flight had drawn tight all the muscles of his face. Maybe it was just the light, but he appeared much older to her then. She could see the fine network of lines connecting the furrows angling from the corners of his eyes, the soft paunch of loose skin under his chin, the gray flecked in his stubbled cheeks.

He was some stranger, an ancient who had crawled into her father's body, and Taria shivered.

She looked at Judy, still leaning against the doorway, and scowled.

* * *

"I won't ever love you," she told Judy.

But in the end that wasn't true. Strangely, it was Judy who became Taria's confidante. Her father continued to retreat from her, as if looking at Taria, blossoming into the image of her mother Gloria, was somehow too painful for him. Her father and Judy married when she was eleven. Taria would never call Judy "Mother," but Judy seemed comfortable and understanding with that. She was younger than Gloria had been—barely twenty years older than Taria herself—and she became more older sister than mother, shepherding Taria through her teenage years with a gentle blend of trust and openness without being particularly judgmental, while Taria's father simply became a person who sometimes grunted in her direction. It was Judy who gave Taria a pack of condoms in her junior year after a late night chat.

"Look, I don't want you to use them," she said. The packet crinkled too loudly in her fingers as she passed it to Taria. "I don't think you're ready yet. But if something happens, I want you to have them with you because, well, things happen quickly sometimes." When Taria did lose her virginity later that year, it was Judy she told . . .

"You're back late."

Taria stopped. Judy was watching television. Blue and erratic light spilled from her bedroom out into the hallway where Taria stood. She leaned against the doorjamb and peered into the bedroom. Judy was sitting propped up on the pillows, wearing the red terry-cloth bathrobe she wore every night. "Sorry," Taria said shortly. She started down the hall to her own room, but Judy's voice pursued her. She stopped again with a sigh.

"I was just a little worried. That's all. At least you beat your dad home—that's the important part. He's still over at Paul's, trying to get his house network up."

Judy smiled conspiratorially at that, as if they shared some secret; Taria just watched her, trying to keep her own face expressionless. Judy patted the bed alongside her.

"Look, I just want to go to my room," Taria said. "I'm tired."

"Please?"

Grimacing, Taria went in, sitting on the edge of the mattress. The television flickered with some historical costume drama set in nineteenth century London. "You really like this shit?" Taria had been experimenting with profanity in the house for the last few months. It still felt strange, cursing in front of her stepmother, and the words never sounded natural, but she felt like cursing tonight, felt like screaming, felt like crying.

Judy didn't like the cursing—Taria could tell by the way her eyes crinkled—but she said nothing. "Like it? Not really. I just figure that if I keep watching, one day it'll take." Judy laughed. "Kind of a vaccination for sophistication. So far, it looks like I'm immune." Taria hadn't laughed with her, hadn't smiled. Judy patted Taria's hand. "So?"

Taria drew her hand back. She knew what Judy was asking, and it was the last thing she wanted to talk about right now. "Hmm?"

"You and Robert."

"What about Robert?"

"Nothing, I suppose." Judy cocked her head, looking at Taria. Even six years after her father's second marriage, Taria still was uncomfortable with their relationship. Under the impact of Judy's scrutiny, Taria scowled.

"What?"

"What's going on with you two?"

Maybe it was just the lateness of the hour, maybe it was just teenage volatility. Taria stood up, arms folded, her face set in careful haughtiness. "Am I still a virgin, is that what you mean? Do you want to know if we're *fucking* yet?" She pronounced the vulgarity with a toss of her head and a glare. She would never have said anything like that to her father. "Well, we did. I even used the goddamn condoms you gave me, too, if that's what you're worried about."

Judy's eyes rose and she opened her mouth as if about to

say something, then she turned her head slightly, her eyes still on Taria. "And now all the magic's gone."

Inexplicably, Taria started crying. She couldn't help it, couldn't hold it back. The emotions battered down all the dams she'd placed around them during the whole evening and came raging out. Somewhere in the midst of the tears, she became aware that Judy was hugging her. Taria shrugged away her stepmother's arms; sniffing, she leaned against the wall. She could see herself in the mirror of Judy's dresser across the room: a waifish seventeen-year-old with smeared mascara, looking sullen and angry; she could see the back of Judy's robe as she stood in front of her.

"Want to talk?" Judy asked. Somehow, she managed to look unoffended by Taria's treatment, her eyes sympathetically moist.

"What the hell is there to talk about?" Taria raged back, her arms flailing as if throwing away Judy's compassion. "He told me he thinks we need to see other people. That pretty much says it, doesn't it? He got what he wanted from me, and now he wants to chase after some other fucking skirt." The tears had started again, and Taria wiped at them savagely with the back of her hand. "*Damn* him!"

"Maybe he's just scared, Taria," Judy said. "Maybe the two of you just got too close too fast, and he doesn't know how to handle it, and this is the only way he knows to retreat. That's the way it is with sex—it always changes things. You think it's going to create a bond, and instead it alters the relationship so much it fractures."

"But he was the first. It was supposed to be something special," she said. The room shimmered in her tears. This time when Judy's arms went around her, Taria didn't resist. She cradled her head in the older woman's shoulder. Judy's hand stroked her back, and Taria could hear the strong beating of her heart through her sobs. For a moment Taria imagined that Judy was her own mother, but then everything shifted around her and she was being held by a stranger and the tears dried as quickly as they'd come. It was so strong an epiphany that Taria was surprised Judy couldn't feel it also, that Judy didn't suddenly let her go in shocked surprise.

But she didn't. "Poor baby," Judy murmured into her hair, and Taria felt her stepmother's lips brush the top of her head in a soft kiss. "Life keeps knocking you around. I know it hurts. You just have to accept the hurt and get through it."

But I won't let *it hurt me*, Taria thought, though she didn't say the words, and she could hear reflections of her earlier selves repeating the mantra with her.

I won't let it.

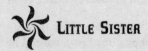 LITTLE SISTER

The Blues seemed to have little sense of privacy.

There were public facilities for elimination, but they were merely small pits in the midst of public open spaces, with no shelter around them. Taria needed to use the facilities after their long walk back from the watersingers; Makes assured her there were no private places, either in the city or within her own residence, nor would anyone care that she used the open hole set to one side on the street. "That is what it's for, Taria-Who-Wants-to-Understand. The tanners will come and take the urine for softening leather, and others will take the excrement for the sourgrass fields. Why would anyone want to waste such a resource?" Dog had given a canine chuckle in Taria's head at that.

When in Rome . . .

Feeling self-conscious and very exposed, she told Dog to turn himself off for a minute, and squatted over the hole and urinated while, within arm's reach, dozens of Blues moved on all sides of her. Small, iridescent beetles snarled around her head, landing and taking off again as Taria batted at them. The ripe smell from the pit wrapped around her.

There was no toilet paper, either. Taria fumbled in the pocket of her pants to find a tissue, wiped herself, and dropped the tissue into the hole. As she stood, buckling her pants, she surveyed the crowds sliding around her—no one watched, no one cared about her embarrassment. "Come on," she said to Makes. "Let's get you that doctor."

Since they'd returned to the city, Makes had said nothing about the watersingers or the confrontation with the kagliaristi. If the Blue was troubled by her wounds, she hadn't told Taria. As they approached the Gruriterash-pali—the huge rambling edifice that the humans had dubbed the Cathedral—they encountered another quartet of the warriors, standing near the entrance: all male, all naked, all with their genitalia twined around one leg. The kagliaristi sent booming notes of sound toward them, and their fingertips glittered with knives. Taria watched them apprehensively, but none of them approached. Makes seemed untroubled by their presence; she simply walked steadily toward the entrance, with Taria following. The kagliaristi stood aside as they approached, saying nothing, but decidedly sinister in the way they swiveled to move with Makes.

Taria was glad when they were within the grounds and the warriors were behind them.

Makes's residence was in the Cathedral of She-Who-Spoke-the-World—though Makes insisted that "cathedral" was the wrong word: the best translation she could offer for Gruriterashpali was Place-Where-She-May-Speak-Again. After they passed the kagliaristi at the gate, some of the younger Blues, whom Taria thought of as acolytes, had come from the building, their booming voices loud and their fingers probing the bandage around Makes's arm. An older Blue had come into the large common room of the temple not long after they returned—she'd removed Taria's bandage and lathered on a greenish poultice before rewrapping it. Makes screamed then, a wordless wail in several octaves at once. Taria had winced in sympathy, hugging herself, but the doctor didn't appear to care at all about her patient's misery.

Taria had no idea what the poultice might be, but the smell reminded her of the hole in the street outside.

"Why were the kagliaristi interested in me?" Taria asked Makes, mostly to try to take her mind away from the doctor's gruff ministrations. Makes's skin shifted to mottled indigo with the question. She was still whimpering as the doctor rebandaged the wound, but her head-crest rose slightly.

"Why are your people so interested in the ones you call the Thunder Makers?" she responded.

"Are you saying it's only because I'm a human and an alien, Makes? That can't be all it is—they're definitely paying attention to you, too. At least I assume that a cluster of kagliaristi standing outside Gruriterashpali isn't there because they're interested in the architecture. What's going on?"

"The Baraaki always interests the kagliaristi. That's all."

"Am I in danger because I'm with you?" Taria tapped her fingers against her pant leg with the question, uneasy. Muscles twitched in her thin face as she clenched her teeth together. "Makes?"

Makes snorted. "You are in danger because you breathe," she said shortly.

"More koans?"

"Mystery is good for the mind. Be glad you have such a wealth."

The Blue obviously wasn't going to discuss the incident further. Taria forced her hands to be still, her jaw muscles to relax. The doctor grunted, said something to Makes, and left them. "You are hurt, too, Taria-Who-Wants-to-Understand. I know that much. Not out here"—Makes touched her bandaged arm—"but inside. I can feel it. You have scars, too, ones that even human eyes miss."

Taria blinked. She didn't know how to answer that. "Makes . . ." she began, then went silent, mouth open.

"You must be hungry," Makes said. "Food's been set out for us. Follow me . . ."

Grateful, Taria allowed the subject to be changed.

They ate supper in Makes's rooms. There had been a slab of roasted, meaty ribs on the table; remembering Makes's comment about the taste of watersingers, Taria confined herself to the bowls of fruit and grain alongside it. She took her plate and went out to the balcony, fitting the vidcam over her eye again, and slowly turned so the camera and Dog could see the panorama.

The city where Makes lived was called Rasedilio-dutherad, which translated, Taria was told, as Oldest-Gathering-Place-Near-the-Quiet-Saltwater.   Rasediliodutherad was built on a series of small promontories rising like the stumps of teeth from the jaw of the coastline. At high tide they became islands, separated from the bluffs of the mainland by a kilometer of shallow water; at low tide a thousand tidal pools glittered in the sandy flats, and you could walk from the shore out to the dwellings. The look of the coast reminded Taria of northern Oregon, where the sea had eroded softer rock away from hard basalt pillars, leaving behind steep-walled islands haunting foggy bays. The Blues had constructed a network of flat-hulled ferries connected to chains anchored to the sea floor that served as a transport system between the islands when the water was high. Arched pedestrian bridges connected the islands closest to each other, while long, winding staircases carved from living rock spiraled down the cliff walls all the way to the floor of the bay.

Taria had learned that each island served a different function. The island she was on now, which she thought of as "Humpback," she understood to be the religious center for all the Blues; "Twin Peaks" was government and administration; "Saddleback" was where all the merchants housed their wares—she had yet to figure out whether they actually sold anything. She'd seen nothing resembling currency changing hands, nor did the Blues seem to barter; they simply took whatever they wanted, calling to the merchant as they left.

Taria found the architecture pleasing—an organic clustering of domes, boxes, and minarets, all made from the same pale green stone and looking more extruded than carved. Still, she could see the marks of chisels, and pieces were fitted together using a white mortar that gave the buildings the appearance of jigsaw puzzles. The buildings were laid out in no order, hanging over narrow, winding streets, none of which ever seemed to intersect another at a right angle. Entrances were wide openings hung with swaying curtains that looked like found material, all of which made pleasing noises when the sea breeze moved them or someone walked through. Noise-making decorations were ubiquitous, hanging from every knob in the walls and filling the air with unmelodious clanks and rustles and chimings. The buildings varied in size from halls that could hold a hundred of the Blues to small rooms barely large enough for two. Taria could only hazard a guess at the functions of the various spaces—there was no clear human analogue to most of them.

Living arrangements were segregated onto various islands as well. "Leaning Shoreward" was the island where all the children lived, along with a constantly rotating shift of teachers/caregivers. A rough semicircle of outer islands was the home for most of the adults, but even after a long conversation with Makes, she wasn't quite sure how the adults were separated, though she knew that there was segregation of some kind—it seemed to be some intricate arrangement of caste and sexual preference.

Altogether, between the two dozen or so islands that comprised this city, Taria estimated there were perhaps two or three hundred thousand of the Blues. This was the largest city, as far as *Lightbringer*'s sensors could detect, though there were several other Blue cities scattered along all the coasts.

Now, Taria leaned out over the railing of the balcony overlooking the bay. There were vines with reddish leaves curled around the stone pillars of the balcony; among them, tiny insects crawled along the rims of papery cups holding a sweet-smelling liquid—as she watched, a white-fly buzzed past and landed inside one of the cups. Before the whitefly could take off again, the insects leaped from rim to rim of the cup, translucent strands trailing from their abdomens, sealing in the whitefly, which batted futilely against the bars of its cage.

Taria moved farther down the balcony, not wanting to see the whitefly's inevitable death, however it might come.

The sun Yin had set, but Yang still dominated the sky as a huge crescent, throwing down a reddish reflected light that was as bright as dusk on Earth. The tide was coming in; already the waves were lapping at the rocks at the bottom of Humpback. A thick fog was coming in off the sea, shrouding the huge, multicolored arc of Yang, hiding the farthest of the islands and muffling the sounds of the city: the jingling of the wind chimes hanging from every available wall; the rattling of the ferry chain; a nearby rhythmic pounding of drums and brassy keening of wind instruments; a faint low droning from out near the islands, which sounded like a chorus of watersingers; the constant low hooting of the Blues as they moved through the warren of buildings, and the clatter and bustle of their daily routines. Under it all was the comforting susurration of the waves.

Directly below, fifty meters down, a courtyard garden of wiry, spindly bushes that looked more dead than alive led to the gate where the kagliaristi still were standing in a cluster, and out into a maze of narrow crowded streets. Clustered buildings huddled like lichens on the steep slope of the island's summit.

Taria was still trying to get a sense of the scale of the city for the video feed, but the static from the camera was getting worse, and the double vision in her optical nerves had brought back her headache. She reached up and touched the contact, letting the vidcam fall into her hand and sighing with relief, though Dog howled in disappointment at no longer being able to see.

"Your city looks like something from a fairy tale," Taria said.

"Fairy tale?" Makes sounded out the words carefully. " 'Tale' I know—another word you use for story. But 'fairy'?"

"A fairy's a mythological creature," Taria answered. "But 'fairy tales' aren't necessarily about fairies—and I know you're going to start complaining about my language again, so don't bother. Fairy tales are archetypes, fables drawing on ancient images and beliefs. Every culture has them."

"Tell me one of these fairy tales," Makes said. She had come out to the balcony herself. Her bandaged arm hung limp, but the other stroked Taria's shoulder and brushed down her hip. Taria fought the urge to move away from the caress.

"All right," she said. "I'll do that—if afterward you tell me one of yours. Is that a fair trade?"

Makes thrummed something that Taria took for assent. "All right, then," she began. "Since we're sitting in a tower looking out over a garden, this is the story of Rapunzel, the way my Gramma once told it to me . . ."

Taria wasn't sure how much of "Rapunzel" Makes really understood. She'd told Makes the unsanitized version of the story, and parts she herself had always found disturbingly odd—the unprotesting ease with which the parents of Rapunzel gave away their child; the witch's decision to lock up the child in a tower for no apparent reason other than to use her hair as a convenient ladder; the sublimated undertones of rape (did the witch use Rapunzel sexually, as the inevitable prince did when he came upon her?)—none of those seemed to bother Makes. Instead Makes was puzzled by the few parts that Taria actually found halfway reasonable.

"Why would Rapunzel want to *keep* her children after the prince made her pregnant?" Makes asked, visibly disgusted by the image, her skin shimmering with pale teal splotches. "Did the witch know that Rapunzel was insane, and is that why she sent her away?"

"Makes, I think you're missing the point—"

"And the prince," Makes continued. "Is sight so important to humans that you would wander lost for years if you were blinded? Couldn't he *hear* where he was?"

"I guess fairy tales aren't exactly the best vehicle to help us understand each other."

"They might be if yours made sense," Makes answered.

Taria laughed at that. "That's hardly fair. I haven't heard yours yet to make a comparison."

Makes pointed out over the bay to an island. "When I was there," she said, "my Keeper-of-Those-Not-Yet-Real would tell us stories that she claimed were Things-Once-True . . ."

Once there was an island where only one Child-of-She-Who-Spoke-the-World lived. Her name was Speaks-Too-High. Speaks-Too-High lived alone because of her voice, which was piercing and sharp, altogether too painful for those around her to tolerate. This made Speaks-Too-High distressed, for she saw the discomfort and pain she caused everyone. The Neritorika of her town, taking pity on the poor creature, ordered her to throw herself from the cliff of her home island so she would die quickly instead of living a life of misery.

But even the sea found the squeals and squeaks she made in her panic to be awful, and so the sea sent a wave to lift her up and carry her away. The sea threw her onto a small island far from everyone, where it was always warm, and there she lived for many turns of seasons, eating whip-tongue worms and dangleberries. Once every turn of the Greater Light, in obedience to her Neritorika's last order to her, Speaks-Too-High would go to the highest cliff of the island and throw herself into the sea, but each time the sea spat her back onto the beach, not liking the sound and taste of her. So Speaks-Too-High prowled her little island, singing mournfully to herself so she would not be left in awful silence. She sang songs of how it would be if everyone spoke the way she spoke. She sang of being magically transformed, so that her voice would be as low as the growling thunder. She sang of returning back to her own home once more.

One day Speaks-Too-High heard the sea toss a shape onto the beach. When she went to hear what it was, she heard a watersinger, but one much, much smaller than any watersinger she had ever heard or touched before, no longer than her own forearm. The tiny watersinger was weak, and Speaks-Too-High thought it would soon die. Speaks-Too-High had found a sharp flake of rock, which she used to cut the dangleberries away from their vines, and she thought that maybe she could use the flake-knife to flay the skin from this tiny watersinger, since she had not had meat in many turns. Even though it was small, Speaks-Too-High hoped the watersinger would still taste good. But when Speaks-Too-High went to cut the watersinger's throat, the watersinger spoke to her in the Language-of-Obedience, saying in a voice three tones higher than any watersinger she had ever heard before: "This one begs you not to kill it."

Speaks-Too-High was so surprised that she dropped the flake-knife. She had not heard another's words in so long that they sounded strange and harsh to her, and to hear them coming from a watersinger's throat was even more startling. Speaks-Too-High thought maybe she had the Disease-of-Too-Much-Greater-Light, which makes you hear things that aren't there. "You will tell me who you are," she told the watersinger in the Language-of-Command, and the watersinger lifted its head.

"This one is the Eldest-and-First," the watersinger answered, and Speaks-Too-High laughed at that, for she had seen the Greater Singers and knew how huge they were.

"Then if you are Eldest-and-First, you will tell me why it is you are so small," Speaks-Too-High answered. "Wouldn't Eldest-and-First have grown to be largest of all?"

"The older a stone in a stream is, the more the water wears it down," the watersinger replied. "Once, ages ago before your kind walked on the land, this one was the Largest-and-Strongest, Speaks-Too-High. No more. This one is worn down by eternity."

Speaks-Too-High was now truly startled. "You will tell me how it is you know my name," she shouted.

"This one has heard you singing these many turns," Eldest-and-First told her. Its voice was hardly audible over the sound of the waves and wind whispering in the prickle-spine trees. "Many times over the seasons you called to She-Who-Spoke-the-World, and though She never answered, this one heard. This one knows your name." Now Eldest-and-First lifted its head again wearily, and all its earlets turned toward Speaks-Too-High, and it no longer spoke in the Language-of-Obedience. "I have heard you singing, Speaks-Too-High, and I know what you have asked, and I have come to give it to you. I will help you, for your voice is like mine, and it has called me. All you must do is sing again. Sing again now, Speaks-Too-High. Sing for me. I heard you, Speaks-Too-High. I alone. I heard you because I gave you life, and now I will give you what you ask."

Speaks-Too-High heard the words of the ancient watersinger, and she shuddered, for she knew what she had asked in her songs. She picked up the flake-knife from where it had dropped on the sand, and with a great cry that echoed over the water and caused the very sea to tremble, she slit the watersinger's throat before it could say another word.

Afterward, she was afraid to eat the watersinger, for if the meat was tough and bitter, she would know that the watersinger had told the truth about itself. She sat and watched the body until the crack-wings covered it in a writhing mass. Then she left.

Speaks-Too-High sang no more, ever again. She made no noises at all. She waited in awful, terrifying silence until her own death found her.

"My God," Taria said when Makes had finished. The sudden, inexplicable violence in the story startled her, made her think again of the kagliaristi, of the missing Ensign Coen. "I don't understand the lesson in that at all. Why would Speaks-Too-High cut the eldest watersinger's throat?"

"How could she not?" Makes answered.

"But the watersinger said it would give Speaks-Too-High what she asked for in her songs."

"Yes," Makes answered, with an almost human smugness. "Exactly."

Taria laughed suddenly, shaking her head. "You are very different, Makes."

"I am the same as I've always been, Taria-Who-Wants-to-Understand," Makes answered. "It's you who are different."

TIME OF TWILIGHT

He who knows does not speak.
He who speaks does not know.

Block all the passages!
Shut all the doors!
Blunt all edges!
Untie all tangles!
Harmonize all lights!
Unite the world into one whole!
This is called the Mystical Whole,
Which you cannot court after nor shun
Benefit nor harm, honor nor humble.

Therefore, it is the Highest of the world.

—Chapter 56, *Tao Teh Ching*

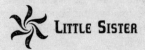 LITTLE SISTER

The small things . . .

"I would like one of those," Taria said to the vendor, speaking the words Dog placed before her eyes and pointing to a display of bright orange and dark blue blossoms. The flowers were tied in bunches at the rear of the stall, with thick pistils of startling and saturated scarlet drooping high over the center of each bunch. Taria had no idea if they were food items, or plants used for medicinal purpose, or simply flowers for display, but they were beautiful and they seemed to match the glory of Yang that hung multicolored in the sky beyond the low buildings. She thought they would look lovely sitting on Makes's balcony.

The vendor said nothing. She simply plucked the bunch from the rack and placed them on a small wooden block. Before Taria could say anything, the vendor plucked a knife from somewhere under her clothing and cut the blossoms from the stems. They cascaded down in brilliance, the petals already starting to shrivel before they even reached the ground. The vendor stepped on them as she handed Taria the empty stems.

Taria took them, too startled to refuse. The vendor seemed to expect nothing further from her; she'd already turned to deal with another client. Taria looked at the decapitated stems, drooling a thick yellowish liquid from the angled cuts. A pungent aroma not unlike licorice wrinkled her nose.

Dog barked in her head, sounding almost like a laugh. Taria laughed with the PIA. She handed the bunch to another Blue who had come up to the vendor, and walked on.

Another reminder this was not home . . .

Makes had told Taria that she was free to roam the area around Gruriterashpali "until Yang touches the water." Despite some trepidation at the thought of being separated from her mentor and guardian, Taria had been eager to see what normal Blue life looked like.

"What about the kagliaristi?" Taria had asked. An image of Alex Coen, his face and body shredded from the finger-blades of the Blue warrior caste, came to her mind.

"Humans are so frightened of things that really don't matter . . ." A noise like rocks grinding came from her throat. "The kagliaristi will not hurt you. I promise you that. Not here."

Makes had touched her then, stroking Taria's cheek the way one might a child's, the touch tender and soft, and Taria had smiled, the specter of Coen momentarily banished.

Trust comes from small things, also. Makes had been right. There were still kagliaristi at the gate—a different group this time—but they let her pass with only a few interrogative bursts of sound.

As Taria walked on into the city, the Blues moved around her in a noisy tide. She could feel the soft impact of sound against her, a constant, tuneless drone. Blues would slide adroitly out of her way as she approached, their arms perhaps reaching out to stroke her shoulder or hip as they passed, as if assuring themselves that this alien creature was indeed there. None of them tried to speak with her, though she heard the incessant chatter of speech all around her. The city was crowded—Taria realized that one implication of the fairy tale of Speaks-Too-High was that Blues preferred to live in close proximity to each other—and for all its lack of technology, the city was as loud as Manhattan in rush hour, with polyphonic voices, wind chimes, the hammering and banging of workers, the calls of a hundred vendors . . .

Someone screamed to Taria's right, a symphonic keening of pain. The sound brought Taria's head up, made her take a step away from the sound and put a corner of the vendor's stall between the horrible uproar and herself. A Blue staggered from a narrow lane, emerging from darkness into the sunlight of the vendor's square. Taria could see open, puss-filled sores on its arms and face, the normally azure skin an ugly, mottled green. The Blue staggered drunkenly, nearly crashing into one of the stalls across the way. She opened her mouth again, venting another hideous, multiple scream. The crowd of Blues in the market square gave her room, none of them touching her as they did the others. Otherwise, no one made a motion to help the creature, who screeched again and fell to her knees near the lane's opening. She knelt there, rocking back and forth and mewling softly.

She fell sideways to the ground. A sound like the failing drone of a bagpipe came from her, then she was quiet.

None of the other Blues reacted. Taria saw business going on as normal all around the square. She crept forward toward the body. Hands touched her as she passed; she shrugged them off. When she stood in the small open space around the Blue, she crouched down in front of her. Fingertips scrabbled on the loose stones of the pavement, but Taria was careful not to let them touch. *Things* moved in the open sores on the Blue's body, like tiny, pale yellow centipedes coiled around each other and writhing obscenely. The Blue's mouth was open, and Taria could hear the faint rasping of a rapid breath. A foul odor hung around her, strong enough that Taria quickly stood back up, her own stomach churning. She took two long breaths, feeling the burning of stomach acid in her throat and willing her stomach to stay settled. "Dog, give me words here. How do I say: 'Excuse me, can you get help for this sick person?' "

A few moments later Dog barked, and Taria grasped the nearest Blue, speaking the words that hung as ghostly lettering in front of her eyes. Her voice always sounded so thin and weak when she spoke in their language, and she couldn't stop the quaver that accompanied it. The Blue sent a quick pulse of sound toward the huddled body on the street, spoke a few words, and walked away from her. Taria, open-mouthed, watched her leave as Dog's translation sounded in her head.

She has nothing to offer me.

Taria asked three other Blues for help, and received a variant of the same answer: *She has nothing to offer me.* When, desperate, she crouched down beside the stricken Blue again, she could hear nothing, no sound of breath, no rise and fall of her chest, no movement at all.

She stood. Around her and the body Blues moved everywhere, and no one paid any attention at all. Taria heard the whine of the first crack-wing finding the corpse.

She left.

"She was infected with blood-larvae, probably from eating old tartseed rinds without washing them. If you ingest the blood-larvae, sometimes death comes that fast, when they emerge. She wouldn't be dangerous unless you touched her, and even then you'd have felt the larvae crawling on your skin before they burrowed into you."

Taria shuddered at the image, remembering the sight of the open sores on the Blue's body and the larvae slithering inside. "But they just *ignored* her, Makes. They . . . they told me that she 'had nothing to offer' them."

Makes seemed nonplussed. Hands slapped her hips. "How else would you expect them to answer?"

"If *you* had asked them, would they have helped? Was it because I'm not one of you?"

"Perhaps, because I am the Baraaki," Makes replied, with a tone implying that the word answered everything. "But only because of that. You dwell too much on this incident, Taria-Who-Wants-to-Understand. There is nothing there to learn."

I disagree, Taria thought, but she sighed, changing the subject. "I've heard the title before, but I don't really know 'Baraaki,' Makes. What does it mean?"

Makes gave a bass grumble from deep in her abdomen; Taria didn't know if it was annoyance or not. "Baraaki is . . . your speech is so thin, Taria, I don't know how you manage to communicate to each other at all . . . I suppose One-Whose-Life-Is-Given-to-Her is close to the translation, but only close."

"The 'Her' in that is She-Who-Spoke-the-World, I assume?"

"Yes."

"So you were chosen to be the Baraaki . . . Does that give you a special relationship with Her?"

Another rumble, deeper and longer this time, with inflections in it of words from the Blue language, though pitched too low for Taria to understand them. "Some things you can ask, Taria-Who-Wants-to-Understand, but I can't answer." In Taria's head a few seconds later Dog yipped at that. Taria raised her eyebrows—a safe enough gesture in front of someone who could not see it.

Some things you can ask but I can't answer . . . So there were embarrassing or taboo subjects for the Blues, too. "We were under the impression that Baraaki means something close to 'priest' or maybe 'archbishop' in our language."

Makes's eyestrip blinked in a long, slow ripple from left to right. "That is one note of the meaning, perhaps, but that's not all."

That seemed to be all she was going to say on the subject. Makes came out onto the balcony with Taria, her hands lightly brushing along Taria's side. The Blue vented air, giving a short, loud hoot that seemed to contain notes spanning Taria's entire range of hearing, a massive dissonant chord that echoed from the nearest island. "It sounds like a nice evening," Makes commented. As an attempt to change the subject, it was clumsy and obvious.

Answer the questions I've asked you. Tell me what happened to poor Coen . . . Taria thought the words but left them unsaid. "What is it you hear, Makes?" Taria asked her. "I mean, in the sense that I'd say 'It looks like a nice evening' or 'It's such a pretty sight'? How would you describe all this?"

Makes gave the baritone hiccup that was the Blue shrug. "I can tell from the way the sounds reflect that it is a night of . . . *harishkameldis*. Thick-Air-That-Is-Wet-and-Confuses-Sound. Fog, in your language. The tones of the chimes tell me the wind is soft, and I can smell its fragrance and know that the *harishkameldis* will be gone soon. The waves touch each of the islands, each with its own song that tells of distant storms, and the way they whisper against the rocks tells me where each island is and how large, as do the chimes and the sound of the wind, and I hear that water rising with each breath we take. The voices of the Children-of-She-Who-Spoke-the-World are pleasant, and tell me that all is well here tonight, and I know where each voice is and sometimes the very person who speaks. Greater Light has vanished but Lesser Light is still there, on the horizon—I not only see its light, but I can feel its presence, so heavy in the air."

As Makes spoke, Taria looked out over the bay, trying to "see" the landscape the way Makes did. She found it impossible. Even when she closed her eyes it was still the visual afterimages she saw, not the aural world of the Blues. She wondered if someone who had been blind for years might be able to approximate Makes's ability, but there was no one to ask—everyone aboard *Lightbringer* was sighted. Maybe that was a mistake; she made a mental note to mention that to Allison in case there was a second ship sent through Thunder.

"That's beautiful, Makes," she said. "I wish I could hear that way."

"If you could hear as we do, there would be many words in our languages you would suddenly understand, because there's no way I can easily translate their meanings." Her hands trailed along the balcony ledge and ran through Taria's hair. "I also know there are words you have that I can't understand—'blue' or 'red' or 'yellow,' for instance. I simply can't grasp—"

Makes stopped. Her head-crest rose suddenly, the earlet holes opening. From well out in the bay Taria heard the beginning of an immense sound. It reminded her of the song of the watersingers that morning, but this time there were far more voices: an entire discordant symphony of bass, cello, bassoon, tuba, trombone, and tympani—low and dark. Taria could feel the subsonics shiver the floor of the balcony. The sound swelled, echoing minor-keyed from between the steep-walled islands, haunting and sad in the fog. The volume was incredible, given the obvious distance from which it must be coming.

"Makes," Taria shouted against the concussive dissonance. Her right hand tingled with a remembered touch. "Are those watersingers?"

"Yes," Makes answered. "There are tens of thousands of them living along the arms of the bay. You can hear one of the Greater Singers, too, the loudest voice on the bottom."

"Greater Singers? I remember you mentioned them in the story about Speaks-Too-High."

"They live in the sea, and sometimes sing with their smaller cousins."

"Do the 'singers do this every day?"

"No." Makes walked slowly back to the balcony door and said nothing more. As the watersingers reached a momentary crescendo, she lifted her head, as if watching something rising from the bay, though Taria knew that her eyestrip could focus on nothing that far away. Then her head came back down and she gave a low, keening drone.

"Come inside, Taria-Who-Wants-to-Understand," Makes said. "The Singers-in-the-Water will be singing for a while yet; I will leave the doors open if you wish to listen. Come, it's time to rest . . ."

Taria heard her name called, a soft cascade of syllables that roused her, though she didn't yet open her eyes, lingering in the dreams.

"Okay, Mama," she answered. "I'm getting up." She stretched out in her sleep, and her mother's hands caught her, her fingers curling around Taria's small, pudgy ones. "I'm awake now," she said. "Give me my hug—"

She opened her eyes. "—Mama," she breathed. Her heart pounded in her chest, and the scene around her seemed less real than the dream from which she'd awakened.

Yang-light flooded the room. Near the door, in a pile of bedding, Makes was sleeping. Through the open windows to the balcony Taria could hear the last fading notes of the watersingers' long song. A hundred chimes fluttered in the wind, and the sea thrashed the rocks far below.

In the light of the gas giant Taria stared at her hand, her bedclothes pooled at her waist. The watersingers had gone silent. She coughed once—a tickle at the back of her throat from the dust of her cover. The sound was loud in the quiet.

It took her more than an hour to fall back asleep.

". . . I'm really fine, and you don't need to worry about me," Taria told Kyung.

It felt too much like a lie, but she was damned if she was going to admit anything else, not after making the decision to come here.

Taria wished she could see Kyung's face, but the neural link didn't allow it. His warm, gruff voice boomed in her head. *"I heard through the grapevine about your little encounter with the warrior caste. From what I gather, Commander Allison's concerned about the implications, enough that he's talked to Merritt. Taria, what if this is what happened to Coen? What if you're in the middle of*

*some social or religious conflict? Maybe you should re-
quest to come back, or at least request that the Blues let
you have a few more people down there with you.*"

She was on the balcony of Makes's rooms. Yang was
gone, but the sun Yin had just risen, throwing golden light
over the bay. The hubbub of the city rose around her, a
clamoring of voices and sounds, but she missed the deep
song of the watersingers. When a few seconds of inner silence went by, Taria realized that Kyung had stopped talking. "I don't need a squadron of unis in battle armor,
Kyung. That's not an option," she answered Kyung, speaking to the morning. After a long pause—two seconds out
for her reply, enough time to listen, then two seconds back
for response—Kyung spoke again.

*"You may not have a choice. Thunder did a little trick
last night, the wormhole opening up all on its own and
sending everyone up here into a panic. We thought something was coming through, but none of the monitoring instruments showed anything. Everyone on* Lightbringer*'s a
little uneasy at the moment. You can understand that.*"

Taria drummed fingers on pants. "Look, whatever tricks
Thunder might have performed don't have anything to do
with me down here. I'm fine, Kyung. No attacks, no acci-
dents, no viruses, not even a lousy cold. I'll tell Allison the
same damn thing if he asks. I'm fine. I signed on for this
and I'm staying. And right now I don't need help."

"We still haven't found Coen."

"There are a hundred explanations for that, Kyung, and
you know it. Chances are, whatever happened to Coen has
nothing to do with the Blues."

Silence. She lifted her head, smelling the breeze and
feeling the sun on her shoulders.

*"Okay, okay . . . Listen, I miss you, Taria. I'm sorry
about the way we said goodbye. I didn't want it to be that
way, didn't want to—"*

There was a sound behind her. "Gotta go," she said into
Kyung's apology. "Dog?"

Kyung's voice trailed on for a few seconds. "—*end with both of us feeling bad. It was my fau—*" And Taria heard Dog bark and the comlink click off. Taria turned away from the sunrise and saw Makes standing near the entrance to the balcony. She wondered how long the Blue had been awake and what she'd heard. "Makes. How are you this morning?"

The alien grumbled something deep in her stomach. "My arm is very sore and tender, but it moves fine. I have an ache in my left shoulder from when I struck the watersinger yesterday, but it already feels better than it did last night. Two of my earlets down the right side are clogged, and I may take some masata root extract for that. However, I'm breathing very well, and I have been in the little-death long enough to be refreshed. I can sense a need to eat something, but—"

"Makes," Taria interrupted. "In our language, 'How are you?' is usually just a greeting. You really don't have to answer at length. 'Fine' is the usual response."

"What if I'm not 'fine'?"

"You probably still tell me that you are. And you might ask how I am, and I might say 'Fine' also."

"And then?"

"Then we can talk about whatever we want to talk about. It's a ritualized greeting sequence."

"If you are not interested in knowing the answer, why should you ask the question, and why should you expect me to lie? That is stupid." Makes shuffled forward until she could touch Taria's face. Taria held herself still and let Makes's hands wander over her body, stroking her gently before the Blue moved past her onto the balcony. "Even in this speech, words are supposed to mean what words mean," she complained. "Understanding your language is like trying to hold sound in your hands."

Makes cupped her own hands, and Taria imagined a sparkling presence hovering there above her azure flesh. "I think you understand it better than you think," she answered. "That's a lovely metaphor."

Makes boomed a low bass note. She didn't seem to be looking at Taria at all, her body facing toward the wall of the building. "You were having a conversation with the Voices-Only-Taria-Can-Hear?"

"I was talking to Kyung, yes."

"What is a 'Kyung'?"

"He is . . ." Taria paused, wondering what she wanted to say or how she should define the parameters of their relationship to Makes. *You don't even know yourself what you want him to be, so don't even try to think of the right words.* ". . . someone I know from *Lightbringer*. A very good friend."

Coward! she railed at herself, but Makes seemed to accept the explanation.

"I didn't understand the words you were saying. Was that the language you use with friends?" Makes asked.

"We were speaking Mandarin," Taria answered. "It's another Earth language. Very different from Shiplish."

Makes boomed; her hands flailed. "For the Time-of-Greater-Light," she said, "I must attend to my duties as Baraaki."

"May I watch?" Taria asked. "It might help me to understand—"

"No," Makes answered, so quickly that Taria knew there was no appeal. "Those in this"—Makes hesitated, as if searching for the right word—"city know who you are. You are free to go where you wish here in Rasedilio-dutherad. If the Voices-That-Only-Taria-Can-Hear can give you the words, you may ask questions of those you meet. I will find you again before the Greater Light is gone if you have not returned by then. Is this acceptable to you?"

Fear prickled her arms as she thought of walking through the city alone. *The crowds, not knowing the lan-*

guage, not understanding what they're saying or their customs . . . She tried to ignore the insistent image of the dead Blue in the market square, of a dead body in a Nanjing market.

"It sounds like you're trying to get rid of me."

"It's important that you go. I . . . I feel this."

"You *feel* this," Taria repeated. "So the Baraaki's a prophet, too." She said it jokingly, but Makes only grumbled deep in her chest and didn't respond. Taria wondered if she'd just insulted her. Taria took a breath, looking at the Blue sidewise.

"Then that will be fine, Makes. I thought . . ." Taria remembered her dream, and the sound of the massed chorus of watersingers. "Is there a way I can get to where the watersingers are? You said that there were thousands of them out beyond the bay . . ."

Makes grumbled deep in her stomach and her eyestrip blinked heavily. "I thought you saw nothing."

"I didn't. But the sound of them . . . I don't know, Makes. I just thought I'd like to see—hear—them again."

Makes blinked and *harrumphed* again. "Then go to where they are. Take the ferry to the next island. Cross the island to the other side, and take the bridge to the island beyond. There you can find boats that can take you to the singers-in-the-water. Tell them that you are the guest of the baraalideish—can the Voices-Only-Taria-Can-Hear give you the words back if I tell them to you?"

"I think so . . ." A second later Dog barked in her head. "Yes," she said.

"Good. This is in the Language-of-Command. Tell them . . ." and Makes unleashed a barrage of words for several seconds. Dog scrolled the syllables across Taria's inner vision.

"All right," she said. "I can manage. You have two languages, then?" she asked, remembering the incident with the warriors.

"We have five." Makes blinked again. "That is not unlike humans?"

"No," Taria said. "That's not unlike us at all." *It just makes communication that much harder*, she thought. "Thank you, Makes. I'll go see the watersingers, then."

Another blink, a growl from deep in the Blue's abdomen. Her hand touched Taria's cheek, gently, and after a moment Taria reached up to touch it. "I would like—" Makes said, then stopped.

"What would you like, Makes?"

There was no answer for several seconds, a silence long enough that Taria wondered whether Makes was going to respond at all. "I would like you to teach me Mandarin. I would like to be able to talk with you the way you talk with this Kyung. In the Language-of-Intimacy."

Taria laughed at the serious tone. *"Shì de,"* she answered. "That means 'yes.' Your first lesson."

"Good. When I know this new language I can help you understand."

"Not until then?"

Low frequencies shivered the floor. "Of course not. How could I?" She seemed puzzled that Taria would even ask.

Taria shrugged. Makes seemed so solemn that Taria couldn't summon the laugh that seemed appropriate. "Then I'll start as soon as I get back. When you're done with your . . . duties."

Makes took a deliberate step back from Taria, and Taria's hand fell to her side with the sudden movement. "Food is on the table. Eat whenever you wish. I will find you later."

With that, Makes turned and left.

Taria spent another half an hour just looking out over the balcony into the morning before going back into the room and breaking her fast: the same offerings as every time before. She suspected she was going to tire of Blue cuisine very quickly. After taking care of the necessities in the hallway hole, she set out into the city.

The sloping landscape of the island was dominated by the massive building of Those-Who-Speak-With-Her at the highest point, with other, smaller buildings huddled submissively around it like lichens anchored on a rock. Humpback, as Taria had nicknamed the island, seemed both louder and more crowded than it had been yesterday. No, not *yesterday*, she reminded herself. Those were Earth reflexes. Here, on the satellite of a far larger world, you couldn't judge the "days" by the passage of the sun—during Little Sister's passage around Yin there would be long periods when the sun wouldn't appear at all. She had yet to experience what Makes called Full Dark, when neither Yin nor Yang appeared in Little Sister's sky.

Taria walked quickly down to the ferry station, the vidcam set over her left eye so she could record her view of the city as she walked. The sky was rippled with gray clouds that partially hid the face of Yang. The tide was in, with waves lapping at the dark rocks near the top of what had been a cliff edge when Taria had first arrived. The ferry was docked there, and she watched the Blues entering the small boat for a few minutes. None of them spoke any words that she could understand, though there were the usual rumblings and grumblings. Taria finally stepped onto the gangplank herself. The Blue who seemed to be the ferry's captain sent a burst of quick echolocational sound toward her, and his hands brushed her side as she passed, but otherwise he made no sign. She took a seat near the front of the ferry. Several minutes later the ferry left in a clanking of chains and an asthmatic huff of steam from the drive mechanism.

Taria estimated that the nearest island—Twin Peaks— was perhaps a half kilometer from Humpback. The ferry took an hour to make that distance, rocking in the swells of the bays, with a raucous clamor from the steam engine and the eternal clanking of the chain rattling through the gears, with the hoots and bellows from the Blues all around her, all of the sound amplified by the roof overhead, which seemed to be made of some kind of plastic. Iridescent green beetles the size of Taria's fist had roosted in the canopy supports, and they made occasional kamikaze strafing runs through the cabin and over the sides of the ferry. Tiny fish as bright as slivers of aluminum foil darted through the ferry's foamy wake; as she watched, one of the beetles hit the water and emerged a few seconds later with a fish clutched in its legs.

The Blues nearest her were continually touching her: a hand stroking her cheek, another sliding down her thigh, yet another at her side. For a moment Taria flashed on China and the crowds in Nanjing, and she shivered, feeling claustrophobic and somehow threatened. She endured the noise and the touching, and was grateful when the ferry docked at Twin Peaks and she could walk out into the relative quiet of the open air again.

Looking out, she could see Humpback and Gruriterashpali—the Cathedral—blurred and softened by distance. Makes was out there somewhere, and Taria felt a quick twinge of panic at being separated from the only person in this world she knew at all. *"Dog?"* she subvocalized, and a few moments later a bark answered her. *"Good. Stay with me. I may need translation."*

Twin Peaks, she knew from Makes's description, was the hub of government for the Blues in this region. It was here that the Neritorika, the Voice-of-Our-Desires resided: the titular head of Blue government and also the head of Makes's group, the baraalideish. There were other Neritorika in other cities, Taria knew, but since Rasediliodutherad was the largest Blue settlement, the Neritorika here was also the most renowned. Taria found herself unimpressed with the seat of power. The building was set prominently enough, alone atop one of the two hills that made up the summit of Twin Peaks, but it was an unimposing structure that couldn't have been much larger than

Makes's apartment within the Gruriterashpali. A pathway of bluish-gray stones led from the dock toward the Neritorika's hill, passing through a huddle of other governmental buildings before ascending the slope. The other Blues who had disembarked from the ferry had already gone in that direction, and the ferry's steam engine was chuffing again as it prepared to depart. Taria hesitated, wondering whether she should just take the ferry back to Humpback and wait for Makes to be done with whatever it was she was doing. *You're here, and you wanted to come here to learn about the Blues and Little Sister. Get on with it. Makes told you there was nothing to worry about.* Taria took a breath, shrugged, and started toward the tangle of buildings, enduring the static-riddled vision the vidcam sent her optic nerves.

Go to the other side of the island and take the bridge, Makes had said, but like a path glimpsed in a dream, the walkway led her into a maze. No sooner had the buildings closed around her in a bewildering array of color and shapes—wind chimes clattering all about—than the stone roadway widened into a square, from which other narrow streets led in at least a half-dozen different directions. She could no longer see the top of the hill, and as she glanced down the streets, she saw that none of them went straight for more than twenty meters before veering off left or right. Blues milled around her, moving noisily on their own business, and whenever one came within arm's reach of her, they touched. Taria had to stop herself from visibly flinching at this public mauling. *I should have taken the ferry back . . . Dog,* she thought, *do we have an orbital image of this place?*

After several seconds a map overlaid her vision. The island *was* a maze, with lanes intersecting at every angle, all of them twisting and turning. The bridge was there, somewhere beyond the cluster of buildings. *Is this accurate, Dog?* A faint whine answered her: *We believe so.* Taria sighed and set off down the path to her right, walking un-

der balconies, upper walkways, and other extrusions that
thrust out over the street at just above head level. The ghost
map stayed with her, turning every few seconds so that the
direction in which she was walking was always "north."
Intent on the map rather than her surroundings, she nearly
walked into a group of a dozen or so Blues as she turned
the final corner leading toward the hill.

"I'm sor—" she began before remembering not only that
apologies were unwanted unless asked for, but that no one
would be able to understand her anyway. She backed away
from the crowd, which broke apart as they all swiveled.
Taria felt herself buffeted by sound waves directed at her.

With a start she realized that this was a gathering of the
warrior caste, the kagliaristi. Worse, among them was the
same male who had wounded Makes on their way to the
city. *Synchronicity,* Taria thought, *and fucking awful bad
luck.*

"Shit," she said aloud. "Umm, I was just leaving. Really.
Sorry," and started to turn to go back the way she'd come.
A deep *harrumph* laden with harsh syllables stopped her.
She understood none of it, but the intent seemed clear
enough. A few seconds later Dog whined in her head.
Can't translate. Taria wasn't surprised. The computer system aboard *Lightbringer* would be working on the recording she had made during the last encounter with the
kagliaristi, but the translation program would need a much
larger sampling of the dialect—if that's what it was—before much progress could be made.

Taria slowly turned to face them again. The naked warrior had stepped forward from the group. The blades on his
fingertips clashed as his hands clenched and unclenched.
The head-crest was fully engorged, the lines painted on it
plainly visible, as if the Blue were reminding her of his status, and the brightly colored coils of his genitalia were
wrapped around his left leg now. Taria contemplated running—maybe she could get far enough ahead of him to
have time to get Kyung's weapon from her pack—but by

then the warrior was already within an arm's reach of her, and when she stepped back, there was a rough stone wall behind her, blocking any retreat.

The barrage of syllables came again, with subsonic undertones that were like soft fists pummeling her stomach. Taria shook her head. "I don't understand," she told him uselessly, but he was already too close to her. She could see the flapping of his nasal vents, could smell his breath, spicy and warm. His eyestrip, riddled with pale blue cells, was hidden for a moment as he blinked. Taria wondered what he saw, close enough now that he could probably focus on her. The metal talons of his fingers touched her, snagging on the fabric of her clothing, first at the sides, then moving up her body. Taria willed herself to remain still, remembering Makes's reassurances that she was safe in the city. The fingertips came up farther, sliding over her breasts. This was not like Makes touching her—the kagliaristi prodded, his fingers insistent, the curved blades held away but still uncomfortably close. Taria knew she was attributing human characteristics to a nonhuman encounter and thus her instincts were entirely wrong, but this touching felt brutal and invasive and sexual—as unwanted as if some stranger had accosted her in an alleyway on Earth and began fondling her against her will. She wanted to strike him, wanted to push him away, wanted to start screaming curses at him. She could feel herself trembling as his hands left her breasts with a last uncomfortable caress, then came up her neck—catching for a moment on the links of her mother's brooch—to her face. The fingertips were warm and almost soft, but she could feel the chill of metal as the bladed tips dragged over her cheeks and into her hair. All he had to do was curl those fingers and rip them back toward himself and she would be laid open, carotid arteries torn and spraying blood as she crumpled to die here on the stones . . .

The melon vendor, screaming at Mama . . .

Fingertip blades clicked hard against the vidcam, knocking it loose. Taria gasped as the vidcam was pulled away from the contacts around her left eye. Her vision blurred momentarily, and she heard the vidcam strike the cobblestones with the bright, distressing sound of shattering glass.

As Taria stiffened, truly frightened now, the warrior's hands moved away, drifting down her shoulders and falling back to his sides, and she let out the breath she hadn't realized she'd been holding. In her head, Dog howled belatedly at the loss of the video feed.

"Taria-Who-Wants-to-Understand," the kagliaristi said, still using the full range of his voice, so that the words hammered at her. He spoke badly, the syllables blurred and wrongly accented—"Tahrier-OO-Unts-OO-Unnerstahn"—but he spoke her name.

He knew her.

"Yes," she answered. "That's me. What's your name? What do you want?"

"Taria-Who-Wants-to-Understand," the warrior repeated, then followed it with another onslaught of Blue phrases.

A moment later Dog whimpered. *Can't translate.*

"I can't understand that," Taria said uselessly, but this time the warrior grasped her arm with one hand. Blades snared cloth and he pulled at her as he started to walk away. The rest of the crowd of Blues simply watched, making their usual grunting and cooing sounds as the warrior tugged at her arm.

"No!" Taria shouted at him, pulling her arm away. Cloth tore, and she felt the tip of one of the blades draw a long line down her forearm. As she cradled her arm, she saw beads of bright red form along the scratch. "Stay the fuck away from me!" she shouted at him, sidling to her left, where an archway led away from the hilltop path. The warrior sent a double burst of echolocation toward her but otherwise didn't move. The other Blues' torsos swiveled, as if they were also watching her retreat.

She felt open air at her back, and moved quickly into the shadow of the archway. The warrior was standing with legs spread wide, the fingertips glinting at his sides. He made no motion to follow her, and Taria finally allowed herself to show her back as she half ran back into the warren of close-set buildings. *Dog, get me back to the ferry. Now!*

When the map appeared again before her eyes, she followed it out of the city and back to the docks. As she waited for the ferry to return she watched the open gates, half expecting the warrior to come striding through them toward her.

But he didn't.

Taria got clambered onto the ferry. She swung into her seat, batting one of the green beetles aside as she scanned the dock area for the kagliaristi. As the other Blues came onto the ferry and took their seats, she finally felt her heart rate slow down. "And you *wanted* to come here," she said to herself as the ferry began the slow journey back. "In fact, you pretty much screwed everything else in your life to get here."

✳ That's Your Real Lover . . .

Taria was twenty-three, in her senior year at Stanford; Eric was twenty-two.

Eric reminded her of her dad, in the pictures of him in his early twenties—short, trim, dark green eyes with a wild shock of unruly red hair above. (And yes, she told herself when she'd first made the decision to sleep with Eric, there are some disturbing Freudian implications in this . . .) Still, the accent was wrong and his voice was tenor, not bass; Eric was from Boston, with a northeastern nasal twang to his voice. Dad—she rarely called him "Papa" anymore— had never lost that strong New Zealand accent. And while her father was a systems tech, Eric was an English major, almost certainly destined for a lifetime of grading under-graduate papers and producing scholarly essays in obscure journals that maybe a hundred of his peers would read.

Taria, on the other hand, already knew what she wanted. She had known for years. That should have been the clue for her. She should have been able to see it coming. She should have known.

And maybe she did, subconsciously. For the first month, she couldn't bear to be away from Eric, and she wanted to make love with him every night. When he wasn't there, she could feel his absence, a hollow in her soul. She wondered what it would be like, being with him for years and years. She forgot the previous failed romances, forgot the promises she'd made to herself every time getting close to someone had caused her pain: *never again*. For a month, maybe two, she set aside the rest of her life to make room for him. But that was all a year ago.

She didn't notice that as she gradually returned to her own goals, her own interests, her own ambitions, there was less and less room inside for Eric.

She didn't notice.

Taria heard Eric enter the apartment, heard the rasp of the key she'd made for him, then the protest of the ancient brass hinges and his footsteps creaking on century-old hardwood. "Hey, love," she said without looking up. The afternoon had dissolved into evening without her noticing. The lamp on her battered desk cast a pool of warm yellow over several magazine and newspaper articles in front of her, and threw a diagonal wedge across the sheaf of handwritten notes alongside the mess. A holocaster—with the newly developed Thunder-resistant interference shields—made shifting light patterns on the far wall. She hadn't turned it off after the newscast, letting the 'caster become mostly unheard background noise. "I was listening to the news and reading." She turned toward Eric, rubbing her eyes. "I guess I kinda got lost. I'm sorry—I was supposed to meet you for the concert—" Taria stopped, seeing his face in the twilight. "Shit," she said. "You're really pissed at me, aren't you?"

His hands lifted from his waist and dropped like stones. "We waited an hour for you, Taria. I finally told the others to go on without us. I figured you'd be here. All this new stuff about that *thing* up there . . ." Eric glanced over Taria to the paper on the desk, scanning the headlines of the articles. His face tightened into a scowl and he shook his head. "I don't know how else to say this, Taria. What we had . . . it's not working for us anymore. When I'm less interesting than some article about sending apes through Thunder—"

"Genetically altered chimps," Taria corrected him. "Not apes."

To Eric's credit, he only smiled sadly at that, his hands

lifting and dropping again. "Chimps," he said. "Whatever. Taria, I'm sorry."

"You don't need to apologize," she said, wondering at the deadness inside her. Why wasn't she crying? Why wasn't she angry? Why wasn't she fighting to make him stay? How could she sit there calmly and let him say goodbye to her? How could she stand to lose the first person in years she'd really let into her life?

But she could. She knew it, knew it because it didn't hurt to imagine life alone again. She wouldn't *let* it hurt. "You don't need to apologize," she repeated, because she didn't know what else to say. She wasn't looking at him anymore. She couldn't bear to look at his face.

She heard him take a step forward. His hand touched her cheek, softly, as if he expected to feel tears there. He crouched down beside her chair. "Taria, I can't compete with this." His emerald gaze flicked over toward the papers on her desk again. "I don't even know how. It's just a damn noisy hole in space."

Taria was shaking her head. She could still feel the touch of his hand. She didn't know why she started talking about Thunder then—maybe it was a safe topic, *her* topic. Maybe she thought that if she could just show him how important it was, he might stay. "Eric, it's an artifact. The probes have proved that. Thunder has a wormhole hidden inside it—do you know how impossible that is? They've proved that it's a gateway to another system. Thunder's a *bridge*, Eric. No one builds a bridge without expecting it to be used."

"I know. And frankly, that terrifies the hell out of me. It would you, too, if you thought about it. Taria, you're obsessed. It's not healthy. There's a part of you, inside, that's broken, but this isn't going to fix it."

Taria ignored even that. "I want to go there. What's wrong with that? They're already talking about building a ship . . ."

"Taria . . ." He gave a sigh of exasperation. "Taria, this

isn't about Thunder or a ship or anything but you and me. You and me."

Taria looked up at him, at the green eyes and wild hair, at the well-remembered lines of his face. She said the words that came to her then, without thinking about them. She felt only their sharp, astringent truth. "There isn't a 'you and me' anymore, is there?"

Eric shook his head. "No. I don't think there really has been for a while."

"Is there . . . someone else for you?"

"No."

She nodded as if that explained things. Something was dead inside her. There was no pain. There should be pain. Ripping away something she'd thought so important to her should be agonizing. But it wasn't. "I'm sorry," she said. "I'm sorry I couldn't be what you wanted."

"So am I," he said, and even that left her numb. She wondered when she'd last cried, and she could only remember that awful day in Nanjing. *Has it been that long? It couldn't have been that long . . .*

"Taria . . ." Eric said again. He stood, and she thought for a moment that he might bend to kiss her, one last time. She raised her chin to meet his lips, but he stepped back. "I'll call," he said. He set her apartment key on the desk on top of the papers and left.

Taria sat there for a long time after she heard the door close. She ruffled the articles on her desk, staring at them without reading them. Then she picked up the phone and dialed, listening to the faint hiss of Thunder through the filters. A familiar, deep and accented voice answered. "Hullo?"

"Dad? It's Taria . . . No, everything's all right . . . Yes, really . . . No, I don't want to talk to Judy . . . Dad? Shit . . ." Taria bit her lip. For a moment she started to hang up the phone, then lifted it again to her ear. "Hey, Judy, it's me . . . No, nothing's wrong. Not really . . . Yeah, I figured he was pretty tied up with work. That's the usual, huh? . . . Eric and me? Not . . . not so good . . ."

She talked to Judy, wishing it was her father, that she could have said what she wanted to say to him: *Dad, I'm asking you to pretend that I'm your little girl again. Tell me a story, would you . . . ?*

But the time for stories had passed long ago.

After Eric, Taria's next serious lover, some two years later, was Nikki.

Taria was pursuing her graduate degree with single-minded purpose—by then the first images of the star system beyond Thunder had been brought back, the sun with its close-orbiting gas giant already dubbed Yin and Yang. With several probes having successfully gone through Thunder, there was serious talk of putting together an international expedition to explore the system, and Taria shifted her classes to give her a chance to be on that team: she added courses to give her undergraduate degrees in Physics and Linguistics, and after graduation was accepted into MIT's graduate program, where the few experts in the fledging, and controversial, field of ExoAnthropology were gathered. Taria became one of their graduate assistants—Thunder consumed her now, the silent roar of that hole in space filling her, and the alien view of its sun in front of her whenever she closed her eyes.

She didn't allow herself to think of what would happen if she couldn't be part of whatever Thunder team was put together. She knew herself to be obsessed, but the alternative was inconceivable.

Nikki, in contrast, took whatever courses interested her, with a degree program ostensibly in Humanities. Taria knew Nikki from a literature class they'd taken together, a dark-haired, dark-skinned woman with a lovely voice and a slightly lopsided smile that Taria had always found sensuous and perfect, and a penchant for fantasy novels that mystified and fascinated the serious Taria. She wasn't sure what strange chemistry caused them to become friends within an hour of knowing each other, but in the ensuing days, Taria and Nikki sought each other out, sharing dinner and stories. Nikki's soul seemed free and unfettered and wild, entirely unlike Taria's own; perhaps that was why Taria found her drawn to the young woman: a reverse twin.

Taria always remembered where friendship became something else, unexpectedly. She and Nikki had gone to the corner teahouse for ginseng tea and appetizers. They ended up talking for hours about everything: from Nikki's years growing up in Louisville to her decision to come out in college; from Taria's early childhood in China and her mother's death to, finally, Taria's relationship with Eric. "Our problem was, we talked at each other," Taria said, "but not *to* each other. Neither one of us listened to what the other was really saying. God, I hate living a cliché."

"Like?" Nikki prodded.

"The example I keep thinking about is really silly . . ."

"I don't care. Go ahead."

Taria shifted in her chair, her hands cupped around her mug. "Okay . . ." She took a breath. "In our apartment building there was a washer and dryer down in the basement for tenant use. One day I asked Eric to take the bed sheets down to the basement so we could wash them. I can remember exactly what I said: 'Eric, we need to wash the sheets. Would you take them off the bed and take them down to the basement?' So he did—that's *all* he did. He took the sheets down, and dumped them there. Didn't gather up anything else to make a full load, didn't put them in the washer when he got down there—just took the sheets off the bed, went down to the basement, and came back up. 'But that's what you *asked* me to do,' he said when I complained." Taria laughed once, and took a sip of her tea. "I know that's really minor, but it was that way with everything. I'd say something, and he wouldn't understand what I was really saying. And I know I did the same with him."

"Men learn a different language," Nikki answered. "We all use the same words, but the meanings are different.

They're the real aliens." She smiled, and laughed at herself as she set down her mug, so that it rattled against the glass tabletop. "Just listen to me."

"I am," Taria answered seriously. She was always serious.

Nikki reached across the small table. She placed her hand on top of Taria's. Their fingers laced together, unbidden, coffee against milk.

That was the start of it . . .

There were times in the next several months when Taria desperately hoped it would never end. There were times, when the sun struck her from a window in the morning, when the wind touched her face, that Taria sometimes sang, just from the joy of it.

> *"E hara i te mea*
> *No naianei te aroha*
> *No nga tupuna*
> *Tuku iho tuku iho."*
>
> *It is not a new thing*
> *Now that is love*
> *Comes from the ancestors*
> *Handed down through the passages of time.*

"You have a pretty voice," Nikki said, coming up behind her one morning. She laid her head on Taria's shoulder and kissed the side of her neck. "What is it?"

"A Maori song my Gramma used to sing."

"You should sing more often."

Taria laughed self-deprecatingly. "Me? No. I didn't even know I was doing it then. My mother . . . she used to sing. All the time. I loved her voice. I don't sound anything like that."

Nikki stroked Taria's back as they stared from the window out to the parking lot of the apartment. Taria had told Nikki about her mother, about China—during the long talks over tea, while they snuggled together late at night. She'd given her all her history, and Nikki gifted Taria with her own in return. "I remember you telling me about her," Nikki said, her breath warm in Taria's ear. "About her singing. But I like your voice. I'd love to hear it more often."

Taria saw her reflection in the glass, smiling back at her. "That was Mama's gift. Not mine. Though you're a very sweet liar."

Nikki gave a growl of mock irritation behind her. Her arms circled Taria's waist. In the glass, Taria saw Nikki's dark, wavering reflection. "You wouldn't sing to your own daughter?" she asked.

"I'm never having kids. Never." The words came out harsh and fast. Taria felt the tears start, unbidden, hearing her mother's voice once again. *They were back at Gramma Ruth's farm, sitting on the porch as the land cooled around them, a breeze coming off the mountains that was chilly enough to raise goose bumps on her arms. Mama saw them and laughed, rubbing Taria's arms and pulling one of Gramma's knitted blankets around her. She could smell the chimney smoke drifting across the field and hear the bleating of the sheep in their pen as Grampa and Papa brought them in, the dogs barking . . . And Mama started to sing, and her voice was clear and high, and there were colors in the sound, bright hues that stayed even when Taria closed her eyes . . .*

"I don't want kids. I couldn't stand to leave them like . . . like my . . ." Taria couldn't say anything more. Her reflection in the glass wavered and swam.

"Ah, love . . ." Nikki said. Her hands turned Taria, who resisted for a moment, then gave in, sinking into Nikki's embrace as she once had into her mother's.

The end, when it came eight months later, didn't seem much different from all the other endings. The pain was the same.

It wasn't the physical aspect. Nikki was as good or better a lover than Eric or most of the men she'd been with before—attentive to her needs, willing to take all the time she needed to simply talk in bed, to become close emotionally as well as physically. Nikki was warmer. Softer.

The ending was, like Nikki, also softer.

"It's time," Nikki said.

"Huh?" Taria asked, glancing up from the application she was filling out. The light from the monofoil screen washed onto her face, making it difficult to see Nikki, standing just in front of her desk. Taria hadn't even noticed her coming into the room.

"Time for me to leave," Nikki elaborated, with that smile Taria still enjoyed, but this time regret sat in the twist of her lips. "Not tonight. Tomorrow, maybe, when I can get my things together. Soon."

"Nikki . . ." Taria glanced from her to the screen—PROJECT LIGHTBRINGER APPLICATION, the words screamed silently as she touched the corner of the monofoil and watched it fold itself neatly into a wafer.

A silent shaking of her head. Highlights from Taria's desk lamp shimmered in the dark strands of her short hair.

"Hush," Nikki said. "What we had was lovely, but I can't compete with what's in here." She touched Taria's head, gently, stroking her hair.

"I don't understand," Taria said.

"You have passion, Taria, and that's exactly what I love in you—those times when you're sitting there talking and your words are all fireworks and lightning and glitter and your gaze is on something only you can see, staring straight ahead like you're daring the world to contradict you. It's just . . ." The smile again, and a touch. "It's not me sparking that passion in you, Taria. It's that thing out there. Thunder. That's your real lover. I don't say that to hurt you, Taria. I don't want to hurt you. Ever. But that's the truth, and I think you'd agree if you stopped to think about it."

Taria clutched at Nikki's hand, pressing it against her cheek. "Nikki . . . God, Nikki, that's not true. It's not."

Nikki's arm circled her shoulder, and she crouched down next to Taria's chair, holding her. "I wish I were wrong," she said, her voice warm and deep in Taria's ear. "I wish I could believe that." Her hand drifted lower, lifting the brooch that hung around Taria's neck. Her dad had given Taria the brooch when she'd left for college; she hadn't taken it off since then. Nikki held the brooch, opening it to look at the wedding picture. "She was beautiful, your mother," she said.

"Nikki, what does my mother have to do with *us*?"

"Nothing. Everything." Nikki sat down on the floor alongside Taria's chair. She laid her arms across Taria's lap, her head on her hands, then abruptly stood up again—Nikki, always in motion. She went to the bookcase, letting her hand trail across the spines. They were mostly Nikki's fantasy books, but now her hand rested on Taria's unkempt section: textbooks and piles of scientific literature on Thunder, clippings of newspaper and journal articles. Since effective shielding from Thunder for computer chips had finally become affordable, the two of them had gone in together to purchase a notebook; its file storage was stuffed with more of the same. "In a year, when they get this *Lightbringer* expedition together, you'll be leaving."

Taria shook her head. "The competition for any slots they have is going to be fierce. The chance they'll take me is small. Minuscule."

"They'd be fools not to." Nikki shrugged. "And you'd go if they asked, wouldn't you?"

"Of course," Taria answered, then realized from the fleeting grimace on Nikki's face that even though this was the answer she'd been expecting, the quickness of her response hurt Nikki more than the admission itself. "I mean, it's not as if we wouldn't be expecting to come back. All the probes, even the ones piloted by chimps, made it through the wormhole and back. I'd be away a few years, that's all."

"And for a few years before that you'd be all caught up

in the preflight stuff, and for another year after you got back—*if* you got back . . ." Nikki shrugged, still looking at the books rather than Taria. Taria could see the tenseness in her back, in the way she held her shoulders, could hear the emotion that quavered in her voice. "I'm selfish, Taria," she said. "I didn't think I was that kind of person, but I am. I guess I don't like being the second most important thing in your life."

"You're not," Taria answered reflexively.

"If I could really believe that . . ." Nikki leaned against the bookcase, arms folded under her breasts, her head to one side. Then she pushed away and went to the desk, touching the monofoil so it opened up again. She touched Taria's name on the first line, a quick stroke. *Delete?* the monofoil asked in response. Nikki looked at Taria. For a long moment Nikki's gaze held her, dark and solemn.

"Delete document," Nikki said, and the monofoil blinked once in response. The file vanished from the screen, and Taria gasped in alarm. Nikki gave a short, quiet laugh. "I think that's my answer," she told Taria, and her smile was at once soft and sad.

"Undo," she told the computer, and the data blinked back into place. "Save document," she said, and leaned down to kiss Taria's head.

"I have packing to do," Nikki said.

Taria told herself that it didn't hurt. She wouldn't let it hurt.

Trevor Spears was never able to understand or forgive his daughter's relationship with another woman. Taria's involvement with Nikki drove a wedge between them that neither would ever again entirely dislodge. In the realm of his morality, homosexuality was a sin and obscene, and rather than talk openly, he simply closed himself off completely. It was Judy who remained in contact with Taria when Trevor refused to talk to his daughter or to allow Nikki in his house. It was Judy who secretly sent money to

Taria when she wrecked her car one rainy night, who met Nikki and Taria for lunches, who returned Taria's happiness in the relationship with a smile.

In many ways, in different ways, Taria responded to Judy as much as she had her mother, Gloria. But she never, in all the years, told Judy that she loved her. Somehow, that would have crossed an interior barrier, broken an old promise that no one could possibly expect her to keep.

Regardless, she never said the words.

Judy came over to Taria's apartment several times in the months after Nikki moved out. "Seeing anyone else?" she asked over coffee and crumb cake one Sunday morning.

"I've had a couple dates," Taria answered, and Judy raised an eyebrow over her steaming mug. "Nothing serious. I went out with an English professor the other night—Jim Baney. We discussed literature preferences at dinner: I like fantasy; he doesn't think anything important was written after the nineteenth century. We saw a foreign movie that he thought was brilliant and I found incredibly slow and turgid; had dessert, latte, and mutual background revelation in the coffee shop afterward, then he dropped me off with a short and almost brotherly good-night kiss. He didn't even ask to come in. I think I'm insulted." Taria grinned at Judy.

"Jim?"

Taria licked powdered sugar from her finger. "I know. A guy. I've also dated a Donna and a Jo Ann. It doesn't mean anything. I've told you—I'm more concerned about the person than their sex. Male, female—they both have qualities I find myself attracted to. Actually, I'm told that sexual ambivalence is regarded as a plus with the *Lightbringer* people—they're screening out people with strong prejudices or intolerance, I understand." Taria lifted a shoulder and reached for another slice of cake. "At least among the civilians," she finished.

"So you haven't heard any final news from them yet one way or the other?"

"No. I know I have the educational background they're looking for, but so do a couple dozen other people. The military's got most of the slots—there isn't a lot of room for people without a uniform and rank. A couple of the people I'm competing with have all of the above, so . . ." Again Taria shrugged. "Wait and see," she said.

Judy set her mug down and took Taria's hand. "I know how much this means to you. So does your father."

"Does he?" Taria asked in a carefully neutral voice.

"They came and interviewed him, too, you know— talked to both of us a couple days ago. That's one of the reasons I came over here today, to tell you about it. Trev told them they'd be fools if they chose anyone other than his daughter."

That's the same thing Nikki said, a few months ago . . . Taria was surprised at the surge of relief that went through her with Judy's words, cooling the edges of more submerged anger and frustration than she'd realized she was holding inside. "He said that, eh? Did he tell them he hasn't spoken more than a dozen words to this same daughter in the last two years?"

Judy nodded slowly, picking up her mug again and sipping before she answered, her hand folded around the streaked blue glaze. "He did. He also told them the estrangement was entirely his fault, that you'd made overtures but he'd ignored them." She sipped again. "He also said that that was a choice he regretted, and that he'd like the chance to try again before you leave on *Lightbringer,*" she said finally, her green eyes watching Taria. "So . . . How's next Friday? You can bring the salad. You could even bring Jim—hey, it might help."

Despite herself, Taria laughed. Reaching over the table, she gave Judy a quick hug, then sat back again.

"I'll bring the salad," she said. "And myself."

Commander Allison didn't like her.

Taria was certain of it from the moment she walked into

his office for the interview. He was exactly the kind of man she disliked herself: stiff, unsmiling, and the creases on his uniform pants were sharp enough to slice bread. Everything about him spoke of stuffy fastidiousness. Even when he ushered her to her chair—placed squarely at the exact middle of his desk—and sat himself, she watched him straighten the dossier on his desk. He didn't open or even glance at it, just placed it in the center of the blank green blotter and folded his hands over it.

"Ms. Spears, I have to say that your university work fits our ExoAnthro profile very well."

"Thank you, Commander. It should; I knew as soon as I heard of the *Lightbringer* expedition that I wanted to be a part of it, and I planned my courses and chose my schools and instructors with that in mind."

All that got her was a nod and silence. Taria wondered if that was a ploy, wondered whether she should hurry into that silence with further explanation or if it was a trap, trying to get her to say more than she should. She blinked hard, started to bite her lower lip in nervousness, then stopped. She waited.

"You're thirty years old. You've never had a relationship last longer than two years. No children."

Taria blinked again. "No children," she answered carefully. "That's correct." The rest was also correct and in her dossier, but she wasn't going to emphasize it by repeating it. The psych report was in there also. She hadn't been permitted to see it—she suspected it contained some unflattering observations, but clearly it hadn't been disturbing enough to get her kicked out of consideration immediately. Gossip had it that Allison would be in charge of ExoAnthro on the expedition, and that the final choice of staff would be his. There were no further interviews scheduled; Taria figured this was it—she would either be accepted or she would be out.

"I'm permitted a wide amount of leeway in this interview, Ms. Spears, so I can ask questions that a prospective employer, for instance, wouldn't be permitted to ask. So . . . why no children?"

None of your goddamn business, she thought, but forced herself to smile outwardly and shrug. *Just get through this* . . . "Children deserve stability and parents who are committed to taking care of them. That's a long-term commitment that I can't make yet. Not with at least two years aboard *Lightbringer* possibly ahead of me."

"Is what happened to your birth mother part of that decision, too?"

Well, aren't you a fucking son of a bitch . . . This time she couldn't manage a smile. She hesitated, wondering where he was going with this. She remembered the long sessions with the psych group. The trauma of her mother's death was brought up more than once. Yes, she'd admitted, you can't have your mother murdered in front of you and not be affected, both in short- and long-term effects. Yes, her interest in Thunder had been piqued and perhaps even cemented because of the circumstances of her conception and her childhood fantasy that her mother had somehow gone there to wait for her. And certainly whenever she'd thought of having children, she'd also thought of how abandoned she'd felt as a young child, how deeply she'd felt the loss of her mother.

Taria took a long breath and loosened her white-knuckled grip on the arms of her chair. "Deep wounds cause scars," she said carefully. "That was as deep an emotional wound that I think someone can sustain, and it certainly left its marks inside me. I'd be lying to you if I said I didn't think about that when I've considered having children. Yes. But it's only one factor among many."

"You claim to be bisexual. Is that a factor, too?"

"No." That came out too fast, too sharply. Taria forced herself to slow down. Allison stared at her, the lines of his face cemented into careful neutrality. He blinked once. "My sexual preferences have to do with other issues than reproduction." She glanced at his desk, barren of any adornment except a silvery cube that looked like it might be a network link. "How about you, Commander? Any kids?"

She asked the question with cutting nonchalance. That at least got a reaction: both eyebrows lifted, like sharp peaks above his eyes. "My family is hardly an issue here."

"No, it isn't," Taria said. "No more than my lack of one. But you *do* have a family, then," she added, to take the sting away from her riposte. She thought it might even get her a smile.

It didn't. It netted her nothing. The eyebrows clambered down to their usual position, and Allison kept his gaze on her. "I'd prefer to keep the conversation about your qualifications, Ms. Spears."

"Then let's do that," Taria answered. "Ask me about my degrees, ask me about what I know and what skills I have. My lack of children and my sexual preferences aren't part of that issue, despite any leeway you might have."

For several seconds Allison just continued to stare at her, blinking only once as his eyes stayed on hers. His lips squeezed together, then opened. "Then let's look at your scholastic history . . ." he said.

Afterward, she was certain she'd blown it. She went home layered in a dark and foul mood, stalking around her apartment unable to even sit down, and punching angrily at the blinking message icon on her monofoil, opened up on her coffee table. The monofoil bleeped once and retrieved the waiting message. She saw the *Lightbringer* logo on the header page and took a deep breath.

She had to read the first line twice to be certain it was correct.

We're pleased to inform you that you have been accepted as a civilian member of the Lightbringer *expedition . . .*

It was signed by Commander Allison.

Taria saw Nikki across the crowded dance floor, dancing with a woman with short blond hair over a startlingly black fan of long hair at the base of her skull. The insistent kick from the bass drum throbbed in the railing under Taria's hand, and synthesized horns shrilled in her ears. Nikki and her companion were dancing close, their eyes locked on each other as they moved, and Taria felt a quick stab of regret and unfair jealousy.

Once, Nikki had danced that way with her.

Nikki looked up then and saw her watching. She leaned over to the blonde and said something in her ear, then made her way across the floor to where Taria stood. The blonde watched Nikki until she reached Taria, then turned away, swaying to the beat.

"She's pretty," Taria said.

"Vicki? Yeah, she is," Nikki answered, leaning close to shout into Taria's ear over the music. "We could talk about the weather, too, if you want." A faint smile took away some of the sting.

"Can we go back there?" Taria nodded toward an alcove where they'd once sat before. "I'll buy you a beer."

Nikki glanced back at Vicki on the dance floor, then lifted one shoulder. "Sure."

In the alcove the dance beat was merely loud. They sat on opposite sides of a small table, their hands carefully not touching. "It's been a long time," Nikki said at last. "I thought you'd be gone by now, up there where they're building *Lightbringer*."

"I leave tomorrow afternoon for the Cape. The shuttle heads for *Lightbringer* on Wednesday."

Nikki nodded as if that explained things, her head down. Then she stared at Taria: blue eyes under black hair. "Why are you here?" she asked.

Taria started to laugh, startled. "You were always direct," she said, trying to sound light and casual and hating the way it came out. Nikki didn't answer; she just watched Taria, who finally spread her hands. "I don't know," she said. "I just thought . . ." Taria stopped. There were too many reasons, none of them particularly well-defined in her mind. "It's my last night here . . ." She stopped again, took a breath, and let the words tumble out. "You were really important to me. If there's one thing I regret about this—what'd you call it?—this obsession of mine, it's that it cost me you."

Nikki blinked. Her hands clenched on the table. "You came to tell me that? Now, when you're leaving?"

Taria allowed herself a tentative smile. "Timing's always been my forte."

"Damn it, Taria . . ." Nikki pushed her chair away from the table, the scraping of wood on linoleum loud even against the drumbeat. Hands sliced air, chopping down across her body. "What the hell did you want? Did you think we'd have a nice, sentimental little conversation about the Good Old Days, drink a few beers and catch up? Or maybe I'd even come home with you for one last tumble in bed before you leave on your great adventure. Is that what you were thinking?"

"Nikki—" Taria started to protest, wide-eyed at Nikki's vehemence, aware that around them others were watching the scene.

"Fuck, Taria. I haven't heard from you in two goddamn *years* except for birthday cards, a few phone calls, and maybe the odd e-mail message. That's not a relationship, Taria. That's not a friendship. I gave you all I had to offer; it wasn't what you wanted then. I loved you; I would have stayed your friend even after I moved out, but you didn't seem to be able to handle that, either. I don't know what you're missing inside, Taria, but I couldn't fill the void, and I doubt that you're going to find it on *Lightbringer*, either. I—"

The fury left her, abruptly. Taria could see it drain from the lines in Nikki's face, letting her shoulders slump. The music track ended in the background. "Nikki," she said into the sudden quiet. Another, slower rhythm began. "I'm sorry. I really am."

Nikki nodded. Her hand lifted, as if she were going to

touch Taria, then dropped again. "I know you are," she said. "So am I. Look, good luck, okay? Send me a card if you get a chance."

Nikki swiveled abruptly and walked quickly away from the table. A hand brushed angrily over her eyes—left, then right—as she maneuvered between the tables on her way back to the dance floor.

When Taria left a few minutes later, Nikki was dancing with Vicki again, holding the young woman tightly in her arms, head cradled against her neck. She would not look up at Taria. She clutched Vicki as if holding a memory.

Though Taria didn't want it to, though she told herself she should be beyond that, the vision hurt.

Saying goodbye to Gramma Ruth was the hardest thing she did.

Grampa Carl had died seven years before. Gramma Ruth had insisted on staying in the small house out in the New Zealand hills despite the worsening arthritis in her hips. "This is my land. I expect to die and be buried on it, very soon. That doesn't bother me, and it shouldn't bother you, either," she told Trevor when he'd last called her on the phone, a year or so previously. Once Taria's father married Judy, he had less and less contact with Gloria's parents, which sometimes bothered Taria. It wasn't Judy's fault—if anything, Judy seemed to prod Trevor when he'd been out of contact with Gramma Ruth for too long. "She's the grandmother of your child, Trev. The least you can do is pick up the phone and call her."

Taria wondered if her father distancing himself wasn't at least partially because of Gloria, since every time he called, it brought back the memories. His own parents were long dead; Gramma Ruth was the only tie Trevor had left to New Zealand, except for the fact that Gloria's grave was there.

That was where Taria said goodbye to Gramma Ruth: on the hill where Gloria was buried next to her father.

"They're still here," Gramma Ruth said, smiling at Taria. After two days with her, Taria still hadn't adjusted to the changes. Ruth moved slowly, painfully, bowed over with a dowager's hump and leaning heavily on a whorled and carved wooden cane. Though her body had become frail, her intellect was still sharp, still alert. It was as if age were compressing her, pulling her inexorably into a tighter and tighter shape, a sun shrinking and collapsing into itself while the core remained bright and hot. "I see their spirits every once in a while, usually early in the evening, standing here and talking with each other, and I know that soon I'll be standing there with them."

In different circumstances, Taria would have protested automatically. *Oh, no, Gramma,* she would have said. *You'll be with us for a long time yet.* But now she only nodded. It was true enough. In all likelihood this would be the last time she'd see Gramma alive. It would be a little more than two years out to Thunder in *Lightbringer*, and even if they simply went there and turned around, another two years back.

When she left this time, she would never see her Gramma again.

It was a blustery day. The wind played with Gramma's long white hair, and she reached up with a withered, large-knuckled hand to brush it away from her face. The graves were simply marked: stone gravestones laid flat on the lush turf, their names and dates carved in polished pink granite. Taria crouched down and touched the incised letters: GLORIA SPEARS. "She shouldn't have died, Gramma," Taria said. "She should be here still, helping you."

"She died because she wouldn't let China become a part of her," Gramma Ruth answered.

Taria lifted her hand from the stone, glancing back over her shoulder at her Gramma. Pale eyes snared in a web of fine wrinkles looked back at her. "Yes, Taria, I know what I said. You can't live within another culture without expecting it to change you. Gloria would never let it in—I could see it. Did she ever learn the language? Did she ever let herself become a bit Chinese? Did she ever really understand how to act and respond?" Gramma Ruth shook her head. "Afterward, I talked to your father. Gloria couldn't understand what the man who killed her was yelling at her, could she? If she had, she'd still be alive, because she would have stopped. She would have realized that he thought she was stealing the melon. I've talked with her about it, since she died."

"Gramma—"

Gramma Ruth glared at her warningly. "You think that's not possible, girl? You think you know everything? You're listening only to the *Pakeha* in you. Gloria knows that what I just said is the truth, and she agrees. Even when she was a little girl, she'd never let the Maori part of her free. She tried to be only *Pakeha* when the Maori part of her soul was shouting to her in pain. She pretended not to hear it. She lived in New Zealand only, not also in *Aotearoa*. I knew—" Gramma Ruth stoppped, and Taria saw a tear form at the corner of one eye. The salty drop swelled, then flowed down the canyons of folded skin. "I knew that one day Gloria would have to face that conflict in herself, had she lived long enough. Her Maori part would insist on being acknowledged. But . . ." Her lips pressed together, opened again. "You have too much of your mother in you, Taria."

"That sounds like a warning, Gramma, but I'd rather take it as a compliment."

Gramma's hand tightened on the head of her cane, but she smiled, a slow thaw in the winter of her face. "It's neither," she said. "It's just the truth."

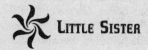 **LITTLE SISTER**

When Taria returned to Humpback, she found Makes outside the main building, surrounded by several other Blues of the baraalideish. Makes held a rod of pale green crystal that was nearly the length of Taria's forearm, the bottom end of it wrapped in a nest of rich black fur, the source of which Taria suspected she knew all too well. As she approached, Makes handed the artifact to one of the Blues, who hurried off with it. The remainder of the group dispersed as well, leaving Makes alone.

"I hear you, Taria-Who-Wants-to-Understand," Makes said, though she still seemed to be "looking" in the direction the crystal had gone. Her voice sounded tired and strained with high overtones, and there was a sag to her posture, while the smell of anise hung strongly around her. She cradled her injured arm, cupping the elbow in her good hand. "Did you find the watersingers? Did your time away enlighten you?"

"It confused me," Taria answered. "It also . . ." She took a breath, remembering. ". . . scared me."

Makes produced an inquisitive grunt from somewhere in her abdomen, a sound lower than anything human.

"The kagliaristi male we encountered after the watersingers—I met him again," Taria explained. She could feel herself trembling at the memory of his hand on her neck. "He knew my name, Makes. He tried to make me go with him. Who is he, Makes? What does he want with me?"

A human would have sighed, or perhaps shrugged. Makes gave a percussive hiccup and slapped her chest with a hand. Her answer, when it came, seemed disingenuous. "How can I know what is in his mind?" Makes answered. "Is that something humans can do? Do you know what's in my head now?"

"No. Who *is* he, Makes? At least tell me that."

A hand fluttered toward Taria, but she was just out of reach. The hand dropped back to Makes's side. "You do not need to know this. It is a thing for my people only."

Training and regulations both required a calm response, a reasoned discussion. Taria paid attention to neither. "Bull*shit*!" she spat out. "He goddamn *knows* me, Makes. He spoke my name." Makes reached out a hand toward Taria, and she slapped it away. "Don't tell me I don't need to know."

"How can I teach you when I can't speak the right language?" Another bass hiccup. Makes took a step toward Taria; her hands touched Taria's waist, her leg. This time Taria didn't move, enduring the touch. "All right. I will try. His name is Strikes-Air-in-Anger. He is—" Makes stopped. Her head-crest rose, and the earlets on the side closest to the bay fluttered. "Come back to my room," she said. "You will be able to hear it from there."

"Hear what?"

"An old thing, but it has to do with what you're asking me to explain," Makes answered. She began walking away into the building; after an exasperated huff, Taria followed.

They wound their way through the tangled, winding corridors of Gruriterashpali. When they reached Makes's room, Makes went out onto the balcony. "There," she said. "Can you hear it? It's very faint from here. The . . . I think your word for it would be 'clanking' . . ."

Taria heard nothing but the waves and the wind, the grumble of distant conversation, the bells and chimes tinkling in the wind, and the everyday sounds of Blue activity.

Makes's head crest was still engorged, with most of the earlets facing one direction. Taria peered that way, toward the steep-walled drop of the closest island. There were . . . twin lines of darkness leading up from the frothing surf and ending halfway up the cliff. Taria wished she had the vidcam as she squinted into the distance. There seemed to be two long links of rusted chain, made from the same greenish metal from which the Blues made their weapons, swaying in the surf from where they were pinioned to rock, perhaps thirty meters higher. Watching the chains lift and fall, Taria could imagine the sound, the dull impact of metal lashing rock. "You can *hear* that, from this distance?"

"Yes. Can't you?"

"No," Taria admitted, then could not resist adding, "but I can *see* them, at least. What's the significance of the chains, Makes?"

"Come back inside," Makes answered. "That story's a long one. We can eat while I talk . . ."

You don't know our history well enough, Taria-Who-Wants-to-Understand. You can't hear this tale with my ears, or feel the words in your Place-Within-That-Weeps. Yes, I know you will try, but I'm such a poor speaker and this is two times the wrong language, and you can't help but hear my story with the ears of your own culture no matter how you try.

When the one you call Commander Allison, whom we named Allison-Who-Speaks-Empty-Words, came the second time, we exchanged our past tales for yours, and we learned how . . . *different* your people were. Have you heard our histories? Ahh, you have . . . Yes, of course it makes sense that Allison-Who-Speaks-Empty-Words would have shared them with you.

Hear this also, then, for it's a tale we didn't speak of before, because it embarrassed us.

I am not even sure where to start. In history—ours or

yours—there are really no sharp beginnings. Every event and action fades into the next and the next, like a line of *dalia* stones knocked over by a child . . . You want to know about Strikes-Air-in-Anger, yes, but to understand him you must also understand what comes before him. Let me think . . .

I will start here, though it's not truly the beginning, either. Parts of this you will already know, but not all. Not all.

We have always had kagliaristi, Taria-Who-Wants-to-Understand. When She-Who-Spoke-the-World created the world and placed life on it, there were still those She made who had a wildness in them, and they became the kagliaristi—Those-Who-Will-Protect. When we Children-of-She-Who-Spoke-the-World lived in small, scattered communities all along this coast, there would always be one or two kagliaristi in the village. They were bound to the Neritorika, the Voice-of-Our-Desires who represent their communities to others and give them life, and they performed their duties for her. The kagliaristi was also the final weapon in the Neritorika's hand, the Cleaving-Sharpness with which she could strike if there was need.

There was rarely need.

For generations whose voices fade into the silence of all beginnings, the kagliaristi existed, their duties ceremonial except when a Neritorika decided that a particularly difficult person needed to correct their ways—someone who withheld their share of the hollow-melon crop, or a sourgrass farmer whose Time-of-Coldest-Winds fireburn had accidentally strayed onto another's yellowbark grove. Usually the simple presence of the kagliaristi alongside the Neritorika was enough. Oh, yes, the kagliaristi were taught the Ways-to-Cause-Pain, and once every few passages there would be need to use those skills, but not for most of them.

Who taught them? The Ways-to-Cause-Pain were taught by the old kagliaristi to his apprentice, one-to-one. If a kagliaristi should die before training a replacement, then the kagliaristi of a neighboring village would do so. Always one-to-one to the next kagliaristi.

What is that . . . ? But Taria-Who-Wants-to-Understand, why would anyone else *want* to know the Ways-to-Cause-Pain? Oh, certainly, someone may have watched the kagliaristi practicing and seen their techniques, and children certainly sometimes play at being a kagliaristi, but why would anyone do that seriously? That would make you kagliaristi yourself, and for us that's not possible.

Ahh . . . I think I understand why you ask. I remember your history, and how we marveled at the sound of death singing through it. When village had conflict with village and the Neritorika couldn't find a way to settle the dispute, when no one listened to her Language-of-Command, then the various Neritorika might agree to let their kagliaristi fight to decide the outcome. "A kagliaristi's wounds are the words of She-Who-Spoke-the-World," as the saying goes. And yes, there were indeed times that a kagliaristi might die of those wounds, but those were few.

And all through this history there were also the baraalideish, those of us whose task it became to listen to She-Who-Spoke-the-World. As our villages became larger and more numerous, the Neritorika became more and more important, until their voices contained the final law. The kagliaristi were used less and less as warriors, though they still performed their other duties.

Two generations ago a kagliaristi made his voice heard . . .

His name was Sees-the-Light-and-Cries.

He was the kagliaristi of the Neritorika here. Sees-the-Light-and-Cries was not obviously marked by She-Who-Spoke-the-World. He was neither stronger, more intelligent, nor more dangerous than other kagliaristi. Sees-the-Light-and-Cries possessed no ambition, no passion that anyone could see. Had nothing changed, he would have served the Neritorika and died alone, without even an apprentice to follow after him.

But passion sought him out, burning and tumultuous.

No one was with Sees-the-Light-and-Cries when this epiphany came. We have only his version of the story. During his time apart from his duties, as a kagliaristi will, Sees-the-Light-and-Cries would often walk alone down to the sands beyond the coastal hills, where he could listen to the wide, limitless ocean, where the only sounds were the waves and the wind, and where he could find watersingers. On one of those excursions, he came upon a strange watersinger, sitting alone. This was a great creature, Sees-the-Light-and-Cries always claimed afterward, far larger and more powerful than the watersingers kagliaristi usually deal with, but still smaller than the huge Greater Singers.

When Sees-the-Light-and-Cries approached her as a kagliaristi will, she sang to him . . .

She sang as no watersinger Sees-the-Light-and-Cries had ever heard before, and it was within her aural display that Sees-the-Light-and-Cries was shown his geas.

Within the song-shapes of this strange watersinger was a message, or so Sees-the-Light-and-Cries claimed. That message was sent directly to him from She-Who-Spoke-the-World. Within the shapes and forms, Sees-the-Light-and-Cries was told that She-Who-Spoke-the-World would soon bring this world to an end. Her long song in the Emptiness-Above-Us would go to silence; in the silence, the world would dissolve into the wind-breath from which it had come. This would happen unless Sees-the-Light-and-Cries took upon himself the leadership held by the Neritorika and the baraalideish. Sees-the-Light-and-Cries would become the Baraaki, though no kagliaristi had ever been the Baraaki. Only then could our fate be averted.

This is what Sees-the-Light-and-Cries claimed She-Who-Spoke-the-World told him through the watersinger. Whether it was true, or simply a delusion, or even an outright lie, no one can tell, because no one else was there.

The truth often doesn't matter, though, does it? What matters is only the reality.

From the time of the watersinger's vision, Sees-the-Light-and-Cries was changed. He left the Neritorika and wandered free through the lands, a rogue kagliaristi. He showed skills no one suspected he had possessed: a natural charisma, a gift of leadership, a voice of fire and passion when he spoke in the Language-of-Command. These became his tools, and in the next few cycles of the Lesser Light, he gathered around him a loyal cadre of other kagliaristi, all of whom had also abandoned their own Neritorika in response to Sees-the-Light-and-Cries's call.

So it began . . . our greatest sadness, right here in Rasediliodutherad, though to someone whose own past speaks of armies crawling over the world like snapbiters in Time-of-Breeding, this must seem foolish. You must hear me, Taria-Who-Wants-to-Understand. You must hear the words beyond my words. The rebellion of Sees-the-Light-and-Cries is the single most bloody and catastrophic event in our recorded history, a tale with which we frighten our children, an event the Eldest never tire of discussing.

Here is how it happened.

When Full Dark came during the Winter-of-Three-Snows, the kagliaristi of Sees-the-Light-and-Cries came to Rasediliodutherad, and to the island of the Neritorika. And I can hear by the pattern of your breath that you have another question . . .

Yes, everyone knew that Sees-the-Light-and-Cries had gathered together the kagliaristi . . . Stop him? How could they have done that, Taria-Who-Wants-to-Understand? Wasn't he a Child-of-She-Who-Spoke-the-World, free to make his own choices? He'd done nothing against the Eldest Laws. He was free to choose his own path, as were his followers. Yes, the Neritorika knew of him, as did all the Neritorika of this region. They knew, and they watched, but they could do nothing. He would not answer to their Language-of-Command.

The kagliaristi of Sees-the-Light-and-Cries went to the island then. They walked to the residence of the Neritorika, that building you tell me your eyes can see even from this distance, and it was there that the horror began. The baraalideish who attend the Neritorika told Sees-the-Light-and-Cries that the Neritorika had refused him entrance and that they must leave. Sees-the-Light-and-Cries only gave a sound of derision and pushed past the baraalideish. The baraalideish, understandably, resisted. Then . . .

The kagliaristi attacked.

In the next few minutes over fifteen Children-of-She-Who-Spoke-the-World died: twelve of the baraalideish and three of the kagliaristi. Fifteen, Taria-Who-Wants-to-Understand. Does that shock you? No, I can hear from your voice that even though you say yes you mean no. You must realize that never in our history had so many Children-of-She-Who-Spoke-the-World been slain at one time. Never. Not due to violence from one of us to another. Even the kagliaristi with Sees-the-Light-and-Cries were shocked by the bloodshed.

The Neritorika's remaining acolytes realized that Sees-the-Light-and-Cries intended to kill the Neritorika, and they fled with the Neritorika to the innermost Speaking-Place. Sees-the-Light-and-Cries pursued them, but the baraalideish reached the Speaking-Place first and barred the doors against him. The kagliaristi now held the compound and entrances to the island, but the Neritorika was barricaded in her Speaking-Place. For five phases of the Lesser Light the stalemate held.

With each rising and setting of the Brightest Light, Sees-the-Light-and-Cries called to the Neritorika with his Language-of-Command, ordering her to leave the Speaking-Place and submit herself to him. Each time, the Neritorika refused, and in her own Language-of-Command ordered Sees-the-Light-and-Cries to leave.

This battle of wills continued, the Neritorika declaring that She-Who-Spoke-the-World spoke only through the baraalideish, while Sees-the-Light-and-Cries invoked his own status. With each phase of Lesser Light a few more of the kagliaristi abandoned the siege, and with each loss, Sees-the-Light-and-Cries's voice became weaker, and the Neritorika's stronger.

On that last setting of Brightest Light, with only three of his kagliaristi still with him, Sees-the-Light-and-Cries again commanded the Neritorika to submit. Again and again he called to her, but his voice could not compel. He knew he had lost.

The Neritorika opened the doors of the Speaking-Place and with her Language-of-Command called to Sees-the-Light-and-Cries to prostrate himself.

Sees-the-Light-and-Cries knew that he had failed. With a cry of anguish, he lay at the Neritorika's feet.

The Neritorika ordered Sees-the-Light-and-Cries chained to the base of the island. He was placed there, screaming that She-Who-Spoke-the-World would yet come to save him, but if She heard his cries, She chose not to respond.

Sees-the-Light-and-Cries drowned in the next high tide.

The Neritorika decreed that his body be left there, a mute warning, until it rotted away or was eaten by the fishes. The chains in which he was secured are those we hear now, Taria-Who-Wants-to-Understand, still clanking their warning with each high tide to those who might consider taking the path of Sees-the-Light-and-Cries.

After Sees-the-Light-and-Cries died, all the kagliaristi affirmed their loyalty to the Neritorika, but it was obvious that the foundations of trust had eroded, like a rock in the waves. No longer could the various Neritorika feel entirely secure, and the kagliaristi knew that Sees-the-Light-and-Cries had come dangerously close to accomplishing his goals. It is whispered that there are those within the kagliaristi who are still followers of Sees-the-Light-and-Cries, even now.

Instead they wait. They wait, they say, for another sign from She-Who-Spoke-the-World, a sign that will tell them what their task is to be. Some kagliaristi say that She-Who-

Spoke-the-World's voice is already weaker, her long song nearly at an end, and that Sees-the-Light-and-Cries was right in his attempt to slay the Neritorika and become Baraaki.

I am afraid that the voice of Sees-the-Light-and-Cries is yet heard within the world.

"Some of us have wondered whether Strikes-Air-in-Anger is one of those who still hear that voice," Makes had said at the end of her tale.

Taria glanced from the stone railing of the balcony toward the faint lines of the chains on the opposite island, and she shuddered. During Makes's long explanation, interrupted often by Taria's requests for clarification, they had finished eating and moved back out to the balcony, where Taria could look over to see the places involved. Makes spoke as if it had happened yesterday, though the fact that the events were two generations of Blues old meant that it had all taken place sixty or seventy years ago. During the tale, Makes's voice had taken on a singsong quality, as if she were reciting. That may have been literally true—the Blues used a written language that had only recently moved from stone carvings, the words represented as braillelike bumps and lines, to incised heavy parchment. All their texts were produced by hand: the Blues had yet to find their Gutenberg. The laborious production meant that most of their historical traditions were orally transmitted.

"In other words, Strikes may be your enemy, and thus mine." Taria was certain now that she knew what had happened to Alex Coen. She could imagine how these kagliaristi might react to finding a human alone.

" 'Enemy' is a word of yours that I don't fully understand. I am telling you that Strikes-Air-in-Anger almost certainly has his own agenda, and that I don't know for certain what he intends."

"If Strikes is so damned suspicious, why is your Neritorika letting him run around?"

Makes vented like a bass calliope. "Didn't you listen to what I said? Strikes-Air-in-Anger has done nothing yet to allow him to be challenged. Would it be different for you?"

"Yes," Taria admitted. "In some places and in some situations. Sometimes suspicion of intent is enough. Aboard the *Lightbringer* it certainly would be."

"You'd punish someone for an action not yet committed? You would punish a person for intent rather than action?"

"If someone was making threats or acting suspiciously, yes."

Makes didn't answer, though she gave another slow blink of her eyestrip. "You are very different," she said, and stopped speaking. Taria forced herself to remain quiet, to accept the silence. After a time, Makes's chest heaved and she issued a long, throbbing low note. "We will go together tomorrow to see the watersingers," she said. "And we will see if someone wishes to stop us."

"Oh my God, Makes! You weren't kidding."

There were thousands upon thousands of the watersingers: like black, moving boulders along the beach; gathered in a crawling heap along a rocky reef a hundred meters offshore; moving like graceful seals through the foamy swells. With the gray clouds overhead blocking both the sun and the gas giant around which they orbited, the watersingers looked like discarded lumps of night strewn on the sandy ground. "No wonder we could hear them all the way back on the islands," Taria breathed, looking down at the scene from one of the cliffs. "All of them singing at once . . ."

"Not all at once," Makes said quickly. "Only a few hundred of them—that's the most I've ever heard." She breathed loudly, as if enjoying the taste of the salt air. "Are any of the Greater Singers out there—I can't hear them from this distance."

"How would I know them?"

"You would know," Makes answered cryptically. "Come this way—there's a pathway . . ."

They'd spent most of the morning making their way over the bay islands to the western arm of the bay. Taria found herself starting at every shadow as they moved through the settlement on the Neritorika's island, expecting at any moment to run into Strikes-Air-in-Anger, but they encountered none of the kagliaristi warriors at all. When they reached the place where Taria had the confrontation with Strikes, she looked around for the vidcam and found it still lying on the stones. She picked it up: glass fragments sparkled and fell like bright jewels from the lenses, and Taria let the device drop again, kicking it away and watching it skitter across the stones.

As they continued to walk among the narrow, winding streets, Taria noticed that the Blues gave the two of them a wide berth, moving to one side or the other of the lane as they approached. She thought for a time that it was her alien presence that caused them to do so, but once, when she stopped to look at a curling spire of red stone set near the base of one building, Makes walked on by herself, and Taria saw that it was Makes to whom the other Blues were giving space.

Is this something else to do with her being the Baraaki, whatever that means? Taria wondered but didn't ask, and she realized something: this was a deliberate, silent insult. The Blues touched. They *always* touched. It was ingrained in them, part of their culture. And yet they were deliberately avoiding Makes as if she were carrying a plague. In a human culture that might be deference; here, Taria believed it could only be an affront. The Blues from Gruriterashpali, the ones who like Makes belonged to the baraalideish, they touched Makes. But walking through Rasediliodutherad, she'd never seen anyone stroke Makes's shoulder or touch her side as they passed.

Taria began to wonder what other details she'd missed.

After a short trip to the inner arm of the bay on another

of the chain-guided boats, the rest of the morning was exhausted climbing up and over the ridge to where Taria could see the open sea, then down to the beach itself. The tide was sluicing out, no longer crashing against the craggy walls of stone that protected the bay. Sandy-bottomed, glistening flats of shallow saltwater ran a half kilometer out to the surf, and most of the tidal pools were alive with more watersingers. By low tide the immense gravity of Yang drew the waters compellingly toward itself, and the sea receded out three times as far as it was now; at high tide it would be two meters deep where she and Makes stood.

Taria didn't remember a scent from her first encounter with the watersingers, but she could smell a cinnamon spice in the breaths of the creatures around her, mixed in with a faint ammonia tang. Looking down—*the small things*—she saw a tiny creature marbled with red and yellow, no longer than her index finger, walking upright on two legs. A quartet of whiplike appendages sprouted from its chest, and as Taria watched, it curled one of the appendages around a mollusk shell and pulled it over, then climbed into the shell and disappeared.

Near her, a watersinger broached the surface of a pool and grunted a bass note in their direction that sounded strangely like a rising interrogative. "Are you *sure* they don't talk?" Taria asked Makes. "The way they sing together . . ."

Another of the watersingers lifted from the wet stones behind them, and as Taria turned to glance at it, she saw several of the nearest animals beginning to stir, as if their presence had aroused them. A sonic grunt from one of the bulls struck Taria, a small fist in her kidney. Another one answered; Taria could feel acoustic waves moving over her body, as if someone were brushing her with unseen fingers. There was no song to this, no coordination of voices, just a cacophony of inquisitive sound. "Makes?"

"I don't know how to answer you, Taria. I hear them, but

I've never been out here alone before—that's something only a kagliaristi would do. I would tell you that watersingers don't talk—that's what I have always been taught . . ." Makes gave a calliope snort. "All animals make noises," she answered, as if reassuring herself.

The watersingers were coming toward them, lumbering satin hillocks. The intensity of their voices was more frightening than their appearance, and the impact of the sound waves was more disturbing than the constant touching of the Blues. Taria backed toward the beach, but Makes was standing still, the brilliant frill of her head-crest lifting as the earlets turned out toward the sea. "There . . ." Makes breathed. Salt air stirred. "There . . ."

Taria saw it then, before she ever heard it.

If she had any doubts about what Makes might call a Greater Singer, they were immediately dispelled. She could only sense the head of it: a yawning emptiness, a black void that seemed to lift impossibly from below the glittering strands of tidal pools like the head of a broaching whale—but she could not truly *see* it. Her eyes refused to focus on that abyss, that hole in reality. Light shimmered and snapped along the boundary, but she could see no details within the apparition—her vision simply refused to accept the thing, as if not willing or able to acknowledge its existence. The beast was defined by absence, limned by reality. She had no sense of distance from it—the Greater Singer might have been impossibly vast, kilometers away; it might as easily have been smaller and closer—she could get no sense of scale, though she could sense the massiveness of the creature, like a pressure against her chest.

There was an undeniable kinship between the Greater Singer and the gathering on the shore. The watersingers— diminished and small in contrast—were ignoring Taria and Makes now, each of their snouts turned toward the Greater Singer, their earlets raised expectantly. The thing was still rising, and now another void seemed to be lifting alongside it, a second creature.

What happened then would shame Taria afterward. There was no thought that impelled her—the emotions that filled her were all hindbrain, all primal. What she felt was animal, something that rose from deep inside her core as the Greater Singers lifted from the sea and earth itself, as if the tidal plain were some vast oceanic depth.

Darkness whirled. The sound of emptiness hammered her ears. Voices cried in languages dead and never yet heard. Taria heard her name, called by a thousand throats, and she could hear each of their separate voices and she knew them. Knew one of them.

Taria!

She gasped. Suffocating words filled her throat. In the face of the inexplicable, she gave no thought to what she did next, responding only to the roiling emotional whirlwind that allowed no other response.

Taria fled. She ran.

Somewhere inside she heard Dog barking in alarm.

Propelled by sheer blind terror, Taria retreated, but her face refused to turn away from the Greater Singers. Gasping, she stumbled over a watersinger who pressed against her, tumbling over the satiny black fur and splashing into shallow, warm water. Taria flailed, spraying sea-foam as she tried to find her footing again. At least the backward fall had torn her gaze away from the hypnotic chasm of the Greater Singers. She didn't dare look back, didn't dare gaze at them again, for fear she'd be lost. Instead she sprinted for the rocks, for the path away from the beach, for anyplace that was away. She didn't know, didn't care, if Makes followed. She needed to be gone from here, away from the panic that slammed her heart against her ribs and ripped the breath from her lungs.

She ran, feeling their presence still rising at her back, hearing the slithering of the watersingers as they moved toward the Greater Singers, the first droning notes of their massed song slithering along Taria's spine. She was on the rocks now and climbing, her breath ragged and loud, her hands abraded and bloody from clambering over shell-strewn stones. She could run now, panting as she forced her legs to move up the path toward the summit of the seaward cliffs, toward the massed, gray clouds.

She didn't stop until she could fling herself to the ground just past the top, where she couldn't see the ocean anymore. She lay there in the dirt, feeling the grit of sand and dust on her tongue, feeling the panic start to clear and the first tendrils of shame rise. Below, she heard the singing begin, with an enormous voice filling the bottom of the long, bass tones: the Greater Singer. The rocks began to shudder underneath her, vibrating in sympathy with the compelling sound. The droning undertone was so low that it was felt rather than heard. Taria's hands trembled against the stones as she lifted her head, and her abdomen throbbed.

"Damn!" she muttered. "Oh, *damn!*" Dog barked again. "I'm okay!" she shouted to her avatar. She could barely hear herself against the din of the watersingers, more and more of them joining the song now, their voices twining around the base of the Greater Singers' voices. The volume was incredible, far louder than the rockets that had launched *Lightbringer*, the decibel level so high that Taria was afraid for her hearing. She pulled tissue from her pocket and stuffed it into her ears. That muffled the sound, but it still hammered at her. "Record this, Dog! Record it and leave me alone!" Taria levered herself off the ground, pulling herself to a sitting position. To either side of her she could see rocks, dislodged by the sonic barrage, tumbling down the cliff sides toward the tidal flats below. Taking a breath, Taria half crawled back to where the path slid over the top of the cliff and forced herself to look back down to the beach.

Crawling night gathered around an abyss she could not see: the watersingers had all pressed against the two Greater Singers. She searched for Makes, and finally saw her, halfway up the path. The Blue had stopped, her head-

crest fully dilated, a bright splash of color. "Makes!" Taria
called, but her voice was lost in the tumult, a whisper
against the shrieking hurricane.

A subsonic crescendo pulsed, shivering the ground under Taria and sending more rocks tumbling. She saw a
boulder the size of her head ricochet from the path not an
arm's length from Makes. "Makes!" Taria shouted again,
but the Blue gave no notice that she heard her.

Something—Taria afterward could never describe it; a
shape glimpsed as if in her peripheral vision even though it
swept directly in front of her—lifted from the midst of the
watersingers below and shot toward the sky, streaking upward and ripping a hole in the clouds through which Taria
caught a glimpse of Yin before the shredded gray billows
came together again. "What the fuck—" she said, staring
upward at where the thing had disappeared into cloud, the
tumult of the watersingers falling for a moment, then beginning to rise again.

Another pulse rippled the ground; and movement again
shivered through the air, shimmering from seafloor to sky.
More rocks fell, and Taria saw a scree of rocks strike
Makes, who tottered and nearly fell, arms flailing as she
fought for balance. "Damn it . . ." Taria muttered, and she
half ran, half slid down the path toward Makes. The fear
that had driven her upward threatened to return, but she
forced it down, forced herself to move. The trip down to
where Makes stood seemed to take forever, though it
couldn't have been more than a minute. Another sonic
pulse shook the cliff side like a cannon blast before she
reached Makes, and Taria stumbled, going to her knees and
putting her arms over her head as more rocks and stones
slid down toward the sea, trailing plumes of dirt. Cursing,
she got to her feet again and went to Makes.

"Come on!" she shouted as she grasped the Blue's arm.
"We have to get out of here!"

Makes didn't seem to react. "Taria-Who-Wants-to-Understand," she said, her voice almost lost in the watersingers' chorus. "Did your eyes-that-see-shapes see? Did you?"

"I did. I don't know what it was, but I saw it. Now we need to get the hell *out* of here!" She tugged at the Blue's arm again, and this time the Blue moved with her. Together they struggled up the path to the summit and over, then down the other side.

The song of the watersingers continued unabated as they moved down the far side of the bluffs. If anything, it reached crescendo, the volume made bearable only by the bulwark of land between them. Periodic sonic throbbings sent shivers from the ground through their feet, and once, when she turned to look back, Taria saw a flash leap from summit into cloud again.

Twenty minutes, maybe half an hour . . . it took them that long to reach the bay, where a chain-boat waited for them. All that time the song continued, rising and falling, though by the time they reached the boat it had faded to a murmur, which suddenly stopped.

"They're done," Taria said, surprised at the relief she heard in her voice. "I can't believe—"

"No," Makes said, lifting her hand. "Not done. Listen . . ."

Taria lifted her head. For a few seconds she heard nothing, then sound, an orchestral swell, welled up, the first notes so deep and low that they thundered just below the range of hearing, the acoustic waves striking her body like a hundred tiny fists. Then her ears registered the sound, still rising in pitch, still expanding in volume and tone. Close, dissonant chords wavered, a rapidly moving melodic line drawn through the air like a ribbon of harmonic color, fading and forming again and again, each time rising a tone higher, each time rising in volume and intensity, a lifting, curling wave of thunderous music that threatened to break over her, that caught her breath and refused to let go, taking her with it up and up until a final massive tonal knot exploded, Taria shrieking with it helplessly . . .

   . . . an emptiness clawing through torn clouds
   . . . a form shimmering in air and gone
   . . . the sound, the sound . . .
   . . . and gone . . .

TIME OF FULL DARK

As weapons are instruments of evil,
They are not properly a gentleman's instruments;
Only on necessity will he resort to them.
For peace and quiet are dearest to his heart,
And to him even a victory is no cause for rejoicing.

To rejoice over a victory is to rejoice over the
*   slaughter of men!*
Hence a man who rejoices over the slaughter of
*   men cannot expect to thrive in the world of men.*

—Chapter 31, *Tao Teh Ching*

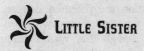 **LITTLE SISTER**

"Bored?"

Tee, Kyung's PIA, sat perched on his desk monofoil. Once, Tee had looked like a miniature of his sister Du Yun, but in the last year, Kyung had changed the avatar's appearance so that she had Taria's features, though he had never told Taria that or let her see his PIA in that form.

In fact, Kyung *was* bored. Life aboard *Lightbringer* was mostly stultifying, deadening routine interrupted at long moments by a barrage of activity, such as when he had taken his Firebird through Thunder ahead of *Lightbringer*, not knowing what might await him on the other side.

Now it seemed that the Yin side of Thunder contained much the same routine as the Sol side.

"A little," Kyung admitted. "It's been a long shift, and I had to run through the system check three times."

"I told you it was a simple data entry error."

"And you were right. I know. Sometimes you sound too *much* like Taria, you know that?"

"I could be Du again, if you'd like."

Kyung shook his head. Taria—he had been attracted to her the first time they had a chance to talk, and by the time they became intimate, Kyung knew that he loved her. Taria was quirky and independent, she could be both funny and loving, and yet there was a pain inside her that she would not let him touch, and the mystery of that attracted him as well.

What he couldn't understand was how easily Taria had left, how quickly she'd agreed to go down to Little Sister, which by necessity would impose a year of isolation on their relationship, not to mention the potential danger. Kyung had known Alex Coen, who had trained with him before *Lightbringer*'s launch, though they hadn't been friends. Coen had been missing for too long now. If they found him, Kyung figured they'd find him dead.

Kyung hadn't wanted Taria to go down to Little Sister, and he'd told her so. "If it's a matter of sex, there's a thousand other people on the ship," Taria had said during one of the arguments. "You can find someone here who'd be willing to take you to bed. I won't mind."

"How can you say that?" he raged back, though he was careful to keep his voice quiet and his face private. Rage was not something you showed easily to another. "I don't want anyone else."

Taria shrugged, looking away. "Fidelity's never exactly been my forte," she answered. "Why should I expect it to be yours?"

Taria infuriated him, ensnared him, worried him.

Kyung was surprised at how large the hole in his world was now that Taria was on Little Sister.

At least his shift was almost over. He could go back to his room, drink a few bottles of ship brew, and watch another movie in the ship library. Maybe, if he was bored enough, he'd go to the fifth level gym and work out, maybe spend some time talking with someone.

An alarm wailed.

At the same time, the floor, the ship, shuddered under Kyung. A massive screech of metal tearing echoed throughout the ship, a banshee scream that went on for long seconds then ended in frightening silence, while a fierce, impossible wind swept through the ship, sweeping paper along in its wake. The ship's living quarters shuddered again as Kyung tried to rise from his seat, and the rotational "gravity" momentarily vanished before the living quarters resumed spinning. The lights dimmed and came back on, and more alarms shrieked even as Kyung finally managed to get out of his chair. No more than fifteen seconds had passed, he figured, but in that short span everything had changed. He knew it.

"My God," Tee exclaimed from the monofoil.

"What?" Kyung asked. "What happened?"

His avatar managed to look stunned. "It's Thunder, Kyung. It just closed off. It's . . . gone. And *Lightbringer* . . . We've been holed."

"What?" Already Kyung could hear klaxons sounding everywhere on *Lightbringer*, and the other PIAs in the cubicles around him were chattering to their people as well. Suddenly there was no boredom. Instead adrenaline surged and a wild energy throbbed in his head as the implications hammered at him.

"Tee, break into the satellite link."

"Kyung, you can't—"

"Do it," he said. "Do it now."

"Taria?"

In that same moment, Taria heard Dog bark wildly in her head. *"Thunder's gone, Taria . . ."* The voice—Kyung's voice—sounded clearly in her head even as she struggled to comprehend the import of that statement, as she staggered from the impact of the abrupt silence around her after the chorus of the 'singers, as she blinked and tried to remember where she was.

As she tried to decide what it was she'd just seen and heard.

"Kyung?" she said, speaking to the air. His voice sounded thin and weak against the memory of the watersingers, like something heard through a bad headset. "Give me a moment, Kyung. I . . . what did you say?"

Seconds went by. *"It's Thunder. The whole thing's just vanished. And there's a . . ."* Kyung's voice faded. Taria shouted back, as if the extra volume could make a difference.

"That's not possible. God, Kyung, you're breaking a dozen different regs overriding the system like this."

"Doesn't matter. This is important for you to know. Thunder's gone, Taria. Worse. Lightbringer's *been damaged. Don't know how badly yet, or why. All hell's breaking loose up here. Full red alert. Be careful down there—we don't know what's happened to cause this. I'll make sure we send . . .* Then Kyung's presence was gone.

"Kyung? Dog?" she called. "What's going on? I need to talk to system support . . . I may . . . I may know something . . ."

Her voice trailed off.

She realized that Makes was there, listening to her half of the conversation. Makes grumbled deep in her chest. "Makes, what just happened?" Taria asked.

Makes's head-crest was still engorged, as if she were craning to hear something. Her earlets were tipped toward the sky. "There's no sound anymore," she said.

"What?"

"The sky-voice. The Voice-of-Her that began on my Acceptance, that made them call me Baraaki—" Makes stopped. Her head swiveled from side to side in a very human gesture. "There is no sound from the Emptiness-Above-Us anymore. What does that mean?"

"I don't know," Taria answered honestly. "I really don't know."

". . . I don't think I need to emphasize just how serious our position is at the moment."

Taria shook her head, even though she knew Commander Allison couldn't see the gesture. She still hardly believed the story he'd told her.

There had been no warning, no signs of trouble. When Thunder closed, a supply shuttle had been going through to the Sol side. The shuttle's hull shattered, and the shock wave from Thunder's collapse had transformed the shards of steel and plastic into a hail of debris moving at frightening velocities. Most of the scattered debris missed, but *Lightbringer* had still been hit several times. Two decks in the living quarters had been holed; thirty crewmembers were dead or missing. Worse, the artificial meteorites had ripped through Engineering in the outer hull, shearing away most of the ship's drive unit and severing control lines everywhere. At the moment the crew had no control of *Lightbringer*. The rules of gravity and motion were inexorable and, unfortunately, easy to calculate: *Lightbringer* was falling in a parabolic arc that would take her, eventually, inward to Yin.

In one singular, awful moment everything had changed. Everything.

"I'm well aware of the seriousness of our options, Commander. Even if we can repair *Lightbringer*—and from what you're telling me, that's in some doubt—we're stuck here unless we can find a way to re-create Thunder ourselves, or we find the Makers and convince them to re-open it."

Taria picked up one of the stones at her feet and flung it out into the bay, watching it splash into the waves as she waited for her transmission to reach *Lightbringer* and Allison's reply to come to her. Taria and Makes had just returned to the Neritorika's island when Dog had yipped in Taria's head and contact with *Lightbringer* returned. Allison had come online a few minutes after. Taria and Makes were still on the rocky beach at the foot of the island, with the tide just beginning to come back in. Before long the beach would be underwater again. At their backs, the stairs up to the settlement were alive with laborer Blues hauling up baskets of hornfish and whiteshells, netted from the tidal pools. The smell of brine and fish was strong here, and the soothing murmur of the waves was laced with the low grunting of the Blues as they worked.

"Or until Thunder opens up of its own accord," Allison said, his voice startling Taria with sudden volume, driving out the sounds of the environment around her. *"Sci-*

enceOps is reviewing all the instrument recordings we have. From what I understand, they all show the same thing. There was no warning here, none at all. One moment Thunder was still there—and the next it just . . . wasn't." Taria heard his exhalation, as if Allison considered it a personal insult that Thunder had decided to close up shop. *"Now, what was this you were telling me about these watersingers?"*

"I wouldn't have mentioned it, but . . ." Taria picked up another rock and tossed it in her hand. There were tiny cilia clinging to the wet underside, wriggling in the air, and as Taria watched, red spores jetted out from them, the breeze off the bay whisking them past her head. Taria dropped the rock. Her nose was tingling, and she sneezed twice in quick succession before answering, "It was the timing. Commander, from what you've just told me, they were singing just before Thunder closed, and when it closed, they stopped. All at once. Yes, it might be coincidence, or maybe they were just reacting to sounds from Thunder that we can't hear, since we know the Blues can—could—hear it all the time. I suspect the watersingers could also hear it, but I don't know. I do know I saw, or I thought I saw, something erupting from the center of them. And the ones the Blues call the Greater Singers . . ." Taria exhaled, took another breath. "Commander, I've *never* seen anything like them. Ever."

"But we've been told that watersingers don't talk," Allison said a few seconds later. *"They have no technology, no tools. They don't create artifacts. Hell, Spears, they don't have hands or eyes, no apparent manipulative organs at all. And they've never attempted to make contact with either the Blues or you."*

"Not in any way that was evident to me," Taria answered carefully.

Pause. Then: *"I would think your hypothesis that they were simply reacting to emanations from Thunder is the most likely, Taria. Occam's razor, eh? But I'll pass the in-*

*formation along to ScienceOps and the rest of the ExoAn-
thro team. Right now I don't know what Admiral McElwan
and the Exec Committee will decide to do. They've already
met twice, but I don't expect anything new for a few days,
when all the reports are in and have been studied. In the
meantime, are you willing to stay on Little Sister? It may
be that we'll need someone down there for negotiations."*

"Negotiations?" Taria took a quick glance at Makes,
who was crouched at the foot of the stairs, her head-crest
down now and her color muted to almost sea-green. To
Taria, she appeared worried. She'd said almost nothing on
the way back from the watersingers' beach, despite Taria's
questions.

*"If Thunder doesn't reappear soon, we'll need to exam-
ine the possibility that it will never return, or not in our
lifetime. Or, in the event that we can't repair* Lightbringer's
*drive system with our resources up here, we couldn't get to
Thunder even if it* does *open again. If that's the case,
then . . . Well, I won't insult your intelligence by pointing
out the obvious."*

"*Commander Allison,*" Taria subvocalized, not wanting
Makes or any of the other Blues to overhear. "*The Blues
made it clear in our previous negotiations that they're not
comfortable with a large contingent of humans being down
here on Little Sister. And you're suggesting we colonize
Little Sister, or at the very least, use it for raw material.
What if—*" Taria stopped, trying to think of how she
wanted to phrase things. "*What if somehow they're responsible for Ensign Coen's disappearance, despite what we
thought. These kagliaristi . . .*" Taria paused again. Allison
spoke into her hesitation.

"*We can't live on* Lightbringer, *Taria. Not forever. In a
few ship-months she'll be too far from Little Sister for the
shuttles to reach the planet; in a little more than a ship-
year she'll be molten slag plunging straight into Yin.
There's only one other option here. Little Sister's a big
enough world for our two races, I would think.*"

"And if the Blues don't like the idea?"

Taria knew what he would answer before he spoke—it was what she suspected any of the unis would say. For that matter, she'd say it herself. She listened to the waves, almost lapping at her feet now; listened to the sounds of the Blues as they went about their work. Out in the swells she thought she saw something dark break water for a moment and dive again with a flash of black fur.

"They won't really have a choice." Allison's voice should have sounded sinister, but the sympathy in his voice only made the words sound more ominous. *"But if it comes to that, it will be our job to convince them that they do, and that the right choice is to share their world."* Another sigh. Taria imagined Allison in his office, fiddling with one of the geodes lined neatly at one side of his spotless desk as he spoke. *"Look, things may never come to that. I hope not. In the best case scenario, Thunder shows up again, we repair* Lightbringer *enough to at least limp home, and we send one of the shuttles to pick you up and get the hell out of here. Let's hope for that. In the meantime, is there anything you want me to relay to anyone up here?"*

Allison knew about Kyung, of course. Allison knew everything in Taria's dossier. "Tell . . . tell Ensign Xiong that I'm all right," she said aloud, "that it really was my decision to stay here."

The waves slid in. Out. In again. *"If you'd like, I'll contact him and switch you over to a private frequency. If there's anything else you'd like to say to him."*

"No." Taria scuffed at the rock-strewn sand. Saltwater pooled in the track of her toes. "I appreciate the offer, but . . . just tell him that. That's all. I'll talk to you later, Commander. Dog, I'm out."

A few seconds later she heard the click of disconnection, and a hum that she hadn't even been aware of disappeared with it. "All right, Makes," she said, turning to the waiting Blue. "I'm done reporting in."

"Then we will climb," Makes answered. "There will be people waiting for us. I know."

Not one of them came near Makes at all.

When Taria and Makes approached the stairs to the Neritorika's island, the laborers on the beach all stepped away, moving aside as they grunted and muttered deep in their chests. And they were otherwise silent—none of them spoke to Makes, none of them talked to another, even though they had been busily chattering not two minutes before. Makes ignored them in return, going to the stairs without a word to Taria and starting the long ascent.

"Makes?" Taria called after her, but the Blue made no answer, continuing to climb. She seemed freighted with a deep worry—Taria knew that equating human emotions to the Blues was dangerous, but Makes had withdrawn since Thunder's disappearance, folding into herself. Taria had no choice: she followed Makes, wanting to ask questions but reserving her breath for the climb. The steps, cut for the longer-legged Blue anatomy, were scaled large for humans, too high and deep to be comfortable. Going down them had been strange enough, but gravity had assisted. Now Taria had to shuffle forward toward the riser, then lift her leg nearly to her knee to reach the next step, pushing herself up with a grunt before shuffling again. Makes was very quickly far ahead of her. As Taria neared the end of the stairs the full tonal range chorus of Blue voices drifted down from above her—Makes and someone else. *Dog?* Taria thought to her PIA. *Can you tell who that is?*

A few seconds later pale translucent letters scudded across her vision: *VOICE ID: Makes. VOICE ID: Strikes.* Then: *I can translate. They are speaking Makes's language.*

That worried Taria more than the simple appearance of Strikes—if Dog could translate, then there was the implication that this was more than a casual meeting. "Go ahead," she told Dog, and hurried up the next few stairs.

Dog had little chance to relay the conversation. As soon as Taria came into view, the two of them stopped talking. Strikes was with an entourage of two other warriors, one of them standing on either side of Makes, with Strikes directly in front.

Strikes stepped aside from Makes and faced Taria. Clawed fingertips glittered in a sun falling through ripped clouds; a fist of dark sound touched Taria's abdomen. He began to speak; after a few moments Dog's translation came to her ears. "Then let me ask Taria-Who-Wants-to-Understand, since you can't answer me. Why has the Voice-From-the-Sky stopped? Is this something Those-Who-Speak-Without-Saying-Anything can tell us? Why did the Singers-From-the-Water sing as they did, with the Greater Singers among them?"

Taria glanced at Makes—her skin was a strange hue, mottled with pale cerulean patches. "Makes, should I answer him?" she asked in Shiplish. "Talk to me. The Voice-Only-Taria-Can-Hear gave me the translation, but I don't know what's going on here or what the etiquette is. Help me."

Makes's voice seemed almost nonchalant, or maybe it was only the fact that the tones sounded so thin after hearing her speak in her own language. "You may answer him or not as you wish, you may tell him the truth or not, Taria-Who-Wants-to-Understand. This is the Language-of-Negotiation, not the Language-of-Command."

You may tell him the truth or not . . . Language-of-Negotiation . . . ? Taria frowned as implications cascaded from that, as remembered fragments of conversation suddenly took on new meanings. *Oh, my God, what I've—we've—missed . . . All along . . .* Strikes took a step toward Taria as she hesitated, the knives of his fingertips clattering brightly, and Taria widened her stance. "Then tell him that I don't have an answer, either. What he calls the Voice-From-the-Sky was the path through which we came from our world to yours, and it's gone now. My people on the ship are trying to find out why, and trying to find out how to open it again. And I know less about the watersingers than you do. Tell him that."

Makes let loose a barrage of sound, and Dog translated. Taria watched Strikes carefully, trying to gauge his reaction, although she knew it was helpless anthropomorphism on her part and her perception was more likely to be wrong than right. Strikes's head-crest rose, his earlets flared, and the eye-ridge blinked heavily a few times. His hands clenched and he rocked from side to side, shifting his weight. His two companions *hoomed* and thrummed, their own hand-blades making noise like silverware tossed in a drawer. After Makes had finished, Strikes slashed the air, his hand-blades whistling sharply. "If Taria-Who-Wants-to-Understand knows even that much, then Those-Who-Speak-Without-Saying-Anything know more than our own Baraaki. Are you shamed by that, Baraaki? Will that satisfy your Neritorika? Did you warn us that the *humans* were coming?" This time Strikes used the English word, breaking it into three distinct syllables: haw-u-mahns: "Did you tell us that the Voice-From-the-Sky was like a bridge in the Emptiness-Above-Us? Did you know *anything* about what She-Who-Spoke-the-World had done?"

The gas giant Yin had nearly set; Yang was quickly following. Double shadows stretched across the rock-strewn field, and the islands painted dark bars over the sun-tipped waters of the bay. The air pulled goose bumps from Taria's forearms, and the salt breeze lashed her hair around her neck.

She wished, for a moment, that she had Kyung's flechette pistol with her now. Even after Makes's tale about the chains hanging in the surf, even knowing the kagliaristi were watching Makes, Taria had thought herself safe from Strikes as long as she was with Makes. Now she wasn't sure.

"I know what I know, and it is enough," Makes retorted. "Since when is it the duty of the kagliaristi to concern themselves with the responsibilities of the baraalideish? Worry about yourself, not the Baraaki."

"I worry about all Children-of-She-Who-Spoke-the-World, and thus I worry about the baraalideish and their Baraaki, as well as Those-Who-Speak-Without-Saying-Anything." Strikes gestured toward Taria again, with a slicing of hands. He touched Makes's neck, briefly, and Taria saw droplets of blood rise where the blade tips dimpled her skin. Then his fingers truly dug in, hard, and Taria gasped, seeing the blades slicing into Makes's neck. Makes made a choking sound as Strike's hand clutched her throat, and blood streamed down her neck. Yet Makes didn't struggle, didn't even raise her hands against the assault. "What does this mean to Those-Who-Speak-Without-Saying-Anything?" Strikes asked, without releasing Makes. The long shadow of his arm slid over Taria's face and she felt her breath catch in her own throat. "Can the human Baraaki answer me that?"

Dog yipped in her head after that translation.

Since the encounter with the watersingers, Taria's reality had shattered; she'd felt it, even if she hadn't been able to put the feeling of disorientation into words. Kyung's warning about Thunder's disappearance and her conversation with Allison—she hadn't let herself feel anything then, too numb from the barrage of the watersingers' grand chorus. Now all the shards and pieces were falling into place around her in a new shape, even as fear for Makes and her own life burned in her gut.

She shifted, she breathed in twin wonder and panic.

Dog! Get me Kyung. Now!

"Makes," she said aloud. "Do you remember how when we first met Strikes, you told me I had to do exactly what you said? Now it's my turn. I need you to follow my lead. You're the Baraaki. You're supposed to know what She-Who-Spoke-the-World is going to do, aren't you? That's part of your duty. You really are the prophet."

There was no answer. Makes hung quiet and unprotestingly in Strikes's bloody grasp, his fingers tight around her neck.

"Makes, listen to me," Taria said desperately. "I need you to do one thing, that's all."

"Taria?"

Taria continued speaking, almost breathlessly, trying to ignore the desperate heave as Makes tried to draw air into her lungs. "I'm also speaking to my friend Kyung, Makes. Wait a moment—" Taria spoke under her breath: *"Kyung, I need your help. I know you programmed the satellites with targeting from our mapping images. There's a little promontory about three kilometers out from where I'm standing, to the north-northwest. I'm figuring that's big enough to be on your maps. I want you to take it out. Spectacularly. And I need a good time estimate of when that will happen."*

Pause. Then: *"Taria, I don't have the authority . . ."*

"Fuck authority," Taria interrupted as Kyung's voice continued over her protest with the time delay.

". . . to do that kind of thing, and things up here are totally insane. You realize that, don't—"

"Commander Allison gave me the authority to do what I need to do down here," Taria continued. A lie. She wondered that she didn't care, that it really didn't concern her that Kyung would probably be pissed as hell if and when he realized that, or that this might kill any career Kyung had. *"I need a miracle, Kyung. Life or death. I don't have time for channels on this one. I need you to do something now."* What made Taria shiver was not the thought of any trouble Kyung might come into afterward as a result of this, but the fact that his fate didn't matter as much to her as that of Makes.

Strikes was saying something to Makes, his voice a quartet of shrill brass instruments. Makes was hardly breathing now. Blood covered the winding cloth around her shoulders, and her color was pale.

"Fifteen seconds from now. A three-second laser burn."

"Thanks, Kyung." she said. *Dog, end link.* "Makes!" she shouted, interrupting the Blues' conversation. Earlets fluttered in her direction from the kagliaristi. She hoped none of them knew Shiplish. "Can you point—no, skip that. Strikes couldn't see you pointing . . ." Taria took a breath. "When I saw 'Now!' I need you to hit Strikes with your hand." When Makes gave no indication that she'd heard, Taria shouted again. "Makes! I'm saying this as your friend. This is important. I need you to do this."

Makes drew another harsh, rattling breath, and Strikes clenched her throat tighter. Taria was certain that Makes had not heard her, that she wasn't going to react, then her arm lifted slowly, her fingers trembling. "Good, Makes." Taria paused, then: "Now!"

Makes's hand struck at the kagliaristi's body, a weak, open-handed slap.

It was enough.

A military laser is invisible, an unglimpsed lance of coherent light that at close range can slice through steel as if it were soft butter, that can sear living tissue to black char with a touch. Kyung had shifted the frequencies slightly, so the beam flickered like violet lightning as it slashed through the clouds in the darkening sky—a visual display that was lost on the Blues but looked impressive to Taria. The beam played over the rock for only a few seconds; in those moments, Taria knew, rock sagged into bright molten slag. The water that poured over the rock from the pounding of surf and rain and was then trapped in the cracks and fissures of the stones vaporized instantly into steam.

At the moment Makes touched Strikes, the top of the promontory shattered, the crown exploding in lava and cloud, fire-snared rocks arcing through the air to splash hissing into the bay. The sound came an instant later, a terrible stony groan followed by the sharp percussion of the explosion, which echoed from the steep hills around the bay, growing fainter with each iteration. Strikes and his companions shouted in alarm with the destruction, their knife-blade hands waving and earlets flattening against their head-crests. A few stones thudded on the grass near them, cracking and steaming as they cooled.

The silence, when it came, was thick.

As a miracle, Taria thought, it was a relatively impressive display.

Strikes vented, a steam-whistle shrill. He released Makes as if she were suddenly molten rock herself and gave a low hooting call that seemed to have no words in it at all. His hands touched Make's bloody clothing at shoulder and chest. Makes barked something to him that Dog could not translate, the words sounding more guttural and sharper than anything Taria heard her speak before. Strikes replied, and this time his voice was quiet and monotone. He gestured to his companions, and they backed away from Makes and Taria as a group, leaving them alone at the top of the island stairs. Taria watched them leave, hoping she'd read this correctly, that this retreat *was* a retreat. And right now, she knew, there'd be a dozen people trying to reach her from *Lightbringer*. "Dog," she said quietly. "Full privacy mode. Keep 'em out." Dog barked once a few seconds later.

And Makes, who Taria thought would be relieved, or thankful, hooted in what Taria knew was cold anger. Her head-crest was fully extended, her skin color deep, and she paid no attention to the deep, open wounds on her neck. "What have you done, Taria-Who-Wants-to-Understand?" she asked, her voice hoarse and strained. "Why did you do this? Do you think that anything the kagliaristi could do to me matters?"

"Makes . . ." Taria gaped, hands wide. "The kagliaristi . . . I thought it would help you. I did it because you're my friend and I thought you were in trouble."

"My *friend*?" Makes snorted, then her earlets flattened and the head-crest settled. "You understand *nothing*. If we are friends, then I need to speak with you in Mandarin, so I can tell you what you need to know." Makes's hands slid over Taria's body from hip to shoulder. The caress was not gentle, and her fingertips left bloody streaks on Taria's blouse. "You have to teach me."

The huge curve of Yang had already vanished and Yin was starting to fall below the clouds piled on the horizon. Darkness was already pooling in the lengthening shadows, with only the top floors of the Blues' buildings still in sunlight.

Out in the bay steam rose from the shattered stump of the island.

"All right," Taria said. "We'll start as soon as we get back home."

✳ TRUST HAS TO BE PART OF LOVE . . .

It was Dog's fault she met Kyung. *Lightbringer* had left orbit a few days earlier. Taria had gone "up" three floors to the strangely pleasant half-gravity where Weapons Systems was located—not a place she usually frequented, but the ExoAnthro planning committee was going over ship resources department by department while drafting contingency plans, and Taria had been drafted to get someone from Weapons to talk to them. She was still in the corridor outside when someone spoke from behind her.

"Hey, I like your avatar. I used to have a dog just like that back home."

First impressions: the powder-blue officer's uniform was just disheveled enough to indicate that at least he was a uni with a mind of his own. Taria saw glossy jet-black hair cropped close in a military cut, and eyes of the same uncompromising hue, but with a softer edge. A stundart gun was holstered on the belt cinching his waist, and he wore both pilot's wings and the bristling cluster of muzzles of Weapons Systems. His nameplate said XIONG. Epicantal folds veiled those dark, smiling eyes, and the smile seemed genuine and slightly lopsided—not a handsome face, but one that reflected an active life. Taria liked the way his cheekbones drew soft shadows on his face, and his Shiplish was accented with tones that reminded her of childhood. If he had an avatar himself, it wasn't immediately apparent—which was normal enough. Most people didn't display theirs as readily as she did. "What's her name?" Ensign Xiong asked.

"Dog," Taria answered.

One eyebrow lifted. He pursed his lips, nodding. Taria waited for the inevitable sarcastic comment: *How creative* or *At least it's easy to remember* or *That's better than "Cat," I suppose.* But Ensign Xiong said nothing. Instead he hunkered down in front of the holo projection as if it were a real animal. "You're handsome," he said to Dog, and pretended to pat the head, grinning as his hand went through the field. "One thing I miss up here is having animals around." That was to Taria. "I know I've seen you before in the preflight orientations, but I don't think we've ever been introduced. What's your name?" he asked, and quickly glanced at Dog. "No, don't tell me. Considering the way you named your PIA, I'll bet I can guess. Human?"

He said it with just the right flippancy, and both of them laughed at the same time. "I'm Taria Spears," she said.

"Kyung Xiong," he answered.

She knew it in that moment. After Nikki, in the months before *Lightbringer*'s departure, there'd been Peter and Paula—the "apostle sequence" she called it afterward—two techs with the project, neither of which had been serious or long relationships. She hadn't felt the Spark with them.

She felt it then, though it scared her. Since her mother's death she'd avoided Chinese men, even though the *Lightbringer* staff was at least half Asian. There were too many memories, too much pain. *Not him*, she thought. *Not him.*

But he smiled, and she stopped listening to the voice.

They had their first real argument somewhere around the orbit of Mars.

"I hate those things," Taria said. "I really wish you wouldn't do that here."

Kyung was sitting at the small table in Taria's quarters. His hair was still wet from the shower and ruffled from the toweling. His uniform pants were on, but above the waist he wore only a thin white undershirt, his uniform shirt hanging stiffly from the chair back. His stundart gun lay in pieces on a towel on the table, and Kyung was polishing each part as he put the weapon back together.

"What?" Kyung asked. "This?" He held up the snubbed barrel of the stundart.

"Yes. I've always hated guns. Always."

Kyung nodded. Snuggled in his arms late one night, she had told him about her mother's murder. She'd cried, and he held her tightly against the pain the retelling always brought with it, the memory she could never forget: the melon vendor breaking free from the crowd, the shouting, the shiny metal of the pistol in his hand . . .

"It's only a stundart," Kyung said. "No one's going to be stupid enough to carry a real firearm while we're on the ship."

"Doesn't matter. It's still a gun."

Kyung gave her a look, and Taria thought she saw scorn mingled with the sympathy. "All right, Taria. Sorry. I'll be more considerate next time now that I know. Let me just finish this . . ."

That could have ended it if she'd just walked away, Taria knew. But the scorn, or perhaps it had only been pity, that she'd glimpsed in Kyung made her set her jaw, cross her arms, widen her stance. "I hate them," she repeated. "I really do."

Kyung's reply was still soft, but there was an edge to his voice now. "I don't. I think they're necessary." His gaze was entirely on the stundart. He fitted the barrel into the firing mechanism with a loud click.

"Necessary? For what, Kyung? They have one function. Period. I've seen them work."

"That's your heart talking, not your head." The handgrip

slid into its slots. Kyung pushed it forward with a grimace: *click.*

Taria's hands dropped to her hips. "Now I'm too emotional? Is that what you're saying?"

"I think you have a lot of emotion invested in this, yes." Kyung placed the darts into the clip, and the clip into the handgrip. He glanced once at Taria as he slid the stundart into the holster on his belt. "I understand why, too. I don't blame you for feeling that way, but it's not the way I feel."

"You like the feeling of power, is that it? Does it make you feel strong?" Taria could hear the shrillness in her voice and hated it, but she couldn't stop the words.

"Stop," Kyung said. "Taria, this is stupid. You knew what I was when we started. And I'm not going to apologize for what I feel or the fact that I'm not bothered by carrying or using weapons."

" 'Bothered'? You make it sound like shooting someone would be a minor annoyance."

"You don't know what you're talking about."

"I know better than *you.* I lost my mother to someone that wasn't 'bothered' by shooting."

"Stop it," Kyung said, shoving his chair away from the table. "Just . . . stop it."

"Why?"

"I don't want to have this argument, Taria. I'm not going to convince you that a weapon is just another tool; you're not going to convince me to give them up."

"Not even if I asked?"

"That's not fair."

Taria knew Kyung was right. It wasn't fair, but she set her stance and stared at him. "Even if I asked?" she repeated.

Kyung didn't answer, not right away. He picked up his uniform and put it on, but didn't button it. He sat. "I'm older than you. When Thunder came, I was six."

"Kyung, that's not—"

His head came up, his black eyes nearly sparked. "Shut up and listen," he said. "I was six. It was bad everywhere when things went to hell, and it was awful in China. I remember it: I remember the crowds, the occasional riots over food or money or supplies, the panic, the lost jobs. There were hundreds of desperate people roaming around then. One day . . . it was summer, hot and still. My parents were gone, I don't know where. My older sister—Du Yun—was watching us; she was thirteen then. I was in my bedroom, so it must have been late in the evening. I heard a commotion at the door, Du Yun shrieking and yelling at someone, my two brothers also yelling, and a deep male voice I didn't know shouting back at them. I was probably asleep; it was like noise heard in a dream, and I don't know how long it had been going on or exactly when most of the shouting stopped. Then someone was tearing through the house, shouting. He came into my room. All I remember is his face, how it was all twisted and red with his shouting. He came over to me, grabbed at me. I remember my nightshirt tearing, and his fingers digging into my arms. I was screaming, too. Taria, I was so *terrified*. He was hurting me and I was screaming for my parents and Du Yun. I was scratching and clawing at him, and when he put his hand over my mouth, I bit him as hard as I could, until I tasted blood. He howled then, and he hit me in the face. He hit me again and again while I screamed and cried, then I didn't remember anything at all. When I woke up, with my cheekbones broken and my eyes nearly swollen shut, I found that the man had ransacked the house, taking everything halfway valuable that he could stuff in a burlap bag. He'd also beaten my brothers, eight and ten years old, unconscious. My sister . . . Du Yun . . . he'd raped her."

Kyung blinked, and a single crystalline line, a tear, outlined the curve of his cheek. "For years after that I went back to that night in my fantasies, imagining I had a pistol under my pillow or that I knew where my parents kept one, that when the man had come into our house, I'd taken the gun and shot him, killed him before he could hurt any of us. Tell me that I'm wrong to think that, Taria. Tell me."

"Kyung . . ." Taria said it softly. She sank to her knees in front of him, her hands taking Kyung's. "You never said anything about that. I am so sorry for you. For your sister and your family. That was a terrible, terrible thing."

"Tell me I'm wrong, Taria." They were both crying now. Taria sniffed, looking up at Kyung's face, shattered with the memory.

If there'd been a gun there, he might have taken it from you, or he might have found it first. He might have used that instead of his fists. The argument was in her head. Taria looked at Kyung, and touched her fingers to her lover's face, feeling the warm moisture there.

"I can't tell you you're wrong," she said, knowing it to be a lie. "I won't."

Taria caught a glimpse of Kyung at the far end of the mess hall and started toward him, weaving through the clusters of unis and civilian staff. It was 1200, lunchtime for the first shift crew, and the mess was crowded. Taria was halfway through the maze of tables when she noticed that Kyung was sitting with someone, that they were involved in a conversation. She was a uni, an officer with the same crossed muzzles on her lapel that Kyung wore: young, pretty, Asian.

. . . the vendor's Asian face, twisted in a rictus of anger, the gun in his hand . . .

Kyung was laughing. His eyes were on the woman's face. He touched her hand as he spoke.

Taria stopped. Silverware clattered against china on her tray. She could hear the silvery flutter of Kyung's laughter through the white noise of a hundred conversations. Kyung's hand reached up. His hands touched her cheek— it was a gesture he had used with her: a touch, a whispered "I love you."

Taria found herself holding her breath, feeling a heat on her cheeks as if Kyung's fingers had touched her. "You sitting here?" someone said behind her, and she startled again, aware that she'd been standing there too long. She didn't answer; she put her tray on the nearest table, then turned and fled the hall. She was about to get on the elevator to E deck when a voice called to her from behind. "Hey! Taria!"

The elevator bell pinged, the doors opened. Taria started to pretend that she hadn't heard the call, then stopped. She let the doors close again.

Kyung was standing in the corridor, his head cocked sideways as he looked at her. "What's the matter?" he asked. "I saw you leaving the mess—"

"Nothing."

"That's bullshit, Taria. Don't give me that crap." There were other people in the corridor, walking to and from the mess—mostly unis, none of them friends, but faces she knew, people she'd spoken with. Some of them glanced at the two of them curiously. Taria took a few steps toward Kyung, who didn't move.

"I just didn't feel like eating right now," she said. She spoke in Mandarin; she packaged the comment with what she hoped was a disarming smile. Kyung simply stared at her.

"This is so high school, Taria," he said in Shiplish. "Am I supposed to pretend that I don't have eyes, or that I can't see that you're upset? I'm not that stupid, and that's not the way friends or lovers should act with each other."

Crewmembers walking by glanced at them. Kyung seemed oblivious to the pressure of their eyes.

"It was stupid," Taria told him, her voice soft and fast. "It was stupid and I know it and I really don't want to talk about it. Especially not here."

"*What* was stupid?" Kyung asked. "I was sitting there with Kwan—" Kyung stopped. He laughed, and the sound was like the clashing of knives. "Kwan. That's the problem, isn't it? Jesus . . ." Kyung swung his arms wide, palms up. "That's it, isn't it? You saw me with Kwan and you thought . . . hell, I don't know what you thought."

"Kyung, listen. I don't care if you're seeing someone else. I really don't. It's not like I can expect—"

Kyung planted a hand on the wall on either side of Taria, trapping her. "No. You listen. Kwan is a friend. My friend. You want to know the truth? Yes, we've even been lovers. For a few months, while *Lightbringer* was still in her construction orbit. Before I knew you. We managed to stay friends, and that's a pretty rare thing. She'll always have that kind of love from me. If that bothers you, then maybe we need to talk about things, but what she doesn't have anymore is the other kind of love, the kind that comes because someone else has become part of your soul, because when you're with that person you can open yourself up both physically and emotionally and let them see all of you. That's *you*, Taria. Only you. You have to trust me in that, because trust has to be part of love, has to be part of any relationship that means anything. Do you trust me, Taria?" His dark eyes were very close to her. They were all Taria could see, at once fierce and soft. "Do you?"

Taria blinked. She wanted to escape, escape the arms that caged her, the eyes that examined her, the voice that made her want to cry. "Kyung . . ." she began, and could go no further.

"It's a simple enough question," Kyung persisted. "I trust *you*. I can tell you that. I trust you or I could never have made love with you. That's the truth."

Taria hated this. She hated the feeling of being captured, hated that for all she knew, others might be watching them, hated that she couldn't find a clear answer inside herself to his question. "Kyung," she began again, "I don't know. Do I want to trust you? If that's the question, then yes, I do. I want that. It's just . . . I'm not good at relationships, Kyung. I'm not. I'm sorry, but that's the truth."

His eyes would not leave. They hovered in front of her:

heavy, unblinking. "Trust me, Taria. That's what it comes down to. Trust me."

Taria nodded because she could do nothing else. Kyung sighed. He leaned forward, and Taria felt his soft lips brush her own. She started to respond, but Kyung had already pushed himself away from the wall. He was still watching her. People were still moving down the corridor. Taria wondered what they'd seen and what they thought.

"I'm going back to talk with Kwan. You want to come with me? She's a great person, and you really should get to know her."

"Kyung . . ."

"It's up to you. I'm going back."

Taria touched his lips with her fingers. "All right," she said. "I'll come with you."

For the first time, Kyung smiled.

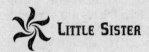 LITTLE SISTER

Over the next several hours, Dog kept Taria appraised of the attempts to contact her. There'd been over twenty contacts by the time they arrived back at Gruriterashpali and the refuge of Makes's rooms. Eventually, Taria figured, they'd pull in one of the net-techs and override Dog's security, but she'd wait until that happened.

It wasn't going to change what had happened—whatever *that* was. Taria still hadn't puzzled out the meaning of the confrontation on the island, and Makes still refused to talk about it—not in Shiplish.

Taria spent the time teaching Makes Mandarin. She found that the Blue was an incredibly quick study, with a nearly mnemonic memory. She explained the four possible tones for each vowel, and how the tone could change one word into another—Makes tended to use too much inflection, and her tones were inevitably pitched too low, but Taria was surprised at how quickly she became understandable.

They were sitting, again, on the balcony. The orbital mechanics of the double system meant that full night came rarely to Little Sister, as either Yin or Yang were usually in the sky. The unrelenting darkness caused the hairs on Taria's arms to rise, a primeval response. There were no moons in the sky—the other three moons snared in Yang's gravitational embrace were below the horizon. There was nothing above Taria but a dusting of stars glimmering in satin, a vast emptiness into which it seemed she could fall forever. Few lights were on in the city or on the other is-lands—Makes had seemed entirely untroubled by the lack of illumination as they'd made their way back to Grurit-erashpali. The streets and lanes below them were loud with the calls of the Blues, but Taria could barely make out their forms in silvered starlight. She held a flashlight from her pack in her hand, but when she'd turned it on, the bright cone of light seemed an intrusion, and the brilliance had ruined her night vision, only making the rest of the dark-ness around seem deeper in comparison. She'd quickly turned it off again, feeding Makes Mandarin words and phrases until she could see all the stars again.

"Spears!"

The voice was an intrusion that made Taria gasp. She wondered how Makes could not have heard it, too.

"Commander Allison," she answered. "I really didn't think it would take you this long."

"You overestimate your importance," Allison answered gruffly. *"Your problems aren't exactly top priority. What the hell's going on there, Taria?"*

"I apologize," she said, "but I didn't really have a choice. Not if you wanted me to be in a position to negoti-ate with the Neritorika. And I really didn't have time to ask for permission. Is . . . is Kyung, um, Ensign Xiong in a lot of trouble over this?" Guilt made her stumble over the words.

"He's not my department or my problem—that'll be up to Commander Merritt. But I can talk with Merritt. Tell me . . . did it work?"

"I think so," Taria answered. She gave Allison a short version of the confrontation, embellishing only when it came to Makes's reaction after the confrontation ended. She didn't mention that the entire action had been done purely on intuition and impulse. She wasn't going to tell Allison that they had essentially propped up the current theocracy and possibly interfered in a sociopolitical conflict. Instead she stressed that she'd felt personal danger, that if Kyung hadn't acted, her own life as well as Makes's might have been in jeopardy. She wasn't certain Allison bought the story, but she also knew that he couldn't directly contradict it, not without downloading her private files from Dog. Taria didn't expect Allison would go snooping in her PIA without following channels and getting permission—which meant he probably wouldn't bother at all.

"I'll talk to Commander Merritt," he said after Taria finished. *"I think I can make a case for leniency, though I'm not happy with your statement to Ensign Xiong that I gave you the authority to do whatever you feel necessary down there."*

"Sorry, Commander," Taria answered, as contritely as she could through a smile. "I apologize. It seemed the time to bend the truth a little."

"Not to mention that you know how uni minds tend to work, eh?" If any trace of amusement seeped into Allison's voice with the comment, Taria was unable to hear it.

"I wouldn't presume to know that, sir," she answered.

"I would advise that you never *make that kind of presumption henceforth. You might be surprised, especially in the face of a crisis."*

"Yes, sir." Taria exhaled, a long sigh. "Commander, can you patch me through to Ensign Xiong's PIA. I'd . . . I'd like to give him my personal apology."

Kyung wasn't available, his avatar informed Taria. The PIA's voice was that of a young Asian woman. "Kyung's in a meeting with Commander Merritt and his immediate superiors," the PIA told her in soft Shiplish. "I'll record your message."

"Shit," Taria said, then switched to Mandarin. "Kyung, I am very very sorry that you're getting the raw end of this. I hope it's not too bad, and I've asked Allison to speak for you. I . . . I feel bad about this, but I really needed you at that moment, and I'm glad you were there and willing. Good luck, and give me a call when you can. I'll tell Dog to let you through. Kyung, I . . ." The next words, the ones that should have come, refused. *I love you.* Simple words, they should have come easily.

"End of message, Dog," she said. "Full privacy mode, except for Kyung, if he calls." Taria wondered if he would.

She felt Makes's hands on her arms, moving slowly from shoulder to elbow, then grazing the curve of her rear. "Your friend . . . you have placed him in difficulty with what you did?" Makes spoke in halting Mandarin.

"*Shì de,*" Taria responded in the same language. "I have. You understood that?"

"Some. Has Kyung asked you for an apology?"

Taria gave Makes a half smile. "I know it's different for you, Makes, but with humans it's really best to offer an apology first. Trust me."

"I already have," the Blue answered. "And so did Kyung." Makes thrummed to herself. "Was that a smart thing for Kyung to do?" she asked.

Taria looked out over the bay without answering. The waves breaking high on the islands' cliffs were phosphorescent in the darkness, glowing white in pale imitation of the stars above. Taria saw groupings that would have been strange constellations had they appeared in Earth's sky. But here the constellations were unnamed, unnoticed by the Blues. They were only stars, not legendary figures of Blue mythology. As far as Taria knew, the Blue cosmology stopped with the concept of the Emptiness-Above.

"I don't know if it was smart for Kyung or not," Taria answered finally. "And I didn't ask myself that question, either, at the time. I guess the truth is, Makes, that sometimes you end up hurting friends more than you'd hurt someone you didn't know at all."

"You asked me once before if I was what you call a 'prophet.' You are maybe closer to the truth than you thought. I was called by She-Who-Spoke-the-World. After all, She had given us a sign at the moment of my Acceptance, and what else could that mean but that I was to be Baraaki? But the truth, Taria-Who-Wants-to-Understand, is that while I've spoken to Her often, I don't always understand what She says to me. Most often, I am empty inside. I don't know what She wants, what She's telling me. That's something I couldn't admit to you with the Language-of-Formality-and-Negotiation. It's only now that I could say it to you. But I am Baraaki, and even the Neritorika listens to me."

Taria sat in the dark, leaning against a wall of Makes's room with her bedding pulled over her legs. The sound of the Blue's heavily accented Mandarin was oddly comforting, like a distorted echo of a pleasant memory. "Then *we* came."

"Then you came," Makes agreed. She was a blackness against the backdrop of stars, standing in front of the open doorway of the balcony. "She-Who-Spoke-the-World had said nothing to me about you. There were only two possibilities then: that I had failed, or that She-Who-Spoke-the-World had failed. The second of those was unthinkable, so it must have been my fault. My fault. The Neritorika knew it. So did the kagliaristi."

Even across species there was no mistaking the sadness in her voice. It pulled at Taria, and she tossed the blanket aside and went to Makes. She hugged her fiercely. Their bodies fit together strangely, with hardness where there should have been softness, and hollows where Taria expected fullness. Taria held Makes for a moment, then stepped back, trying to see some expression in her shadowed face.

"What was that?" Makes asked.

"Something human friends do," Taria answered. "If it offended you, I'm—" Taria stopped. *No apologies.* "Tell me if that bothered you," she finished.

"No." Makes gave a low hoot, a soft ululation. "It was . . . not unpleasant."

Taria gave a soft laugh at that. "Good. That'll have to do, I guess." Makes's fingers found Taria's head and moved through her short hair. "Why did Strikes call me Baraaki?" Taria asked Makes. "Is that what he thinks I am—your human counterpart?"

"That *is* what you are."

Taria stepped away, shaking her head. "No, Makes, I'm not. I'm nothing even close to what I understand a Baraaki to be. Surely you realize that. And it's certainly not something I want to be. I don't believe in *any* god, yours or mine."

"It was nothing I *wanted* to be, either," Makes answered.

"Makes, I'm sorry, but you can't drag me into—"

Taria heard a sound at the open archway to the hall. She snatched her flash from her belt clip and swung it in that direction, thumbing it on. In the cone of light, a young Blue stood. She was naked, and on her body were ridges of what looked like gray paint, set in swirling figures that covered her from neck to crotch. "Who is that?" Taria asked.

"A message." Makes had already moved toward the young female. Bursts of quick speech came from them, and Makes ran her hands over the painted body, tracing the paint lines slathered over the flesh.

Reading, Taria suddenly realized. That's what Makes was doing—reading a message painted on the body. When she was done, Makes rubbed her hands hard over the unresisting messenger, smearing the paste and rendering unreadable whatever had been written there. Another harsh burst of sound from Makes—what Taria recognized now as the Language-of-Command—and the young Blue retreated wordlessly, leaving them alone again. In the cone of Taria's flash Makes stood silent, her hands stained from the body paint.

"Makes?"

Makes *hroomed*, her voice loud in the darkness around them.

"We must go to the Neritorika," she said. "Both of us."

The building stood atop a stony hill, all strange angles and curves. It appeared almost organic, as if someone had taken a pile of exotic fruit and placed it on a canted pillar, enlarged everything, then turned it to hollow stone.

There was a flight of stone steps leading up to the Neritorika's dwelling. Makes paused at the foot of the stairs in the night darkness and clapped her hands sharply. A cascade of echoes followed which made Taria gasp in wonder—the sound was like the twittering of birds, as if Makes had wakened a sleeping flock with her handclap.

"Makes, that's lovely," Taria said in Mandarin. "How does—"

"Later, Taria-Who-Wants-to-Understand," Makes answered. "Do as I do. Strike your hands together with me."

She clapped twice more, with Taria mimicking her. Each time the echo-birds answered, and as the reverberations of the last clap died in the hillside, the doors opened above them.

The two Blues who held the doors had rings of twisted copper wire fitted around their head-crests, adorned with tinkling shards of pottery that filled the air with clashing and chiming as Taria followed Makes up the stairs. The attendants reached out as Makes approached, their hands stroking the Baraaki as she entered, and also touching Taria. No words were spoken by anyone—no greetings, no introductions. Taria clamped her jaw around the hundred questions she already had for Makes and followed her into a large hall. Like most Blue interiors, it was plain to the eye, since the Blues had no ability to appreciate painting or other visual decoration. Instead it was decorated with sound: a vicious cold draft from off the bay swept through the door, jangling wind chimes that hung from hooks along the wall and sending treble notes chasing each other through the interior. The hallway led back into unguessed black depths, and the floor seemed to angle downward, as if descending into the hill on which the building stood. Only the first few meters were illuminated: by dim starlight and the weak yellow glow from one of Yang's other moons.

The doors clanged shut.

Immediately Taria was surrounded by pitch-blackness, and she heard the fading timbre of the wind chimes as they settled once more. "Makes?" she whispered, and her voice sounded impossibly loud and panicked. Once, years ago, she, her father, and Judy had gone to Mammoth Caves in Kentucky. In the middle of the cave tour the guide had gathered the group around her and turned off the lights. Even then, in those few seconds, Taria had felt as if the weight of the earth above them was closing in around her—she felt the same sense of impending suffocation now. Dog barked in sympathetic alarm in her head. Taria could hear the rustling of the Blues around her, and a hand grasped hers: Makes. "I can't see at all," Taria said.

"Hold my hand," Makes whispered back. "Use your ears—they can guide you."

Taria concentrated on her hearing, closing her eyes so she wouldn't have to confront the darkness around her. Concentrating, she found that she *could* hear, that she could determine the directions of the sounds and tell, to some extent, how far away they were. The rows of chimes hung along the walls were like an acoustic channel, leading off in the distance ahead of her. She could hear Makes's breath in front of her, and the clinking sounds the two acolytes made as they walked farther into the building. She felt Makes squeeze her hand, and she started to walk with her, the tightness in her throat relaxing slowly.

They were descending a slope: Taria could feel that. As they walked, twisting downward and to the right—she realized that only a small portion of this building had shown aboveground—they passed openings leading off the main hallway. Taria was pleasantly surprised to find that she could *hear* the openings—a change in the echoes, a sudden absence of wind chimes on one side or the other—as well as *feel* them: the touch of a cold breeze on her arms, a prickling sensation in her skin. She could hear other Blues moving within the space also, in the rustling of their body-wraps, in the persistent low hooting of their echolocation, in the occasional exploratory touch as one passed close to them.

If her eyes could not see, at least the rest of her senses could find some pattern in the environment around her. She was not entirely lost. She relaxed the death grip she'd been keeping on Makes's fingers, though she did not let go.

Still downward, a little more steeply than before, and now to the left. There was a smell now, a salty taste to the air currents: brine. There was another, fainter smell as well, one that seemed familiar to Taria, though she couldn't place it. She could hear the lapping of waves on stone, and a faint illumination came to her eyes, a drifting green-yellow phosphorescence that was down and to her right. It took a moment for Taria to realize what she was seeing: glowing algae on the surface of a pool. The corridor was now open on the right, winding around and down the walls of a large chamber in which the pool of water sat. As they descended, she could glimpse more of the room: a floor of plain brown tiles, walls that looked more natural than made. The water filled one end of the room, and Taria could see an opening in the wall through which moonshine glittered on the wavelets—an exit out into the bay. The algae grew along the walls, the glow ending abruptly several meters up, and she realized that this room flooded with each high tide, the algae-glow demarking the tidal line.

The room was chilly and damp. Taria's nose wrinkled, and she sneezed abruptly, and again. If this was the Neritorika's chambers, these were not comfortable accommodations. She far preferred Makes's rooms back at Grurit-erashpali. Ahead of her, Makes and the attendants halted. Taria blinked, trying to bring the room into focus in the dimness. A shape moved in the shadows of the far corner, with a sound of damp flesh scraping over tiles . . .

Makes and the attendants clapped their hands together. The sudden, reverberating noise startled Taria. "Neritorika," Makes said, her voice trumpeting the title in several octaves.

The Neritorika came forward, and this time Taria did cry out in surprise.

The Neritorika was not a Blue.

The Neritorika was a watersinger.

Dog, Taria whispered in her head. *Patch this through to Allison. I've totally missed something here. God, have I missed something . . .*

The Neritorika was not like any watersinger Taria had seen before, but she was undeniably kindred—since Taria saw no sign of external male genitalia, she decided she would think of the Neritorika as female until someone said differently.

The Neritorika was larger than the watersingers Taria had first seen, but much smaller than the Greater Singers she'd glimpsed on the beach. Where the watersingers moved like a seal on the land, the Neritorika walked upright, with a waddling gait that reminded Taria of a penguin. She stood half again as tall as Taria, her fur seeming to hold a darkness deeper than the night that swaddled the room; now that she was closer, Taria could see tiny blue-white sparks glimmering underneath the silken hairs. The forepaws were more flippers than hands, clenched near her breasts. Her face was hairless, with a prominent head-crest that was lighter in hue than the rest of her, though Taria could not tell in the algal gleam what color it might be. Like the other watersingers, she had no eyes or eyestrip at all. As the Neritorika made her way across the tile toward them, she sent booming waves of inquiring sound that Taria could feel, rippling over her body.

And the Neritorika, unlike the watersingers, could speak. The Neritoka opened her wide mouth and began talking; after a lag of a few seconds, Dog began to translate. She spoke in what Taria now knew was the Language-of-Formality-and-Negotiation, the dialect the Blues had used when they first met with the *Lightbringer* contingent.

"Makes-the-Sound-of-East-Wind, Taria-Who-Wants-to-Understand. You have come as asked. That is good."

The Neritorika sidled close to Makes. She leaned over Makes, her flipper-hands sliding along the Blue's head-crest. "Baraaki," she said. "She-Who-Spoke-the-World chose you. Is now the Time-of-Dispersion?"

"I don't know," Makes answered, and Taria heard the strain in her voice. "You ask the wrong Baraaki."

"Then should I ask the Baraaki-Who-Can-Call-Destruction?" The Neritorika turned, and now she bent over Taria. The Neritorika's hands touched her head—the caress was gentle, just tousling her hair, and Taria could smell a faint and pleasant spice-musk coming from the Neritorika's body. She felt strangely safe in the Neritorika's presence, as if the pheromones exuded by the creature had a calming effect. Taria reached out herself and touched the Neritorika's fur. Her hand tingled as she stroked the satin softness of her massive flank, and blue fireflies outlined her fingertips. Deep basso waves of sound surrounded Taria, as if she were being embraced by a host of invisible hands.

"Makes, what should I do?" Taria said softly in Mandarin.

"Answer the Neritorika. I will translate for you," Makes answered. "Speak Shiplish."

Taria looked up at the face of the Neritorika, unreadable in its utter alienness. The dampness of the chamber still bothered her, and her nose was starting to run. Taria sniffed and rubbed her sleeve across her nose. "First, I am not a Baraaki."

The Neritorika seemed amused by that.

"You do not get to choose that title for yourself," she answered, "so it is not something you can deny. And secondly?"

"How do you know I called destruction?" Taria asked. "How do you know what I did?"

"How do you know that the wind is cold or the sea as warm as mother's milk?" the Neritorika answered after Makes had spoken for Taria. "I feel. I hear. I know. Listen . . ."

The Neritorika took a step away from Taria. Lifting her head, she sounded a soft, low tone like a pedal note on an organ. Her mouth opened wider, and the tone swelled while other notes joined it. The sound echoed in the room, filling it, oscillating and growing louder until Taria's own heart began to throb in time with the slow rise and fall, her blood pulsing with it. The sound filled her head, driving out everything else: she couldn't think, couldn't hear Dog, could pay no attention to anything but the sound, the swelling atonal massiveness taking her up and holding her, capturing her . . .

There was something in front of Taria, floating at chest level, something she could not see at all. She could feel the shape of it, shimmering under her touch. Taria traced the outline: a human head, maybe done in half scale, with flowing long hair that seemed to spread out on a hard, rough surface, as if someone were lying on her back, the head turned slightly toward Taria. She let her slide wonderingly downward, exploring the impossibility: a neck, the frilled collar of a blouse giving way under her fingers, the lamb's-wool collar of a coat, partially open, the swell of breasts . . . With a shock, Taria knew what—who—this was. She let her hands continue down: a warm, thick wetness between the breasts made Taria cry out in a sob.

The acoustic sculpture shifted under her touch, becoming a sudden jagged sharpness, like the knife edge of broken pottery. Taria snatched her hand back.

She was aware that the Neritorika's song was gone, with the last vestiges of it fading as she listened. Whatever had been in front of her vanished as well. Taria glanced at her fingers, half expecting to see them stained with blood, but her skin was unbroken. She reached out to the empty air where the sound-sculpture had been—there was nothing there at all now.

Taria looked up at the Neritorika.

"When something is lost, there's pain," the Neritorika told her. "That is something you know."

Mama's body, lying on the pavement, the blood . . .
"Yes." Her voice cracked with a stifled sob. "I know."

"That is the way I hear you," the Neritorika said. "That is your sound. There is a space in you that you've chosen to leave empty and silent." The Neritorika gave a loud *huff* of sound, then changed the subject disconcertingly. "What will happen next, Baraaki-of-Others, now that the Voice-From-Above is silent?"

"We can't go home," Taria answered simply. She was too tired to try to dissemble or lie. "So we will make a home here."

"We asked only *you* to stay with us. Not the others."

"That won't matter," Taria answered bluntly. "We'll come anyway."

The Neritorika seemed to draw herself up with that statement. Her next words jarred Taria. "That," the Neritorika responded, "would be a terrible mistake. *They* wouldn't like that."

TIME OF THUNDER

Tao never makes any ado,
And yet it does everything.
If a ruler can cling to it,
All things will grow of themselves.
When they have grown and make a stir,
It is time to keep them in place by the aid of
    nameless Primal Simplicity,
Which alone can curb the desires of men.
When the desires of men are curbed, there will be
    peace,
And the world will settle down of its own accord.

—Chapter 37, *Tao Teh Ching*

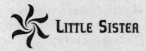 **LITTLE SISTER**

They came down, as Taria had known they would.

Of course, she was instructed to say nothing, to give the lie of omission, the same lie they'd given when Alex Coen had been sent down. She was to keep secret the fact that more humans had arrived on-world. When the hovercraft came for Taria, she told Makes—in Shiplish—that she was expected back on *Lightbringer* to meet with Commander Allison.

It didn't matter that the hovercraft was obviously an atmospheric craft. That kind of technological insight was beyond the Blues.

The encampment was half a continent away from Rasediliodutherad or any of the other Blue settlements, which were all coastal. *Lightbringer* landed its first contingent in the interior, in a grassy valley nestled between the ridges of the continental spine. It was a beautiful site, Taria had to admit—as picturesque as anything she'd seen back home: snowcapped mountains of gray stone looming over shaded green foothills, pristine creeks running from the slopes down to the looping cradle of a blue river.

But it was not Earth. Not with the colorful storm-whorls of Yang hovering above. Not with the distinct bluish tint to the grass. Not with the tiny, winged nuisances that swirled around the tent looking more like miniature furry rodents than insects.

Taria sneezed.

"The hover pilot told me you weren't feeling well," Commander Allison said. He sat stiffly at one end of the long table set under the tent, a monofoil screen aligned at careful right angles to the edges. His end of the tent ended at the airlocks to the quickly expanding home base.

Taria blew her nose with a tissue, which she left on the table, as she'd been asked to do. Someone from Med, dressed in a biohazard suit, would pick it up later and put it in a sterile plastic bag. "Just a cold," she answered. "No worse than anything I've had back home."

Taria sat at the other end of the table, with the landscape open behind her. Here, Dog was visible again, with the holographic arrays set around the tent area. She reached out to touch her avatar's image, feeling the tingle of the field as her fingers approached his ruff. She knew that if she extended her hand toward Allison, she'd feel the gelid, invisible barrier of the environmental shield: Allison sat in a microcosm of *Lightbringer*'s environment, protected from Little Sister by the barrier and a difference in air pressure that held Little Sister's atmosphere away like an unwanted embrace. The occasional winged rodent that blundered into the barrier sizzled and then dropped to the ground.

This was the same arrangement they'd used in their first meetings with the Blues. Now it was Taria who was seated on the other side.

The alien.

"Still, this is something we need to watch carefully." Allison's voice was carefully neutral. "We don't know the microbiology of this world at all, or how it will react to us. And we still don't know what happened to Ensign Coen."

"I knew the risks when I came down, sir. We talked about them at length, if you remember." *And we don't know what our microbiology's going to do to this world, either, and I don't remember us mentioning to the Blues what happened to the native people when the European settlers hit the Americas.* "I have my medkit. If things start looking more serious than a head cold, I'll let everyone know. Right now, the worst I've had was a slight fever two ship-days ago, after I met with the Neritorika." Taria stroked Dog's ruff and tried not to sniff. "Is that what it's come to, Commander? We're definitely coming down here, all of us?"

He tried to hedge the truth, but Taria saw it in the pained, quick squint of his eyes. "It's still uncertain. Admiral McElwan hasn't made her decision yet. Right now, we're still trying to gain control of the drive system. Environmentally, everything's been repaired."

So we're drifting in a little doomed bubble of Earth that's heading for the sun, and it's not going to get fixed. We're trapped here. Unable to stop the reflex, Taria sniffed again. The airlock door opened, and she saw a heat-waver response around Allison as the barrier reacted. Kyung stepped out, dressed in khaki. "Ahh, Ensign," Allison said. "Since you're here early, I'll catch up on my log for a bit and then let you get back to your duties. Taria, I'll be back in ten minutes—we have a lot to discuss." Allison nodded to Taria and gave Kyung a salute as he passed back through the airlock.

Taria gave Kyung a tentative smile. *"Ni hao ma?"* she said: How are you?

Kyung didn't answer immediately. He sat down in Allison's chair and slid the monofoil away. He looked at Taria and ruffled his hair with his hand. "I wish I could touch you," he said. "I really do. I've missed you, Taria. I've really missed you."

She knew she was supposed to respond in kind. Instead she shrugged and ducked her head so Kyung couldn't quite see her eyes. The polite Chinese way—never quite say no to anyone, or reveal exactly what you're thinking . . . "I know. But you have to stay away from all those icky alien viruses," she said. "I . . . I never really thanked you for helping me when I called. How's it been?"

Now it was Kyung who shrugged and glanced away for a moment. His hands were folded on the table, but his thumbs tapped together impatiently. "Not too bad. I got reamed by Merritt for breaking protocol, and they moved me off Satellites. I don't think I should expect to get a promotion anytime soon, but at least I kept my rating. But my request to come down to Little Sister went right through. Guess they figured that was a sort of punishment, doing the shit work to set up things here." He shrugged again, and looked directly at Taria for the first time. "What else could I do, Taria? You said it was life or death. I *had* to."

But it wasn't, really. Not for me, anyway. "I know. I put you in an impossible position and I'm sorry. And I also appreciate your reaction. I wish I could have thought of something else at that time."

"I understand. I'm not angry or upset. I'm glad you thought of me. I'm glad I was there to help."

Placid, bland words. Both of them were fairly certain that everything was being recorded; which only made the awkwardness more pronounced. There were worlds more to say, and they were exchanging pleasantries like society matrons over tea and cookies.

One of the flying ratlets hit the barrier and expired in a tiny shriek. They both watched it fall to the floor, the delicate translucent wings shriveled and black.

"I keep hoping that we'll find the Makers, or that Thunder will open up again and we'll have the drive ready," Taria said. She gestured toward the hills around them. "That this won't end up being our home."

"I have a few friends in ScienceOps. Frankly, they sound pretty resigned to Thunder staying gone. The grunts in Engineering don't act very optimistic at the moment, either. And I understand the Blues aren't happy with the thought of us as neighbors."

Taria shrugged. "The Neritorika wasn't pleased, but she didn't seem so much angry as annoyed. She seemed to indicate that the kagliaristi would be upset. '*They* wouldn't like it,' she said. Which tells me that's what happened to poor Coen."

"And they're armed with what? Spears and long fingernails?" Kyung sniffed. "They might have been able to overpower Coen, all alone here, but not if we come in force. There won't be much either the Neritorika or these kagliaristi can do about it."

"Wonder how we'd feel if the Makers came to Earth and said the same thing? 'All they have are puny lasers and atomic weapons . . . ' "

Kyung laughed quietly at that. They sat for a while in silence. Taria sniffed and blew her nose again.

"Are you doing all right?" Kyung asked. "Otherwise, I mean."

Taria wondered what he really wanted her to say. *I've missed you so much, Kyung. I love you* . . . She couldn't say any of it. She hadn't missed him that way, not in the midst of being on Little Sister. No time to think of love . . . or she wouldn't allow herself to think of it. "I've been fine. Too busy to think about much but the Blues." She saw the slight sag in Kyung's shoulders and the way his lips tightened, and suddenly wanted to share herself with him, to help him understand. She hurried to speak. "There's so much here to learn, Kyung. God, I can't even imagine how little we know. Whenever I think I've figured something out, there's a twist. Something I've missed. The Neritorika not being a Blue—we all just *assumed* . . ." Taria lifted her hands and let them fall back to the table. "There's something here, Kyung. Something we need to know, maybe even linked to Thunder and the Makers. I mean, the Makers must have known the Blues were here—anyone who could make a wormhole like that *must* have noticed them. Maybe they even contacted the Blues, in some way that the Blues can't or won't tell us. There's *something*. I've felt it all along, and now I'm sure of it. I just don't know exactly what it is. But I'll find out. I will."

He was watching her with a smile on his thin face. "What?" Taria asked.

"All at once you're animated, you're all energy and light. You have passion. Interest." Kyung's smile evaporated. "I guess I should be heading back in. Allison's going to want to grill you about the Neritorika and Little Sister." He pushed away from the table and stood. Ratlets stirred from their perches in the outer folds of the tent with the sound, buzzing past Taria's head. "I miss you, Taria," he said again.

"I miss you, too." It was the smallest gift she could give him.

Taria hoped it was actually true, but something inside her wouldn't let Kyung touch her own emotions. Instead she sneezed.

Kyung asked to take her back. They spent most of the trip in meditative quiet, separated by the bulwark leading to the front of the craft where Kyung sat at the controls. That was mostly Taria's choice. She had a headache that had grown progressively more severe as Allison quizzed her, and the noise of the hover only made it worse. Kyung put the hovercraft down next to the bridge leading over to the first island of Rasediliodutherad. A crowd of Blues tending the adjoining sourgrass field listened to them land, sending inquisitive grunts in their direction. *"Be careful, Taria,"* Kyung's voice said inside her head.

"I will," Taria answered. Moving her head to get up sent a throb of pain through her temples. "Thanks for the ride back."

"My pleasure. Maybe the next time we can actually sit in the same place; I can hope, anyway." The door clicked open and stairs unfolded. Taria climbed out of the craft. Once clear of the rotors, she could see Kyung in the airtight pilot's compartment, doubly protected by his flight suit and helmet. He waved at her; she waved in return as Kyung gunned the motor. Jets whined and the rotors sliced

air, and Kyung was gone, the throbbing quick beat of the shuttle slowly fading to the east.

The dust kicked up by the rotor wash caused her to go into a fit of sneezing and nose-blowing—at least that was what she told herself. Her headache screamed at the abuse. When she recovered, Taria headed toward the islands. She hadn't told Makes when she'd be back, not knowing how long Allison would hold her. She'd been gone a full ship-day, sleeping in a sterilized field tent just outside the building. Yang still dominated Little Sister's sky, a little lower in the west now, with just the top quarter of the gas giant showing above the hills. A long, pale shadow trailed Taria as she walked along the bridge.

Halfway across, she entered the shadow cast by Grurit-erashpali, and she wondered whether Makes was there, perhaps standing on her balcony and listening to the sounds of the city below her. There was a Blue moving across the bridge toward her, though the figure was half lost in shadow. As the Blue approached, Taria stopped.

It was a kagliaristi. Taria wasn't certain, but he looked like Strikes. "Fuck," she whispered to herself. At the moment, the Blue seemed to be "looking" in the direction of Kyung's hovercraft, so it was most likely the noise that had brought him this way. She stopped, hoping he would pay no attention to her.

The ploy didn't work. Taria sneezed, a quick reflex that came and went before she could even begin to try to stop the impulse. She felt the acoustic waves hit her a few seconds later, and the kagliaristi moved toward her. "Fuck," she said again, sniffing. "Dog? I'm going to need translation help here." Dog barked in her head—much more quickly, now that there was a local relay for the network.

It was definitely Strikes. "Taria-Who-Wants-to-Understand," he said in his poor parody of Shiplish, stopping a few feet away. Then he rattled off a string of words in what Taria assumed was the Language-of-Command.

Dog's whine a few seconds later confirmed that the PIA

couldn't translate the words. "Great," Taria said. "Wonderful. I feel like crap, and I have to have a conversation with Mr. Steel Fingernails all alone out on the bridge." Taria sneezed again, and tried to sidle past the kagliaristi; Strikes slid sideways to block her, raising his hands so the fingernails glittered in the pallid light. He reached toward her face and she backed away a step.

"Dog, give me words here. I need to tell him that I'm on my way to Makes, that I want him to leave me alone." A line of translucent phonetic syllables appeared a second later, appearing to overlay the scene in front of her as Dog stimulated her optic nerves. Haltingly, Taria spoke the phrases. Strikes's eyestrip blinked in a slow roll as he listened to her, and the kagliaristi grumbled around her.

Then it was Strikes who spoke, finger-knives clashing in front of her. This time Dog could translate. "You speak in the wrong language. You are commanded to come with me."

"No," Taria answered in Shiplish, and spoke the syllables Dog provided.

"You must. It is important for you."

"No." Again. "Not a chance. I need you to move aside."

Strikes barked something in the Language-of-Command, and knife blades clashed again. One forefinger snagged cloth at Taria's shoulder and held as she tried to retreat. Strikes's other hand had her now, blades curling around her forearm. One blade was streaked with a dark, oily substance, and that blade dug into Taria's arm. "Hey!" she shouted in alarm and pain.

Taria felt her body freeze and stiffen in response to the attack. She started to tell Dog to call for Kyung—maybe he could bring the hover back in time—but though Dog barked in alarm in her head, the words didn't come.

Taria had taken a few self-defense courses in college. One instructor had a simple mantra she repeated often: *If you're ever attacked, keep breathing, and then hit the bastard with whatever part of your body is still loose.*

Taria screamed, ignoring the pain that lanced her forehead with the sound. She kicked Strikes as hard as she could, her foot smashing into one of the several sacklike structures around his hips.

The reaction was far more dramatic than she expected or hoped for. Strikes made a sound like a leaking pipe organ. His hands were suddenly no longer on her. Taria ran past him, listening as she ran, but though Strikes continued to howl behind her, he didn't seem to be pursuing her. When she reached the end of the bridge, she paused and looked back.

Strikes was still out there, still venting either pain or surprise or both.

Taria hoped it was a *lot* of pain. She coughed, out of breath. Dog barked inquiry.

"I'm okay, Dog," she said. "I guess that worked. At least it's easier to kick 'em in the balls when they have lots of them."

Her arm was burning where Strikes had cut her, as if the cut had been quickly infected. "Great. That's all I need on top of this cold." Taria scowled. The sky seemed darker. The ramparts of Gruriterashpali were doing a slow, lumbering dance in front of her. Taria blinked. The ground rolled underneath her, and Yang seemed to add no light at all to the sky.

"I think I need to sit—" she began, and her knees gave out. Her head bounced once on the stones, but she hardly felt it. "—down," she finished, and giggled as she sprawled on the ground. She squinted into the darkness, seeing a darker figure against the sky. "Hey, Strikes," she said. "I fell—"

But the world had already collapsed into blackness, and Taria went pinwheeling away into nothingness.

The hover swung away from the Blue city and arrowed back toward the interior. Once a few dozen kilometers rolled underneath the craft, Kyung could no longer see any

signs of the Blues at all. Little Sister teemed with life, as
did Earth, but the Blue population hadn't moved inland, instead spreading along the shores of the single large continent. Now that he was alone, Kyung allowed his avatar to
become visible. The miniature Taria perched on the instrument console and smiled at him. "ETA for Little Sister
Base is thirty-seven minutes," she said.

"Thanks, Tee."

She does miss you, you know. Even if she won't say it.

Kyung lifted one corner of his upper lip under the flight
mask. "Sometimes I wonder. I hope you're right."

I am, though—Tee stopped, frowning. *Kyung, something's wrong.*

The words were like a blow to his stomach. "What?"

*Taria. Dog just told me he's lost contact with her; she's
no longer in the net at all.*

The fist that hammered Kyung's stomach grabbed his insides and twisted. "Shit. Tee, please double-check that.
Maybe it's just a com glitch."

*I already have. She's gone. The connection was severed
suddenly.*

Kyung's fingers tightened on the arm of his chair, trembling. He could feel the thrum of the hover's engines
through the neural net, throbbing like a part of him, and he
felt an urge to swing the craft around and head back to
where he'd last seen Taria. It was an effort to keep that impulse from leaking into the command pathway. The hover
banked slightly with the unspoken desire, and Kyung
brought it back on course. "Is Allison aware of this?"

A hesitation. *He is now. I just told the Cube.*

"Patch me through to him."

Allison's voice was, as always, calm. "Ensign, I'm very
busy at the moment."

"I know, Commander. But Taria—"

He got no further before Allison interrupted. "Ensign,
this could be nothing more than a com breakdown or a failure in Spears's neural patch."

"Commander, I can be there in fifteen minutes. Less. If there *is* a problem—"

"If there *is* a problem," Allison echoed, "then we absolutely want to be careful how we respond, for everyone's safety, including Taria's. Ensign, you will return to base. You will pick me up, and we'll return to the Blue city. Together."

"Sir—"

"Ensign, you have your orders. You barely managed to keep your position after the last time you . . . ahh, decided to improvise. I assure you that you won't be so lucky a second time. Do I make myself clear?"

"Abundantly," Kyung answered. "Sir." Kyung took a breath. "End connection," he said to Tee.

The hover thrummed under, around, and in him. He could imagine turning the craft in a wide arc, opening the engines to a full-throated scream as he rushed back to the city, a scream that Kyung could feel bottled up in the pit of his stomach.

Kyung? Tee said, and Kyung glanced at the small image of Taria on his console.

He swallowed the scream. He kept the hover on course.

And he wondered whether, afterward, he would hate himself for this.

Somewhere, someone with a bass voice was humming tunelessly and scraping rocks together. Her eyelids didn't want to open; when they did open, the light sent spears of pain of through her head. She couldn't feel the rest of her body, and when she tried to lift her head, she ended up coughing. The spasm sent white curtains of agony through her, and for a time she went away again.

When she awoke once more, the person was still humming, but the light didn't hurt as much, and though her limbs felt as heavy and thick as logs, she could at least move them. But it was cold, so cold . . .

Dog?

There was nothing but silence in her head. *Dog?* She queried again, but there was no answering bark. She felt the back of her head—her hair was stiff with matted blood and some other substance she couldn't identify. There was a large, tender bump on her skull, but her head didn't hurt at all. A blow on the head could have damaged the neural net—that would explain Dog's absence. Someone in *Lightbringer*'s tech support should also have noticed the detached PIA—with any luck, someone would already be looking for her.

Someone was still humming and scraping rocks. Taria realized that she was in a half cavern—a hollow under a cliff. There were rocks strewn about, and behind her was a stone beach and the mouth of the bay opening to the ocean, which in turn merged into the haze of the horizon. She sat facing the beach—hugging herself against the cold, she turned to look deeper into the recess under the cliff.

She saw Strikes. And she gasped.

Not from fear, not from pain or cold, but from surprise. Under the canopy of the cliff wall, someone had done something wondrous. All around were large stones, some a meter or more in length, but balanced precariously atop other rocks, sometimes stacked five or six high in impossible, delicate positions: larger rocks balanced on far smaller ones; misshapen masses of stone set on a single point. The stacks looked as if a breath would send heavy rocks tumbling—the nearest pile to Taria was a large round boulder, on top of which a tapering, rough, upside-down triangle of granite perched on its apex so that it rose well above her, as if captured in a momentary stasis. The contrast of massive, unworked stones set on end and somehow placed on their long ends was stunning, a ballet of frozen motion.

This was sculpture. This was art.

And the artist was Strikes, Taria realized. He was working as she watched. He was holding a jagged slab of rock, fitting it atop another, smaller rock that was already balanced on a piece of shale. His hands—the finger-blades

missing now, Taria noticed—delicately moved the rock
back and forth as if he were feeling for its center of gravity,
the motions delicate and slow, though Taria knew the rock
must weigh twenty kilograms or more. Strikes grunted, a
low *hrummm* that resonated in the cavern, and stepped
away.

The rock stayed in place, caught in balance.

Taria wanted desperately touch the stone, just to feel that
balance, and yet she knew that if she did, the pressure of
her fingers would inevitably push the stone off-center and
send it all crashing down.

If this was art, it was compelling but yet ephemeral—a
strong wind would ruin it all.

*You need to go, before he notices you're awake. Find
Makes, find a warm bed to crawl into, and maybe Dog will
come back when the swelling goes down . . .*

The thought made Taria stir and try to get to her feet.
The movement betrayed her. The ground beneath the shel-
tering roof was littered with fragments of stone, and they
shifted noisily under her as she stood. She swayed, feeling
nauseous, then fell back to her knees and threw up—
quickly, violently, and noisily. When the spasms passed,
she spat and wiped her mouth on her sleeve. Her head was
throbbing with a migraine that threatened to make her sick
again. Strikes was watching her; he'd moved closer while
she'd been sick. Again she tried to stand up, if only to
move away from the sickening smell of the vomit, but the
muscles in her arm were shuddering and she was suddenly
freezing. All her muscles ached, and she could feel the heat
when she put her hand at her forehead. "Damn . . ." she
said aloud. "My pack . . ."

She looked around for the backpack, which held her
medkit, trying not to move her head too quickly. Strikes
was listening to her, and Taria somehow found that funny.
"You did the thing with the rocks?" she said to him, not
caring that he couldn't possibly understand her. "I like it.
Really, I do." She tried to stand and managed to get upright

this time, though she staggered on the loose scree of rocks under her feet. "But I must be going."

She found herself giggling, and couldn't stop. "Tah-tah, now. I had a wonderful time, but it's too cold here. I don't know how you stand it without clothing, though I imagine if human males had cocks long enough to wrap around their legs, they'd go naked, too, just to show them off." Taria chuckled at the thought. "Am I rambling?" she asked, waving her hand. She sat down again, a little heavily. "*Umph!* Sorry, I guess I'm getting tired. It's so damned *cold.*" She shivered again, hugging herself and drawing her knees up to her chest. Her head, though, was on fire, and nothing was funny anymore. She lay down on the stones. "God, I feel like shit." Her eyes were burning and heavy, feeling almost too large for their sockets, and she could not keep her eyelids open. The migraine was outlining everything in strange colors.

"Here . . ." Taria felt her mother's hand on her shoulder. "Poor baby. Take this. Come on now, darling." Taria opened her eyes, squinting at the familiar shape before her, holding a cup. She took it and drank—bitter, thick fire crawled the length of her throat, and she nearly gagged. "It's okay . . . There there . . ." Her mother's voice grew fainter and fainter, though Taria could still feel her touch, lingering on her skin.

"Mama?" Taria called after her, but her eyelids were closed again, and the bed felt so warm that she couldn't move.

Someone was singing, deep and low. "Papa?" Taria called, but he only kept on singing. She could see him, standing by Mama's coffin as they loaded it on the plane, and he sang long bass notes to her, his body huge and black, sparkling with amber flecks of light. He sang, and Taria felt the song wrap itself around her, throbbing in and through her, and the song drifted in her blood and filled her with a soft warmth.

She saw shapes in the song, saw her mother's face, and

her hand touched her again. "Drink, darling," she said, and Taria drank the liquid fire again while the song droned on, carrying her like a dark, glowing river.

Carrying her.

The song.

The long, low song.

She had no idea how long she'd been asleep or how long she'd been dreaming. Taria lifted her head; her eyelashes were thick with gummy deposits, and her mouth was so parched she could not even swallow. She rubbed at her eyes, and finally managed to get some spittle in her mouth.

She was still in the cave, surrounded by Strikes's "sculptures" of balanced rocks, but she couldn't see anyone. "Hello?" she called, and heard her voice sounding cracked and hoarse. Someone had covered her with a blanket. Her blouse had been opened, and an aromatic unguent was smeared across her breasts. She felt frantically around her neck—the chain with her mother's brooch was still there, and Taria held the jewelry, grasping the silver curve of the brooch tightly in her fist while she glanced around.

A wooden bowl of partially eaten fruit sat nearby, along with a mug that still held a bit of water. Taria sniffed it— there was a sharp, astringent smell to the liquid that brought back memories. She remembered someone making her swallow something. Her mother? No, that was impossible. It must have been the fever causing hallucinations. There were flashes of consciousness, of being sick, of voices around her, but Taria had no concept of how long she might have been delirious.

Her backpack was missing, which meant that her med-kit, Kyung's weapon, and the backup monofoil with its hardware network connection were all gone with it.

"Hello?" she called again. *Dog?* she queried inside her head.

No one answered either call. Taria sat up, waiting until the dizziness passed and she could take inventory. Her bladder clamored for attention—that was suddenly the first priority. She tried standing, and though her legs were unsteady and every muscle protested, she could stand and take a few steps. As to the rest—she could walk, but she was weak, and she would occasionally shiver, as if a fever were lurking just under her awareness.

Moving behind a large rock, Taria unbuckled her pants and, crouching carefully, relieved herself. The urine burned, as if it had been a long time since she'd last urinated. *How long have I been out? A ship-day? Two?* Without Dog, she had no way of knowing, not without the monofoil in her backpack, wherever Strikes had hidden it.

Afterward, Taria moved away from the overhang, going down to the beach. The tide was well out now, and the beach was exposed—pebbly stones leading down to the water—but here and there she could see tracks: a Blue's foot, and also a trough of sand with deep flipper marks on either side—a watersinger dragging itself back to the ocean? she wondered. The beach itself was only a small arc that ended both left and right in sheer cliff walls. Ahead there, the waters of the bay were empty all the way out to where it gave itself to the open ocean. The ocean swells stretched empty before the huge arc of Yang, with a cold spray accompanying the salt breeze in her face. The curving arms of the bay were far too distant to reach by swimming.

No way out. Not that way. Even if she were fully recovered, Taria didn't think she could scale those cliff sides without equipment. She could swim out along this island's coastline and hope she could find a way up a little farther down, but for all she knew, the steep rock walls could go on for kilometers and she'd drown due to cold and exhaustion before she found a place to land.

She looked back at the darkness of the overhang. Strikes got in here somehow, had brought her here. Taria made her way back into the shadows underneath the cliff, walking slowly and carefully. *Like old Auntie Li,* she thought.

The ground sloped down toward the right, and Taria followed the slope deeper into the overhang's shadow. The sharp ridges of snout-shells lined the rocks below her feet now, which meant that this section of the cave was submerged at high tide. Well back in the overhang and maybe another ten feet downslope was an opening in the rock—a true cave entrance that was for the moment dry and open.

Taria glanced back at the bay, at the curving line on the shore that designated the high tide line: the water was a good hundred meters away. She estimated she had at least another few hours before she had to worry about being trapped by the rising water, and without light she couldn't go far inside in any case. She made her way down to the cave entrance.

Someone used the cave, and had been doing so for years: the rocks before the entrance were worn smooth and glossy, and while algae grew along the sides and on the roof, the floor was clean. To Taria's eyes, it looked as if something large had been dragged through here over and over until the stones were polished. *Watersingers?* she wondered.

"Hello?" she called again at the entrance. She listened to the faint echo of her voice. Somewhere beyond, in the blackness, water lapped at stone, and something heavy was moving.

Taria hesitated, unsure. Her body ached: when she felt her forehead it seemed cool enough, though she could feel the weariness in every muscle. But . . . Strikes, it seemed, had taken care of her, had nursed her through the worst of the illness. She was alive, when it would have been simplicity itself to kill her, if that were his intention. That knowledge made Taria fear Strikes less than she had—he'd had been given the opportunity to hurt her, and instead had cared for her. And those sculptures . . . She looked back upslope to where they stood, perched precariously. Whatever Strikes might be, those were the creations of an artist. That by itself didn't preclude violence—she had read too much history to believe that—the classic samurai warrior also studied calligraphy, Zen painting, or flower arranging. But seeing Strikes's contemplative side gave him a sympathy, a fullness that her vision of the kagliaristi had always lacked.

She would be wary of him, but she was no longer afraid.

Her hesitation worked to her advantage. As her eyes adjusted to the dimness, Taria realized that the algae was giving off a faint green phosphorescence, the same glow she'd seen in the Neritorika's chamber.

The Neritorika's chamber was deep under the summit of the island, with a passageway leading out to water, and it flooded at high tide . . .

Taria looked again at the worn, slick stones of the cavern floor, crouching down. There were small tufts of shimmering black hair caught here and there between the rocks—if not the Neritorika herself, then definitely watersingers.

Taria stood, took a breath, and went in.

The rock under her feet felt slippery, and she kept one hand on the moist surface of the wall to steady herself. The glow from the algae, as her eyes continued to adjust to the darkness, was sufficient to give a general image of the passage, if not to see details. The ground sloped slightly downward, and perhaps twenty steps from the entrance, water covered the floor. She went forward to that point and crouched down again at the edge of the still water.

The passageway continued on, relatively straight, sloping down until the roof came within a meter of the water's surface well back. It seemed the passage then opened up into a large room, though the emerald light was so dim and spectral that she couldn't be certain.

She held her breath, listening. There was . . . *something*, a damp and heavy scraping. She started to call out, and stopped herself in mid-breath. She took another breath, letting her hand trail in the water and watching the ripples moving out from her touch. The water was chilly but not too cold.

Taria rose, exhaled once, and took a step forward, wincing and shivering involuntarily as water slipped through the laces of her boots. The water continued to rise as she moved on: to her knees, to her waist, to her chest. She took another few steps—the water was no deeper, so she continued, half expecting with every step that the bottom would suddenly drop out from underneath her. Her clothes were soaked and heavy; she wasn't entirely certain that she had the strength to swim, if it came to that. The algae's glow gave the water an eerie, translucent quality, and a scum of the stuff floated on the surface, coating her with glowing specks of green.

The air changed suddenly. She felt a breeze on her face, and a smell that she recognized. Everything opened up on either side of her, the space widening out. For a moment the details were too dim for her to see. She could hear something, someone moving nearby, could hear the chuffing of a breath and the sounds of movement. Taria stopped, blinking. This was . . . familiar. Though the glow was fainter here, as she waited she began to see the outlines of the room.

The Neritorika's lower chamber. She was standing in the Neritorika's pool.

And the Neritorika and Strikes were both there as well.

She stared for several moments before she understood what she was seeing. Strikes was clasping the Neritorika from behind, and the Neritorika was moving along the back wall of the chamber. There were handholds along the wall, and the Neritorika periodically pulled herself up the wall, until her bulk towered above Strikes. The strange, wet sound that Taria had heard from the passageway continued, and Taria saw that along the wall were pale, oblong lozenges as long as her forearm, all at various heights, as if they'd been glued to the rocky surface.

Strikes moved along behind the Neritorika, occasionally stroking her back, and Taria saw that his genitals were no longer wrapped around his own leg. The long tubular structure snaked around the Neritorika's trunk.

The strange scene fell together for Taria: she remembered playing in the pine woods behind her house in Pensacola in the springtime. A creek ran through the property; in the spring, the spadefoot toads would come out and mate, the smaller male clutching the female like a terrified rodeo rider as she hopped along to the water's edge. There, the female laid her jellied clusters of eggs, attaching them to rocks or plants. The strands of eggs waved in the water, the black specks of the nascent tadpoles just visible inside them . . .

Taria, startled, took a breath. Cold, bright water rippled around her.

The Neritorika was laying eggs, and Strikes was fertilizing them.

Which meant that everything she and the *Lightbringer* crew thought they knew about the Blues was terribly, incredibly wrong.

Kyung knew why Commander Allison had very nearly not let him attend the meeting.

If it were up to him, he'd have already strangled Makes—despite possible biological contamination, despite orders, despite the rift it would undoubtedly cause in interspecies relations.

To Kyung, the Blue was irritatingly evasive. Her answers to each of Allison's questions were hedged, as if Makes was performing some verbal martial art.

Taria's PIA was still missing in the net, and she hadn't used the monofoil in her pack. Once they'd landed, Allison used the outside speaker system to request that the Baraaki come to meet with them. Makes had come to the hover within the hour. She stood outside; Allison and Kyung, behind a transparent air-shield covering the cargo doors, sat inside the shelter of the hover.

"Baraaki," Allison said after the quick introductions. "I thank you for coming, and forgive us for intruding on Little Sister without your permission. We are concerned about Taria, who was returning to you. Have you heard her?"

Makes lifted her arm to point at Kyung. "The Friend-of-Taria took Taria-Who-Wants-to-Understand back to *Lightbringer* to hear you," the Blue said, her Shiplish almost artificially well-pronounced.

"Yes, Baraaki," Allison purred with a glance at Kyung. *They are not to know that we're on-planet,* he'd cautioned Kyung on the way to the city. *Taria made it very clear that the Neritorika was uncomfortable with the idea, and we're not going to tell them otherwise until we have to, especially with Ensign Coen's fate still unknown. Is that understood?*

Kyung understood. He didn't like it; he didn't like *any* of it right now, but he'd nodded.

"However," Allison continued, "Kyung also returned Taria from *Lightbringer* some time ago, and we have not heard from her since."

"Taria sometimes did not want to hear the Voices-That-Only-Taria-Can-Hear, and she told them to leave her alone."

"That's true, but the network—the Voices—would still be able to know that Taria was connected to it. She is not. She didn't return to you?"

"No," Makes replied simply. If the Blue was concerned, Kyung could not hear it in her strange voice.

"Would you know where she might be?"

"No."

"Is there some other authority here who we should contact for help? We know Taria met a kagliaristi."

"I know now, and I will tell the other baraalideish and the Neritorika. That is all that can be done."

"We are concerned that Taria may be injured or perhaps very ill," Allison persisted, with a glance at Kyung. "A blow to the head might have caused her to lose contact with the . . . the Voices-Only-Taria-Can-Hear. A severe fever might have done the same."

Or she might be dead. Allison didn't say it, but Kyung could hear the unvoiced thought. "I brought Taria here, Baraaki," Kyung broke in. "Right here. She got out of the hover by that bridge over there, and I saw her as I left. There were a couple Blues working the fields there. They saw—heard—me; they had to notice Taria. You may not care, but I most emphatically do, and we *will* find her."

"Ensign," Allison said sharply. "That will be quite sufficient."

Kyung flushed as he set his jaw, muscles bunching. "Sir," he said, his voice clipped and short, but Allison had already turned away from him.

"As you can hear, Ensign Xiong is quite concerned, as am I," Allison purred, sounding to Kyung's ears like an oily, too-smooth salesperson. "I'm sure the Children-of-She-Who-Spoke-the-World can understand that, and would feel the same if our positions were reversed."

The strange, wriggling earlets on Makes's head-crest were still pointed toward Kyung. "You speak to Taria in Mandarin, in the Language-of-Intimacy," she said. It took Kyung a moment to realize that the Blue was talking to him—the eyestrip gave no visual cues.

"Yes," he said, feeling Allison watching him carefully. "I do." *And what the hell does that have to do with this?* he wanted to add, but Allison's stare made Kyung hold back.

What Makes said next surprised Kyung. "I do also," she told him in Mandarin that mimicked Taria's accented tones. "That is something we share with Taria-Who-Wants-to-Understand. I will find her, if I can, because of that. Because she has helped me, and keeping face demands it."

Kyung hesitated, then gave a slight bow of his head that

he belatedly remembered the Blue could not possibly see. *"Xiexie,"* he said: Thank you.

Taria realized she must have made a sound as she started to back out of the Neritorika's chamber: a splash of glowing water, a breath. The Neritorika turned, Strikes—still intimately attached to her—moving with her. The Neritorika grumbled something in her own language, but without Dog, Taria couldn't translate the words. When Taria didn't answer, the Neritorika vented air, then spoke again. "I hear you, Taria-Baraaki," she said.

Impossibly, she spoke in Shiplish.

But I am not a Baraaki, she wanted to answer. Taria hesitated, part of her aching to flee back the way she'd come, but there was nothing there but the crescent of a beach, the cliffs, and a rising tide. There was no escape that way.

Nor this. Strikes's head-crest was raised and the earlets fluttered in her direction. The finger-knives were missing, but Strikes still looked muscular and formidable, especially weakened as she was. Even if she managed to get past Strikes, Taria remembered all too well the twisting, unlighted passages that led down here. She would never make it back to the surface, not before she was captured or became hopelessly lost. She was effectively trapped.

"I hear you also, Neritorika," Taria answered. "I didn't think you knew my language."

"It's something you didn't ask. Come here," the Neritorika said. Blue firefly sparks shimmered in her black fur as she spoke. Her words were unmistakably a command, strangely compelling, and Taria had taken a step toward the Neritorika before she realized it. "Come here," the Neritorika said again.

Water swirled around Taria as she walked toward the two, coiling streams of bright water in her wake. Strikes had withdrawn from the Neritorika, his flamboyant genitals wrapped again around his right leg as he waited. The water shallowed as Taria approached them, then she stepped out of the pool, dripping water on the stones and shivering in the chill, hugging herself. Now that she was close, she could see the Neritorika's eggs: the hand-sized dark shape of the fetus, a yolk sack partially surrounding it. They looked gelid, and were losing their translucence as she watched. Already the first eggs had turned opaque. In the glow of the algae, they looked almost gray.

"We were wrong," Taria said. She glanced from the Neritorika to Strikes. "We thought . . ." Her teeth were chattering, she took a breath.

"Yes," the Neritorika said. "You didn't understand." She had moved, without Taria realizing it, and was now standing alongside her. Taria could feel the heat from the Neritorika's body warming her. She wanted to do nothing more than come closer to the Neritorika, to fold herself into that warmth. The Neritorika's thick arms went around her, as if she had heard the unspoken wish, and Taria allowed herself to be pulled in. The Neritorika's fur was silken fire, and Taria burrowed into it. A smell of spicy musk clung to her, not unpleasant but strong, and her skin was more oily than Taria remembered from their last meeting. But the Neritorika was warm, and bright sparks flew wherever she and Taria touched. "Does that help?" the Neritorika rumbled.

Taria felt more than heard her voice. "Yes," she whispered. "Thank you."

They remained that way for what seemed to be minutes. The Neritorika didn't speak, but she gave voice to long, throaty notes spanning several octaves at once, singing like the watersingers she resembled. Taria was content to stay there, to let the heat soak into her and listen. The bass notes throbbed against her body, an aural massage. She thought she heard Strikes moving about the chamber, but she didn't look up, staying clasped in the Neritorika's embrace. She felt, for the moment, safe and protected—like a child, she realized, curled up on her mother's lap.

After a time, the Neritorika's song ended and her arms relaxed around Taria. Reluctantly, Taria stepped away. Her clothes were still damp, but some of the chill had left the air. Her muscles ached, her sinuses pounded, and there was an uncomfortable absence in her mind where Dog usually resided. Taria wanted nothing more than to lay down and sleep. "You still have your illness," the Neritorika said. "The Heat-From-Within was bad enough that I thought you would die, but Strikes-the-Air-in-Anger would not let that happen. The kagliaristi saved your life, but there's more to do. You are different, and your body doesn't respond to the herbs as ours do."

Taria glanced at Strikes, who listened from a few feet away. She remembered the way the crowd had ignored the Blue who died near the vendor stand when she'd been out alone in the city, how they'd said the dying Blue had "nothing to offer." She wondered what Strikes thought she had to offer. "Then let me thank Strikes for nursing me through the fever. But now I need to let my people know where I am. If they come looking for me, they may not be . . . gentle about it."

"No," the Neritorika said, a dark explosion of a word. "They may *not* come here. Only you."

They're already here, she wanted to tell the Neritorika, but Allison had stressed the importance of keeping that secret. "Then let me tell them where I am, that I'm all right. That way they'll stay where they are. My backpack—"

"No."

"Why, Neritorika?"

"Because I don't wish it," the Neritorika answered.

There seemed to be no easy answer to that. A hundred questions crowded Taria's head, and she didn't know which one to ask: *Why did Strikes bring me here? Why did he take care of me? You don't even look like the same species, and yet Strikes is fertilizing your eggs—how is that possible? Do you really hear my thoughts? What are the*

Greater Singers? Did they have anything to do with Thunder vanishing? Her head hurt and the questions would not hold still long enough for her to ask.

Instead Taria went to the wall and looked closely at one of the eggs. It was entirely opaque now, the surface hard in appearance. She wanted to touch it; she lifted a hand and then stopped, looking back at the Neritorika—if she noticed the gesture, she didn't react. "I'm . . ." *sorry*, Taria was about to say, then started over. "I didn't intend to interrupt you, not while you were . . . well . . ."

The Neritorika's hand stroked Taria's side. A step away, Strikes waited. "Reproduction is private for humans?"

"Usually, yes. Is it the same for Children-of-She-Who-Spoke-the-World?"

"Sometimes." The Neritorika's hand continued to stroke Taria. "I haven't yet decided whether this is one of those times. You are . . . new. And you are changed from what you were."

"And if you should decide that this *was* one of those private times, what then?"

"Then Strikes-the-Air-in-Anger would decide what to do with you, since he is most like you."

"You told me that he just nursed me back to health."

The Neritorika vented air. "If you think that would stop him from ending your life if it were necessary, then you don't know the kagliaristi at all."

"I am the Baraaki, and I will speak to the Neritorika," Makes said in the Language-of-Command. "You will escort me to her." The audible glow from the Lesser Light—invisible to the humans—pulsed in shimmering, dark waves around the Neritorika's hilltop, the reflections from the building forming an aural image. Makes-the-Sound-of-East-Wind wondered how strange the world must appear for the humans, whose range of hearing was impossibly narrow. The high tones of the Language-of-Command sent sharp spearlike ripples through the aural-light toward the baraalideish who stood there.

The baraalideish felt the challenge pulse hard against her chest, for she took an involuntary step backward. She gave the soft, lower-pitched sound of negation, but Makes-the-Sound-of-East-Wind could hear the waver in her voice, which left the challenge still pointed and sharp. Disobedience to the Baraaki would not be condoned unless the Neritorika had given specific instructions otherwise, and the fact that this one could defy the Baraaki told Makes-the-Sound-of-East-Wind that the Neritorika had expected her arrival.

Which in turn made Makes-the-Sound-of-East-Wind suspect that the Neritorika knew about Taria-Who-Wants-to-Understand and what had happened to her.

Makes-the-Sound-of-East-Wind had made the inquiries she had promised to Kyung-Who-Speaks-in-Fury. The field workers had indeed heard Taria-Who-Wants-to-Understand, and they had told the Baraaki that Strikes-the-Air-in-Anger had met the human at the bridge. She had been ill, they said. They had heard her coughing and the sound of sickness in her breath, and they could see the Heat-From-Within that shone from her—bright enough, they said, that they were surprised the human was even alive. That alone hadn't worried Makes-the-Sound-of-East-Wind; she had been with the humans enough to feel that their body temperature was higher than her own, so she assumed that Taria-Who-Wants-to-Understand might well survive a fever that would kill a Blue. But she had fallen, the field workers claimed, and Strikes-the-Air-in-Anger had taken her away—to where, of course, they didn't know.

She felt her skin cool with that news, and knew that the field workers saw it, too, though they said nothing.

Makes-the-Sound-of-East-Wind then made inquiries among the kagliaristi. Even her status and Language-of-

Command had done little with them. None of them claimed to have heard Strikes-the-Air-in-Anger since Taria-Who-Wants-to-Understand had returned, nor would they suggest to Makes-the-Sound-of-East-Wind where she might listen for her.

As Baraaki, she had ordered the baraalideish of Gruriterashpali to make inquiries within the city—it seemed no one had heard the human at all.

The humans were impatient. Already Allison-Who-Speaks-Empty-Words had returned twice to ask Makes-the-Sound-of-East-Wind whether she had found Taria yet. Once Kyung-Who-Speaks-in-Fury had accompanied the other human, but he was obviously distraught at the news, and the next time it was another human who brought Allison-Who-Speaks-Empty-Words. Makes-the-Sound-of-East-Wind had heard the threats that lay under the human's thin tones. She remembered how Taria-Who-Wants-to-Understand had destroyed the small island with a word, and she worried.

The Baraaki had prayed, as well. It seemed the only choice she had left. But She-Who-Spoke-the-World was as silent to her Baraaki as the sky-voice. All the doubts she had felt for over twenty cycles now began to assail Makes-the-Sound-of-East-Wind again, and she meditated for a long time before she could calm herself enough to leave her chambers. The silence from the Emptiness-Above-Us mocked her, and though the other baraalideish said nothing, Makes-the-Sound-of-East-Wind knew that the baraalideish passing outside her chambers had heard her entreaties to She-Who-Spoke-the-World. They all knew that the sky-voice that had made her Baraaki remained silent. The latest failure of the Baraaki would be whispered throughout the Gruriterashpali.

Makes-the-Sound-of-East-Wind could think of nothing else to do but go to the Neritorika. She would confess her failure; she would ask the Neritorika for help.

If the Neritorika would hear her. "You will escort me,"

Makes-the-Sound-of-East-Wind said again to the baraali-deish, but the guard still made no move.

"This one desires to obey," she replied obsequiously in the Language-of-Obedience, as status demanded. But though the baraalideish took another step back under the Baraaki's verbal assault, she then planted her feet. Makes-the-Sound-of-East-Wind heard the iron inside her stance. "But the Neritorika gave this one explicit commands, and though it pains this one to deny the Baraaki what she desires, this one must obey the Neritorika."

Makes-the-Sound-of-East-Wind wanted to turn and walk away, even if it meant that she must go back to Kyung-Who-Speaks-in-Fury and Allison-Who-Speaks-Empty-Words and admit her incompetence. Instead she stomped on the ground once to indicate her annoyance and persisted. "What I have to say to the Neritorika is of utmost importance, and your impertinence and disobedience harms all of the Children-of-She-Who-Spoke-the-World. If you will not take me to the Neritorika, then you will go to her yourself and tell her that I wait to speak with her, or tell one of the other baraalideish to do so. I order this as your Baraaki."

The poor guard visibly shuddered and took another step backward before stopping, waving her arms so that Makes-the-Sound-of-East-Wind saw the eddies in the aural-light. "Even that small task this one cannot do, Baraaki. The Neritorika was very explicit about her wishes not to be disturbed."

Makes-the-Sound-of-East-Wind stamped her foot again. "You must," she insisted, but this time the baraalideish did not even reply in the Language-of-Obedience, but the Language-of-Formality, and Makes-the-Sound-of-East-Wind knew that she had lost. "I cannot, Baraaki," she said. "I hear your concern, but it is not possible. I will tell the Neritorika that you were here when she emerges from her chamber, but that is all I can do."

Makes-the-Sound-of-East-Wind could only reply in the

same language. "Then I ask that you do so. Tell her that the Baraaki must speak to her immediately, that it has to do with the humans and the one called Taria-Who-Wants-to-Understand. Tell her that."

The baraalideish made the sound of acceptance then. "I will, Baraaki."

Makes-the-Sound-of-East-Wind sounded her own agreement and went down from the hilltop, each step sending waves shuddering through the sound-landscape around her. She didn't know what she would tell the humans. She didn't know how they would react once they knew that Taria-Who-Wants-to-Understand was still missing.

She didn't know, and She-Who-Spoke-the-World would not tell her.

"Let me go, Neritorika," Taria said.

It must have been hours later. Taria had hesitantly taken a draught of some green, thick liquid from Strikes, after the Neritorika had insisted it was medicine that would help her. The stuff had tasted awful, salty and somewhat fishy, and a few minutes afterward she found herself unable to stand, unable to talk without slurring her words, unable to keep her eyes open. She must have been moved at some point; when she awoke, she was on a balcony along one wall of the Neritorika's chamber and water was sloshing halfway up the walls, submerging a number of the eggs the Neritorika had laid. From the tidal marks on the wall, from the way the glowing algae stopping growing at about the same point, she knew this must be high tide. The way out to the beach lay a good three or four meters underneath the surface, and the beach itself would be nearly gone, only the barest strip left and Strikes's rock sculptures threatened by the waves.

"I am not holding you, Taria-Baraaki," the Neritorika answered. "No one is holding you." The Neritorika stood near the edge of the balcony. There was no rail, no ledge there—the balcony simply ended, with a ten-meter drop to the cold, glowing water below. Strikes was nowhere to be seen—he'd been gone when Taria woke. A few strides away, cold air flowed from the mouth of a passageway that emptied out onto the narrow balcony. Taria kept her back to the stone wall, wanting the comfort of the solid, harsh rock.

"Then take me back. Or have one of your baraalideish escort me. I'm . . . I'm feeling much better." That was at least partially true. She could still feel the fatigue in her muscles and a residue of the fever deep inside. But her head *was* clearer now, though a mist obscured her memories of the last day or so, made them seem impossibly distant and long ago.

"I can do that," the Neritorika answered. She seemed to take a long breath, a whistling that rose slowly in pitch. Her midnight fur rippled along her spine, and the collar of earlets flicked back and forth. "But if you go, will your questions be answered?"

"I don't have questions."

"You do. I hear them in your breath. Listen around you, Taria-Baraaki. It is often dark for you, and when you can't see, you think you can't understand. The world may be dark, but the world is never silent. It always sings. There are things here for which you can't even phrase the question, for you don't even realize your lack of knowledge. If you go, if I call the baraalideish now and have them take you back, you will never know them."

Wavelets slapped at the walls. The greenish light of the algae swayed and moved, alive. The eggs attached to the wall which were above water were now yellow and opaque, no longer gelid. *Listen around you . . . The world always sings . . .* Taria closed her eyes. She could hear the movement of the water, the echoing *plunk* of droplets falling from somewhere close by. She could hear her own breath flowing, the quiet rasp of cloth as she moved, the

Neritorika's harsher, louder breath. Even more softly, she could hear the hollow sound of the cave's own respiration, the flow of air through the passageways.

And underneath, sotto voce, there was something else, something she would not have heard had she not been listening for it: the chorus of watersingers, far away and distant. Taria was not even sure she really heard the song—it was nearly drowned out by the faint ringing in her ears, and when she tried to concentrate on the watersingers' melody, it faded away entirely.

"There is so much you don't feel," the Neritorika said. Taria's eyes flew open, she gasped. The Neritorika's voice seemed impossibly loud, obliterating the subtle nuances of sound she had discovered. "You are awash in vibrations, and you only notice such a narrow range of them. The world sings to you, the Greater Light and the Lesser Light add their own voices, and you cannot hear them." The Neritorika paused. She took a step closer to Taria, so that Taria could smell the spice odor of the creature and could see the blue sparks twinkling deep in the satin fur. "What did your mother say about singing, Taria? What questions might she have asked?"

Despite his frustration, Kyung almost felt sorry for Makes. The disappointment in the Blue's voice was so deep and heartfelt that he couldn't be angry with the Baraaki at all.

Which was just as well. Allison would have pulled him at the first indication of an outburst, and had Makes been anything but perfectly contrite, the outburst would have been inevitable. Taria had been missing for over forty-eight ship-hours now, and there had still been no contact from her or Dog. *Lightbringer* was still tumbling through space—it appeared more and more certain that the crew would need Little Sister as a haven.

They didn't need a hostile race to complicate the situation.

Makes had insisted on talking to Kyung alone, and Allison grudgingly permitted Kyung to go to Makes in the Gruriterashpali, with Kyung encased in a biohazard suit. The suit was uncomfortable and the faceplate kept fogging up, so that Kyung saw Makes and her rooms through the slight haze of his own breath. A vidcam was mounted on the visor, allowing Allison to monitor the meeting, and Kyung's avatar Tee was closely linked to the Cube.

Kyung suspected that half of ExoAnthro and a good portion of Admiral McElwan's staff were also silent observers.

Makes insisted on speaking in Mandarin. It was obvious that Taria had taught her the language—Makes had Taria's accent and mistakes in tones. She spoke the language like a New Zealander who had learned the language early and was out of practice. Kyung had no illusion that this gave them any privacy; he knew that even if Allison didn't know Mandarin, the ship's network did, and the Cube was feeding everyone a running translation.

"I have searched for Taria-Who-Wants-to-Understand, and I have spoken to those who saw her last. No one will tell me where she is." Makes vented air, almost like a human sound of frustration. "Strikes-the-Air-in-Anger is also missing, or the kagliaristi will simply not tell me where he has gone."

"Then we find this Strikes and we'll find Taria." Even knowing Allison was listening, the worry and anger still tumbled out. "Tell *me* where to find him."

"You would kill him," Makes answered. Kyung couldn't tell whether that thought bothered the Baraaki or not. "I hear the anger in your voice. What would that solve? How would that make things better?"

"I wouldn't kill him," Kyung said. *Not right away, anyway* . . . "I want Taria, not revenge." A pause. "Unless I can't have Taria. Then I suppose revenge will have to do. Is that something you understand, Makes?"

In his head, Tee hissed. *Kyung, careful . . . Allison's getting edgy after that last comment . . .*

"No," Makes said. "I understand the word and what it means, but not the emotions that go with it. It's nothing we do."

Kyung glanced from the window to the balcony and beyond, to the cliff of the Neritorika's island, with the sea high against the rocks. What he wanted to see was hidden somewhere underneath the blue-green waves. "The chains . . . the story you told Taria about how the Neritorika hung the kagliaristi. That wasn't revenge?"

"If you think so, then it's clear you don't understand us at all," Makes answered.

Kyung drummed his fingers against his thighs, staring at the fabric of his blue uniform pants without seeing it.

"You care very much for Taria, Kyung-Who-Speaks-in-Fury."

"Yes." Kyung nodded. "Is there someone you care about the same way? Is there someone you love?"

"Not in that way," Makes answered, and Kyung could detect neither sorrow nor regret in her voice, only a soft statement of fact. "That way isn't possible for me. For us."

"You don't understand revenge, you don't understand love. How can you help me, Makes?"

The words came in high, singsong Mandarin. "Is that all life is for you, either revenge or love?"

Despite himself, Kyung smiled. "Now you sound like her, Makes. No. Of course not. Life is a thousand other things. But can you understand what I feel?"

"No. No more than you can understand what I feel. We're not the same; we can never be the same. But I *can* take you to where I believe Taria is. I think I know where to find her."

"When? When can you take me?"

"Now," the Blue answered softly. "We can go now."

From inside came Allison's sudden, growling voice. *"No, Ensign. No. I know what you're thinking, I understand your feelings, but you can't. Find out this location from the Baraaki, and we will put together a response team—I'll make certain you're part of that team. In the meantime, you will return to the shuttle in ten minutes— you only have half an hour of air left in your suit, and you're up on the safety factor we agreed on. That's an order, Ensign."*

"Now?" Kyung answered Makes. "Are you certain Taria's there?"

"Certain? No. But I can't think of where else she could be if she is still alive," Makes answered.

There was only one choice in his heart. Only one choice he could make. "I'll go with you."

"Ensign, you are jeopardizing Taria's life by doing this, not to mention your career. If she's already dead, you can't help her; if she's not, then you endanger her by going without backup and resources. Don't be foolish here."

"You're listening to the Voices-Only-Taria-Can-Hear," Makes said. "You hear them also?"

"Yes. I'm afraid I do."

"Taria didn't seem to like what they said."

Inside the hood of the biosuit Kyung smiled at that. "I can understand. Will you take me to where you think Taria is, Makes? Will you take me there now?"

"Ensign . . ."

"Yes," Makes answered.

"Consider this another experiment, Commander," Kyung subvocalized through Tee. Kyung touched the seals of the biosuit's helmet, and air hissed. He pulled off the helmet and shook his head. "Let's go," he said to Makes.

Little Sister's air was sweet and cool, a breeze ran fluttering fingers along his skin from the window, and Makes smelled faintly of licorice and spice. Kyung took in deep draughts of the atmosphere, as if he could take in Taria's presence with his breath.

With the tide down, the Neritorika had gone back down to the pool level. She made no effort to force Taria to come with her, but Taria had followed her despite that, feeling she had little choice. Strikes had returned to the balcony, and he accompanied them.

The Neritorika immediately went to examine the eggs she'd laid along the wall. Taria watched the Neritorika stroke them (fans of translucent flesh between the fingers—a swimming creature's hands), then Taria examined them more closely herself. They were cemented to the stones by glistening strands. The ones highest along the wall had been out of the water entirely; the lowest had been submerged ever since the waves had first lapped over the edge of the pool.

The bright specks of algae clung to and around the lower eggs, coating them. They glowed fiercely in the dark, brighter than the algae on the stones, as if the life inside fed the light. Two of the eggs were laid at the midpoint of the water line, and these eggs were larger than the others, with a pale mottled blue in the otherwise white shell.

Strikes was at her shoulder. Taria could feel the occasional touch of his hand and the pressure of his locational grunts against her body. At least the fever had gone, even if she still felt weak. The Neritorika had said that she owed Strikes her life, and she wondered why he had bothered with her. But those questions she didn't ask. Instead she moved closer to the Neritorika, watching the azure sparks within the night of her fur.

"Neritorika, I don't understand. On my world some creatures lay their eggs in the water, and others on the land, but not both. Won't the water drown the low eggs, or won't the high ones be too dry?"

"If I laid them all high or low, then they would all be the same when they hatch," the Neritorika answered.

"All the same?"

"All Children-of-She-Who-Spoke-the-World, or all Singers-From-the-Water, or all Neritorika. It is the water that determines which."

Taria's breath snagged itself deep in her chest. The implications fluttered her heart, made the blood pulse in her temple. She remembered Comparative Biology classes— remembered how they'd looked at egg-bearers, how the amount of heat a crocodile egg received determined the sex of the embryo . . . "You're all the same species, aren't you? We've completely missed that: the eyestrip, the way you use hearing, the multiple range of your voices . . ." She remembered Makes killing the old watersinger on the beach: *The meat of Singers-From-the-Water tastes good* . . . Her stomach recoiled, remembering the slabs of pinkish flesh on the food trays in Makes's room. *You can't judge,* she told herself. *That's the first lesson you learned, and the hardest. Think of all the animals on Earth that will eat their own kind.*

Taria felt Strikes's hand graze her shoulder again, sliding down her side almost possessively. She glanced at him, realizing that the only males she'd ever noticed in the Blue community were also kagliaristi.

Kagliaristi. Not simply "warriors," but also males. Makes had given them the hint during the second meeting, when she and Allison had spoken briefly about sex. *So if a person is not-male, they are female and you would not use "he"?* That's what Makes had asked Allison, and Allison had told Makes that she was correct—because for humans, that would be true. A person "not-male" was female. Therefore Makes was female. Therefore all the other Blues except kagliaristi were female.

Simple. And in this case, wrong.

Makes had thought she'd understood the terminology; the humans had thought they'd understood Makes's interpretation, and they'd all been wrong. "Makes *can't* reproduce, can she? None of the Blue . . . Children-of-She-Who-Spoke-the-World ever lay their own eggs. None of them will ever have the kagliaristi fertilize them. They're not able to have offspring at all."

"No." There was neither surprise nor condescension in the Neritorika's voice. Just a low, many-toned negative.

"Do they know this, the Children-of-She-Who-Spoke-the-World? Do they know how they—you—reproduce?"

"Of course. My baraalideish will come for the eggs when it's time and help them hatch. The hatchlings who come from the Eggs-of-the-Children will be taken to the Keepers-of-Those-Not-Yet-Real until it's time for them to choose their Guardian-of-the-Right-Spirit and their Life-Task. The hatchlings from the Eggs-of-the-Singers will be given to the Singers-From-the-Water who will come here for them."

"And you, Neritorika? What are you?"

The Neritorika laughed. Taria had never heard Makes laugh, had never heard any of the Blues give voice to amusement. But "laughter" was the only way Taria had to describe the wash of pure, joyful sound that came from the Neritorika's mouth with her question, a sound like cold, bright water cascading over granite boulders, like wind rushing through a stand of mountain pines. "I am one of Those-Who-Change. The rare ones. At the moment, I am Between," she said. "I wait to Become."

"Between where? Become what?"

The Neritorika seemed to consider that question for a moment, then she lumbered toward the pool, moving ungracefully across the stones to the water. "Come with me," she said, and dove into the water. In the water, the Neritorika was fluid and quick, her dark body cutting through the slate-gray waves. "Come with me," she said again as Taria hesitated at the edge of the water. "You need to see them again."

"I'm still cold," she said. "The water—"

"Come with me," the Neritorika said again, and dove under the water. Taria stood at the edge of the pool, shaking her head, her clothes still damp and clammy from her last immersion. She heard a voice, a song, coming from the tunnel that led out to the beach where Strikes had left her. The song echoed in the darkness, a high voice Taria remembered too well.

"*Po atarau, e moea iho nei . . .*"

"Damn it," she said, hot tears filling her eyes. "Damn it, that's not fair."

She let herself down into the pool, grimacing as the frigid water covered her. She half swam, half waded in pursuit of the Neritorika and the voice.

Allison took several long, slow breaths. He clenched his left hand into a fist, feeling the pressure of fingernails against palm. "Enter into the record that Ensign Xiong disobeyed a direct order and has violated the regulations set down by ExoAnthro for contact with an alien race."

So entered, the quiet, calm voice of his avatar answered.

Allison glanced at the faces of the ExoAnthro team's avatars, which were gathered around the table with him while the actual team members were still aboard *Lightbringer*. "I will need each of you to give a deposition of this incident to your PIAs," he said. "You may also be called upon to testify at a disciplinary hearing."

Each of the avatars nodded, and he heard a muttered "Yes, sir" from the group. Allison relaxed his hand. He could see four curved indentations in his palm, bloodred against white. "I'll take overall responsibility for this. Obviously, my decision to allow Lieutenant Xiong access to the Blues was a mistake." Allison exhaled sharply through his nose. "I will continue to monitor this situation, and we'll record the lieutenant's PIA feed. You will all be given access to that information, of course. For the time being, there's no reason to hold your avatars here. Thank you for attending, and I will discuss this further at our regular 1800 meeting this evening."

The son of a bitch, he added to himself. *I should never have let Spears go down there in the first place, should have kept to the original plan that only unis would have direct contact . . .*

One by one the avatars blinked out of existence, until Allison was seated alone at the table, with only the plain geometric shape of his own avatar visible. "Give me Ensign Xiong's PIA feed," he said to the Cube, and heard the soft tone in his head that meant obedience. There was only silence on the channel, though—Kyung was not talking to his avatar, nor was the avatar actively doing anything in the network.

Something shimmered on the gray wall, like a movement caught in the corner of his eye: not so much dark as a total absence of light, though there was an afterimage of bright blue-white sparks. Allison blinked and stared; there was nothing there but wall. He rubbed his eyes—dealing with Xiong had been stressful, and he was tired. Still . . . "Security check," he said to the Cube.

There was a pause, then the scratch of a voice in his head: Perez, head of the marine squad. *"Personnel are accounted for, Commander, except for Ensign Xiong. All the sector alarms are showing green. Something up, Commander?"*

"No. Not really. Just . . ." Allison sighed and blinked heavily again. The wall was still a wall. ". . . checking on things," he said. "Thank you." He pushed away from the table. The room was small—everything here was small and tidy and clean. Of the *Lightbringer*'s complement of some fourteen hundred men and women, only two dozen were downworld on Little Sister, living in the temporary shelter—two dozen and one, Allison corrected himself, assuming Spears was still alive. Two dozen and *two*, if Coen was also still alive somewhere.

Frankly, Allison hated the place.

Lightbringer smelled of people, of sweat and life and breath, of steel and life. Down here the air was scrubbed and antiseptic, and it smelled of . . . nothing. There was life all around them—alien, yes, but life nonetheless—and yet they held it away with sprays and scrubbers and walls. They bathed it in radiation and heat and antiseptics. Like a mollusk huddling in whorls of bright color, they blanketed themselves in a fragile shell and cowered inside it.

The truth was that Allison almost envied Xiong and Spears their freedom, their ability to smell and taste and move unencumbered in this world.

There was a sound, a low note throbbing almost below the range of hearing. Allison narrowed his eyes, cocking his head to one side as he listened. Yes, there it was again, below . . . no, all around him, moving now away to his left, toward the rear of their encampment.

"Perez?"

"We hear it, Commander. We're checking . . ."

The sound continued, louder now and with a complex shifting of tones built into it. Allison could feel the floor trembling under his feet in response, and when he placed his hand on the wall, he could feel the throbbing through the plastifiber. "Earthquake?" he asked the air.

"No, sir. The seismic monitors are all quiet. Whatever this is, it's extremely localiz— Shit!"

"Perez?"

There was silence in his head for a moment, but Allison heard the new sound, a ripping, tearing metallic shriek, and the whole building seemed to lift and drop a few centimeters. Allison staggered, off balance; the table and chairs all scraped across the floor, moving nearly a half meter. The projected image of the Cube, disconcertingly, remained where it was, hanging in space now. An alarm in the corridor outside started hooting; the power went off, then came back again. "Perez?"

No longer in the system, came the quiet, calm voice of his avatar, followed almost immediately by another. *"Commander, this is Ensign Ballior. Lieutenant Commander Perez is . . . gone, sir. The whole back canopy and half the rear wall were just ripped away—he was standing there, and he and three of the others are . . . just gone. Christ . . . I swear there's something moving out there. What should we do? I don't know what to do, sir!"* The voice was loud and increasingly shrill and Allison could hear the fright in it.

Allison had never been in combat. He was a tech officer, and his service had been largely behind a terminal or in the classroom. Nothing he'd done had prepared him for this, and he had no answer for the man. Allison's breath was caught in his throat. The alarm was still wailing, and the low rumbling had quieted. *Is it over?* he wondered. *Is this a weather event, or some kind of earth slippage? Is it done?*

Then the low roar started to build once more, like a mad bass chorus singing a cluster of dissonant half-tones, and the floor began to shudder again. In his head, Allison heard shouts and screams. The building bucked, this time sending him down and throwing the tables and chairs against the far wall. The power went off, and stayed off this time, and red-tinged emergency lights came on from the wall-strips. In his head Allison felt the local intranet collapse with a disconcerting moment of static before his neural net flicked over to *Lightbringer*'s remote access. Someone close by was screaming. "Broadcast," Allison shouted to the Cube, then heard his own voice echoing in his head through the network as he spoke. *"This is Commander Allison. All personnel move immediately to* Galileo. *I repeat, all personnel to the shuttle.* Galileo *crew, prepare for immediate departure as soon as everyone's aboard."*

Retreat. Flee. Words that matched the panic rising in his chest. Allison pushed himself off the floor and went to the door—it ignored him, and he had to manually wrench it open. There were people in the corridor, jogging with concerned faces toward the exit to the shuttlecraft, and Allison allowed himself to be caught up in the flow. He was coughing from the dust thrown up by the building's shaking, and air moved against his face—they were breached, then, and they were all breathing Little Sister's air.

Allison felt a moment of panic, then forced himself to take a slow breath. *We're heading for isolation, then, when we return to* Lightbringer. *I can deal with that. I'll have to deal with that. The important thing is to get out of here.*

"Let's go! Move!" he shouted to the others in the hallway, waving a hand at them and following himself. The air was chilly now, and carried the sharpness of ozone.

The sounds came again, and the floor shook itself. He could actually see the ripple moving down the hallway toward him, dying in a wave of cracked plastic just before it reached him. Allison stared in horrified wonder for a moment. The alarms went silent, abruptly, leaving them in eerie silence except for the continuing low growl that seemed to permeate the entire site. *Move! Get out!* he broadcast, not knowing whether he was talking to himself or the rest of the crew.

Allison turned a corner, moving at the back of the crowd through the dining hall, then into the Decon chamber which led to the shuttle tube. *Galileo* itself was connected to the building by an umbilical passageway; it was still intact, and Allison ran through it to the open hatchway. Hands pulled him inside. "The net says you're the last one, Commander. Thirty seconds or less to takeoff. Better grab a seat—Benander says it's gonna be a rough ride."

There were maybe a dozen people in the passenger compartment—if the full crew of three was aboard, that meant only fifteen people had made it to the shuttle. Allison's stomach churned. He nodded, then pulled himself up the ladder toward the pilots' compartment. The pilot—a woman Allison assumed was Benander—turned once to glance at him, then returned to barking off the flight checklist to the navigator. An observer's seat was still vacant and Allison took it, strapping himself in and looking out the tiny window. The glass was fogged with scratches and filmed with dirt, but he could see the building. Whatever had hit it had torn away half of it, like some jagged claw cutting through the structure. Plastibeams jutted out like broken teeth from where the roof was sheared away, and sheeting curled like paper in the wreckage.

There was movement out there, too, and Allison rubbed futilely at the glass in an effort to see better. Something . . .

A glimpse of darkness shot with blue sparks, a huge, shimmering arc that seemed to rise from the ground like it was the surface of the sea, a moving thing that made his eyes ache when he stared directly toward it, as if it were more an absence, a void in his sight. At the same time that hideous low, mad chorus began again, and this time Allison felt *Galileo* itself shudder under the sonic assault.

"Let's move!" he shouted to the pilot, who glared at him and continued her litany. Outside, the apparition had disappeared, and Allison wondered whether he'd really seen it. Vibrations shook the ship, rattling his teeth with a protest of steel and plastic . . .

. . . then a new roar intruded on the song of destruction from outside, and the ship began to move as Benander rammed the throttles full on. Wild acceleration slammed Allison back in his seat and he could barely turn his head to look out, but he thought he saw the building collapse into rubble as the vertical lift jet shoved them away from the ground. The nose lifted, the main jets shrieked, and they were away and turning, and the sudden, deafening wail of the orbital thrusters was the most wonderful sound he'd ever heard.

The beach was much the same as Taria remembered, though the relentless waves of high tide had destroyed Strikes's exquisitely balanced sculptures. The stacks of boulders were all knocked down, half buried in sand brought in by the tide. The Neritorika was down near the beach, several meters away. Taria shivered in the breeze, her soaked clothing cold against her skin and goose bumps puckering her forearms. Yang was hidden behind a mask of gray, lowering clouds that seemed to make the wind even colder. Grimacing, Taria moved toward where the Neritorika stood, half submerged in the now quiet surf.

As Taria approached, the Neritorika sounded a cluster of low, dissonant notes, holding the notes for a long breath while the sound echoed from the cliffs that flanked them on the inlet. When the echoes had faded, the Neritorika sounded them again, and this time, faintly, there was an answer, almost more felt than heard, a rumble that shivered the rocks under Taria's feet.

And something began to rise from the surface of the water, a shape Taria had seen once before: a Greater Singer.

As before, it lifted from the shallow water as if it were rising from a bottomless sea, its bulk far too large to be contained in the water alone. As it rose, the volume of its call increased, and Taria shouted against the thunder of it, staring even though she could not look directly at the thing—it was like looking into a blind spot. There was nothing there, though light flickered along the edges of it and points of blue-white seemed to gleam inside the blackness. She would have described it as dark, but it was more than darkness: it was Absence.

And the voice: as before, it was a cyclone of sound, containing within it whispers of a thousand voices, calling words that lingered half understood at the edge of recognition. Again Taria thought she heard her name, and she took an involuntary step back, then another, retreating before the apparition, before this Absence that was also Presence, screaming futilely against its roar. She started to turn, started to run as she had before, then forced herself to stand, to face it . . .

. . . but the Neritorika had already stopped singing to it, and the Greater Singer was lowering itself once more, the voice quieting, the thundering of it diminishing with each moment until it was gone and there was nothing there anymore but the quiet rollers from off the bay: undisturbed, unbroken—as if nothing had ever been there at all.

Taria was breathing hard and fast, as if from some long exertion. She glanced at the Neritorika, at the black fur and the blue light dancing within it. "You're one of them, aren't you?" she said. "You're a Greater Singer."

"I may be a Greater Singer, one day," the Neritorika answered. "Not now."

"You can talk to them, though?"

"No. I can call to them, and they to me, and they can hear me as they hear the Singers-in-the-Water, but I don't know their language. I don't even know if they use language as we do. The truth is, we are as insubstantial as the wind to them, Taria-Baraaki. How can I say this?" The Neritorika vented air, splashing in the surf. "They exist in more places than we do."

"In more places? I don't understand."

"I don't really, either, though I am beginning to feel it, as I begin to change." The Neritorika lifted her arms: up, sideways, back. "We are high, we are wide, we are deep. They are more."

Memories of college physics classes returned to her: there'd been one professor who was both attractive and gifted with the ability to make the esoteric understandable to noninitiates taking the course to fill degree requirements. Taria had had little interest in the science, but the class was interesting and engaging, and she managed to learn despite herself, and went on to earn her degree. Professor Greene talked of string theory, which while uniting the discrepancies between general relativity and quantum theory, between the physics of the very large and the very small, also required at least nine spatial dimensions as well as time. He discussed Calabi-Yau shapes, which were mathematical descriptions of folded-up extra dimensions. He spoke of black holes and wormholes in space and theories about the construction of Thunder.

"More than three dimensional," Taria said. "You're saying I can't really see them because I'm missing a spatial component."

"Why is what you *see* so important, Taria-Baraaki? Sight is such a small thing. The Greater Singers do not see at all, not in the way you're talking about. The Greater Singers are More in other ways beyond sight. Hear them, Taria. Listen to them and know that the part of the Greater

Singers' voices that you hear is only a portion of their full voice, an echo of the whole. They are More."

The song, the shapes arcing toward the sky, Kyung calling me not five minutes later to tell me that Thunder was gone . . . "They built Thunder," Taria said, no longer even feeling the cold wind. The truth was heat and fire. "The Voice-From-the-Sky was theirs. They're the Makers."

The Neritorika snorted, a sound like low brass instruments. "I think so," she said. "I truly think so."

They hadn't even left the Gruriterashpali before the uproar and chaos sounded in Kyung's head. "What's going on?" he asked Tee in Shiplish, and his avatar's voice came back sounding strangely calm against the urgent broadcast voices of the net.

The encampment is under attack. Commander Allison has called for evacuation.

"Under attack from who?"

They don't know.

"Kyung-Who-Speaks-in-Fury, what's the matter?" Makes asked in Mandarin. They'd come to a halt in the inner courtyard. Other Blues, the baraalideish who were attached to the temple, moved around them, always reaching out with their hands to touch. Kyung still tried to avoid the hands, though Makes just stood there, touching in return. Kyung especially tried to stop them from touching the backpack strapped around his shoulders. *A fucking constant grope party,* he thought.

He couldn't tell Makes the truth, not without admitting that the humans were on-planet. He might jeopardize his own safety and career, but he wasn't about to put anyone else at risk.

"Nothing," he answered Makes in the same language. "It's nothing."

"That's not true," Makes said. "I can hear that's not true." She hissed something in her own language and her posture dropped.

"All right, it's not precisely true. But it's nothing to do with us." Kyung hoped he was right. But Makes didn't move, didn't resume their walk. Her eyestrip rolled in a long, slow blink, and she hissed again.

"You cannot lie in the Language-of-Intimacy," she said. "It's not permitted."

Kyung didn't consider her answer; the words just came out. "Makes, I don't really care what you think I can or can't do. If I lied, it's too damn bad. Right now, I'm worried about Taria. That's all. Let's find her and get her out of wherever she is."

When Makes spoke again, it was in Shiplish, and the color of her skin had paled. "You are the friend of Taria-Who-Wants-to-Understand. That is why I help you."

Kyung shrugged. "Then let's go help Taria while we can."

Kyung thought that the Blue hesitated, or maybe it was just the way they were. Makes didn't move at first, then started walking again toward the open gates of the temple, with Kyung following. As he walked he spoke softly to Tee.

"Tee, what's the status?"

There was a distinct pause, which told Kyung that the local connection to the net was gone. *The base has been destroyed. Allison is on* Galileo *heading for* Lightbringer. *Six of the base camp personnel are missing.*

"Shit! Who were the hostiles?"

No one knows. There are conflicting reports of large moving shapes in the area but no one has a good description. The video feed on the shuttle cameras is being analyzed.

Sudden, suspicious guilt assailed Kyung, and he frowned as he and Makes made their way through the streets toward one of the island bridges. *"Did something I did cause this? I don't know how it could tie in, but the timing . . ."*

No, Tee answered. *At least no one has suggested that.*

Right now I don't think you're much in anyone's thoughts at all.

Kyung laughed aloud at that, a sound without much amusement, and Makes turned to look at him before swiveling back without a word. *"I'll try to stay that way, but I have a suspicion that it's not going to be possible. Let Allison know that I'm aware of the attack, and if I have any new information to give him, I'll pass it on through you."*

Tee didn't answer immediately, beyond a grunt of acknowledgment. *They already have a netsnoop on me. You want me to try to get rid of it?*

"No. They'd just stick another one on you we wouldn't be able to see. Privacy mode for now, Tee."

Privacy on. Good luck.

Kyung was fairly certain that luck wasn't going to be enough.

Impatient but unable to hurry Makes, he followed the Blue through the narrow streets of the island, enduring the constant touching of the Blues they passed, though he noticed that once they were off Makes's island and on the bridge to the next island over, the Blues stopped touching Makes and actually seemed to avoid her. The air was full of their grunts and *harrumphs*, and it seemed that every few seconds Kyung could feel the soft impact of a sonic inquiry hitting him. In the distance watersingers were singing, a low chorus that sounded more like a drone than music to Kyung, though Taria had claimed to find it interesting.

"Is it always this noisy here?" Kyung asked as they moved through the city. He spoke in Mandarin; Makes answered in Shiplish.

"The world is made of sound," she said. "If there were no sound, there would be no world."

"What about deaf people? Aren't any of you Blues ever born deaf?"

"Some are born deaf, yes." There was a strange inflection in the sentence, and Kyung frowned.

"What happens when they become adults?"

Makes made a strange motion with her body, almost a ripple from shoulder to waist. "They don't become adults," she said.

"They don't . . . *become* adults?"

"No."

Kyung hissed, stopping in the middle of the bridge while Makes continued walking. "You *kill* them?"

Makes stopped. Her earlets wriggled in Kyung's direction. "No," she answered. "They kill themselves."

"They kill themselves." He said it flatly, without the rising interrogative.

"Yes," Makes answered, just as flatly.

"I don't understand you people at all."

"Then we are . . . how would you say it . . . ? Even?" Makes started walking again. Kyung stood on the bridge, watching her and listening to the sounds of the city around him. A pair of Blues approached them, grunting low pulses of sound, and Kyung felt the impact on his stomach.

"I don't think we're even at all," he muttered to himself. He hurried after Makes, jogging for a few moments to catch up to the Blue. "I think you're way ahead of the game."

It was starting to drizzle, a chill damp wind that carried spatters of rain from the overcast skies, but Taria continued to look out to the gray rolling waves where the Greater Singer had appeared. "If the Greater Singers are the ones we call the Makers, then I must speak with them," she told the Neritorika. "If they made Thunder once, they can open it again. We wouldn't be trapped here. We could go home."

The Neritorika seemed amused by that. "Why would they care about you at all?"

A spray of rain sluiced over them. "Some . . . some people on my world thought that Thunder was an invitation to us. We thought that the Makers were giving us a way to contact them. We watched Thunder for a long time before we went through, and we never saw anything or anyone coming through to our side, so we believed it had been made for us to go through."

"You think everything is about you."

Taria almost smiled. "I'd say that's a pretty common human failing. You don't share it?"

Nasal vents fluttered and the Neritorika vented air that steamed in the chill, a rising wind tearing away the fog of her breath. "We do. And we're also usually wrong, too."

"Then what *was* Thunder?" Taria asked.

"You would need to ask them: the Makers, the Greater Singers."

"You told me that you can't talk with them."

"Not as I am now, no," the Neritorika answered. "But I will change the way I am." The Neritorika paused; a hand reached out to touch Taria's face, the alien's flesh wonderfully warm. "You will change also," she said. "You've already begun."

"What do you mean?"

The Neritorika vented air again. Taria thought it sounded like laughter. "Did you think that you could breathe in this world and not have it become part of you? Did you think you were so large that Little Sister would bend to you instead of the reverse? It's already started for you, Taria-Baraaki. You have already begun the journey. Trust me, Taria-Baraaki. I've gone before you, and you must trust me."

The Neritorika had come entirely out of the surf now, the tips of her fur pearled with bright water. Taria brushed a hand against the fur: water cascaded over her hand, and she felt again an electric tingling in her fingers. "I don't know you well enough to trust you."

The Neritorika waddled up the beach toward the opening to her chamber. She stopped where the stones Strikes had balanced were scattered on the ground. Her earlets flicked in Taria's direction and her low voice rumbled against the sounds of the surf. "There is trust, or there is death, Taria-Baraaki. There are no other choices."

It was starting to rain, and the weather had gotten colder, enough that Kyung wished he'd brought along the jacket that was in the hovercraft. The wind lashed them with cold droplets, and already the thin fabric of the jumpsuit he'd worn under the biosuit was damp. His short dark hair was matted to his head. Makes, at least, seemed to pay no attention to the rain at all, even though the stained white wrapping she wore was dappled with dark splotches. "We should have brought an umbrella," Kyung called to her.

"Umbrella?"

Kyung shook his head. "Never mind. Maybe I can start a business after we're done here. How much further, Makes?"

Makes sent out a long blast of focused sound, moving her body from side to side. She swiveled to face a hill just ahead of them, a building set in its rocky summit, and sent a trumpeting of sound in that direction. "There," she said.

The building looked to have been constructed in the same manner as the temple on the other island. Kyung decided that he didn't care for the Blue aesthetic in architecture: a steep, wide, and much-worn stone staircase rose to a landing. There, a door was set to one side, just enough out of square that it looked wrong, as if the builder had tried to make a rectangular door but lacked the right tools. Windows studded the rock wall at various heights and in various sizes, adding to the haphazard appearance. The roof canted downward, until it met the grassy slope of the hill several meters from the front wall. The whole thing was unpainted—*everything* in the city was unpainted—which made everything look worn and somehow shabby to Kyung's eyes.

At the bottom of the stairs Makes stopped and clapped her hands, which started a cascade of high-pitched echoes that startled Kyung. She clapped twice more, then started to ascend, with Kyung moving carefully around the puddles and up the slick stairs behind her. Before they reached the landing, the door opened and another Blue dressed in a cloth wrapping much like Makes's emerged from the darkness beyond. An ornate ring of coppery metal was wound about her head-crest, and shards of porcelain hung from it, the whole arrangement ringing like mad wind chimes as she moved.

The Blue addressed them. The only thing Kyung understood was the word "Baraaki." Kyung said softly to the air, "Tee, can you give me a translation?" A few seconds later his avatar's voice sounded in his head.

Sorry. I don't have access to those files.

"Contact the Cube. Tell Allison I need it."

Checking . . . Tee's voice faded. The two Blues were still talking. Makes's voice was rising, and the words didn't sound the same: the tones were more guttural, sharper. *I have access now, Kyung, but this isn't translatable.*

"Why not?"

According to the file notes, Taria discovered that the Blues use five separate languages, depending on the social situation.

"You're a great help."

The voice came back without a trace of sarcasm. *Thank you. By the way, Commander Allison wants to talk with you.*

"He just wants to lecture me. Not now, Tee. Out."

Whatever Makes and the other Blue were saying, the conversation was dying down. Makes seemed to have made her point. The other Blue retreated back into the building, but left the door open. "Makes, what's up?"

A sound burst struck Kyung's left shoulder, and Makes swiveled, the Blue's head-crest facing him. "I asked that the Neritorika meet with us. I said that I must know where Taria-Who-Wants-to-Understand is, and that I must speak with both of them."

"And?"

"She has gone to deliver the message. We must wait."

"Then at least let's wait out of the damn rain." Kyung moved toward the door. Makes slowly followed. Kyung stepped inside.

The interior smelled. It stank of moisture and living be-ings and long use. There was a faint spice of brine in the complex odor, along with spices that Kyung could not identify. It was also dark—the only light came from the windows and the open door, dissipating into blackness not ten steps farther in. They seemed to be in one large room, with the floor sloping downward under their feet, as if the building itself was burrowing into the depths of the island. Moving air ran fragrant fingers over Kyung's face, a faint breeze welling from the black interior. He could hear movement, could hear the hoots and grunts and bellows of several Blues somewhere nearby, but he could see nothing. Makes was entering the building, and her shadow sent the room into eclipse.

From the darkness Kyung heard the clashing of steel and a firm step. He took a step back, putting a hand on the standard issue 9mm pistol on his belt, then moved his hand back to the less lethal stundart gun holstered behind it. From back in the bowels of the building a form emerged into the pale light of the entrance: a kagliaristi. A warrior.

His voice was loud and booming as he spoke to Makes. Kyung stared at the knives on his fingers, at the filed teeth, at the tattooed and broad muscular chest crisscrossed with white scars, at the colorful and massive genitalia wrapped almost daintily around his leg. A moment later Tee's voice provided the translation in Kyung's ear: "Why have you brought another one of Those-Who-Speak-Without-Say-ing-Anything here?" the kagliaristi said.

"Strikes-the-Air-in-Anger, this is Kyung-Who-Speaks-in-Fury," Makes answered. "He looks for Taria-Who-Wants-to-Understand." Kyung scowled at hearing the name Strikes—even before Makes told him that the

kagliaristi had been seen with Taria just before her disappearance, he'd heard that name. It had been all through
Taria's reports, and mentioned in their occasional conversations.

"Taria-Who-Wants-to-Understand is no more," the
kagliaristi answered, and with the words, Kyung's breath
left him, as if a massive fist had taken hold of his lungs and
squeezed. Nausea twisted his gut and he tasted bile at the
back of his throat. He started to speak and his voice broke.

"I need . . . I need to see the body, Makes. Tell him that."

"Kyung-Who-Speaks-in-Fury would still see her," Tee
translated after Makes had spoken.

"No," Strikes said. He started to turn, as if to leave
again.

Kyung shouted, his fingers digging into the kagliaristi's
shoulder as he lurched forward. He could feel the alien's
skin, hot and almost scaly to the touch, and the rippling
cords of muscle underneath. He pulled at Strikes. The
kagliaristi resisted, and Kyung pulled harder. This time he
did turn. In that last second, almost too late, Kyung heard
the bright chatter of steel.

He let go of Strikes and let himself fall away, but the tips
of the finger-blades still caught him, slicing from the right
side of his neck and ripping through the cloth of his jumpsuit to the left shoulder. Had he not turned his face, had he
not been moving away from Strikes, those keen edges
would have caught him fully and ripped out his throat.
Kyung cried out, letting himself continue to fall backward
into a quick roll. He came up crouching, the pistol gripped
in both hands. *"Ta mada,"* he cursed in Mandarin. Blood
was streaming down his front; he could feel it hot and wet
on his skin, and he fought the temptation to touch the
wounds, to see how badly he was hurt. The gun trembled in
his hands, pointed at the kagliaristi's chest.

"You *fucker!*" he screamed at Strikes in Shiplish, and he
intended to pull the trigger then, to send the son of a bitch
to whatever hell or god awaited him, but the pistol seemed

impossibly heavy, almost falling from his hand. Though he willed his finger to move, to pull the trigger back, his body would not cooperate. Kyung staggered, the gun now pointing at the floor, his vision blurred. "Fucker . . ." he said again, but his voice sounded slurred and he wasn't sure whether he was still seeing Strikes or not.

Kyung tried to force himself to stand up, but then the floor came up and hit him in the face, and he didn't remember anything at all.

"Do you trust me?" the Neritorika asked.

Taria didn't know how to answer. The Neritorika had taken an earthenware jar from an alcove in her chamber. The jar, even in the pale, emerald glow of the algae, was plain: slightly lopsided, the opening canted to one side, the walls indented with finger marks, and the clay itself unadorned with the glassy swirls of a glaze or painted decorations. There was a symbol carved into the side, like someone had taken a stick and drawn in the damp greenware before it had been fired.

The handle of a ladle protruded from the opening of the jar. When the Neritorika took it and stirred, a blue radiance welled from the container, limning the Neritorika's fingers. "What is that?" Taria asked.

"Change." The Neritorika lifted the ladle: viscous, bright liquid dripped: a glowing gel. "Transformation, or perhaps simply Death. Sometimes one, sometimes the other, depending on the person's readiness. Will you taste it?" Her voice reverberated in the darkness, the sound of moving water echoing through the caverns. A flaring droplet slid from ladle to jar.

Taria backed away a step. "Why should I?"

"Because you are Taria-Baraaki. Because when it is their time, every Baraaki and every Neritorika must taste of this." She boomed a low trill that Taria felt to her bones. Her head-crest lifted, and she seemed to be listening to something Taria could not hear. "I will take it along with you, because it's also *my* time. I've laid my eggs, and the Baraaki has come. It's the Time-of-Dispersion."

"The Baraaki has come? Makes is here? Where? I want to see her."

"She is coming here now." The Neritorika lifted the ladle slightly, and a slow stream of bright liquid cascaded over the lip and back into the jar. "There isn't much time. You must believe me in that. Do you trust me, Taria-Baraaki?" she asked again.

"You want me to take something you admit could kill me, and you can ask that question?" Taria gave a dry cough of laughter. "You have a strange sense of humor, Neritorika. I think I'll wait for Makes."

"This is the only way to talk with them, Taria-Baraaki. This is the only way."

"I'm not doing it, Neritorika."

The Neritorika didn't answer. Instead she began to sing, her mouth wide as a chorus of voices welled forth, each taking its own note. For a moment it was only noise, then Taria felt the waves of acoustic energy buffet her as the Neritorika turned. She sang to Taria, the song buffeting her like wild surf so that Taria staggered back a step. Then the song changed, became more focused. An unseen hand touched Taria's cheek, and in the midst of the song a voice spoke in English. "Taria . . . little darling . . ."

Her mother's voice.

"Stop it!" Taria shouted at the Neritorika. She slapped at the air in front of her, as if the unseen apparition were drifting smoke, and she could feel an arm, a face, long and flowing hair . . . Her hand moved through the body, the hair prickling on her forearm.

"Taria . . ." the voice whispered again. "Trust me . . ."

"Damn you!" Taria shrieked, her voice shrill against the roar of the song. "Stop it! Stop it!" She ran forward, battering her fists against the alien's side, feeling the warm, damp fur tingling against her clenched fingers, smelling the spice of it, hearing the song and a part of her wanting desperately for her mother's voice to stay, for it to be real. "Damn you!" Taria was crying now, deep wracking sobs, and the song had stopped. The fading echoes of her voice competed with the soughing of tidal water. Taria pushed at the Neritorika, whose earlets flicked in her direction. The jar the Neritorika held in her hands splashed glittering liquid over her fur and Taria's arms. Taria flung the liquid away as if it were burning acid.

"Stop it," she said again, more quietly this time.

"I have stopped." The Neritorika moved as if to touch her, and Taria stepped back, hand out. "It's my time, Taria-Baraaki. I'm asking you to travel with me, because that's the only way you'll come to understand. The only way."

"How did you . . . My mother . . . I heard her, felt her . . . How did you do that? *Why* did you do that?"

"You will understand if you trust me. If you drink this." She lifted the jar once more.

"No. Not . . . yet. I can't."

"The rocks wait. And before they make up their mind, the rain and wind erode them away to sand and dust, and their time is past."

"I'm not rock. I'm flesh."

The Neritorika snorted, low and long. "Then you've even less time, don't you?" She lifted the ladle up and the liquid poured bright over her lips, twin streams glowing down the fur on either side of her mouth. She swallowed, and dipped the ladle in the jar again, holding it out to Taria.

"No," Taria said.

The Neritorika said nothing.

"What happens now?" Taria asked. "What happens to you?"

"I will become, or I will not," the Neritorika answered.

"Become what? A Greater Singer?"

"Simply . . . Beco . . . umm . . ." The Neritorika's voice was slurred. She continued to speak, but the words were either in the Blue language or were so poorly enunciated that Taria could no longer understand the Shiplish. A few moments later she staggered, dropping down to the floor on all fours like the watersinger she resembled. She lifted her head, the mouth opening as if she were beginning to sing, but the chorus of notes was cracked and broken, the notes no longer legato and sustained, but choppy. Her fur bristled like the spine of an angry dog, and the Neritorika gave a sound that could only have been a moan of pain.

"Neritorika . . ." Taria came over to her, going to her knees alongside the alien. The Neritorika's pain seemed to be increasing: her arms flailed, her flippered feet slapped at the stones, and there was no song in her voice now, only a cry of agony. Taria felt helpless, not knowing what to do. She reached out to stroke the Neritorika's fur, as she might a cat, but sparks snapped, leaping from fur to her fingertips. Taria cried out in surprise and pain, snatching her hand back. Muscles contracted wildly along the Neritorika's body and more sparks flared along the crests of the waves of fur. "Neritorika!" Taria cried again, then lifted her head to call into the darkness of the caves. "Can anyone hear me! I need help!"

Only the mocking, faint return of her own voice answered her.

The Neritorika's breath rasped and gurgled from her throat. She started to struggle, attempting to sit up. Taria tried to help her, ignoring the painful crackling of static electricity along her arms and body as she pulled at the Neritorika's body. She was lighter than Taria would have imagined, as if most of her seeming bulk was fur. The Neritorika wheezed, gasping for air. She started to fall back sideways, her body sagging, and it was all Taria could do simply to break the worst of the fall. The Neritorika lay on her side on the wet stones, in the verdant glow of the algae, surrounded by her eggs.

For a moment she rallied. She lifted her head, and

though her voice was still slurred, Taria could understand the words. "Sometimes, despite what you wish, the answer is no."

Her head dropped, like someone dropping a small boulder. Taria could hear the dull impact of flesh, bone, and fur on the stones. The Neritorika was very still.

"Neritorika!" Taria jostled the creature, and the body responded to her push like a sack of sand. "Damn it . . ."

Taria stopped, holding her own breath.

She could hear water. She could hear her own heart slamming against her ribs. She could hear the shimmering echoes as her foot scraped stone.

There was no other sound.

"Oh, damn . . ."

There was one place he could be himself—behind his face. Inside himself, he could be alone, he could allow himself to be free: to smile and laugh, to weep, to shout.

Only now there was another voice inside him, and he was not alone anymore.

Kyung! it was saying. *Kyung!* Repeating his name, over and over.

"What?" he muttered angrily in reply. "Get out of my head."

Kyung!

It was Taria's voice, and with the realization, Kyung allowed himself to smile. "Taria! I came down after you—"

Kyung! This is Tee.

"Tee?" Memory returned first: the daggered hands of Strikes raking his neck and shoulder, the collapse into unconsciousness. Kyung could feel movement, could feel the pain of the wounds on his upper body. He heard the sounds of footsteps echoing, caught the odor of Blues in the cold air. Someone was carrying him. He could feel arms underneath his body, supporting him, but he could see nothing. At first Kyung thought it was because he had just awak-

ened—he blinked, but though he felt his eyelids move, it
made no difference. Everything was darkness around him.

The panic slammed into him in the next moment, and he
twisted away from the hands holding him. The movement
ripped the wounds open again, and as he sucked in a breath
against the pain, he felt himself falling. The fall was neither hard nor high, and his hands slapped damp stone. He
rolled, coming up to a crouching position. A burst of low
sound erupted in the darkness.

"Kyung-Who-Speaks-in-Fury, I couldn't hold you. I'm
sorry."

"Makes?" The voice came from his right. Kyung didn't
move. He put a hand to the side of his neck; it came away
sticky and wet. "Where am I? What happened?"

"We are approaching the Neritorika's chambers. I carried you here after you fell into the Silence-That-Was-Not-
Sleep."

"I can't see," Kyung said, and he heard the panic woven
in his voice. Makes heard it as well, for sympathy was
warm in her voice when she answered.

"There's nothing wrong with your eyes. Taria-Who-
Wants-to-Understand couldn't see in the tunnels when she
came here, either. Listen, if you can't see."

Kyung let out a breath he hadn't known he was holding.
*You're underground, and the Blues don't need light to see.
You're fine. It's just dark . . .*

Something—someone—else moved, to his left, and
Kyung heard the metallic rattle of finger-knives: Strikes.
With that, anger flared, and Kyung's hand went to his hip.
The pistol was back in its holster, and the stundart was still
on his belt as well. He didn't know if Strikes didn't realize
these were weapons or if the Blue considered him so little
a threat that it didn't matter; Kyung didn't particularly care
which. He didn't intend to let Strikes get close enough to
use the hand-blades again.

Cautiously, Kyung stood. He tried to lift his left hand

over his head in case the roof was low, but more of his wounds threatened to open again and he stopped. *Listen*, Makes had said, and he did. The cavern sounded spacious enough, with slow, distant echoes reflecting back from every sound. As he paid more attention to the web of noise around him, he realized that he could sense Makes, an arm's length away, and that Strikes was a few steps distant on the other side. Standing now, he could feel the slope of the floor beneath him, and from the darkness farther ahead there was the faint sound of moving water.

Kyung felt his breath settle into his center. *Nothing to fear . . .* Even if he couldn't see, he could still maneuver, he could still sense the world around him. Another deep, calming breath, letting it out slowly through pursed lips, and Kyung felt his muscles relax. He could still feel the pain of the cuts, but he could hold it at a distance. He reached out into darkness until he felt Makes's arm. *Tee*, he thought, and felt the scalp prickle of the neural web activating. *Where am I, Tee?*

In the caverns under the Neritorika's island, Tee answered. *You're almost at sea level at the moment.*

Can you get me back out?

I think so. I monitored your movements and should be able to backtrack.

Good. I may need your help to do just that. "Let's go," Kyung said aloud to Makes.

"Strikes will lead us to the Neritorika," Makes said.

Strikes might die before then.

Kyung smiled inside at the thought, behind his face.

Taria heard the shuffling of several footsteps on the balcony, and she glanced upward. In the eerie shimming illumination of the algae, she saw that Strikes was there, and Makes, and . . .

"Kyung!"

"Taria!" Kyung half ran, half slid down the winding stone ramp to the lower level, meeting Taria in mid-stride.

They hugged each other fiercely, until Kyung pulled away with a soft grunt of pain.

"God, you're hurt . . . Jesus, Kyung . . ."

"It looks that bad?" Eyebrows wrinkled; his eyes narrowed.

Taria shook her head reflexively. "No. Yes. There's a lot of blood, but I'm sure it looks worse than it is. If I had my pack . . . God, Kyung, what are you *doing* here? What's going on out there?"

Kyung tilted his head at Taria. It seemed that the movement hurt him—Taria saw fine lines form at the corners of Kyung's mouth for an instant before he hid the pain away and smiled. "What the hell do you *think* I'm doing here? I'm looking for you. Taria, you feel so warm . . ."

"I've been sick. Some kind of fever. I'm still not quite sure how I feel."

Kyung pointed at Strikes, descending the ramp ahead of Makes. "That bastard with the fancy cock told me you were dead."

"He did not say that," Makes boomed. "He said that Taria-Who-Wants-to-Understand is no more. And that is true enough. The Neritorika named you Taria-Baraaki."

"Fucking semantics," Kyung spat out. "What was I supposed to think?"

"You were supposed to think no more than what was said," Makes answered placidly. "Taria-Baraaki, where is the Neritorika?" Makes let out an inquisitive, locational grunt.

Taria glanced back to where the Neritorika's body was huddled on the stones, a dark hummock of glossy fur. "I didn't kill her," Taria said. "I didn't. She . . . she took something."

Strikes had reached the floor of the cavern now, sending out a quick barrage of sound. His earlets flicked back and forth, and he moved quickly to the Neritorika's body before Taria could say anything else. He reached down and stroked the fur, a constant low murmur coming from him,

and he straightened once more. He spoke, a flurry of unintelligible words. To Taria, they sounded angry. "Makes,"
Taria said. "Tell Strikes that I didn't *do* anything. The Neritorika drank something, and it killed her. She even tried to
make me drink some of it. You need to tell that to Strikes.
Right now."

"He knows," Makes answered.

"Then tell him to back away," Kyung broke in. Strikes
had risen again and started to approach Taria and Kyung,
still murmuring. Taria saw the glint of metal in Kyung's
hand. "Tell him that he isn't going to get close enough to
me to use his claws again, Makes. I'm not giving him a
second chance to hurt us." Strikes took another step, and
Kyung grimaced, bringing the weapon up. "Makes, damn
it—"

Taria heard Makes say something quickly to Strikes,
then Strikes answered back. "He is not afraid of you."

"He doesn't have to be afraid," Kyung answered. "He
has to know that he'll be dead in another two steps."

"Kyung . . ." Taria touched Kyung's shoulder. "Don't do
this."

Strikes took another step toward them. "He's not giving
me a choice, Taria."

"He doesn't understand, Kyung." No answer. Another
step. It was then that the image flashed on her: *the crowd
parting as the melon vendor pushed through, the silver
glint of the small handgun, the shouting, the bark of the
gun* . . . She moved in front of Kyung, pushing his hand
down. "Kyung, don't." Kyung started to push her aside, but
Taria held tightly. She could feel Strikes just behind her,
could hear the sound of his daggered fingers and smell the
odd scent of his breath. She shivered: as Kyung struggled
against her, as Makes *hrummed* and boomed, as Strikes put
a hand on her shoulder. Taria could feel the chill of the
blades.

She held very still, her eyes on Kyung, watching herself
in Kyung's dark brown pupils. "Don't," she whispered to

him. "He's helped me. If you could see what he made . . . the stones . . ."

Her fingers loosened on Kyung's hand, her fingertips still touching his arm. Taria could see Kyung's nostrils flare and the tightening of his eyes. Strikes's hand was draped over her shoulder, and Taria saw Kyung's eyes flick anxiously to the hand-blades and back again. "Please . . ." Taria said. "Trust me."

A blink. A sigh. Kyung's hand dropped back again. "I still owe him," Kyung said.

Strikes's hand slipped from Taria's shoulder. She reached toward Kyung and hugged him again, pulling him tight to her. "Thanks," she whispered into his ear. "Thanks for coming for me."

Allison put on the VR goggles, and the meeting room snapped into existence around him. There were two other people in the room, on two of the other sides of the square table: Commander Merritt, in charge of the marine contingent of *Lightbringer*, and Commander Ivanovich of Systems. When Allison appeared, they both seemed to lean away from him, as if even his virtual presence could contaminate them with whatever he'd inhaled on Little Sister.

A chime sounded, and Admiral McElwan's image shivered into view in the remaining chair. Serena McElwan was called the Cold Lady, though never to her face. Allison couldn't recall ever having seen her smile. She was sixty-three, with short-cropped white hair, eyes of green ice, and a lean body that she exercised daily. Allison had seen a few of those workouts in the Officers' Gymnasium—she seemed to go through the routine without joy, her face looking as bored as if she were reading some junior officer's mundane report while sweat soaked her T-shirt and muscles shivered from hard use in her arms and legs. She would move from machine to machine, following an unvarying schedule, with one of her aides spotting her when she went to free weights. She was unrelenting, pushing herself through sets that would have left Allison exhausted and defeated.

She was as unrelenting with the staff of *Lightbringer*. She had a well-deserved (in Allison's opinion) reputation for being harsh but fair, and for making rapid-fire decisions that had so far in her career proved to be the right ones.

Allison admired the woman. He would not have had anyone else sitting in her chair, nor did he have the slightest desire to ever sit there himself. He'd been in few meetings with McElwan, but like all officers, he knew the routine—wait for the questions to come to you, and answer them as briefly as possible. If the Admiral wanted to know more, she'd ask, and she was desperately impatient with those who dissembled or circled a subject a few times before getting to the point.

"What happened down there, Commander Allison?" she said. Her voice was umber and silk. It nearly purred; Allison knew it could also cut with a remorseless edge.

Allison shifted in his seat under her emerald stare. "I don't know precisely," he answered, which was only the truth. "We were attacked, but by who or what, I was unable to determine. I only caught a few glimpses, and we all heard the sounds. I haven't had a chance to review the images from the shuttle's cameras."

"*I've* seen them," McElwan snapped, like a teacher scolding a neglectful student. "I've also reviewed the satellite images. Everything's consistent with what you described in your report. Are these the Greater Singers that Spears has described?"

So she's come to the same conclusion I have . . . "Can I say that for certain? No. Is that what I suspect? Yes. Definitely."

"Then we have a larger question—are they animals who attacked because we were in their territory or they mistook us for part of the food chain, or are they sentient beings with hostile intentions? Your thoughts, Commander?"

The Admiral expected answers to her questions, but far

more dangerous than sidestepping those questions was to give her misinformation. "We don't have enough data to make that determination, Admiral," Allison answered. "I've already put everyone in ExoAnthro on finding the answer."

McElwan grunted at that. She blinked once as she stared at Allison, then her image swiveled in her seat as she turned to Ivanovich. "Has anything changed with the status of *Lightbringer*?"

Ivanovich's dour shake of his balding head was answer enough. His Shiplish was tinged with a strong Ukrainian accent. "No. We have limited maneuvering capabilities, and that's all. The drive system remains offline." He shrugged then, a simple lifting of shoulders that was more expressive than any words. "In my opinion, it will stay offline."

Allison could see that McElwan expected that answer—undoubtedly she'd been receiving reports all along regarding the damage to the ship, but it was news that sent icy spiders crawling down Allison's spine. He'd known the damage was extensive, but it appeared that the expectation that it was repairable was a fantasy. Allison stroked his chin.

Suddenly Little Sister and its inhabitants had taken on far more importance than anyone had expected. "Has the decision point changed at all?"

Ivanovich shook his head again. "Still the same. We have no more than two ship-weeks before we're out of shuttle range of Little Sister. We've already started stripping the essential systems and packing them for transport downworld."

"Commander Merritt, what about Weapons Systems?"

"We've begun taking out whatever can be shifted to field-based use." Kalim Merritt was a tall man of African heritage, with skin the deep, rich color of aged mahogany. His voice was the same dark, low tone.

"Can you handle these . . . things?"

Allison caught a glimpse of teeth as the man smiled. "We'll know when it happens, Admiral."

"That's not precisely the answer I was hoping for."

"It's simply the truth, Admiral. I don't expect any trouble—whatever those things were, they didn't look to be armed or shielded. The stuff we have . . ." Merritt lifted a hand and let it drop again. In the VR simulation, his hand hit the tabletop, but there was no sound. "It should be no contest, but we won't know until it happens. I've already told Lieutenant Commander Irumaki to put together a team to retake our beachhead on Little Sister."

"Good," McElwan said immediately. "We need to find out now what we're up against, before we're in a position where all of our options are gone. Commander Merritt, you'll have the lieutenant commander get his team ready to go downworld immediately—use two shuttles, one to land and one for support in case of trouble. They may take whatever they feel they need and go back down to what's left of our encampment. Recover the bodies of our crewmembers, if they can be found. And if they find those creatures, whatever they are, they will deal with them as the situation warrants. Is that clear?"

"Very clear, Admiral. I'd like Commander Allison to be involved also, since he's seen these creatures, and Irumaki may need ExoAnthro input."

Her gaze of pale sea ice went to Allison. "Is that acceptable to you, Commander? You've already been exposed to Little Sister's environment. While you can certainly still perform your onboard duties while you're in the Isolation Chamber through your PIA and VR conferencing, it seems logical to send you back to Little Sister."

What should we do? I don't know what to do, sir! Ensign Ballior screaming as those things killed him, the sound of them . . . Allison blinked, realizing that McElwan was expecting an answer and he was still sitting there, listening to the remembered sounds of destruction. "Admi-

ral—" he began, and stopped. She was still staring at him.
"Yes, Admiral. That's fine. If you need my help there."

He didn't know what she was thinking. They were only
there in simulation, but he wondered if she could smell the
fear on him.

Her gaze finally drifted away from him, going to each of
the others in turn. "Then that is all for now, gentlemen,"
she said. "You will give me or my avatar any updates."

She vanished; one moment there, and the next her seat
stood empty. Merritt vanished a second later. Allison
reached up for his link visor and pulled it off.

He was in his own room in the Isolation Sector, seated in
his own chair, and he was sweating.

Taria-Baraaki and Kyung-Who-Speaks-in-Fury were
wrapped in each other, and Makes-the-Sound-of-East-
Wind moved past them to where Meat-that-Was-Once-the-
Neritorika lay on the stones. She could hear no breath, and
when she sent a quick burst of sound over the body, the returning waves were perfectly aligned where they passed
over the abdomen—the Neritorika was not breathing. The
sound burst had painted the clay vessel alongside the Neritorika, and Makes-the-Sound-of-East-Wind moved to it
with quiet drones of sound, the patterns of sound distur-
bance giving her a shifting, three-dimensional auditory image of the room. Strikes-the-Air-in-Anger had moved
away from the humans; Makes-the-Sound-of-East-Wind
felt the kagliaristi's presence in the waves of sound in the
cavern and in his own sounds striking her.

She could hear each of them, like rocks set unmoving in
a pool of rippling water. She heard the eggs laid carefully
on the walls of the cavern, and the sound of them made her
own barren abdomen ache.

This will never be your task, her body seemed to say to
her. *Your burden is elsewhere.*

Makes-the-Sound-of-East-Wind crouched down near

the Neritorika, dipping a finger in the clay jar and tasting the thick liquid inside. The fluid ran down her tongue like points of slow fire, the acrid taste vanishing an instant later. "This is *jika*," she said aloud. "The Neritorika has gone beyond."

Strikes-the-Air-in-Anger was standing beside her now. Bladed hands slid down her back, the edges reversed so that she felt only the chill of the metal. She heard him slip the blades off the fingers of his left hand, dropping them to the stones with a clatter. His hand closed around the ladle lying alongside the jar. He dipped it into the *jika* and brought it out again. Makes-the-Sound-of-East-Wind heard the hissing effervescence of the liquid. "I give you the *jika*," he said to Makes-the-Sound-of-East-Wind, and he spoke in the Language-of-Intimacy to her. Makes-the-Sound-of-East-Wind had so rarely used that language with anyone except the Neritorika, and hearing the words spoken by a male, with his odd high tones, was so strange that she almost did not understand him. "You are no longer the Baraaki."

"No," Makes-the-Sound-of-East-Wind said sadly. "I am not. Strikes-the-Air-in-Anger, thank you for your help."

He gave a low hoot that was laden with modesty. "You were the Baraaki. How could I not do as you asked?" His hand slid over her shoulder and around her head-crest, flattening the earlets for a moment so that the world went momentarily silent. Makes-the-Sound-of-East-Wind gasped at the audacity of his touching her that way, something only true intimates would do. It was disconcerting, that touch, blocking off her world so that for that instant it seemed only the two of them existed. He was so close to her that she could see the mottled pattern of his skin through her eyestrip. "Now you will be Calabaraaki. You will go Beyond with the Neritorika." His hand touched hers, and she felt the hard, slick surface of the ladle's handle. "Here. Here is the *jika*."

"Not yet," she answered. "Not yet." She gently pushed

away the ladle and lowered herself down alongside the
furred body of the Neritorika. She stoked the fur, feeling
the softness of it and the way it moved through her fingers,
the sparking tingle that no one could explain. *I will be like
this*, she thought. *I will be like this if I survive and I will
understand what it is like to be More.*

If I survive. And if she failed, she would know none of it,
and someone else would be named Baraaki and given the
jika in her place, and would become Calabaraaki or also
die in the metamorphosis. The fear caused Makes-the-
Sound-of-East-Wind to shudder, and she pushed away the
feeling, knowing that if she let it consume her, she would
be entirely lost.

She pressed down on the Neritorika's chest, thrusting
her hand down through the downy underlayer of fur. Her
fingertips throbbed once, then again. Yes, the Neritorika's
heart still beat, slowly but strongly, as it should. Touching
her, Makes-the-Sound-of-East-Wind could sense the
greater connection of the Neritorika to the life-web.
Faintly, she felt the subterranean voices of the Greater
Singers, calling to the Neritorika-Who-Would-Become,
their voices faint and somehow troubled. Makes-the-
Sound-of-East-Wind frowned—they should have already
come, the Greater Singers. Their presence should have already filled this chamber to ease the Neritorika through the
transformation. Makes-the-Sound-of-East-Wind didn't
even know if the Neritorika could find her way through
alone: that was not the way it was done.

Something was wrong.

"Makes-the-Sound-of-East-Wind, you should take the
jika," Strikes-the-Air-in-Anger said from behind her, and
even in the Language-of-Intimacy, his voice was edged
with command.

"I can't. There is . . ." Makes-the-Sound-of-East-Wind
pushed her hand harder against the Neritorika's body. The
flesh tingled against her own, feeling as if it could merge
with her own flesh, painlessly and effortlessly; as if, were

she to push hard enough, she could thrust her hand entirely into the Neritorika and hold in her fingers the throbbing red muscle in its cage of bone. Makes-the-Sound-of-East-Wind lowered her head-crest, flattening her earlets down so her world contracted to that touch, that contact with the Neritorika. This was how she meditated back in the Grurit-erashpali, trying to feel the elusive pattern of All-Life-Here and determine where the patterns led. Touching the Neri-torika, Makes-the-Sound-of-East-Wind knew now how full the Neritorika's contact was with that pattern, and how frail her own contact had been, how diminished and faint. She could hear the sounds of life far away, and the patterns were far more complex and difficult to understand. She had thought herself gifted as the Baraaki, but now she experienced directly what she'd always known intellectually—she had taken only the first step of many, and she might never reach the end of that journey.

She let herself fall into the pattern that leaked from the Neritorika's body. She could feel the Greater Singers, and knew that their attention was elsewhere, farther out in the world, where the web was strangely tangled and the sound of it was muted, distorted and blurred like the sound of a cracked bell.

Makes-the-Sound-of-East-Wind knew that pattern, though she had heard it only in much quieter tones. She gave a quiet, disconsolate hoot and brought her head-crest back up, her earlets rising. She sent a burst of sound toward Taria-Baraaki and Kyung-Who-Speaks-in-Fury. "Those-Who-Speak-Without-Saying-Anything have lied to us," Makes-the-Sound-of-East-Wind said to Strikes-the-Air-in-Anger. "They've already come here."

Even as she said the words, she felt the sudden movement of the Greater Singers, surging so strongly toward the patterns that were Those-Who-Speak-Without-Say-ing-Anything that Makes-the-Sound-of-East-Wind pulled her hand away from the Neritorika with a startled inhalation.

* * *

There was nothing there.

The only way Allison knew that this was the same place where, a scant half ship-day before, the first human settlement on Little Sister had stood were a few scraps of plasti-steel stuck in the thorny branches of the bushes. The rest—the beams, the furniture, the fabric, the bodies they'd left behind—had vanished. Already, in the circle where the shuttle *Galileo*'s laser had sterilized the earth, the first vanguards of native life were making their return: green tendrils curling from the dirt, and crawling lines of bright yellow insects pinwheeling over the dirt on oarlike stubs of legs.

The wind freshened, and a jagged flap of plastisteel came loose from its branches. When it hit the ground, the sun-colored pinwheels pounced on it, like piranha on a young steer. As Allison watched, the shivering mass devoured the plastisteel. He couldn't even see how it was done—dissolving the substance with acidic enzymes, or slicing it to pieces with teeth or hidden claws—they were so thick around the piece of debris. The entire process couldn't have been much longer than a minute, then the plastisteel was simply gone and the pinwheels returned to their swirling lines, moving jerkily across the dirt.

Allison decided he was going to be very careful where he stepped.

"Commander, you're sure this is where . . . ?"

Lieutenant Commander Irumaki, encased in an armored suit, was standing alongside him. Allison wore a simple biosuit, a precaution that seemed at best redundant, since he'd already been exposed to Little Sister's air, but it kept the others from being exposed to him. Allison nodded to the mirrored visor. "This is it," he said. "Watch out for the little yellow bugs."

"It doesn't look like there's anything here to recover," Irumaki said over the private command channel, then Allison heard him tongue his transmitter to the broadcast band as he waved a hand at the marines exiting *Galileo*. "You all know your assignments. Secure the perimeter. I want one of the heavy lasers set over there, near that rise. Avoid the local fauna—I don't care if it's a goddamn ant, kill it before you let it on your suit. We don't know what's happened here, and until we do, no one's taking any chances or I'll send you back to *Lightbringer*. If you see something you don't like, inform me immediately. You know what to do—let's do it."

Marines scattered, all of them moving slowly in their armor. Irumaki stayed where he was, scanning the horizon. The command channel clicked open again. "You picked a picturesque place, Commander Allison," he said. "I went to graduate school in Santa Fe, and this reminds me of New Mexico."

"I'd have said the same until a while ago. Now it doesn't remind me of New Mexico at all."

Allison thought he heard Irumaki chuckle. "I guess not." His booted foot scuffed at the dirt, and Allison thought the grains of dust wriggled before they settled back into place. "You said the things came from underground?"

Allison was still staring at the dirt. It wasn't moving. It was just dirt. He let out a breath. "Yes," he answered. "I think so, anyway. But it's not like they were burrowing. It was more . . . I don't know. Have you ever seen a whale surfacing? That's what it reminded me of—like something coming out of the ocean, then going back under, and the sea—the earth—closing over it again like it had never been disturbed."

He couldn't see Irumaki's face beyond the golden sheen of the visor, but he could feel the man's eyes staring at him. "That's not possible, Commander," he said.

"I know," Allison told him. "I know. But it's what I saw." Allison shivered; he wondered if he was coming down with a cold.

He wondered if he were coming down with Taria's cold.

"New Mexico," he muttered.

"What?"

"Nothing." Allison glanced back down at the dirt. It *was* moving, a faint trembling, and he could feel it through his feet as well. The yellow pinwheels were capering away, as if a hurricane wind were propelling them. "Shit . . ."

Irumaki felt it as well, and went back to the broadcast channel. "Barrett, Hanashiro, is that laser online yet?"

A voice hissed in Allison's head. "A few minutes yet, sir."

"Now, people," Irumaki barked. "We need it now. *Hajime!*" He was already moving, starting to run toward the end of the shuttle where the laser emplacement was being erected. There was a weapon in his hand now, a multi-snouted beast strapped under his armored right forearm. "Commander Allison, you might want to head back into *Galileo*. This doesn't exactly look like an opportunity for negotiation."

Allison very much wanted to go into the shuttle. He very much wanted to leave Little Sister right now. He'd started toward the open shuttle bay when he heard the subsonic rumbling begin.

He saw the first form lift as if rising from a green and brown sea, a rounded blackness shot through with light, an emptiness that he couldn't see, couldn't hold in his vision.

He heard the song begin.

He heard the first scream.

The agonized shriek came from the far side of *Galileo*, and mixed with it was the mechanical whine of a turret servo. "Now! To your left!" Allison heard Irumaki shout. "Now!" Small-caliber weapons were firing—to the right, at the front of the shuttle.

The song swelled and shrieked. Something rose up in front of the shuttle, something Allison could not see, rising swiftly from the earth. There should have been an awful ripping of soil and rock, but there was nothing but the song. The song was deafening now, a droning so low that it was felt rather than heard. The furious sound shook Allison's insides, made his teeth rattle. Metal groaned and the shuttle jerked and tilted, nose down as if the ground had melted underneath the machine's front struts. Allison pulled out his own weapon. The blackness reared up in front of him, blinding, and he fired into it, pulling the trigger back and holding it back, letting the gun buck again and again until it clicked dry and empty.

The laser screamed treble against the bass roar of the blackness, tearing a line of white brilliance through it. But the blackness held the light, then closed around it.

There were more screams.

The song roared, vibrating in every fiber of Allison's body.

And the blackness consumed him.

TIME OF SONGS

The movement of the Tao consists of Returning.
The use of the Tao consists of softness.

All things under Heaven are born of the corporeal:
The corporeal is born of the Incorporeal.

—Chapter 40, *Tao Teh Ching*

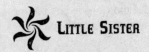

LITTLE SISTER

Taria heard Makes gasp and lift her hand away from the Neritorika's body as if shocked. "Makes," she called to her in Mandarin. "I'm sorry the Neritorika's dead. If I'd known what was going to happen, I would have stopped her."

"How can you say that to me in Mandarin?" Makes answered, speaking in Shiplish. There was unalloyed anger in her voice, an unmistakable hue of fire. "How could you lie to me in your Language-of-Intimacy, and not tell me about the other humans?"

Taria flushed. *Shit, she knows about Allison and the others . . .* "Makes, what's—" Taria started to say, but then Kyung gave a cry of alarm, holding his hand to the side of his head.

"Taria . . ." Kyung looked at her. "My God . . . *Galileo*'s under attack. The network's in an uproar, and they've just slammed down all the security walls. This is worse than the first attack."

"First attack? Attack by what?" Taria asked, wishing that she could contact Dog, that she could listen for herself. "Are we being attacked by the Blues?"

Kyung shook his head. "By . . . something else."

"It is the Greater Singers," Makes answered. Her earlets moved from Kyung to Taria. "You promised us, Taria-Baraaki, all of us. You said that you wouldn't come here without our permission. That's what Allison-Who-Speaks-

Empty-Words told us, and that's what you said to me, also. In Mandarin you told me. But your people came here anyway."

"Makes, you don't understand. I didn't have any part of that deci—" Taria began, when a blast of angry sound interrupted her.

"We understand all that we need to understand," Makes said, the multiple tones of her full voice nearly rendering the words unintelligible. "You called me friend. You taught me your Language-of-Intimacy. But it meant nothing to you."

"It meant everything to me, Makes," Taria said desperately. "You have to believe me. You are my friend. I didn't mean for any of this to happen, none of it. But you have to understand the position we're in. The Voice-From-Above is gone, and we're trapped here in a broken ship, and if we don't come to live here, we'll die, all of us."

"Then why didn't you ask?"

Taria spread her hands, knowing the gesture meant nothing to Makes or Strikes, even if they noticed it, but unable to help herself. "If it had been my decision, I would have, Makes. But it wasn't. And who should we have asked? You? The Neritorika? The Greater Singers, who we didn't even know existed?" Taria sank down to the ground, exhausted, the fever starting to burn in her again. Kyung stood over her, just behind. "I can't argue this anymore, Makes. I'm too tired and sick, and it's *done*. I can't change what's happened, and neither can you. All I can affect is what we do from here."

Makes took the ladle from Strikes's hand. Sparkling liquid sloshed. "That's true enough," Makes said. "But you still have no trust in us, or you would have taken the *jika* when the Neritorika asked. Now it's my time to take *jika*. It's your time, too, Taria-Baraaki. I ask you in the name of this friendship you claim to have, or was that just another of your lies?"

With that, Makes lifted the ladle to her mouth and drained it. She plunged it back in the clay jar and brought it out again, holding it toward Taria.

"Show me you friendship," she said in Mandarin.

He came back to chaos.

He coughed, wrapped in tendrils of acrid smoke that tore away and vanished in a hurricane wind. He couldn't stand against the fierce gusts, but on his hands and knees he lifted his head.

Galileo was lifting, groaning and creaking as its vertical lift jets screamed and vomited great billowing clouds of flame and exhaust. *Help!* He screamed inside to the Cube, to the network, but there was no answering tingle, only silence inside. "Help!" he screamed aloud, but his voice was lost in the banshee shrill of the shuttle's liftoff.

Allison staggered upright. He remembered . . . what? The creature rising up from the ground, a searing absence dancing in front of him, a void in reality that advanced like a tsunami and swallowed him in its midnight crest. Then . . . there were only flashes, brief moments . . .

. . . feeling the neural web sparking and flaring in his head, a white-heat agony . . .

. . . the sense of free fall, of plummeting from some incredible height toward an unseen ground . . .

. . . the feeling of being torn apart, of fingers or something ripping through him though there was, impossibly, no pain . . .

And the tsunami passed him, leaving him crumpled on the grass as if it had never been there at all, the chaos still screaming around him. Time must have passed, but he had no idea how much. He could hear nothing but what his own ears told him—the net had gone silent in his head.

"Help!" he shouted again, uselessly, waving his arms at the underbelly of the craft. "By God, don't leave me down here! Irumaki!" The shuttle was still rising, its shadow

growing, and there were at least two of the creatures still
moving below it, doubled humps of nothingness moving
across the plain a hundred meters from him. Aching white
light spat from *Galileo*'s nose: laser cannon drew flaming
lines across the ground, and twin flares cast smoky spears
toward the ground—tactical torpedoes. One laser touched
the mound of blackness of one of the creatures. For a moment the outline of it glowed, fiery light sputtering around
the edges of it. One torpedo exploded a few meters away in
a fireball; the other struck the other mound of blackness . . . and it vanished as if it had never been.

Allison had seen a laser cannon slice steel like a cutter
through soft cheese. He had seen torpedoes vaporize target
drones in a ball of fire. All of them did nothing, nothing to
the creatures.

They howled, the monsters. Allison saw shapes and
shifting forms in the contours of the creatures: a head, figures. He heard a roaring crescendo in the Wagnerian, hell-
ish roar of the Greater Singers. They shrieked mad
imprecations toward the sky, a blaring torrent that shivered
the air, made it seem to Allison that he was viewing the
scene through a veil of shimmering water. He could *see* the
sound, the bass waves pounding against his body like a
wild surf, outlined in dust, and he knew that he heard only
the edges of it, that if the full force of it were directed at
him, it would deafen him, would tear him apart.

Galileo howled back at the creatures, a voice of vibrating steel and clashing beams. For a moment it hung there,
a monster belching smoke and fire in the air, its massive
shadow a pale imitation of the moving darkness below,
then, impossibly, it began to break up under the sonic
attack.

An engine casing broke away from the hull, dropping in
a gout of gray-black fumes. *Galileo* canted over to one side
as a stubby airfoil shattered and threw brightly colored
confetti into the air. The nose of the craft dropped, a jagged
crack opening from cargo doors to the cockpit. Allison saw

dark figures spill from the rift in the hull, flailing arms and legs as they fell.

Galileo fell with them, a stricken bird. Allison watched, seeing the ship roll, cartwheeling ass over nose as it plummeted, and he knew, in that instant, where the fatal trajectory would land.

He could have run. He could have flung himself to the ground. He did not. He stared transfixed, watching the wreckage streak toward him, wondering what it was going to feel like to die a second time.

The ground rumbled below him. Allison looked down and saw darkness rising up toward him . . .

Kyung could barely concentrate. The network had gone wild in his head, Tee was shouting something at him, and Taria was reaching for the ladle of glowing poison. "No!" he shouted, reaching for her hand. "Jesus, Taria, that stuff killed the Neritorika."

"The Neritorika isn't dead," Makes said. Her voice sounded odd, as if she were forcing it from her throat, and the azure of her skin had shifted hues, so dark that it nearly seemed black. "She is simply waiting. Taria-Baraaki, drink. Quickly, if you wish to truly understand."

"No!" Kyung shouted again, tightening his grip on Taria's forearm. "Taria, you can't do this. I can't believe you're even thinking about it. Look what it's doing to Makes already." The Blue was shaking now, the ladle trembling in her hand as she held it out.

"She's my friend," Taria said, her voice too calm. "And she's right; I haven't trusted her. Let go of me, Kyung."

"No. I can't let you do this. I won't stand here and watch you die."

Taria looked up at Kyung, her pale eyes sad in the shimmering undersea light of the cavern. The corner of her mouth lifted. Kyung's arm ached, and he knew—they both knew—that she could pull loose of his grip if she wanted. "Then go. Go back to *Lightbringer*. I've made my choice."

"Taria—"

"Let me go, Kyung. I have to do this. I have to know. Or don't you trust *me*?"

He frowned. "That's not fair, Taria."

"I don't remember any 'fairness' clause when we signed the contracts for *Lightbringer*, Kyung. I do recall signing a couple dozen releases against getting hurt or maimed or dead. It's the chance we both took when we signed up for this." Surprisingly, she laughed then, a bright sound in the darkness of the chamber. "Hey, you were the one who decided to take off his biosuit against orders." She looked at his hand clutching her arm. He let her go, and she touched his face gently. "Stay with me?" she asked.

Kyung nodded.

Taria took the ladle from Makes.

She drank.

The taste was snow melded with lava; it was dust and earth and fruit sagging open with ripeness. The taste was more complex and overwhelming than anything she'd ever experienced before, the electric fire of it almost painful as it sloughed over her tongue, overstimulating the taste buds so that they burned. The stuff was as thick as mucus, and Taria had to force herself not to gag as she swallowed. She could feel its fiery descent down her throat, searing like dry ice, and she cried out in surprise, wondering whether she would ever be able to swallow again. "Taria!" she heard Kyung cry out, and she lifted her hand, taking a tentative breath.

"I'm . . ." Taria's stomach churned, and she forced herself to hold down her gorge. "I'm all right. I think so, anyway." She glanced over at Makes. The Blue was crouched down, doubled over and shaking, and Strikes was standing alongside her, stroking her back and head-crest. "Makes?" Taria called, but the Blue didn't answer, going to her knees, her color gone to a green-brown as dark as a bruise.

"How do you feel?" Kyung asked. He was standing in

front of her, his hands on her shoulders, his dark eyes staring at her with a frightening intensity.

"I'm fine," she said to him. "No different." But it was already a lie. She could see the bloody line running across Kyung's neck and shoulder, and it glowed, like lava in a volcanic crevice. Her stomach was cramping, her muscles constricting in waves, causing her to hunch over suddenly with a groan. "Oh, fuck," she said, and tried to laugh. "That hurt. That really hurt."

"Taria, throw it up. Get rid of it."

She wanted to. She wanted to listen to him, but she knew it was already too late. She could feel the *jika* coursing through her, a hundred lances inside her body, twisting and changing whatever it touched. Taria was suddenly very frightened, so scared that she lifted her hand to her mouth to choke off the sob that threatened to escape. Kyung was holding her, still talking, but she couldn't understand the words he was saying because the *jika* roared in her ears. Her fingertips dug into his shoulders and she felt like she could press through him, as if she could slip between the spaces of his cells. The Neritorika's chamber was so bright that she had to squint against the brilliance, and she could hear the Neritorika's heartbeat, a reverberating *doom* like the stroke of a gigantic bass drum. Everything was hypersensitive: even her skin seemed to sense every nuance of the air movements, to feel the very fibers of Kyung's shirt.

She was aware that she was no longer standing, that she had collapsed to the floor of the chamber, but it didn't matter. She was inundated by sensation, overloaded. Kyung was talking to her, and she could only look at him. She opened her mouth to reassure him but couldn't speak the words.

The *jika* was fire, and it consumed her, and she was too tired now to respond, too exhausted by its conquest of her body. She closed her eyes because the light of the algae hurt too much. She let her hands fall away from Kyung.

Taria fell into herself.

*   *   *

Kyung watched Taria crumple and fall unconscious. He watched her and could do nothing but hope that she wasn't dying, that she wasn't already dead.

He shouted in wordless pain and worry, still cradling Taria in his arms. Tee shouted with him. Strikes was standing near Makes, who also had collapsed, and he hooted something to Kyung that Tee translated belatedly. "We must take them back," Strikes was saying, and he was already crouching down, lifting Makes's body with an effort, hissing like steam through a calliope's pipes. "You will carry Taria-Baraaki."

"If she's dead, you'll die, too," Kyung said. "That's a promise." It felt good to say the words, even knowing Strikes could not understand them. If revenge was all he had left to him, then he would take what empty comfort it offered. Kyung scooped his arms under Taria. She felt too light, or maybe that was just adrenaline. Her arms hung limp and her head lolled. He pressed his ear against her and was reassured by the thump of a heartbeat. But her breath was so shallow that he could barely see her chest moving, and her pulse fluttered like a dying bird. Her eyes were moving behind her closed lids, and her skin burned with the fever, impossibly hot against the skin of his arms.

Strikes was already striding up the ramp toward the balcony and the archway to the caverns through which they'd come. Kyung looked around him again, at the sickly illumination, at the pool of water that was now lapping higher, at the body of the Neritorika. Strikes, as if he sensed what Kyung was doing, spoke. "The baraalideish of the Neritorika are coming to tend to her—she is not our duty. We will watch over these two. Follow me."

You have no choice. You can't care for her here. At best, maybe Fancy Cock knows what he's doing and can help Taria; at worst, you can take her to the hover and hope that Lightbringer *will send down a shuttle for the two of you.* Kyung cradled Taria tightly to him. He wasn't sure how long he could hold her with his injured arm, if he could carry her all the way back across this island and the next, but Strikes wasn't waiting to see if he was responding, and Kyung knew that the impenetrable blackness of the caverns would have been a maze in which he would become hopelessly lost. He forced away the thought of pain and started up the ramp behind Strikes, subvocalizing to his avatar as he trudged up the rough slope.

"Tee? Patch me through to sick bay. I'm going to need advice and help."

Just a moment . . .

He would get Taria to a safe place, then he would deal with the rest.

Her gut was filled with burning acid, and the screams and sounds of destruction were knives in her chest. Knowing that her staff and Commander Merritt were watching her, Serena forced herself to show nothing of it on the outside. She clenched her lips tightly together and blinked once, heavily. She caught a glimpse of herself in the polished tabletop—it always surprised her to see an old, wrinkled and sour face, not the younger image she seemed to carry in her head. She grimaced, and the furrows in her cheeks and forehead creased deeper in her flesh: *the Cold Lady*.

"Cease fire!" Merritt was barking to his avatar, an eagle perched on the table in front of him. "Damn it, if there are survivors down there, we don't want to kill them ourselves." In one of the 3D simulation windows hovering over the table, the satellite weaponry around the globe of Little Sister went from red to green. There was nothing but static in the various windows showing views from the cameras in battle helmets and the shuttle. Serena closed her eyes briefly: *Get rid of them*, she thought to her PIA, and when her eyes opened, the windows had all vanished.

There was silence in the room. They were staring at her, all of them.

McElwan's own avatar spoke in the voice of her long-dead husband, Tomas. *We still have network contact with four of the people on the ground. That's all . . .* A bare four out of thirty-one, and one of *Lightbringer*'s half-dozen shuttles totally destroyed. This had been costly. This had been far, far too costly.

The knives dug deeper in her, and bitter failure oozed from the open wounds.

"Commander Merritt, tell Mahaffey to take *Hawking* down from her support orbit. We'll need an evac team from their crew: volunteers only. Grab anyone still alive and any bodies and get out. I want them on the ground no longer than ten minutes, and the shuttle will take off at the first sign of hostiles whether everyone's aboard or not—we can't afford to lose another ship. Is that understood?"

"Yes, ma'am." Merritt's eyes closed, and McElwan knew that he was talking to Mahaffey through his PIA— like McElwan, Merritt was old enough that internal network access was far easier without the sensory interference of sight. When his eyes opened again, they were hard and angry. She knew what he was thinking; she was thinking it herself.

We've just lost the first battle with a new enemy, and unless we can find a way to win the next one, we are all of us dead. "All right," she said. "*Hawking* should be back here in something less than eight hours. I want a complete analysis of the recordings we have of this, and we will meet back here at 0930 for a debriefing. Communications, get a message to those downworld that *Hawking* will be there within the hour. I want to talk with them personally in a few minutes. In the meantime, I need to speak with Ensign Xiong." Serena glanced down at the image of herself in the tabletop. *Old. Tired. And scared that this time you don't know what you're doing . . .*

She looked back up. They expected nothing of her but the appearance of strength and certainty, and the appearance was all she could give them. "All right, people. Let's move. Let's get some answers and be back here at 0930."

* * *

"We need to know more about these Greater Singers. I can't condone your actions, Ensign, but in the long run, you've put yourself in a good position for us, if you can get us that information. You will keep me informed. Have your PIA contact mine if you have anything. Anything at all."

"Yes, Admiral," Kyung answered. He continued stroking Taria's forehead. She was sweating so heavily that Kyung was worrying about dehydration.

"All right, then. Hawking *will be picking up the survivors of the last attack within the next fifteen minutes. If there is any hint of another attack, we will have the satellites saturate the area once everyone's clear.* Hawking *should be nearing the coastal mountain range by 2300; you will evacuate Spears at that time, and* Hawking *will return her to* Lightbringer."* There was a pause, and Kyung thought for a moment that the Admiral was finished. He started to speak, but the Cold Lady's voice returned. *"The decision to stay on planet or to return with Spears is yours, Ensign. I won't order you to stay, since once* Hawking's *returned, we would be at least six hours away from you. But we may need someone down there. We don't have much time before we'll have to abandon* Lightbringer, *and once we do that, there's no turning back."*

Kyung glanced down at Taria, at the sheen of sweat across her face and the rictus of internal pain touching her features. "I understand. I'll stay, Admiral, once I get Taria out of here," he said.

He could almost hear her nod, imagining her dour face and gray eyes. *"Thank you, Ensign. I'll inform* Hawking *to listen for your hover's signal. Out,"* she said, and she was gone.

Kyung stroked Taria's hair back from her forehead, the strands wet and dark. "We've got you set, at least," he told her, and got up from where he was crouching near her bed. He went across the room to the balcony overlooking the islands and the bay. The rain had stopped, and through the

broken ranks of clouds he could see the mottled, parti-
colored face of Yang. There were flying creatures darting
through the misty, low clouds, but they looked more like
reptiles than birds. Watersingers were wailing their low,
wild chorus somewhere in the cloud-wrapped arms of the
bay, and bright chimes were clanging in the stiff breeze
coming off the water, points of sound coming from all over
the city spread below him. For a moment, looking out over
the landscape, he could understand how Taria had claimed
to find the world beautiful. Little Sister was familiar on the
surface: land and water, mountains and sea—yet once you
scratched below that initial perception, everything was
changed and alien.

He hoped Little Sister's strangeness wasn't about to kill
her.

Kyung didn't know where Makes was. Strikes had led
them all back to the Gruriterashpali, and the baraalideish
had escorted Kyung to this room. One of the baraalideish
could speak a little Shiplish and said that she'd send a Blue
doctor in to see to Taria. Eventually she came back with
another Blue that she said was the doctor, but after looking
at Taria, touching her enough that Kyung started to feel uncomfortable, and hooting and muttering, the doctor left her
alone. The Blue spent more time with Kyung, looking at
the long cuts from Strikes's hand and putting a cool salve
on them that Kyung had to admit eased the pain and allowed him to move more comfortably. The baraalideish
told him that the doctor said Taria was "still changing," and
would return sometime later. Kyung had asked after Makes
and Strikes; Strikes was gone, and Makes was also "changing."

Kyung was left alone, sitting next to Taria and trying to
catch up on the events with *Lightbringer* and the *Galileo*
fiasco through Tee. Then Admiral McElwan had called.

Kyung wanted to break something. He wanted something physical to confront, something he could see and
touch and feel and conquer because there was nothing he

could do to help Taria. She would live or not; the answer was out of his hands, and Kyung felt useless.

He gripped the wall of the balcony, his fingers pale with effort. The orange and yellow fur of a fungus clung to the stones alongside his hands. As Kyung stared down at his hands, he realized that the outline of the fungus was shifting, moving away from the warm intrusion of his hands, the edges of the growth undulating like a slow amoeba.

Familiar. Strange.

From the other room there was a moan and a muffled call. "Kyung?"

"Taria!" He hurried into the other room.

Stopped.

She was sitting up, the covers pooled over her waist. Her head was up, her eyes open, and they were no longer green. They were colorless, blending seamlessly into the whites. "Kyung?"

"I'm here," he said, going to her and taking her hands. He gazed at the milky eyes; they moved, seeming to track him, but she was looking over his head, not at his face.

"Kyung, I can't . . . I can't see." Her voice quavered, and he could hear the fright in it. Her hands clutched his tightly. "Everything's . . . different. So different." Her head tilted, and she seemed to be looking around the room.

"Taria, you'll be all right. *Lightbringer*'s sending down *Hawking* for you, and they'll take care of you. We're leaving in about an hour. I'll get you out of here, Taria. I promise."

She didn't seem to be listening to him, or rather, she seemed to be paying attention to far more than him. Her mouth was slightly open, and he could hear her breathe, quicker than he remembered. "Taria?" he said again, but she didn't answer.

The sound, the sound . . .

For a few brief moments she hadn't realized she was blind, because the world moved around in aural waves: the scratching of cloth as she moved, the swell of air over the blankets, the harsh breath of Kyung beside her. A thousand sounds, individual and defined and placed in acoustic space inside her head, sounds more complex and shaded, both higher and lower, than any she'd heard before. She could sense the emptiness of the archway leading out to the balcony, and the way the sound reflected less sharply from the wooden door of the room. She knew it was her own room in the Gruriterashpali, knew it because she heard the familiar placement of the furniture in the reflections of sound. She knew that Makes was in the next room, because she could hear the Blue's breathing, wafting in from outside through her own balcony, and more faintly through the cracks in the stone walls.

She knew, but she could see none of it, and her breath caught in her throat and she felt panic clutch at her chest again. Kyung had been talking and she'd heard none of it, lost in reverie. She held tightly to his hands. "Taria?" he asked. "How are you?"

This time when she spoke, she realized that her voice was fuller than she remembered, with a rich timbre that had never been there before. "I still can't see . . ." she said.

"I'm getting you back to *Lightbringer*," Kyung said. Strange, Taria thought. She'd always thought of Kyung's voice as deep and resonant, but it sounded so *thin*, with such confined tones. "They'll check you out there—"

". . . but I can *hear*," she said, interrupting him. "My God, how I can hear things, Kyung." Distantly, she knew she should be more afraid, more frightened, but if there was fear in her, it was hiding in the changes inside her. She could feel the changes, still working, a slow, crackling fire, a living presence. She threw the covers aside and stood. She could feel her own presence in the room, a solidity in the air. She coughed, and the sound was glorious, radiating outward and coming back to her a hundred times altered and shifted. She took a step, Kyung's hand a warmth on her arm, then another.

"Taria?"

"I'm all right. You can let go. Let me try this."

"Where are you going?"

"To see Makes." She stopped, and a short laugh escaped her. She realized that she shouldn't be so giddy, so calm. She should be terrified and concerned—she could feel those emotions underneath, waiting, but she could push them aside. "That was the wrong verb, wasn't it? 'To see . . . ' "

"We need to get out of here in just a few minutes, Taria. The hover's sitting just this side of the mainland bridge." She could hear the pain twined through his voice, and under it the core of his affection for her, and she didn't want to tell him. She stopped, and stroked his face with a hand. Beard stubble rasped like sandpaper over her palm, and the feel of his body was as thin as his voice, as insubstantial. She thought that if she wanted to, she could pass her hand entirely through him with little effort.

What are you thinking? What's happened to you? You love him. You know it.

She did. She'd never quite known how to tell him before, and now, now she was certain she couldn't, because she no longer even knew who she was herself. Part of her was Taria, part of her was something she knew not at all.

Changed.

"I'm not going, Kyung," she said, trying to make her voice as thin as his own and not succeeding. Whatever had altered her had touched her vocal cords as well.

"You *have* to go, Taria. You can't even see."

"I know," she said quietly. "And part of me is scared as hell about that. I don't expect you to understand this, because I don't understand it myself yet, but another part of me isn't concerned at all, because it knows that I'm all right, that what I've lost has been compensated for."

"You're right. I don't understand. Taria, McElwan is sending *Hawking* for you."

"Then tell her I don't need it."

"I don't want to do that."

Taria paused. Heat flared inside her, from heart to center, and she wondered how she could say the next words without hurting him. In the end she simply said them, with as little inflection as she could manage. "It's not your choice to make, Kyung."

She didn't need sight to imagine how Kyung suddenly hid himself behind his eyes, and she could hear the pained intake of breath that she would never have noticed before. She turned and went into the corridor, half expecting him to follow her, but he didn't. She paused, one hand on the wall—the grainy texture like a range of mountains under her fingertips; she felt as if she could slip her fingertips into the valleys, sink deep into the stone—then went on. The corridor was bright with long echoes, the next doorway a hole in the sound, and she moved into it. There were two Blues in the room, and she knew from the sounds of one that it was a male; the other's breath was longer and deeper and complex.

"Makes," she said, but it was Strikes who spoke.

"Taria-Calabaraaki," he said. The new title made no sense to her beyond saying that she had changed, and she was all too aware of that. Taria could sense Strikes's acoustic shape, could hear it from the reflections of ambient sound, and his footsteps told her that he was moving away from her and out onto the balcony, leaving her alone with Makes. Taria crouched down alongside Makes.

She could sense the alteration in Makes's breathing as she came closer to her; Taria knew that the Blue was aware of her, though she was still sleeping. "What did you do to me, Makes?" she asked. The words cracked the emotional dam inside her, and Taria sobbed with the crashing, rising emotions. She felt hot tears filling her eyes and sluicing down her cheeks. "God damn it, I can't *see*!" she shouted, and for a moment the acoustic world-shape around her wavered and vanished and she was truly blind, wrapped in darkness and lost. "What have you done to me! God, I'm so scared, I'm so fucking *scared* . . . "

Someone touched her from behind, and Taria gasped—she hadn't heard anyone approach. Kyung's arms went around her, and she turned into him, accepting the embrace and crying openly now, giving herself to the comfort of being with him. "Kyung," she said into his chest, "I don't understand any of this."

She felt his lips brush the top of her head, and his arms tightened around her. "I know. I don't understand it, either. That's why I want you to go back to *Lightbringer*."

She lifted her face toward him, lifting her finger to his face and tracing his expression, trying to fit the lines under her fingertips into an image of him. Her hands slipped around the back of his head, and she drew him down to her, kissing him softly. "That's exactly why I have to stay," she whispered to him. "This is where the answers are for me, not back at *Lightbringer*. I'm sorry." She kissed him again. "Can you understand that?"

"No," he said. "But I can trust your feelings."

She laughed and sobbed at the same time, wiping away the tears with the back of her hand. "Thanks," she said.

His arms pulled her close again, and she leaned into the embrace for long moments, enjoying the feel of him, the smell of him, the texture of his skin and clothes against her. As she calmed, she felt the acoustic contours of the room shimmer back into existence around her. If she could not truly see, she could hear fully again. She could hear the strong beat of Kyung's heart, loud in the chorus of sounds, and she took a long breath. "I'm okay," she said at last. "At least as okay as I'm going to be for the time being."

She stroked his back, then let her hands fall down to his waist. His arms relaxed around her, and she took a step back with another long breath. "Thanks," she said. "For taking the chance. For coming for me. For being here."

She could hear his smile. "You know why I came here."

She smiled back. "Yeah. I do." She touched his cheek once more: stubble and soft, warm flesh. "I do." Turning, she went to Makes again, kneeling down beside her. She touched the Blue once more, and again Makes's breathing altered with the touch. Skin against skin: Taria's hand tingled where her fingers were spread against Makes's chest. She pressed harder, feeling the tingling spread up her fingers to the palm.

"Jesus, Taria, what are you doing?" she heard Kyung exclaim behind her, but she ignored him, pressing harder.

It was like pushing her hand into a box packed tightly with tiny plastic pellets. They gave slowly, reluctantly, against the pressure, allowing her hand to slide inside, but her hand was composed of pellets also—as she put pressure on her hand, it slid into her as well. The tingling was to her wrist now, and she could feel a throbbing pulse, a convulsing muscle under her fingertips. Makes stirred, and Taria pulled her hand back with a gasp.

She touched her right hand with a fingertip of her left, expecting—fearing—that she would feel the hot slickness of blood coating it, but the skin was dry. "My God," she breathed.

She heard Makes sit up, groaning. For the first time, she heard the full, varied sounds of a Blue, the automatic tonal pulses that seemed to give acoustic light to the room. In the brilliance, Taria could hear nuances she had missed before: the tiny alcove on the east wall; the curvetail webs festooning the ceiling; the knobby texture of the walls.

Makes's voice was hoarse and broken, but she spoke in Mandarin.

"*Chi fan le ma,* Taria-Calabaraaki," she said.

"*Chi le,* Makes-Calabaraaki," Taria answered.

Being dead was not what he expected.

Allison had been raised Catholic, and if he hadn't been extremely diligent in pursuing that faith, he still believed.

Death was supposed to bring a meeting with St. Peter, and entrance into either heaven or hell.

It was not supposed to be a void alive with voices.

They came from all around, these voices, and though he knew they weren't speaking Shiplish, he could understand them. They sang, and the music contained images, and images were words and concepts and thoughts, and he heard them, finally, as words inside his head. There were at least a dozen voices here with him, and maybe as many as a hundred. "Am I really dead?" he thought to them, and crystalline laughter answered from dozens of throats.

"Yes," they answered. The affirmation came from everywhere and nowhere, echoing: *Yes, yes, yes, yes* . . . "As you mean it, yes. Your body is gone, but we have kept the structure of your thoughts. Think of it as . . ." The voices paused, and Allison felt them touch his consciousness, riffling through his thoughts and memories like they were a stack of cards. ". . . as a virtual image—everything you've experienced captured, and all the connections retained. We hold you together inside us, by our choice."

"And once you let me go, I'll be gone."

"You are already gone," they sang to him. "You haven't realized it yet. You are—" Allison felt the prick of intrusion as the voices rummaged through his memories. "—a phantom, a ghost, a wisp of electricity, a set of data."

He felt a wash of deep sorrow pass over him, the realization that this consciousness was a short-lived chimera, that his life was truly ended. The voices faded, returned. "Ahh," they crooned. "So that is 'sadness.' "

There was no answer he wanted to give to that. He felt invaded, emotionally raped. He wanted to lash out, but where there should have been the awareness of body, the tentacles of spinal nerves and neurons, there was only an aching emptiness. "Why am I here?"

"Because we need to know," the voices answered. *Know, know, know, know* . . . "Here," they said, and Allison felt his awareness opened. He saw/felt the world, a matrix settling around him, complex and varied. He sensed the clusters of Blue towns around the rippling expanse of the great seas, felt the grazing herds moving across the interior plains, felt the linkage of it all: the interconnection and meshed energy of the life there. Above and around the matrix was the pressure of radiation and gravity from the gas giant Yang, and the sharper, searing barrage from the sun Yin. *So that is how they see the world . . .* he thought, and more amusement rippled through the space around him. "No," they sang back to him. "That is only the part that your mind is capable of holding. Here, do you feel this?"

The matrix shifted around him, and he felt a darkness within it, a rip in the fabric through which the life energy could not flow. Pain flowed outward from it, a radiating hurt that made Allison's mind draw back. "That's us," he said suddenly. "That's our encampment here."

"That is what we felt, yes." The voices paused, and for a moment Allison feared that they'd left him entirely, that in the next moment they would cease holding him and his consciousness would vanish. But he could still feel them around him, and here and there, caught in the matrix like him, he could feel other phantoms like him. He knew them: Irumaki, Barrett, Harashiro. He knew the voices were talking to them also, that they were all there for the same reason and would all be discarded when that reason was gone.

Dead. All of them.

"Tell us," the voices whispered. "Tell us about *Lightbringer*. Tell us about the ships you brought down here. Tell us what you intend. Tell us about yourselves."

"No," Allison thought back at them. "You want us gone."

"Yes," they answered, and Allison could hear no emotion at all in their voices. They weren't angry, weren't sad, weren't amused. There was neither revulsion or pity. They sang, and Allison heard the dissonance where the song touched the dark presence of the humans. "Tell us."

"No." Allison tried to hide the knowledge within him, tried to bury it under a deluge of other thoughts, but even as he did so, he felt the touch of the voices, felt them go into him and take what they sought.

"Ahh," they sang, and he thought he heard satisfaction in the many-voiced chord. "So strange. So odd. So . . . fragile."

"What are you going to do?" Allison asked them. He could feel their attention drifting from him already. One by one each of the individual awarenesses inside the Greater Singer was turning elsewhere, and he knew that as soon as they left entirely, their hold on him would dissolve and he would be swept away like a tendril of fog in a passing zephyr. "What are you going to do?" he asked again, desperately this time.

"Nothing," came the faint reply. "We will do nothing unless your people force it on us. Those on your ship are doomed; we've seen it in your mind and the minds of the others. But you have billions more, so why should it matter? Leave us alone, and we will do nothing."

"We can't leave you alone," Allison cried out to them as they drifted further from him. "We can't. We have to come here if we want to live."

The answer came to him faintly, as if it was a breath of music heard in the distance. "We can't let you do that," they said. *Do that, do that, do that, do that . . .*

"We must," Allison tried to say to them, but they were gone. "No . . ." he cried, but the word died, and the consciousness that held him together opened its hands and let the winds of emptiness break him apart into dust and dreams.

"I don't want *Hawking* down for longer than ten minutes. No more. If there's no one to grab, make it less. Understood?"

Hawking was piloted by Mahaffey, who had taken the first Firebird through Thunder. McElwan wished the heavily shielded and armed Firebirds were capable of atmospheric flight, but if anyone could handle a shuttle in a crisis, it was Mahaffey. Her avatar was a tiny Mdab, the Celtic warrior queen. Serena could see Mdab standing on a console in back of Mahaffey in the window hovering over her desk. Mahaffey was grim-faced under her shock of unruly red hair. "Not a problem, Admiral," she said. "We'll get 'em, get out, and then we'll head to the city to grab Spears. I'll see you in seven hours. Less."

"We'll be waiting for you."

The window with Mahaffey closed. *Give me images from the shuttle cameras*, she thought.

Here you go, Serena, Tomas's voice replied, and a half-dozen windows opened up in front of her. Two of them showed little but the shreds of clouds through which *Hawking* was descending; the other four gave various views of the ground rising up to meet the shuttle. McElwan leaned her elbows on her desk, holding her head cupped in her hands. Below was a pastoral plain and the haze-blued peaks of the mountains in the distance, then, disturbingly, she saw the wreckage of *Galileo* scattered in a fan of black across the grass. If there was anyone left alive, McElwan couldn't see them. *Infrared*, she thought to her avatar, and the view shifted. McElwan squinted, hoping to see pinpoints of heat. There were several, and she felt hope rising until Tomas's voice spoke in her mind, even as she realized there were too many of the points of yellow. *Sorry, Serena. Those have already been ID'd as native herd animals. There's nothing below moving that shows the shape or heat signature of skirmish armor.*

If her people were down there, then, they were cold and still.

"Damn it . . ." She took a long breath. Already *Hawking*'s landing jets were kicking up dust and obscuring the landscape. She waited, listening to the feed from Mahaffey and her crew as they landed the shuttle.

"All right, that's it . . . Kinopo, get your squad in posi-

tion and strapped down; we're going to hit hard and fast. As soon as we touch, I'm opening the bay doors and you're out. Ten minutes, and we're gone. Understood? Good. Frank, have you got body locations? Squirt that over to Kinopo. We're . . . oh shit!—"

McElwan saw it at the same time from the nose camera's window. A mountainous darkness was rising from the ground, and the wail of sound from it could be heard even through Mahaffey's feed. The wild banshee keening of the thing shrilled in the audio, overloading the circuit. McElwan could hear nothing else, and when a second later the automatic compression cut in, the sudden decrease in volume was nearly as shocking as the noise itself. Faintly, McElwan heard Mahaffey shouting, and the camera windows showed another Greater Singer rising to starboard.

McElwan waited for the searing light from the satellites to slice into the Greater Singers—the weapons systems were supposed to give fire support at the first sign of trouble, but nothing happened. McElwan pounded the table. "Weapons! Where's *Hawking*'s support?"

"Admiral, the satellite comlinks went down. We're trying—"

McElwan didn't let him finish. "Mahaffey! This is McElwan—get the hell out of there! Now!"

She didn't know if Mahaffey heard her, or if it was already too late. The landscape in the windows yawed sickeningly in front of her, the perceived motion so compelling that Serena gripped the side of the table in response. The song shrilled; the nose camera went to static, then two others followed. McElwan shouted herself, standing and staring helplessly at the other windows, which showed a pinwheeling of horizon, sky and ground, a kaleidoscopic whirling of blue and green and blue and green and—

They all went dead at once. Six windows spat static and white noise at her.

McElwan sat. She took a breath, spoke to her PIA. "Do we have contact with anyone down there? Anyone at all?"

There are still twenty people with net links, Serena. None of them are conscious. Serena, you must have a dozen priority queries coming at you.

"Keep them out. I don't want to talk to anyone."

McElwan sat again. She could see her hands trembling on the tabletop, and she stared at them, looking at the knobby joints and the fine mesh of wrinkles in the skin. For the first time she felt old. She stared at *Hawking*'s camera windows, hissing in front of her, hoping that one of them might clear again.

"Windows out," she said quietly, feeling her voice gone raw from shouting. One by one the windows vanished. She sat there in the dark for minutes, her eyes closed.

The Cold Lady allowed herself to cry.

"We don't have any choices, Ensign. You're about an hour away with the hover; we're at least six. There are eighteen people who we know are still alive."

From the balcony Kyung glanced back into the room. Taria was talking with Makes. At least he assumed they were talking—their heads were close together, and he could hear a high murmuring that sounded like voices but was pitched almost too high for his hearing. Taria's hand moved as she talked: Kyung still didn't believe what he'd thought she'd done—he would have sworn that Taria plunged her hand deep into Makes's chest without either one of them seeming to be hurt by the experience.

He doubted that this was going to be the strangest thing he saw down here. He watched Taria, and he worried. She seemed so . . . placid about what had happened to her. Kyung imagined himself in her position, and the thought of being blinded and changed made him shiver. He would be railing and furious, terrified and angry . . .

"Ensign Xiong?"

The uproar in Kyung's head had been ferocious, the net wild with the awful news about the attack on *Hawking*. He still couldn't believe all that Tee had relayed to him. Kyung had known Bea Mahaffey almost as well as he'd known Taria, and he and Kinopo had roomed together while the *Lightbringer* crew was going through initial training. To think of them both dead . . . A hard, cold anger filled Kyung's belly, and his decision was quick and firm. "I heard you, Admiral," he said. "I'll go. Can I get any support at all from the satellites?"

"According to Weapons, the comlinks and redundants are dead. Fried. We lost all communication with them a few seconds before the Greater Singers attacked Hawking. *We don't believe it's coincidence. It's as if they knew about the satellites and exactly how to disable our communications with them. I can't and won't pretend that we can help you with this, Ensign. If you see anything at all threatening, you can return to the city and no one will think worse of you.* Tycho Brahe *is already on the way, and will retrieve you, Spears, and any of the survivors."*

"And after that?"

Kyung knew she didn't want to answer. The pause went on far longer than the distance between them warranted. For that matter, he hardly deserved an answer—he was facing disciplinary action on return. But her voice came back, and it sounded flat and resigned. *"We don't have time or resources for patience or subtlety,"* McElwan said: the Cold Lady. *"We will learn to deal with these Greater Singers quickly, or we won't."*

"I think I understand, Admiral."

"Do you?" Another pause. *"I'll be observing through your avatar, Ensign. Out."*

Kyung took three slow calming breaths, listening to the droning, low song of the watersingers coming from over the bay—they'd not stopped singing since he and Taria had returned. Through the torn clouds, he could see the red and orange-swirled face of Yang. Out near the Neritorika's island, he saw movement: dozens of black-furred watersingers moved there, like dolphins slicing through the waves. For a moment he thought he saw a larger darkness moving below and with them, but when he squinted and moved closer to the stone railing to peer across the water, both the dark shape and the watersingers seemed to have disappeared.

"Taria," he called, and left the balcony.

"What?"

"How are you doing?"

Her strange, dead white eyes seemed to find him. Makes was sitting up in her bed, her arm stroking Taria's shoulder as if they were lovers. "You know, if you'd asked me that back on *Lightbringer,* I'd never have noticed all the undertones and color in your voice. They say more than the words. What's wrong, Kyung?"

He thought of telling her everything, but saying it would make it real, would make him have to deal with the grief and panic he was feeling. "I need to leave. I'll be back in two, three hours."

They'd been speaking Shiplish, but Taria shifted abruptly to Mandarin. "What's happened, Kyung? What aren't you telling me?"

"I have to go now, Taria, and I really don't have time to explain. I need to know if you'll be okay here while I'm gone."

Taria's hand touched Makes's head-crest, her skin pale against the vibrant orange there. "I'm as safe here as anywhere, Kyung. But I think I need to go with you. I think we all do."

"I don't need your help with this, Taria. It's something I have to do alone."

She cocked her head. She seemed to be staring somewhere off to his left.

"You can't lie to her in Mandarin, Kyung-Who-Speaks-in-Fury," Makes said from her bed. "Do you think she can't hear the lie?"

Taria stirred, standing. She lifted her head, as if listening to the air. "You need us, Kyung," she said. "You can't meet the Greater Singers alone."

*   *   *

The hover shrieked and battered at the air with its rotors, so loudly that Taria wanted to hold her hands over her ears. She knew now why the Blues had never developed enclosed vehicles: she was lost inside the hover, trapped in a noisy hell that made it nearly impossible to hear where she was. It was like being blindfolded and shoved into the trunk of a car.

For the first time in her life Taria truly understood the conflict Gramma Ruth had felt within herself. Part of her wanted to scream in panic, and she could hear that voice deep inside her. She knew that if she paid no attention to it, if she tried to ignore it, it would eventually surface and force her to acknowledge the fear. She knew that eventually that would have to happen anyway, that she would have to sit down and open herself to those feelings and let them run their course.

For now, she shoved that all too human part of her deep into herself and closed her ears to the howling. "Behind her face"; it was something Kyung should have understood.

She did little during the flight but curl up in her seat and wait for it to be over. And when she felt the bump of the hover touching ground, she was out of her seat quickly, grabbing a medkit and rushing outside as soon as the hatch doors opened.

Taria could hear the sullen *whup whup* of the rotors slowing. Behind her, she could hear Makes jumping down from the hatch and sending her inquisitive bursts of sound outward. Kyung followed them: the click of a weapon being loaded was loud as he exited the hover.

The sound of the rotors radiated outward, illuminating the wide meadow in which Taria stood. In the echoes of the sound she could sense the tangled wreckage of *Hawking*, a few meters to her right. Someone called, a weak voice heavy with pain. Taria hurried toward the sound, dropping to her knees in the tall grass. Hands clutched at her own, sticky with drying blood. Taria could smell the sharp scent of it. "Taria! Thank God! My legs . . ." the voice said, and Taria recognized the voice as Kwan, Kyung's friend. ". . . they're both broken, and I'm bleeding pretty bad . . ."

"We're here, Kwan. We'll get you out. Here, take this . . ." Taria fumbled in the medkit for the cylindrical shape of the morphine injector. If Kwan had survived the two hours since *Hawking*'s destruction, then Taria figured the bleeding wasn't critical, and though the smell of blood was strong, it wasn't overpowering. "Give me your arm," she said to Kwan, then pressed the top of the injector against her shoulder, hearing the hiss of the ampule as it broke. Kwan's breathing became steadier, slower. "Hang on for a few more minutes," Taria said. "I'll be back for you. I promise."

Taria stood up, turning as she listened. Makes and Strikes had moved away from the wreckage, standing farther out in the grasses that rustled in the fitful wind. Kyung was nearby; she could hear him breathing heavily as he shoved aside scraps of the hull. "Kyung, I've got Kwan over here. She's okay for the moment—let's keep looking." Already, she knew there was another body just to her left, knew by the shape of the hole in the sound of the rustling grass, and she moved toward it. The movement, the reaction, were all unconscious. For the moment, she'd forgotten that she couldn't see. It was enough to hear, to touch, to smell, to have an acoustic image of the landscape in her head.

She crouched alongside the body. This one was dead, she knew—there were no breath sounds, no movement, and the coppery blood smell blotted out everything else. She reached gingerly toward the body: there was no heat radiating from it. Almost, she touched it, but held back, not knowing what she might feel, not wanting to have to imagine the details of death.

She stood again, hearing Kyung nearby with Kwan, and she stopped. "What's the matter?" Kyung asked. "Taria?"

Makes was humming to herself, but there was another undertone, something that filled the air, seeming to come from everywhere.

"They're here," Makes boomed in the hush. "They're here."

"Back to the hover!" Kyung shouted. "Come on—grab Kwan and let's go!"

It was already too late for that. Taria heard the Greater Singer lift from below. If she could not see it, all of her other senses screamed alarm: the fire-crackling as it moved through the earth, the thunderous bass of its voice, the electric crackling against her skin as it rose up in front of them, huge and massive. Off to the side she heard Kyung rip his pistol from its holster. "Kyung! Don't!" she told him, but she heard the cough of the weapon. If there was a response from the Greater Singer, a change in its furious singing, she couldn't hear it. The Greater Singer didn't attack them; it simply waited there, and it sang. The sound of its voice pounded at them, the waves of rippling sound pounding at Taria's body so loudly that she was lost in it, engulfed.

Kyung had gone to Kwan; Taria heard the woman cry out as Kyung lifted her up and started to carry her to the hover.

Hands stroked her shoulders, her waist: Makes. She felt the Blue's passing touch as she strode past Taria toward the Greater Singer. She was singing also, a thin strand in the symphonic battering of the Greater Singer. "Makes!" Taria called to her, but the Blue didn't respond. Taria strained to hear the sounds of her movement through the Greater Singer's voice. The Greater Singer's song changed as Makes approached: the volume lowered while the pitch shifted up, matching Makes's own singing pattern. "Makes!" Taria called again.

It was the Greater Singer who answered. "Taria," it called, its voice singing, and the voice was familiar and aching. "Taria," it said again.

"Mama?" Taria whispered. She started walking toward the sound, toward the bulk of the Greater Singer.

"Christ, Taria, what the hell are you doing!"

She heard Kyung shout at her, but he was too far away to stop her now. She kept walking, feeling the presence of the Greater Singer rising before her, a gray wall that pressed against her skin, sparking. "Taria," it called again. She held out her hands toward it, feeling the tingle as they touched the slick, almost silken flesh of its body. It opened to her, the flesh opening like a dry wound in its side . . .

. . . and she entered.

Serena didn't notice Dimitri Ivanovich entering her office, as her attention was entirely on the window she'd opened above her desk. She'd watched the images from the hover's nose camera a dozen times now, each time hoping that she'd see something different, notice something she'd missed before that would help her. She was late in the sequence: the window showed nothing but swirls of brown dust and a confusion of jerky images of the Greater Singers, but she could hear the audio: the final minute of Ensign Xiong's transmissions over the net. Kyung was shouting at Taria Spears, warning her back from the Greater Singers. She evidently hadn't heeded the warning, or couldn't; Xiong's cry of despair, a long, wailing *"Nooooooo . . ."* followed, then his panting breath as he tried to run, carrying his wounded crewmate.

The dark bulk of a Greater Singer filled the window. First there was a moment of black with blue stars, then static. The audio continued for a few seconds more—Xiong cursing as the Greater Singer swallowed the hover, more panting, then . . . then . . .

. . . nothing.

"Close the window," McElwan said, and the window vanished. She glanced up and saw Ivanovich standing near the door. "Dimitri," she said. "Come on in. Have a seat." She took a breath. "Is there anyone down there still alive?"

Ivanovich came over to her desk and pulled a chair up from the floor. He sat with a sigh. "Sorry, Serena. All the personal net connections are gone. The satellite communications are still out, so we can't get a visual. There's no way to tell for certain, but I suspect . . ." He paused, grimaced. ". . . not."

Serena closed her eyes, steepling her hands over her nose. *More deaths laid at your feet, old woman. More spirits to haunt you at night . . .* "I'm going to order *Tycho Brahe* to go into orbit around Little Sister but not to land unless we know there are survivors. I don't want to lose another shuttle. We can't afford it." She glanced at Dimitri again. "Did you get the chance to run the scenario I mentioned?"

Commander Ivanovich had the grace to look troubled, an expression that settled uneasily on his full Slavic face. Serena wondered if her own face held the same grim sourness—she expected it did. "I ran them, Serena." The two of them had been involved in the *Lightbringer* project for the last five years, and Ivanovich was one of the few people Serena actually considered a friend. In private, they'd long ago ceased using titles. When Dimitri was in the room, Serena usually turned off Tomas as her PIA—as if Dimi's presence might make the simulation of her late husband jealous. "I still don't like the idea."

"Neither do I." She gestured at the desk in front of her, strewn with monofoil crystals. "I've been looking at every alternative anyone can put forward, no matter how farfetched." She picked up one of the crystals. "Here's one. We could use the shuttle engines to push us into a stable orbit around the sun—but the oxygen supply is finite, and all that effort buys us is maybe an extra half year while giving us a slow death by asphyxiation. On the other hand, at least *Lightbringer* remains as a mausoleum and warning to anyone else who might come here." She let the crystal fall back to her desk and plucked another from the pile.

"Here's another: Donahue up in Engineering believes

that we could attack the Greater Singers acoustically . . . if we can put together a large enough amplification system, if we can create exactly the right projection equipment, if we can figure out exactly what frequency or frequencies might hurt the Greater Singers, if we could understand their biology a whole lot better than we do, if we could get the whole array in the right place and the right time and if we could get these Greater Singers to come to it. Sounds like a hell of a lot of 'ifs' to me." The crystal dropped back with a stony *clink*. Serena glanced over at Dimitri.

"And you tell me that we're not going to be able to repair *Lightbringer* with the resources at hand—not in time, anyway. Has that assessment changed?" She didn't need an answer; the pain in his face and the way his hands clutched the arms of the chair were enough. "So tell me, will my scenario work?"

Slowly, Dimitri nodded. "It will work. I ran most of the simulations myself, so we wouldn't have people gossiping. If we take our remaining shuttles except *Tycho Brahe*, pack them with the nukes we have on board, and slam them into Little Sister in the right place in the right sequence at the right speeds, we do what the Cretaceous asteroid did on Earth and severely alter the environment. The impacts will throw cubic miles of rocky fragments into low orbit and torch the forests over most of the continent. Over the next several days, the fragments will reenter the atmosphere, the larger pieces still retaining enough heat from the impact that they'll be glowing white-hot—a rain of molten rock. The atmosphere of Little Sister will heat up dramatically for several days. Sulfuric acid generated by the impact will be thrown into the atmosphere, and the rain will have the pH of weak acid across the continent. The simulations say that the *least* we'd do is take out ninety percent of the life on the planet; at the far end of the projections, nothing much survives at all. It would take the Blues and Greater Singers decades to centuries to recover, if ever."

Serena took a long slow breath. "So," she breathed.

"I thought that was the answer you wanted to hear."

"It was. It's just not the solution I want."

Dimitri reached across the desk and touched her hand for a moment before leaning back in his chair again. "Then don't do it. We'll abandon *Lightbringer*. We'll use the shuttles ourselves and take everyone down, and either deal with these Greater Singers or die trying. That way, at least *we* have a chance." Serena could hear the excitement in his voice, his willingness to fight even against long odds. Then Dimitri shrugged. "The other way, your way, the scenarios say we *all* die."

"Maybe not. If Thunder opens up again—before we reach the limits of the shuttle's range for Little Sister—we'd still have *Tycho Brahe* to take us through."

"You think that's a likely scenario?"

"No," Serena answered quickly. "I think we'll all die. But from what we've seen of them, do you think it's likely that we can handle the Greater Singers?"

Dimitri paused. He took a long breath. "No. Nothing we had hurt them, and they knew enough to take out the satellites before we could use them. But at least—" Serena raised a finger to stop him, but Dimitri finished anyway. "—we go out fighting."

"*Your* way," Serena answered, "we're all dead anyway, *and* those things are still here. Spears had come to believe that they're the Makers, and I'm inclined to agree with her. Which means they're free to open up Thunder again and come through to Earth, without anyone at home knowing what they're like and how dangerous they are. The Greater Singers have already demonstrated how they react to us. How many would they kill before we stopped them? *If* we stopped them." Serena shook her head. "Dimi, let's say that after we throw the shuttles at Little Sister, we abandon *Lightbringer* and bring everyone and all we can salvage down to the planet with four crowded trips from *Tycho Brahe*, ten ship-days or so afterward. What do your scenarios say then?"

"Little Sister will be a mess from the shuttle impacts. The ecology of the planet will be wrecked and won't stabilize for one hell of a long time. Fires will still be burning, the temperatures will still be high . . ." Dimitri shrugged. "Our chances of survival would be incredibly low. And if we *haven't* taken out the Greater Singers, well . . ."

She looked at Dimitri and spread her hands wide. " 'Low' but not nil. Dimi, when I took on this assignment, it was made very clear to me that the prime duty was to make sure that our own world wasn't put in jeopardy by whatever was beyond Thunder. And now I'm afraid that may be the case. Am I being paranoid, Dimi?"

"I don't know," he answered. "None of us can really answer that yet."

Serena nodded. She fiddled with the crystals on her desk. "And we don't have time to find out. Which means, I'm afraid, that I will have to assume the worst. Will you start getting things ready?"

Dimitri pressed his lips tightly together. He pushed himself up from his chair. "I still don't like it," he said.

"I don't see that we have a choice."

"Is that a choice you're willing to make, with the consequences not only for yourself but everyone else aboard *Lightbringer*? It's not revocable, Serena. Once you send those shuttles out, our fate's set and we have only one course of action. I . . ." Dimitri shook his head. "I don't know that I could give that order, knowing I'm probably killing everyone else here."

"I know. But I could. I *will*, if *Tycho Brahe* tells me that no one's alive down there." Serena smiled at Ivanovich, sadly. "I suppose that's why they call me the Cold Lady, eh?"

✳ Inside the Belly of the Beast . . .

Her mother sang.

> *"E hine hoki mai ra*
> *E papa waiari*
> *Taku nei mahi*
> *Taku nei mahi*
> *Hei tuku roimata*
> *E aue e ka mate ahau*
> *E hine hoki mai ra . . ."*

> *Return to me, girl*
> *Sighing and grieving*
> *Is what I have been doing*
> *Is what I have been doing*
> *Here are my tears of woe*
> *Alas I will die*
> *Return to me, girl . . .*

Taria answered, singing the last line of the song in unison. *"Maku e kaute o hikoitanga"*—I will count your footsteps. When the last echo had died away, she called out softly. "Mama?"

"In here, darling."

Taria realized that she was standing in the tiny entrance-way of their apartment in Nanjing. She turned right and

337

saw her mother sitting in the wooden chair with the carved dragon's head at the back, the tail broken as it always had been. Her mother smiled at her, opening her arms, and Taria ran to her. Mama folded her into her body, and Taria fit as she always had. She sobbed in happiness.

"This isn't real, is it?" she said through the tears. "I feel you, I *see* you. And I'm four again."

"No," Mama said, stroking her hair. "It's not real. I wish it were. I wish it could be, darling. But it's not."

"Am I dead?"

A laugh. "No, love. You're not dead. You've been taken in—as Makes-the-Sound-of-East-Wind has been taken in, as the Neritorika was taken earlier today."

"You're a Greater Singer, then."

Mama laughed. "Not me. I'm a memory. A wisp of thought. A voice for many others, who are, yes, the Greater Singers."

Taria reached up and stroked her mother's face, her hair. Mama's skin felt warm, her hair silken, and light glittered in her smiling eyes. Taria sighed, wanting to cry again. If it was an illusion, it was so real, so compelling. She could stay here; she *wanted* to stay here. "Why are you doing this?"

Her mother shrugged, a gesture that Taria remembered, achingly. "I—we—don't truly know. Because you are different from the others. Because the Neritorika called you Taria-Baraaki. Because Makes-the-Sound-of-East-Wind is our Calabaraaki, and she speaks to you in the Language-of-Intimacy. Because you have Become, as only the Calabaraaki or Neritorika should be able to Become, and that makes us wonder about you. Otherwise, we would take you in to destroy you."

"Why? Why are you attacking us?"

"Because you're not part of this world. Because your presence disturbs the—" Mama hesitated. She cocked her head to one side, as if thinking, then smiled down at Taria on her lap. "Remember the bell you had—how lovely it sounded until it cracked. Then—"

"Then it sounded 'just clunk.' " Taria smiled momentarily at the memory. "Yes, I remember."

Mama smiled, too. "That is what your presence on this world is to us: a crack in the bell. We knew that when Allison-Who-Speaks-Empty-Words sent down the first one of you, and when we removed it, everything was fine. When you were here, it was different—you changed the sound, but you added another tone of your own, something alien and odd yet still compelling. But the more of you who came, and the more things you placed here, the larger the fissure became, until we couldn't ignore it."

"Mama . . ." Taria began, then shook her head. Despite the reality of the illusion, despite the reality of the image before her, this wasn't Mama and it wasn't her speaking, but someone else. "We don't have a choice. Not if we want to survive."

"That's what Allison-Who-Speaks-Empty-Words told us," Mama said.

"Allison? Allison's here, too?"

"Not any longer. He's dead." Another shrug, and with the movement, Taria felt a chill, the visceral realization that this was *not* Mama. She pushed away, getting off her lap, and when she stood, she was no longer four. "We know what's happened to *Lightbringer*," the vision of her Mama continued as if nothing had happened. "We are sorry for that and for our part in it, but there are billions more of you elsewhere, so the fate of so few of you doesn't matter. If we let you come here, in time there will be more and more of you, and the world wouldn't sing anymore."

"It's a world. It's large. There should be enough room for us all."

Mama smiled again, spreading her hands wide. "Is *your* world as it once was, Taria? Is there room enough for us *there*?"

Taria decided that question was rhetorical and didn't

need an answer. "Then send us back. You made Thunder, didn't you? Open it again and send us back."

"We made Thunder, yes. But to let you go back . . . ? You would let all the rest of you know that we are here." Mama smiled gently. "You'll forgive us if we don't trust you quite that much."

"We'll come here anyway. We'll bring everyone aboard *Lightbringer* here. I know the Admiral—she won't think she has a choice."

Mama shifted in her chair. She seemed to look out the window, and Taria glanced that way—outside was Nanjing, as she remembered it, the building as brightly colored as a child's imagination. "You've already sent two of your shuttles here. Do you think the others will fare differently?"

"No," Taria admitted. "Then why are you talking to me, if you've already decided what you're going to do?"

Mama looked at her, her face alight with a broad smile. She sang again, her voice full with a hundred others.

> *"Te whenua te whenua*
> *Te oranga mo te iwi*
> *No nga tupuna*
> *Tuku iho tuku iho."*
>
> *The land, the land*
> *is the life for the people*
> *Comes from the ancestors*
> *Handed down through the passages of time.*

"Do you remember that?" Mama asked. The echoes of the song seemed to continue, wafting in the air.

"Yes. *'E Hara I Te Mea'*—It Is Not a New Thing. Gramma Ruth used to sing it to me. So did . . ." *You*, she almost said. ". . . my mama," she finished.

"We made this land. When we came here—only the Eldest can remember that time—this place was barren and lifeless. We gave it life and form, and now we have ripened fully again. So we opened the pathway, and we found on the other side another planet like this one once had been, one we could take and change. That's the way it's always been—the largest planets have children, and we can take those infant worlds and change them, and when we are full and ripe again, we find another."

"Only this time, *we* came through," Taria said.

Mama laughed, a sound of ironic amusement. "Nine other times we've made the passage. Nine other dead worlds we took, and made them whole so that they can sing, a process that can take millions of your years. We've seen other worlds with other life-forms, but never life that could leave their own world. We did not expect *you*. We did not even notice you until you came, and even then we paid little attention to you until you destroyed the rock in the harbor. Then we knew that we had to watch more carefully."

"That still doesn't answer my question."

"You are Calabaraaki. That is why we brought you here."

"Makes called me that; and Strikes called Makes 'Calabaraaki.' I don't understand the term."

"When we are ready to put life on another world, there is always a Calabaraaki. It is the Calabaraaki who will be sent through, who contains the song of life." Mama smiled again. "She is the parent. The seed from which everything else comes. The Calabaraaki is sent through last, when the world's been prepared to receive her."

"And me? What is a human Calabaaraki?"

Mama shrugged again. She stood and took a step toward Taria, and her hand rose as if she were about to caress her cheek. Taria took a step back, not allowing her to close the distance. Mama's hand dropped back to her side. "We don't know, darling," she said. "That is what we need to find out."

Mama was holding her hand. She was four again, and they were leaving the apartment in Nanjing. "Where are we going, Mama?" Taria asked.

"Just for a walk," Mama answered, and they plunged into the crowds. Nanjing was as Taria remembered it: the dense crowds in the streets and around the sidewalk vendors; the chattering in the three dialects common to the city; the smells of people and charcoal grills and bus exhaust; the swirl of occasional bright clothing among the usual dark jackets; the chill of the autumn air. Taria could understand the occasional snatches of Mandarin, and she looked up at the dark-haired Asian faces around them, holding on desperately to her mother's hand.

A feeling of uncertain dread nagged at Taria, and she tugged on Mama's jacket with her free hand. "Mama, let's go home."

"We can't, darling," Mama answered. She didn't look back at Taria, but continued to push her way forward through the throngs. "I have to get something. Stay with me now, understand."

Taria clutched harder at Mama's hand, not wanting to get lost, not wanting to lose Mama.

They were down near the Yangtze now, at the edge of the market around the docks. The voices around them were louder, more strident. The smell of grilled fish wafted past them, delicious and salty, and Taria realized just how hungry she was, how hungry they all were. The money Mama and Papa brought in barely paid for all their expenses, and they subsisted on rice and a few vegetables, occasionally supplemented with fish or chicken. She heard her belly rumble in acknowledgment of the smells.

She was suddenly aware of the desperation all around her. She remembered the long hot and dry summer that had just ended, the way it had been difficult for everyone in Nanjing to find food, the hushed tones Mama and Papa used when they talked of food riots in the nearby towns.

There was a hunger in the crowd, and it scared Taria.

Mama pushed forward, and Taria saw a pile of muskmelons just unloaded from a small boat. The crowd surged forward at the same time, pushing, and Taria was torn away from her mother. "Mama!" Her mother glanced up, snatched the melon from the ground, and pushed back through the crowds toward her. A man shrieked at Mama as she tried to push against the crowd. "Thief!" he shouted in Mandarin. "You're stealing my melon!"

Mama glanced back, but it was obvious she didn't understand. She tried to smile at Taria, though Taria saw the uncertainty in the way she looked back in apprehension. "Look, Taria! This will taste good at supper tonight." The man seemed to have disappeared. "I need to find the vendor to pay—"

"Mama, he's back there," Taria said. "He thinks you're—" *stealing the melon*, she started to say, but in that same moment, the man pushed through the ranks of people around the melons. He brandished a pistol, the silvered barrel glinting in the sun as he moved into a quickly emptying lacuna in the crowd.

"Mama!" Taria shouted, and she was no longer four. She was herself, and she knew what would happen, remembering the terror of that day, and she had Kyung's stundart in her hand, the weapon he'd placed in her backpack when she left for Little Sister. She glanced down; the top of the stundart glinted blood red at her: it was set to full discharge, to kill rather than stun. She brought it up, shouting wordlessly: as her mother started to turn, startled, as the crowd moved away, as the melon seller came out and pointed his own gun.

He was Kyung. The realization came in the instant before she could pull the trigger. It was Kyung glaring at her mama, his face twisted in a rictus of anger. It was Kyung who waved his gun about, then brought it down ... down ... still shouting at her mother to give back the melon, to turn around ... down ... shouting in Mandarin that Taria could not translate quickly enough ... down ...

She could stop it, this time. She could save her mother's life. All she had to do was take Kyung's life instead.

The moment was frozen, Kyung trapped in mid-shout,

his finger just starting to tighten around the trigger, the weapon still slightly lifted. The people stood around them in a ragged circle, some running away, others staring in horror or fascination or fear, and Mama was just starting to turn back to the vendor/Kyung. But without moving her body, trapped in mid-motion, she spoke to Taria.

"You have to decide, darling."

"This isn't real."

"Isn't it? Have you already decided what we are or aren't capable of?" The voice was soft, gentle, and infinitely sad.

"Kyung wasn't there. I didn't have a gun. I was four. I couldn't do anything about it."

"You can *now*. And you must decide. How should this play out, Taria?"

"You're not *real*, Mama."

"I can be real. We could make it real for you. You would have me back. You could start over again." The empathy in the voice throbbed, rich and full. There could only be truth in that voice, there could only be concern for her.

"By killing Kyung." Taria cried the words, tears shivering the scene before her. She was frozen, too, unable to move, unable to break this spell.

"I promise you that you wouldn't know it was Kyung, not afterward," Mama said, and Taria knew that to be true, knew it beyond possibility of question. The words were a song, and the song was a promise. "You'd be four again, Taria, and it would be the two of us, and Papa, and we could go back to New Zealand and be with Gramma and Grampa again. Whatever you want. It's your choice, but you must choose. Are you ready, Taria?"

"Wait!" Taria shouted, her voice breaking in a cry, a wail, but the tableau was beginning to dissolve now, the figures blurring back into motion.

"Choose!" Mama said. "Now, darling. Now. Do you trust me, or do you trust him?"

And the roar of Nanjing sang in her ears, and Kyung

brought the weapon down, and her mother started to spread her arms wide in horror. Taria, sobbing, pointed the barrel of the stundart at Kyung's chest.

The gunshot sounded loud, a thunder in silence.

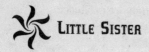 LITTLE SISTER

Since Dimi had left, a headache had asserted its presence. Serena pretended to ignore it, but now—watching *Tycho Brahe* arrive in orbit around Little Sister—she could feel the throbbing in her temples, each beat of her pulse another shiver of pain.

The pilot of the *Tycho Brahe* was Theo Davies, who had flown the third Firebird through Thunder. One of the Firebirds was with him now, riding shotgun for the shuttle. Davies was confident and almost cocky—he couldn't have been anything else and been chosen to be aboard *Lightbringer*—but Serena thought she could detect a certain apprehension in his voice as he slipped his shuttle into orbit. She spoke softly, trying to keep the headache at bay. "Davies, if there's *any* sign of hostility, you will take your ship out of orbit and head back to *Lightbringer.* The Firebird will engage first to give you time. Is that clear?"

"No one likes to run, Admiral," Davies answered a second or two later, but before Serena could retort, he added: "But I understand my orders. I'll bring her back."

"Good. See that you do." Her head throbbed. Serena had several windows open with various views from the cameras and instruments aboard *Tycho Brahe.* None of them looked encouraging. There was no sign of the hover, of Xiong, Spears, or any of the survivors of *Hawking*, or of

346

the Greater Singers. The land below seemed untouched except for the gouged, blackened grass where *Hawking* had crashed, and the huge, black curve of a Greater Singer moving slowly through the landscape as if it were water. "Is there *any* indication of survivors?" she asked Tomas. "Anything at all?"

Her PIA's voice was grim and clipped. *We have Systems reviewing the data. The network's already decided on first review that there's no one alive down there except the Singer. Commander Ivanovich is asking for enough time to allow* Tycho Brahe *another pass.*

Dimi doesn't want to give up. He knows the cost of that answer. She thought the words, but didn't allow Tomas to hear them. Serena assumed that the security on her PIA was tight enough that no one could intercept her interaction with Tomas, but there was still a chance that someone had cracked it—too many talented people were aboard *Lightbringer.* The light from the various windows was limned with hazy sparks, and Serena closed her eyes. "Tell Commander Ivanovich that he can have the extra pass, as long as *Tycho Brahe* is not threatened. If we can't detect survivors on the second orbit, then *Tycho Brahe* will return here."

And then I'm going to take out Little Sister and almost certainly seal our own fate, she finished, silently. She watched Little Sister's landscape rolling underneath *Tycho Brahe*, and she rubbed her temples with her fingertips. The west coast was just coming into view: down there were clusters of Blue cities.

All of which, once she gave the order, would fall under the barrage of tsunamis and a cloud of angry ash. The Blues would pay back far more than a thousand to one for the lives of the humans the Greater Singers had killed. Serena didn't even truly know if the Blues were responsible, or if the Greater Singers were actually connected to them biologically or culturally. It didn't matter, because the weapon with which *Lightbringer* threatened them could not discriminate between them, or between any other life-forms on Little Sister.

Serena felt each of those lives as if she'd already killed them, each another needle in her forehead, each adding to the agony in her head. She couldn't open her eyes, couldn't bear the thought of letting in the stabbing light.

"Let me know when *Tycho Brahe*'s made the next orbit," she said to Tomas. "And have the clinic send me up some NoPain tabs."

Done, Tomas's voice said. *The medicine's on the way.*

Serena suspected that nothing was really going to take away the pain in her head. The tabs might blunt it, but the pain was deeper than medicine could reach.

"Serena?"

Serena touched the contact on her desk, and the light in her office went from dusk to early evening. "Sorry, Dimi," she said. "A headache. It's mostly gone now." She waited. A beat. "I heard. Tomas told me."

He stood near her in the dimness, a shadowed, heavy presence, his voice dark and comforting. "There are still other ways, Serena," he said. "We don't need to do this."

She smiled at that. "It's not 'we' in any case, Dimi. Just me. I get to shoulder the blame and the karma. And I don't think I have a choice."

"Give me more time to go over the data, to make sure there's no one left down there."

"Is it going to make a difference, Dimi?"

She saw his shrug. "No." He nearly growled the word. "I don't think so."

"Is everything ready?"

"Yes. All you need to do is give the order."

The headache was threatening to return, and Serena started to rub her temples when Dimi moved a step toward her. His thick, muscular fingers touched either side of her forehead, caressing gently. He'd never touched her before, not like that, and she started to draw back, then stayed where she was, glancing up at him. His eyes glinted in the murky room light. "Should I stop?" he asked.

"No. It feels good. Thank you." She looked up at him again. "I have to do this, Dimi. If I do, I know I'm probably sentencing everyone here to death, over a thousand people. I know that. But if I don't and the Greater Singers decide that they're mad at Earth, then how many millions might end up dying? I don't have a choice. I'll note your objection and the objections I expect to hear from others in the log we'll leave in permanent orbit around Little Sister."

His fingers banished the throb of the returning headache. "This is no way for you to be remembered."

Serena reached up and took his hands in her own, bringing them down in front of her. "Tomas," she said to the air, and her husband's voice answered in her head.

Here.

"Order *Tycho Brahe* back to *Lightbringer*. And . . ." She paused. Dimi was watching her, silent. ". . . launch the other shuttles."

Done. A faint shudder ran through the ship, rattling the decking. Serena sighed, her gaze still on Dimi, her hands still clasping his. "I'm sorry," she said.

Dimi nodded. He brought her hands to his lips and kissed them, then pulled away. "The terrible thing is that we'll never know whether we made the right decision or not."

Serena put her hands on her desk. She could still feel the touch of Dimi's lips on her fingers. "Maybe," she said. "But I think it would be more terrible to actually know."

Kyung!

Tee's voice was loud in his head. Disoriented, Kyung spun around. He was standing on the grassy field, with the tangled wreckage of *Hawking* around him and the smell of smoke and burned fuel lingering in the air. Kwan was lying on the ground near him, and the hover stood seemingly untouched not far off. The dark, rounded hulk of a Greater Singer loomed nearby, like brooding night. "Taria?"

Kyung called, then shouted, watching the Greater Singer. "Taria!" There was no answer.

"Tee," Kyung breathed, crouching down beside Kwan; he touched her neck and felt a strong pulse: she was alive. "Where's Taria?"

Don't know. You were out of the net for almost five hours. Hold on . . .

Another voice came through the network relay. *"Kyung, this is Davies in* Tycho Brahe. *We're heading back to pick you up. Hang on—I've got an ETA of about forty minutes. Then we really need to get the hell out. McElwan has heavy-duty ordnance coming in."*

"Theo, you'd better hold off. I've still got one of those Sing—" Kyung heard a sound, like miles of cellophane being crumpled by a giant hand; when he turned to look, the Greater Singer was gone. There was nothing but unbroken ground in the valley. "Damn . . . All right, Theo. It's gone, at least for the moment. I have Kwan with me, and Taria should be here somewhere, too. I'm going to try to get the hover up and stay in it until you get here."

"On our way, my friend . . ."

"Taria!" Kyung called again. He lifted Kwan up. She groaned through dry, cracked lips, and her eyelids fluttered. "It's okay, Kwan," he told her. "It's okay. They're coming for us. We're getting out of here." He didn't know if she heard any of it; her eyes had closed again. He carried her to the hover, stopping twice to rest and scanning for signs of Taria or the return of the Greater Singer. He called for Taria each time, each time more frantic when there was no answer. *Almost five hours out of the net*, Tee had said. So much time, and he remembered none of it, nothing between the initial appearance of the Greater Singer and now. "Taria! Come on, love! Answer me!"

Kyung prowled through the wreckage. There were other bodies there, all of them dead—judging from the wounds and generally mangled appearance of most of them, he assumed they'd died in the crash. Local insects had been at them as well: there were wriggling, tiny forms moving in the wounds—orange bodies attached to bright blue heads, forming nests of white fiber in the body cavities, or black dots like sesame seeds that would suddenly fly up from a bloody carcass as he passed, leaving a stench of terrible corruption in their wake. Kyung retched and fought his stomach.

Taria wasn't among the bodies. Kyung widened his search, moving out from the wreck of *Hawking* into the surrounding plain. He found no one else alive at all.

It made no sense. The Greater Singer had swallowed up the whole area inside itself. Kyung remembered that moment, vividly—the feel of being enveloped, the sparking, electric sensation as the thing had contacted him. But it left everything else as it had been: himself, Kwan, the hover, the wreck. Everything but Taria. And Makes, though Kyung was hardly concerned with the Blue's fate.

Five hours the thing had held him . . .

Kyung was still searching when he heard the sonic boom as *Tycho Brahe* entered the atmosphere. A few minutes later he heard the wail of jets and saw the dark speck of the shuttle with its contrail. He waved his arms as the shuttle moved closer, its landing jets just beginning to fire.

"Gotcha on visual, Kyung. Thought you were going to be in the hover."

"I was looking for Taria. She's still missing."

"We don't have much time here. Admiral's orders. Any more signs of the Singers?"

"None, Theo. It's been quiet. I assume you have medical with you; you're going to need triage with Kwan. Everyone else I've found is dead. I've got the bodies flagged, the ones I could find, anyway."

"The bodies stay. We touch down, we get you and anyone else who's alive, and we go. Everything else stays."

"Theo, I just need a bit more time. Taria was here, and the Singers haven't taken anything else with them. She should be here—"

"I'm sorry, Kyung. Really I am. But you've had all the time the Cold Lady's gonna give you. We'll pick you up by the hover."

"I can't leave, Theo. Not yet."

"No choice, man. No choice."

"Taria!" Kyung shouted again, desperately. The shuttle banked and settled; the landing jets shrilled, pounding the ground with waves of heat as *Tycho Brahe* lowered itself. Landing struts groaned as they took the shuttle's weight, and the cargo bay opened. A dozen marines in powered skirmish armor spilled out. Voices shouted in his head: *"Let's go! Move it!"* Kyung found himself picked up, still shouting for Taria, as others retrieved Kwan. He was still calling for Taria as hands pulled him into the shuttle, as the voices shouted inside him, as the vertical jets kicked back into life and the deckplate lurched underneath him, as medics in biohazard suits swarmed around him and the bay door shut, severing his last glimpse of Little Sister.

❄ LIFE IS ACCIDENTAL . . .

She remembered . . .

Mama sagged like a broken puppet. It was the same vision Taria had held in her memories for so long, the sight gouging open the emotional scar tissue with which the years had coated it. Taria screamed—*"Mama!"*—watching her mother's body spin under the impact of the bullet while blood soaked the front of her jacket. The melon lay broken on the ground, her hand splayed out toward it. The gun smoked in Kyung's hand; stricken, Taria dropped her unused stundart. She ran forward—she seemed to be four again—and crouched down beside her Mama, lifting her as she'd wanted to do that morning, cradling her and sobbing. "Mama, don't die, Mama. Please . . ."

Mama's face turned toward her, and she smiled. "You surprise us, darling," she said.

"Mama, I'm sorry! I'm so sorry . . . I couldn't . . . Please don't die again!" She looked up at Kyung, desperate. "Help me, Kyung," she said. "You have to help me."

Kyung didn't move. A long, low drone echoed, a thousand voices filling the dissonant chord. Everything was changing around her, the market square and the crowd dissolving, then ripping like a mist in a sudden wind, her mother becoming smoke in her arms. The song shifted, altered itself, and the sound hammered at Taria like a blinding light, unrelenting.

When it ended, abruptly, Taria was blind again, lost in darkness. For a moment she panicked, her breath fast and her chest tightening. She was still sobbing, and the remembered weight of her mother was reflected in her cupped arms. *Listen* . . . a voice whispered in her head, and she did. The darkness seemed to recede as she shifted her attention from her eyes to her ears and her other senses. Her skin prickled with warmth: Yin was out, even if she could no longer see the visible light. There were rocks and sand under her feet—she could hear the crunch of wet gravel and thick sand as she took a tentative step, arms out—and there was the smell of saltwater in the air. There were watersingers nearby: she heard them splashing in the surf, and somewhere close a bull had started singing. One by one other watersingers joined in, a low melody like an incantation. She was alone otherwise. She listened for Kyung's breath, but heard nothing. "Kyung?" she called out. "Kyung!"

There was no answer.

Her skin prickled with the presence of a Greater Singer. She could hear the crackling, fiery sound as it rose from the beach in front of her.

"You *have* changed." The voice, in accented Mandarin, was familiar, but it came from the brooding hillock of the Greater Singer.

"Makes?" she said, and underneath her confusion was rage at the way her mind had been twisted and used.

"Makes . . ." The voice repeated the word, as if turning it over on its tongue and marveling at the sound. "Yes, that was a name we used." A hundred other timbres rode in her words, shadows of other voices. "Part of us was Makes."

"You goddamn son of a bitch!" Taria screamed at the Greater Singer. Her voice cracked, and she rubbed at the tears fiercely, glaring toward the space where the Greater Singer rested. "Where is Kyung? What did you do with him?"

"He isn't like you. We couldn't make him part of us, as we could you. We left him behind."

"Dead?"

"Alive. His life or death isn't ours to decide."

"No. But you'd let *me* kill him, or was he just another dream?"

The Greater Singer growled low and soft. "Kyung was real, Taria-Who-Wants-to-Understand. But he and you were given different images. For Kyung, he was back in the Neritorika's cavern, and Strikes saw that the Neritorika was dead and he moved toward you. Kyung saw the kagliaristi's finger-blades, and he shot him—"

"You *bastard*!" Taria shouted the word, screaming the invective at Makes. She wiped at her blind eyes and felt tears smear across her cheeks. Her voice cracked on the word, breaking. "You played with us, lied to us. If I'd used the stundart, I'd've killed Kyung, and you would have let me do it."

"Yes." The Greater Singer's voice—Makes's voice—was unperturbed. The watersingers were still singing, and at least one more Greater Singer was somewhere close; Taria heard its thundering voice join the watersingers. "But we didn't lie to you. Had that been your choice, we would have kept you within us. We would have let you live out whatever life your mind and memories devised. We would have kept our promise."

The anger and sorrow still shrilled in Taria's voice. "You'd have given me a fucking *false* life, not a real one."

"You wouldn't have known the difference. Can you tell us for certain that *this* is not a 'false' life, another inner dream?" Makes almost seemed to laugh, a sound Taria had never heard her make before. "You can't. It's a disturbing thought, isn't it?" The Greater Singer throbbed a great bass tone that Taria felt in her stomach. "When we were Makes, I told you that you would change. We kept that promise, too."

"Fuck you! You blinded me!"

"You were given more than sight."

"It's not what I *wanted*."

A burst of sound hit her chest like a soft fist. "You chose to let your mother die rather than kill Kyung. Was *that* what you wanted? No, don't say anything. We can hear your anger, and we understand it. We understand so much more now."

"Is that what it all was, some kind of fucking test? I hope you goddamn enjoyed it." Taria took a step toward the Greater Singer, wanting to strike Makes and force the Blue to feel her anger. She punched blindly, feeling her fist contact the surface of the beast then press within as if pushing through a thin membrane. Her skin prickled, then the tingling entered within her skin, as if the Greater Singer had entered her as easily as she had entered into it. Taria pulled back, cradling her fist to her chest, and started to cry again, more from frustration than sorrow. She sat down hard on the beach, shivering in the cool, wet wind and wiping at her eyes. She could hear the watersingers moving toward her, could feel the warmth as they circled around her: their fur incredibly warm and soft and comforting, their singing a pliant embrace. "Makes . . . Makes, I'm scared. I'm so goddamn *scared*."

"For humans, it's almost too simple," Makes answered. "You exist alone. To make more of you, you need nothing but a male's sperm and a female's egg and the decision to reproduce. You stay alone. There is no greater whole that requires you to be part of it." The Greater Singer vented, a great, concussive blast of air that sounded like an explosion. "Not for us. Kagliaristi must have Singers-in-the-Water to give their seed vitality. Neritorikas must have kagliaristi to fertilizer their eggs. Greater Singers do not reproduce at all, but wait to see which of the Singers-in-the-Water or Children-of-She-Who-Spoke-the-World can Become when they take the Water-That-Changes. And the Water-That-Changes is filled with the Life-Too-Small-to-

Hear—you would call them 'viruses,' I think, though they are more that that—who live within the Greater Singers. And when it is time, the Greater Singers wait for the Calabaraaki, the Seed-of-a-New-World, to take her in and send her on."

"You."

"Yes." The Greater Singer paused. "And you."

Taria shook her head. The watersingers huddled around her. "Not me. Makes, that can't be."

"We asked you once to trust us, Taria-Who-Wants-to-Understand. Trust us now." The Greater Singer moved closer; Taria felt it, felt the pressure and tingling of it pushing against her, felt herself leaning back away from the intrusion and then . . . then . . . relaxing with a cry.

She let herself be taken in.

. . . Mama pushed forward, and Taria saw a pile of muskmelons just being unloaded from a small boat. The crowd surged forward at the same time, pushing, and Taria was torn away from her mother for a moment. "Mama!" Her mother glanced up, snatched the melon from the ground, and pushed back through the crowds toward her. A man shrieked at Mama as she tried to push against the crowd. "Thief!" he shouted in Mandarin. "You're stealing my melon!"

Mama glanced back, but it was obvious she didn't understand. She tried to smile at Taria, though Taria saw the uncertainty in the way she looked back in apprehension. "Look, Taria! This will taste good at supper tonight." The man seemed to have disappeared. "I need to find the vendor to pay—"

"Mama, he's back there," Taria said. "He thinks you're—" *stealing the melon*, she started to say, but in that same moment, Mama interrupted her.

"Oh, there he is . . ." The vendor had pushed through the crowds, still screaming at Mama. She dug into her coat pocket and held out a handful of bills toward the man. The vendor snatched two of the bills away, still grumbling. Mama put the rest of the money back in her pocket. "Let's go home," she said. "We'll share this your papa when he gets home."

"But Mama . . ." Taria started to protest. Confused images filled her mind. The vendor . . . why would his name be Kyung? A gunshot, Mama falling on the ground . . . but Mama was holding her hand, and they were walking back through the crowds toward Nanjing Gate, strolling toward the apartment through a day that was beautiful and noisy and brilliant.

. . . She sat at the table with Mama, but she wasn't four anymore. Pieces of muskmelon adorned a plate in the middle of the plain linen tablecloth. She remembered the plate, pale yellow with a floral display around the edges. The edge of the plate was chipped; every plate in the set was chipped by the time they left China. Taria took a wedge of the fruit: sweet juice filled her mouth as she bit into it. "I missed you," she said. "All those years, Mama. All those times I wanted you to be there, to have you to talk to and share my life."

"It wasn't your fault, darling," Mama answered. "It wasn't my fault. It wasn't even the melon vendor's fault. It just was. Life is accidental. We get what we get, and we can't worry about how it's all going to end, because we don't control that." Mama picked a piece of fruit herself. "Your father did what he could, you know. Judy was good to you, also. And Gramma Ruth."

"I know. I know." Taria sucked at the tips of her fingers and plucked another piece of melon from the dish. "I miss Gramma Ruth, too."

. . . "I miss you also," Gramma Ruth answered. "But I never left. Not really. Only the *Pakeha* part dies; the Maori part remains." She swept her arm wide to indicate the hillside overlooking the old homestead. They were sitting on Gramma Ruth's gravestone, and Grampa Carl and Mama's graves were on either side. "They're *all* still here, part of them. I see them sometimes. I talk with them. You hold us, Taria. You hold us all. *They* know it."

The night sky was filled with bright blue sparks and the sound of singing. They sat and watched for a few moments, silent. Gramma Ruth put her arm around Taria.

. . . and her father shifted, and her shoulder cooled as he moved his arm away. Taria turned to him. "I would have given you anything you wanted," she said. "I wanted so much to please you, because you were all I had left. All you had to do was ask, but it seemed like we talked less and less over the years, until we didn't talk at all—not about things that mattered."

Papa shrugged. It was his usual response. They were sitting on the porch of the house in Pensacola. As Taria watched, a lizard skittered along the railing and down into the palmettos. "I didn't know how to talk to you. I never wanted to hurt you, but the longer it went on and the older you got, the more there was to say and explain, and the harder it was. Eventually I even stopped worrying about it." His hand lifted and fell back into his lap like a stricken bird. His dark eyes found hers and then drifted away again, uncomfortable. "I'm sorry, Taria. It was hard for me to say the words, and that's my fault, not yours." He reached over and touched her hand. "But I have something to ask you now."

In the night sky, streaks of light burned amid the blue sparks. Taria watched them, wondering how to answer. Part of her wanted to scream at him, to tell him that, goddamn it, it was too late for that, that the overlay of the bad years had eroded most of her affection for him. "What?" she finally asked, gruffly. "What is it you want?"

. . . "That's a question I never had to ask you," Nikki answered. "Hell, I always knew exactly what you wanted. I could see it, every time something came on about that damned Thunder. You cared more about a frigging hole in the sky than me. I knew I could never love you enough to make you see me instead of it."

"Nikki, I *did* love you."

She smiled, that lopsided grin that had always made Taria's heart melt. Nikki's fingertip grazed along the line of her jaw. "You loved me as much as you could. I know that. It just wasn't enough—not for me. Not for you, either, when it came down to it."

"I'm sorry."

Again the smile. "Don't be. It's the way you are. It's why we're talking to you now. See . . ." Nikki pointed at the sky. The light trails were still there, swirling through the blue sparks and arrowing toward her. Nikki lifted Taria's hand, and she could feel them, hot and violent. She could follow the trails backward, toward a hardness in the void. "We need you to take care of those."

"Just send them away," Taria said to Nikki. "Can't you do that?"

"No. We've tried. Go ahead, push at them."

Taria did, but the hardness of the moving streaks passed through her hand. "There, you see," Nikki said. "When I left you, Taria, when I knew that I had lost you to Thunder, I didn't try to hurt you. They've lost you, and they try to hurt us."

"They don't understand. They're afraid. *I'm* afraid."

"There's no reason to be afraid. Not of me." Nikki lifted her hand, and Taria caught it in her own.

"I know," Taria answered softly. "What do you want me to do?"

. . . "Trust me," Makes said to her in Mandarin. Blood was drooling from parallel, long cuts on her arms, deep wounds that Taria knew Strikes must have inflicted on her.

Makes tried to take a step toward her and staggered, and Taria rushed forward. "Let me help you," she said. She started to reach toward Makes, but Makes had taken Taria's hand instead. Blue sparks stuttered where their alien skins touched.

"There," Makes said. She lifted Taria's hand. "Feel it as we do."

And she did. She felt the wash of noise in a thousand frequencies, felt how it radiated outward from *Lightbringer*, and she followed it back, feeling the neural web return to life in her mind.

✳ LITTLE SISTER

He was standing next to the med-unit covering Kwan's sleeping body.

Kyung!

"What's up, Tee?"

Dog's back in the system. At least I think it's Dog. She's . . . changed.

Kyung's breath hissed between his teeth. *Tycho Brahe*'s drive shuddered the floor plates under his feet. He glanced around; there were cameras in the bay, and the medics could walk in at any moment. He subvocalized, leaning over Kwan's med-unit so no one could see the faint movements of his lips. *"Is it Taria?"*

That's what Dog says.

"She's alive, then . . ." The relief Kyung felt surged through him like cool water. He stroked the curved plastic cover of the med-unit as if he were touching her body. *"Tell Dog I need to talk to Taria directly. I can get Theo to head back and pick her up. There's still time, I think . . ."*

Dog says that's not possible. But she wants me to run interference for her before the net snoops find her and shut her down.

"What's Dog after?"

Access to the shuttle controls.

"*Ta mada.*" Kyung spoke the curse aloud in Mandarin, then tried to cover it by crouching down and reaching

362

through the cover of the med-unit to take Kwan's hand. He imagined the shuttles launched from *Lightbringer* striking Little Sister, spewing dark clouds high in the atmosphere and spawning firestorms . . . *"Tee, I can't do that. I don't even know if it's possible."*

Dog said that you'd say that. He said that Taria says that you need to trust her, trust that this is the right thing to do.

Kwan's hand clasped his. He thought he saw her eyelids move. He wondered if she was remembering *Hawking*'s destruction, the barrage of sound from the Greater Singers bringing the craft down, the lines of cutting lasers slicing through them without harming them at all. He doubted that Kwan would call back the shuttles, if the decision was hers.

There was no good decision here. There was only intuition and hope.

Air shimmered in front of Kyung, like a desert's heat waver. A distorted, wispy voice emerged from the waver. "Kyung, you should remember that you once said that you weren't the uniform you wear. I always believed that. I still do."

"Taria?" Kyung managed to husk out.

"Yes," the air whispered back.

"How?"

"Words are just moving air, Kyung. A song or a word or a promise or a question—they're all the same. Yet it's so difficult . . . so hard . . . I can't . . ." The waver vanished. There was only air in front of him again. Kyung found himself breathing hard and fast. He reached out, as if he could touch Taria. He waited, but Taria—if it *had* been Taria—didn't return. Finally, he went back inside his head. *"Tee, tell Dog we'll come back and pick her up."*

She tells Dog she doesn't need to be rescued. Not if you let Dog do what she's asked.

"Dog can't *do it. The security's going to be way too tight."*

Dog thinks she can beat the security. She just needs

time. And she's running out of it. Tell me, Kyung. Yes or no. We need to know now.

Kyung's fingers tightened around Kwan's. Two of the medics came back into the bay, wearing their biosuits. Kyung stood up and waved to them. He remembered the heat waver and the husk of her voice. Yes or no . . . how could he choose any other way? *"All right, Tee. Yes. And Tee, tell Dog . . . tell Dog to let Taria know that I love her."*

She said she knows, Tee answered.

Kyung thought that was all he would hear. Then Tee's voice came again. *She says that she's sorry it took her so long to realize it, but she loves you, too.*

Dog yelped in pain, and Taria watched dark lightning crackle around her PIA's form as it crumpled and died. Tee had vanished a few seconds before, smashed under the attack from net security as she tried to protect Dog and give her a few more seconds of access time—Taria hadn't known that Kyung had formed his PIA in her image, and it was like watching her own death. The truth was that in the year and a half they'd been together, she'd never really paid attention to how much Kyung cared for her, and guilt stabbed at her, an obsidian blade. She reached toward Dog as the black, hooded forms of the security watchdogs hurried toward her slain PIA, and she snatched the glowing core of light from Dog's paws. She held up the ball of radiance, marveling at the glow, then hugged it to herself.

Bitstreams ran through her, threads of light weaving patterns. She followed them, taking in the song of data and finding the links to the shuttles streaking toward Little Sister. The system watchdogs gathered around her, making darting attacks that she ignored despite the stinging pain. The watchdogs snarled and yapped alarm: they weren't sure who this presence in the net could be, or how to eradicate it. She could sense the opening of the net, the sudden prying of human hands trying to block her.

Yes, there it is . . . Taria knew that the Cold Lady

wouldn't have launched the shuttles without an abort option—she would want that last bit of caution, a fail-safe
against mistake. Taria opened that command, sent it arrowing outward like the gaseous shell of a nova. When the
snippet of code touched the moving hardness of the shuttles, it flared. She pushed, and shuttles fell away from their
paths, as if she were scattering a handful of seeds.

Taria heard the pulse of relief from the Greater Singers,
heard the wail of alarm from the watchdogs and the system
operators.

Taria let herself drop out of the net, tumbling through
the Emptiness and falling back to Little Sister, into the
welcoming embrace of the Greater Singers. She was
standing on water near the beach where she and Makes
had first heard the Greater Singers, but her body was dif-
fuse and airy, a part of the greater whole, with no particular form of its own except the shape her mind imposed
upon it. Waves lapped over and through her ankles, and
she felt neither the chill of the sea nor the touch of the water. Makes appeared alongside her; the Blue's head-crest
was erect and colorful, all the earlets pointed toward her.
She gave a *hroom* of welcome and reached out as if to
stroke Taria's body as she always had.

There was no sense of flesh, only a shivering, an electric
tingle: two ghosts embracing. "We're part of them now,
aren't we?" Taria asked, and Makes's eyestrip convulsed in
a blink.

"Yes," she said. "We thank you, Taria-Calabaraaki. This
was not something we could have done ourselves."

"Then show me that my trust in you was warranted,"
Taria replied. "Show me."

Taria was answered with a drone note from the watersingers: the Song-of-Preparation. A few seconds later
the Greater Singers loaned their powerful voices to the rising symphony, a song louder and more complex than any
Taria had heard before.

"Sing with us," Makes said. "Join with us now."

"You'll go through," Taria said. "Your DNA, your genetic structure, your racial memories—you'll send that through as the catalyst, the start of more life. That's what the Calabaraaki does."

"So you understand." Makes's mouth opened in a nearly human smile. "Yes. But you are also Calabaraaki. *Both* of us will go."

"Makes . . . I'm not the same species as you. What would happen if I go with you? Would life even start there at all?"

"We don't know," Makes answered. "But there's only one way to find out. Sing, Taria-Calabaraaki. Sing with us."

Taria opened her mouth.

She felt her own voice intertwine with the whole.

It was then, in the center of the circle, that Taria heard-saw for the first time the form their song created.

She gasped in wonder and delight.

The Cold Lady was not cold at all. She was heat and fury, and her very presence threatened to sear Kyung's skin. Even the two marines who flanked Kyung shrank back a half step as the Admiral stalked to Kyung, who hid himself behind his face as she approached, shielding himself from showing any emotion. He endured her burning stare, her stern examination of his features, and the scorn that imbued each word she spoke.

"Does it bother you to know that you've killed us, Ensign Xiong?"

"I don't agree with that assessment, Admiral." They'd given Kyung a biosuit before they allowed him out of the isolation unit. The stiff fabric rubbed against his skin, and the faceplate seemed to smear his vision. His voice was muffled and dead.

"Who the *hell*"—McElwan stopped pacing and glared at him—"elected you God?" She didn't wait for an answer, but turned abruptly and went back to her desk. A window was open above and to one side. She looked at it, and the view changed to show the achingly bright ball of Yin. Inside Kyung's head there was only silence. Tee was dead, his net connection severed. McElwan pointed at the sun. "That's where we're headed now. There, or to Little Sister so the Greater Singers can kill us."

"Taria's still alive, Admiral. She's with the Greater Singers."

"Yes?" The scorn snarled in her voice. "Or have you just been duped by them?" McElwan pushed her chair away from her desk with an expression of disgust. "Listen," she said, and sound filled the room, the roar of the Greater Singers. "We still have a few bugs down on Little Sister. Listen to them, Ensign. There must be nearly a hundred of the damn things, all gathered together in the bay. We would have taken them all out. All of them." The song, if that's what it was, rose and fell, so loud that Kyung could barely hear the Admiral's voice over the cacophany. "By regulations, I could have you court-martialed and executed. Are you aware of that, Ensign?"

Kyung nodded. He remained hidden behind his face, behind the hood of the biosuit.

Something moved in the window above the Admiral's desk, eclipsing Yin and the stars. A darkness . . .

Kyung realized what it was in the same instant that the Admiral's face went distant, as she heard the commotion within the net, as he heard the Greater Singers' song reach a shuddering crescendo. Alarms hooted throughout the ship, nearly drowning out the Greater Singers.

Thunder . . . Silent, blacker than night, immense . . .

Its yawning maw opened directly before them.

TIME OF SILENCE

Attain to utmost Emptiness.
Cling single-heartedly to interior peace.
While all things are stirring together,
I only contemplate the Return.
For flourishing as they do,
Each of them will return to its root.
To return to the root is to find peace.
To find peace is to fulfill one's destiny.
To fulfill one's destiny is to be constant.
To know the Constant is called Insight.

—Chapter 16, *Tao Teh Ching*

Unpowered, unable to change course even if they'd wanted to do so, *Lightbringer* tumbled through Thunder. The passage was uneventful, almost quiet. They fell into the satin night of the wormhole: there was a moment of cold and blackness and disorientation, and when they could see again, the stars had changed and the brilliant, banded orb of Jupiter loomed nearby and Ganymede floated almost within touch, seemingly larger than Jupiter itself. A familiar yellow sun burned in the distance.

Nearby, lights winked on the metal hulls of the support ships they'd left behind months ago.

"This is *Demosthenes* calling *Lightbringer* . . ."

Home. They were home.

Kyung watched the several windows arrayed above the Admiral's desk. He was still there, though the guards had been dismissed an hour ago, just before they fell into Thunder. *Home.* Kyung let out a breath that momentarily fogged the faceplate of his suit.

"I was wrong," Admiral McElwan said to him. "We all were."

Kyung couldn't answer. He had no words.

"I'm sorry we had to leave her behind," McElwan said. "We all regret that."

"She said . . ." Kyung took another breath, staring at Thunder. "She said that she didn't need to be rescued. She knew."

McElwan nodded. In the window showing Thunder in a false, enhanced spectrum, coruscating light shimmered as a quartet of energy pulses shot out from the gateway. A new window opened and tracked them, swinging wildly away from Thunder to center on Ganymede, its surface piebald: half of it a pattern of grooved, silvery terrain covering liquid water oceans; half darker and pockmarked with craters. The edges of the satellite were faintly blurred with Ganymede's thin atmosphere. The pulses merged into one, and lanced downward to the satellite's surface. Through the lenses of the cameras, they could see a huge cloud of water vapor billowing outward from the point of impact, near one of the huge, shallow palimpsest craters.

The Admiral glanced away from the window to Kyung. "The support ships are telling me that there's been sudden volcanic activity on Ganymede for the last few days. Odd atmospheric events. When Thunder closed, when we were trapped on the other side, they recorded a large pulse coming from the mouth of the anomaly and striking Ganymede." McElwan pressed her lips together, sat her chin on steepled hands. "They're asking me what to do."

"Leave them alone," Kyung answered. "Just . . . leave them alone. Let's find out what they can do. Maybe we can even learn something from them."

McElwan nodded. Kyung thought for a moment that she almost smiled. "I think that's my inclination, too."

Thunder spat light again, more violently this time. The pair of pulses emerged, the camera tracking them. One of the orbs of flickering light suddenly banked away from the other, then swooped back to loop around the other. It was a familiar maneuver, a hotdog maneuver. Kyung laughed aloud and McElwan's head swiveled toward him. "What?" she asked.

The pulses raced toward Ganymede, descending into the rising silver cloud.

"What?" McElwan asked him again.

Kyung watched the light spiral down onto the surface of

Ganymede. "Somebody's come home," he said. Behind Ganymede, behind *Lightbringer*, Thunder collapsed in upon itself again, the wormhole's throat collapsing convulsively.

There should have been sound, but there was only silence.

Appendix

The Characters

Alisa	co-worker of Taria's in ExoAnthro
Commander Allison	Taria's superior on *Lightbringer*, head of ExoAnthro (called "Allison-Who-Speaks-Empty-Words" by the Blues)
Jim Baney	Taria's boyfriend after Nikki
Ensign Ballior	redshirt from the security force on Little Sister
Barrett	redshirt from *Galileo*
Benander	pilot of shuttle *Galileo*
Alex Coen	Ensign. First human to stand on Little sister. Gone missing.
Colin Daniels	co-worker of Taria's in ExoAnthro
Theo Davies	third pilot of the Firebirds that first went through Thunder

Dog	Taria's Personal Interface Avatar (PIA)
Donahue	tech in Engineering
Donna	person Taria dated after Nikki
Du Yun	Kyung's sister
Eric	Taria's boyfriend at Stanford University
Harashiro	redshirt from *Galileo*
Lt. Commander Irumaki	in charge of assault team on Little Sister
Cmdr. Dimitri Ivanovich	head of Systems aboard *Lightbringer*
Jo Ann	person Taria dated after Nikki
Kelsey	Taria's next-door neighbor "friend" in Pensacola
Kinope	redshirt from *Hawking*
Kwan	friend of Kyung's aboard *Lightbringer*
Lisa	friend of Taria's in Pensacola
Bea Mahaffey	first person through Thunder in one of the Firebirds, and pilot of shuttle *Hawking*
Makes	Also Makes-the-Sound-of-East-Wind. The Baraaki of the Blues. Becomes the Cal-abaraaki.
Admiral Serena McElwan	Leader of the *Lightbringer* expedition. Her avatar

	speaks with the voice of her deceased husband, Tomas.
Commander Merritt	Kyung's superior aboard *Lightbringer*
Neritorika	"Voice-of-Our-Desires," head of the Blue community
Nikki	Taria's lover at MIT
Paula	person Taria dated before Kyung
Lt. Commander Perez	head of marine force on Little Sister
Peter	person Taria dated before Kyung
Robert	Taria's boyfriend in Pensacola, to whom she lost her virginity
Rosie	simulacrum that helped Taria learn the Blue language
Sees-the-Light-and-Cries	famous kagliaristi warrior who was executed by his Neritorika
Strikes-Air-in-Anger	kagliaristi warrior
Carl Spears	"Grampa," Taria's grandfather
Gloria Spears	"Mama," Taria's mother
Judy Spears	Taria's stepmother
Ruth Spears	"Gramma," Taria's grandmother

Taria Spears	also "Taria-Who-Wants-To-Understand"
Trevor Spears	"Papa," Taria's father
Suni	co-worker of Taria's in ExoAnthro
Tee	Kyung's PIA
Vicki	Nikki's girlfriend after Taria
Kyung Xiong	Ensign. Taria's lover aboard *Lightbringer*, also called "Kyung-Who-Speaks-In-Fury"
Auntie Li Xouyin	woman who watched the young Taria in Nanjing
Zachary	co-worker of Taria's in ExoAnthro

The following sections were excerpted from ExoAnthro notes entered by various crew members. Since the notes were logged in prior to the return of *Lightbringer* to Earth's solar system, there are occasional discrepancies with facts uncovered late in the expedition.

THE BLUES' LANGUAGES

Unlike Shiplish, the English-creole spoken by the crew of *Lightbringer*, the Blue languages consist of five distinct dialects, and the use of a particular dialect reflects the social situation involved. Some words are shared within the dialects, but pronunciation and emphasis changes, and it is not always possible to say the same thing in two different types of speech. For instance, in the Language-of-Command you can say "Bring me that dish." However, in the

Language-of-Obedience you would be forced to say something along the lines of "If it would not offend you, would
it be possible for this Person-of-Little-Consequence to be
given that dish?"

Language-of-Formality-and-Negotiation
Used for negotiations, when status is not clear, or
when the situation is not certain. This is perhaps the
freest dialect, as you are also permitted to exagger-
ate, lie, or evade, and the speakers understand this.

This is the speech that the Blues, understandably,
used when first contacted by the *Lightbringer* humans, and the one the humans learned. It is very
similar to the Language-of-Neutrality, but contains
additional frills of etiquette and is more formal in
structure.

Language-of-Neutrality
The common language, used in everyday speech between relative equals.

Language-of-Command
Used only in a dominance situation. The use of the
Language-of-Command indicates that the speaker is
emphasizing his or her superior status to those being
spoken to, and obedience is demanded. Should the
person being spoken to respond in the Language-of-
Obedience, then the relationship of superior/inferior
is implicit. If the person being spoken to, however,
also responds in the Language-of-Command, it indicates a conflict that must be resolved, either through
negotiation or violence. For this reason, the Language-of-Command is used sparingly.

Language-of-Obedience
Use of the Language-of-Obedience indicates that the
speaker understands his or her lower status. In this

language, requesting someone else to do something can only be done in a most circumspect manner—there are very few action words, and one cannot even refer to him- or herself in the first person.

Language-of-Intimacy
Used only by the closest of friends.

A BLUE VOCABULARY (BASED ON THE LANGUAGE-OF-FORMALITY-AND-NEGOTIATION)

It should be noted that the Blue "words" are at best approximations of the sound in their own language, which contains tones and pitches which the human voice cannot reproduce. Some of the content of a word is contained in both the pitch and inflection of the voice. Thus a human speaking a Blue language unaided is akin to listening to a toneless, inflectionless recitation of English, pitched uncomfortably high.

Baraaki	*One-Whose-Life-Is-Given-to-Her.*
baraalideish	*Those-Who-Speak-With-Her.* A religious group in the Blue culture, who currently hold most of the political power as well.
Children-of-She-Who-Spoke-the-World	The Blues' name for themselves.
Emptiness-Above-Us	The sky—with their inability to focus except at extremely close distances, the Blues

have little conception of anything in the sky above them other than the sun and the gas giant planet around which they orbit.

Greater Light · The sun the humans call Yin.

Gruriterashpali · *Place-Where-She-May-Speak-Again*. The chief "temple" of Those-Who-Speak-With-Her.

Guardians-of-the-Right-Spirit · Also part of a Blue's chosen extended family. The Guardians-of-the-Right-Spirit are those Blues who a person chooses during their long pubescence to aid their Mother-of-Name in guiding them to their adult occupation.

kagliaristi · *Those-Who-Will-Protect*. The military arm of Blue government, ostensibly under control of the Neritorikas.

Keeper-of-Those-Not-Yet-Real · Those who care for Blue children.

Lesser Light · The gas giant the humans call Yang.

Mother-of-Name · The person in Blue culture who a youngling chooses just before puberty to guide the child through to adult-hood. The Mother-of-Name will at some point give a young Blue the name she will bear for the rest of her life. An adult Blue will still feel an obligation of sub-servience to their Mother-of-Name.

Neritorika

Voice-Of-Our-Desires. The head of Blue city govern-ment. Each city has its own Neritorika, though the Neritorika of Rase-diliodutherad, the largest city, is also the unofficial leader of all Neritorika, as well as the baraali-deish.

Place-of-Walking

The single large continent on which the Blues live.

Rasediliodutherad

Oldest-Gathering-Place-Near-the-Quiet-Saltwater. Capital city of the Blues in an eastern bay of the conti-nent.

Sees-the-Light-and-Cries

Historical figure. A member of Those-Who-Protect who rebelled unsuccessfully against Those-Who-Speak-With-Her.

She-Who-Spoke-the-World

Chief god of the Blue pan-theon.

Singer-from-the-Water	The creatures the humans call "watersingers."
Singer-of-the-Acolytes	The "priest" of Those-Who-Speak-With-Her who is in charge of the acolytes given to the organization.
Small-Companion-to-the-Lesser-Light	The world the humans call Little Sister, on which the Blues live.
The-Little-Death	One of the several names for types of sleep—the deepest state.
Things-Once-True	Mythology. Fairy tales. Fables.
Time-of-Full-Dark	When neither Yin nor Yang is in the sky.
Time-of-Lesser-Light	When the sun Yin has set but Yang still is in the sky.
Time-of-Most-Light	When both Yin and Yang are in the sky.
Wermasthaibrezhzorilak	An apology phrase in the Blue language that means: *"I-have-wrongly-placed-my-will-on-you-and-offer-the-repentance-desired."*

BLUE PHYSIOLOGY & PSYCHOLOGY

The way in which the Blues interact with each other and the environment around them is entirely divergent from the human model. Though we share the same basic five senses, the ways in which they are ordered are vastly different.

	Human	Blue
Primary Sense for interacting with environment	Sight	Hearing
Secondary Sense for interacting with environment	Hearing	Touch
Primary Sense for Intimate Contact with another	Touch	Sight
Secondary Sense for Intimate Contact with another	Taste	Smell
"Alert" Senses	Sight	Hearing
	Smell	Taste
	Hearing	Sight

Cascading from the above are thousands of differences in cultural response:

Blues touch all the time: other people as well as objects. Hands are constantly in motion.

Sight is an "intimate" sense for them, due to the inability of their visual organs to focus. It is only when they are in extremely close proximity that they can sense the details of another's features—and that is most likely an arousal factor for them.

To see if food has gone bad, where we would first smell it, the Blues first take a small taste. Their stomachs are far more tolerant of bacteria.

Because their hearing range goes well above and below ours, and because they are capable of producing sound within that full range (and of making more than one tone at a time), the human will—at best—be only able to produce "baby talk" in their language without computerized assistance.

Information is carried in their language not only in the word, but in pitch and volume as well—stress on syllables is even more complex than stress in any human language.

They find our language "thin," with not enough meanings conveyed in each word. Translating Blue to Human involves long "word-sequences" that are attempts at communicating the various levels of meaning contained with the word. Expressing an extremely detailed and precise concept in Blue takes much less time than conveying the same thought in Shiplish, because component meanings are given simultaneously: through primary pitch, through inflection, through the use of additional tones added to the syllable, through volume.

Art: There are no "paintings" in Blue art. "Fine" art is 3D or aural. Decorative art—as we might have on everyday objects like china—is either tactile (raised surfaces) or audible (attached things that create sound).

However, we do come together on *music*—Blue music is recognizably "music" to us, though again, theirs covers a much larger total range.

THE BLUE RELIGION

Anthropologically, it's interesting that all Blues have in common the same religion, from as far back as we have been able to ascertain. This is entirely unlike our own history, where religions and gods have come and gone, and where there is still much religious diversity. The Blues—all of them, no matter where on the continent they live—share a common mythological ground, a racial memory that has formed their image of their primary god: She-Who-Spoke-the-World. Whereas we humans, since at least primeval times, have tended to shape our gods after our own image, it's also interesting that the Blues have not followed this pattern. Instead, their chief god most resembles a huge and divinely powered watersinger. The fossil record on Little Sister reveals that far larger specimens of watersingers once roamed the coastal waters and the tidal plains of Little Sister—did the nascent Blue population witness these huge creatures and fold them into their own creation myth, pulled from their common racial memory?

Whether or not that is the case, the quasireligious organization of Those-Who-Speak-With-Her came into existence over three thousand years before the arrival of the humans on Little Sister. Those-Who-Speak-With-Her, the baraalideish, were able, via the religious authority invested in them as speakers for the chief god of their pantheon, to create a power structure between the scattered Blue settlements, though they were still under the command of the local Neritorika.

The Blues moved quickly from a tribal structure to a stable theocracy. Unlike human history, Blue history is without the horrible repetition of war after war after war. There were certainly conflicts, and at times those conflicts involved physical violence, but it was nearly always on a smaller scale. There are political intrigues, but they involve individuals or at best small groups; there were coups, but they involved dozens or at best hundreds of individuals, not thousands. No vast armies crawled like flies across the landscape of Little Sister, spreading blood and carnage. The history of Little Sister is the history of a land mostly at peace with itself.

LITTLE SISTER

The landmass of Little Sister, which the native Blues call Small-Companion-to-the-Lesser-Light, is concentrated almost entirely in one large continent that nearly girdles the planet's equator. The continent, which the Blues call simply Place-of-Walking, is about the size of Eurasia in square kilometers, but stays mostly within the tropic latitudes of Little Sister, resulting in a relatively temperate climate for the Blues, since the overall average temperature of Little Sister is nearly ten degrees colder than that of Earth.

With the exception of the deep deserts and more mountainous regions, there are Blue settlements scattered throughout the main continent and even on some of the larger islands. As with us, there are urban centers—though the largest are far smaller than any of Earth's major cities—as well as smaller settlements and farmland.

LITTLE SISTER FLORA & FAUNA

beetle-birds	Small birds with armored, beetlelike bodies.
crack-wing	Noisy insects that feed on carrion.
curvetail	A small bird that, like a spider, has spinnerets that can weave a fine web to snare flying insects. Curvetails live inside Blue residences, and are tolerated since they keep the insect population in check.
dangleberry	A vine that bears bright blue fruit hanging from long thin stalks.
Fat Man's Hands	A plant with thick, pink tubular stalks that wriggle, lifelike, when touched.

fisher-fly	An insect that dangles an iridescent "lure" from the end of its tongue.
fishing beetles	Iridescent green beetles the size of a person's fist, whose main source of food is small fish.
fleasnappers	Tiny, biting insects that move in swarms.
hornfish	A staple of Blue diet. A large fish with a pair of doubled "horns" on the head. The horns are actually air chambers, which the fish uses for ballast.
horseslugs	Legless, muscular creatures used by the Blues to pull carts and similar loads.
licorice flowers	A flowering plant that when cut exudes a strong scent much like licorice. The Blues don't care for the flower, but use the stems for some unknown purpose.
masata	A root the Blues use to make an analgesic.
pinwheels	Small, yellow insects with oarlike legs that roll across the ground in search of food.
prickle-spine trees	Medium-size trees with orange-yellow bark, festooned with bright purple, finger-long spikes.

red spores	Tiny spores that cling to the underside of rocks in the tidal zone. Can cause pulmonary infections in humans.
snapbiters	Mammalian creatures the size of a large dog, that run in packs and are especially dangerous to approach in their breeding season.
snout-shells	Barnaclelike creatures that live on rock an' under the sand in the tidal zone.
sourgrass	A tidal-zone grass.
sticky-weed	Grassy growth whose lacy seed pods are liberally coated with a gluey sap.
whip-tongue worms	More properly snakes than worms, with brightly patterned yellow and black scales and a long red tongue used to snare small rodents.
whitefly	An insect, resembling an Earth fly, startlingly white in color.
whiteshells	A mollusk with translucent shells that turn bright, opaque white once the animal has died.
windowsill worms	A colony creature that is actually a ball of hundreds of tiny, hair-thin worms, with iridescent red beads at the

end of their bodies. Together, they look almost like a wad of salad sprouts. When disturbed, or when they sense prey, they quickly break apart and spray a thin mist from their mouths that quickly sets into a stinging net. Should the net catch an insect, the colony will devour it.

winged rodent — Exactly what it sounds like. Indigenous to the inner high plain of Little Sister.

yellowbark — A type of tree with bright yellow bark that peels much like a sycamore tree.

Matthew Farrell
Notes from the Cube

*My main character, Taria Spears, "plays a hunch" in
Thunder Rift—and ends up making an explosive discovery about the nature of the alien race who built Thunder.
This could never have occurred, though, if another character hadn't played a similar hunch, unbeknownst to
Taria. Commander Allison, the by-the-book military
man, takes a substantial risk in sending Taria downworld
to interact with the Blues. As I wrote this novel, I prepared a lot of background material that, while critical,
doesn't directly appear. Here's a look at a fragment of
that hidden background: excerpt from the PIA log of
Commander Allison, ExAnthro, of the research vessel*
Lightbringer.

—Matthew Farrell

**Transcript of conversation with Admiral Serena
McElwan, 32AT/5/15 14:56:**
    McELWAN: I just received your final crew list, Commander. I have to say that I'm concerned about one of the
choices.
    ALLISON: Spears.
    McELWAN: Spears, yes. I thought that after the Selection
Committee's level of concern with her suitability, why
would you choose her over the other final candidates?
Spear's psych profile: her mother's murder, her bisexuality,
her attitude toward her, her inability to form stable rela-

tionships. . . . This is a small community we're building here, Commander. We can't afford outsiders.

ALLISON: I don't disagree, Admiral.

McELWAN: But . . . ?

ALLISON (after a pause): Do you ever play hunches, Admiral?

McELWAN (laughing): Hunches? You're telling me that *you* are playing a *hunch,* Commander? Now you are surprising me.

ALLISON: Yes, I am. If I'm wrong, well, Spears is merely one of many in ExoAnthro—she can't have too adverse an impact. I want her on my staff. I'm prepared to justify her selection further if required.

McELWAN: No, No, Commander. You know the needs of ExAnthro, and ultimately you're the one who will deal with the consequence, not me. You're certain?

ALLISON: Considering what we're going into, Admiral, I don't think any of us can be certain of anything. But she's the best choice I can make.

Transcript of conversation with Lt. Commander Everett Nelson, Pysch, 33AT/11/4 09:03:

NELSON: . . . in short, I think it would be a considerable mistake to permit Spears to go downworld with the Blues.

ALLISON: It's not like she's making the request out of thin air, Everett. They've *asked* for her. *Her* specifically.

NELSON: I know that—though why is beyond me. Look, you ramrodded Spears through the Selection Committee when *my* recommendation—and damn near everyone else's—was that she didn't fit. She's a maverick. Mavericks are dangerous. I've heard rumors that she disobeyed direct orders—*your* direct orders—right after the passage while ExAnthro was making its first survey.

ALLISON: She did. She's also not military, so orders don't have quite the same weight for her that they might for you or me. And if she hadn't done that, we might not have noticed the Blues for a long time.

NELSON (snorts): Right. What is it with you and Spears, Allison?

ALLISON: Are you going to sign off on the request, or aren't you?

NELSON: All right. I'll sign, but I'm going to note my concerns in the log. And I'm going to ask you again, as a friend, to reconsider. Be careful. I think this has the potential to blow up in your face. Spears should never have been on this ship in the first place; don't compound the mistake.

ALLISON: She's not a mistake. Not sending her would be the mistake.

Transcript of conversation with Taria Spears, 33AT/11/4 11:12:

SPEARS: You're kidding. (Pause.) Well . . . I have to say that I'm, uh, surprised.

ALLISON: So am I, frankly. To tell you the truth, Spears, I don't support your going downworld. To me, it's one less person involved in the search for the Thunder Makers, and you're going to tie up resources I'd rather put elsewhere. But you made the request; my superiors have signed off on it.

SPEARS: Permission to speak frankly, Commander?

ALLISON: You're a civie, Spears; you don't need permission. Say your piece and get the hell out of my office.

SPEARS: I'm telling you again, Commander—the Blues may be the key to the Thunder Makers. I don't know how, I know I don't have the hard facts to back that up, it's just a gut feeling. . . .

ALLISON: I don't believe in 'feelings,' Spears. But—

SPEARS (interrupting): I'm quite certain you don't.

ALLISON (ignoring her comment): But I do agree with you that there are best practices we can glean from your interaction with the Blues. *That* is the only reason I can see for this. You have tonight to reconsider your request.

SPEARS: Good. (She starts to leave. Stops.) Thank you, Commander.

ALLISON: Thank the Admiral. It's her signature on the release.

(The door closes behind Spears. There are three seconds of silence before Allison speaks again.)

ALLISON: Good luck, Spears. Recording off.